The Last Summer

Chan Howell

Fulton Books, Inc.
Meadville, PA

Published by Fulton Books 2020

ISBN 978-1-64654-446-2 (paperback)
ISBN 978-1-64654-447-9 (digital)

Printed in the United States of America

On the Map

Frankie Winslow and my dad have told me the story of the 1980 Swansville Red Raiders state championship game so many times I feel like I was at the game despite the critical fact that I was not even born yet. I would make my debut roughly sixteen months later. The story seems more like a legend than something that actually happened.

My parents, much like most of the local youth and high school kids, gathered at Rocky Point Pier to listen to the game on the radio. Red Solo cups were to disguise the teenagers that were drinking alcohol in the event the authorities or someone's parents showed up unannounced. No adult was concerned with the local teens at Rocky Point Pier. They ignored whatever teenage cocktails were drunk as everyone expected the night to end in a celebration. A small bonfire made the trees dance across the water just before the sunset. The adults gathered at the back of the cove at Winslow's to do the same. Only a small caravan of parents and relatives made the trip to Chapel Hill to watch the game in person.

Radios echoed off the water at Rocky Point Pier. The boys that now considered themselves men, who had played on the team a year earlier, controlled the crowd with shouts of "Close your mouths or leave!" Baseball was serious business to those that almost won a year prior. The night was heavy and mostly silent, until something happened in favor of the Red Raiders.

My dad said, "We lived and died with each pitch, and the fact we trailed most of the game made everyone nervous."

My parents sat on a blanket under an old oak tree and quietly listened as the innings slowly passed. The adults at Winslow's cared little that the town youth were drinking alcohol just up the cove. Most of the adults sipped from flasks to calm their nerves.

One year earlier, the Red Raiders fell in the state championship game, and most of the folks in town thought the chance at baseball immortality had passed. Tonight's game was a rematch and a shot at redemption. We still had a dominant pitcher, but his home-run-hitting older brother had graduated. Jacob Hartley represented our last and best chance now that his brother was gone. Swansville was not known for baseball, but a win would put the town on the map. The Hartley brothers had brought attention to the brown water of Pisgah Lake.

The local church radio station broadcast the game, and the AM radio station was interrupted with static throughout the broadcast. The Methodist preacher and his brother stumbled through the game. Every time there was a break in the action, Reverend Callahan would ask, "Why is Jacob Hartley not on the mound?" His brother Peter would answer, "It doesn't make sense to keep your best pitcher in left field." Jamie Hartley paced the shoreline while his future bride tried to settle him down. She did little good as usual, and Jamie's face turned scarlet with each step.

Jamie was banned from all of Swansville High School's athletic events due to a fight earlier in the year. He was only able to give advice by shouting at the radio and hoping the frequency somehow reached his younger brother. Swansville High School was glad he was gone. Jamie was exiled from all sports and school functions. Two fans from our conference rival shouted taunts at Jacob while he was injured when an errant foul ball hit him while he was warming up on deck. Everyone was silent until Jacob gained consciousness, while the rival fans openly mocked him, shouting, "Delay of game cupcake!" among other insults. After the game, Jamie confronted the opposing fans. The grandfather and father of a rival player were behind the insults. The story went that the opposing fan told Jamie, "I guess you are trying to hold on to your glory days by holding your brother's hand." A melee ensued, with Jamie breaking the old man's arm. He was not arrested, but the penalty of not being able to watch his younger brother was far worse than a jail sentence or any community service.

Jacob had pitched 15 2/3 innings over the last three games, and his arm was ailing. It achingly hung by his side while he patrolled left field. The former baseball players knew why Jacob was in left field, but the rest of the crowd shouted at the radio, "Coach Burkhard, you're a fool! Put him in! There is no tomorrow!" Jamie scowled at any comment that would be perceived as negative. No one dared making a direct comment at him, and everyone avoided eye contact in effort to keep Jamie's wrath from turning their direction. The red cup he sipped from made him more volatile, and his fuse was shorter than normal. His date would occasionally walk up and kiss him as he paced the shoreline. Her kisses did not seem to settle him down, but it did slow his vibrant pace.

The Swansville Red Raiders were down 2 to 0, heading into the fifth inning. The crowds at both Winslow's and Rocky Point Pier began to sense a repeat of the previous year's title game. Reverend Callahan opened the fifth inning with "For those of you back in Swansville, hope and faith are two pillars of our lives. Don't fret. We can still win." His words floated into the night air like ashes from a dying bonfire. No one wanted to hear a sermon, and the crowd at Rocky Point Pier booed.

Jamie Hartley threw two large bundles of wood on the fire, then doused it with gasoline. The fire raged and popped as he said, "We have nine outs. We can do it!"

The crowd cheered as one lone boy shouted back at Jamie, "Let's hope your brother can deliver. You surely couldn't!"

It was rare for someone to challenge either of the Hartley brothers, and the crowd looked in the direction of the boy that made the foolish remark. Jamie shouted, "You'll find out one way or another!" Jamie's date ran over to the other boy and told him to stop. She grabbed his face and pulled him down to her level, then whispered something to him. Whatever she said seemed to work. The blue-eyed beauty was successful. She was able to quiet her older brother, George. Others in the crowd were shocked her brother even showed his face on this side of the lake. George sulked away quietly, but his red Solo cup still had some courage left in it.

The Swansville Red Raiders scored one in the top of the fifth, and now the deficient was only a single run. The heat from the fire forced my parents away from their spot under the old oak tree, and they struggled to hear the rest of the game. My dad told me, "I felt like I missed those last two innings." The tension in the air was more prevalent than ever. Swansville scored two runs in the top of the sixth on a no-name sophomore's double. The sophomore pitcher for the Red Raiders was running out of steam, and we still needed six more outs.

Reverend Callahan ran out of words and pointed the microphone toward the crowd. The crowd at both Winslow's and Rocky Point Pier started shouting at the radio. My dad said, "The shouts must've reached old Coach Burkhard, because he called for Hartley to take his place on top of the mound." Reverend Callahan's brother Peter was so excited he shouted, "Jesus Christ, here he comes!" Jacob Hartley was sent to the mound to get the last six outs of the 1980 state championship. Jacob had little trouble in the bottom of the sixth inning. He struck out two of the West Lee Dragons as the third Dragon bounced weakly to first.

The mood at both Winslow's and Rocky Point Pier began to sense the outcome. Jacob Hartley had given everyone confidence. Car horns began to the fill the night air, much to the chagrin of the folks actually trying to hear the ending of the game. The former Swansville baseball players were not happy trying to hear the last inning over all the noise. The Red Raiders were unable to add to their lead, and the game's outcome fell squarely on Jacob Hartley's magical right arm. He had to get three more outs, and he had to face one of the top hitters in the state.

Jacob Hartley walked the first batter of the inning as he winced in pain. Reverend Callahan declared, "Hartley looks tired, and I pray he can get three more outs."

Jamie Hartley shouted, "Damn, Callahan, have a little faith!"

My dad said he shouted, "Nine more strikes!" and Jamie told the crowd, "Silence!" and everyone listened.

Jacob was able to get a weak ground ball to third, but the tying run made it to second base with the All-State Dragon heading to the plate. Reverend Callahan said, "I am not sure what is happening, but it looks like they are going to let the winning run on first." Jacob intentionally walked the best hitter in the state. Boos floated down from the stadium in Chapel Hill. George openly shouted, "Bunch of cowards!"

The word *coward* riled the crowd.

Jamie Hartley looked at his date and told her, "Tell him to leave, now."

Reverend Callahan shouted, "Two outs!" as Jacob struck out another Dragon. My dad always said he could tell something was about to happen. He knew the muffled radio call of the last out was inevitable as Jacob Hartley still had three more heaters left in his arm. The real drama was between Jamie Hartley and his date's older brother.

Just as Jacob Hartley was winning the 1980 North Carolina State Championship, his brother was defending his honor. George had called a Hartley a coward. Reverend Callahan made the call just as Jamie approached his rival. The static-filled winning call from Reverend Callahan was missed as the crowd begged Jamie not to do anything crazy. Jamie stood back until his rival jerked his date by the arm, insisting she leave. She begged Jamie not to do anything to her brother. My dad said, "I remember the fireworks from Winslow's popped over the Brown Water just as Jamie Hartley broke his future brother-in-law's jaw." The night sky lit up, and shadows were cast on the faces of the kids at Rocky Point Pier. No one at Rocky Point Pier heard the final call of Jacob Hartley striking out the last batter in the 1980 state championship game.

Jamie Hartley was arrested after the ambulance picked up his future brother-in-law. Jamie's date and future wife slept on the steps of the town's small police station. She did not have to wait until morning. Jacob returned a hero just after midnight, and the team bus made a lap around town. No one wanted the night to end, as the citizens of Swansville honked their horns at the team bus. Jacob was able to use his instant celebrity to get his brother out of jail without posting bail.

Four months later, the town erected a sign "Welcome to Swansville, Home of the 1980 State Baseball Champions." Jamie Hartley and his new bride left town the same day.

Gray Beards

The gray in my beard made its first appearance this past year. It obnoxiously challenges me until the razor's blade gives me a false sense of victory. My wife always objects to my decision to try to look younger. She says she likes the older me, but I tease her because she did not like the younger version. The gray in my beard doesn't remind me that I am growing old as much as it reminds me of a gray-bearded baseball coach. He was much older than I originally believed. I will turn thirty-eight years old on September 7. Time is starting to catch up to me. I feel the aches of a father, and I yearn for the ailments and heartbreaks of my youth.

Time, unfortunately, has no sympathy, and it refuses to slow down. The moments that I wish would have lasted longer are the first memories the villain of youth attempts to steal. It is relentless. Some memories, thankfully, will be the last to lose their grip as I tell some of those stories daily. I fear the day their grasp loosens and they let go, leaving me with no tall tales to recount.

I have only felt special a few times in my life. The first time was the summer of 1994. That summer seems like it happened yesterday, and I pray it will be one of the last of my memories to fade.

Twenty-five years ago, before puberty and girls were an obsession, my friends and I experienced the longest summer of our lives. We did not spend our time chasing girls, swimming at the lake, or playing video games. We gambled our summer vacations away for the chance at baseball immortality. Our time was spent on clockless baseball fields. Time stood still for us that summer, and for some the clock has remained broken. I was not the main attraction, and I never would be. I felt insignificant when I was twelve, but that summer, everything seemed to change, although I was not even the main character of my own story.

My midlife crisis unexpectedly called me. I was asked to get thirteen boys that are now men together one more time. The summer we were twelve was nothing short of magical. It all started on a baseball field across from a lake at a dead-end road. We stared down countless foes on our way to transforming into something more than just your average twelve-year-olds. The summer of 1994 was the first time I read my name in the newspaper, knowingly lied, and began to notice a girl. My mission was to get my old teammates together to turn back the clock and to chronicle our epic summer on baseball diamonds across the South.

Many of my former teammates were still living near Swansville, and they would not be difficult to find. I had lost touch with many of them despite the fact they lived nearby. My new circle of friends were the fathers of the kids I now coach. I am the old man to the much younger fathers. I embrace it. Many of these guys have heard how the summer of 1994 unfolded more than once. It is the rerun of my life. I never tire of reliving that summer. My teammates that moved away would be easier to track down than those that are still around. The big water and the brown water flowed the same direction, but it created a massive divide, and Swansville has been split for a long time. I assume I was chosen to round up everyone since I really never left. My wife jokingly calls me the mayor of the Brown Water.

The 1994 MLB strike was on its way, and our national pastime was about to come to a screeching halt. Baseball fans in America needed a team to follow, and due to some luck, magic, and a new arrival, we would be on the marquee for most of the summer. We went from the local paper to the national news almost overnight. It was the first time in my life I was a dinner-table topic instead of my sister. My parents relayed our baseball exploits, and everyone in town began to learn our names. Our team picture is still hanging in the entrance of the town bank and the post office.

Baseball was in our town's blood. The decade prior, our local high school team had a five-year stretch of deep playoff runs. Most of our parents remembered the baseball glory days of the 1980s; thus, when we showed promise, the bandwagon filled quickly. We became local celebrities by the middle of the summer. We reluctantly rode the wave of fame until it finally broke when the school bell rang the following August.

Our journey through all-star baseball tournaments became the spark that ignited friendships beyond the baseball diamond. Baseball was the easy part of our ever-changing lives. We could always set foot on the diamond and all our future conflicts magically disappeared. Baseball was the foundation of our friendships even though it created enemies. I barely remember the last time we all shared a baseball field, and it will be scary revisiting old wounds. My task of reuniting everyone would be difficult, and memory lane would not be easy to navigate. I will have to find old enemies, old allies, old heroes, and especially, old friends.

The Brown Water

The small town where I grew up began to change thirty years before I turned twelve. My friends and I felt the lake's impact more than anyone. The nearby river was dammed in the summer of 1920, just as Babe Ruth arrived in New York, departing Boston but leaving a famous curse in his wake. Pisgah Lake was created, and Swansville became a dot on the map. Swansville is the town where the road and the lake end.

Pisgah Lake's original owners did not allow development. All they wanted was to provide electricity to the ever-growing North Carolina countryside. In the 1950s, development was finally permitted. The dam was sold in 1969, and the new owners agreed to allow development of roughly 70 percent of the lake the following year. The people of nearby Charlotte migrated like ants taking over a Dr. Pepper spill at a picnic. The slow march started on the big water, then the ants headed our way. It was easy to spot these transplants due to their foreign cars and their bigger boats.

Our section of the lake was the farthest from the dam and directly across from the mouth of the river. Tinker's Creek was named after the first postmaster and cousin of the famous Chicago Cub Joe Tinker. Eli Tinker eventually became the mayor. Outsiders called Tinker's Creek Cubbie Cove, except the folks from the big water. The big-water snobs called Swansville the Brown Water in an attempt to insult the town. Many locals embraced the insult. Almost everyone wore the badge of being from the Brown Water with pride.

The ants began to make their way to the Brown Water by the early 1980s. Pisgah Lake was a finger lake; thus, it was spread out. It was developed from the bigger sections of the lake down to Swansville. Cubbie Cove was opened for development, and our small town and small school started to drastically change. Only a small portion of the lake reached town, but the back of Cubbie Cove was its heartbeat. Swansville collected the trash that drifted down from the big water.

In 1986, the brown water of Pisgah Lake brought a new hospital just as Bill Buckner was letting a ball pass through his legs to keep the curse of the Bambino alive. A new road and an exit off the highway eliminated the isolation of Swansville. Now, less than ten years later, a new middle school was set to open in the fall. A ground-breaking ceremony was scheduled for a new high school on the anniversary of Joe Carter's game-winning 1993 World Series home run. The town's population was just over four thousand the summer after my sixth-grade year. Most folks lived in the rural areas or now the ever-expanding lake. The kids that lived on or near the lake would be going to a new school next fall. Classmates and teammates would soon be rivals, but for now we had one last summer together.

During the summer, most of my friends and I could be found at one of three places, the closed-public-access Rocky Point Pier, Scarborough Memorial Park, or Winslow's. Rocky Point Pier was closed after a teenager mysteriously went missing three years earlier. Ben Lee Chapel was last seen riding his bike to the pier. His body was never found. Ben Lee Chapel's shoes were found five days later on a small island at the mouth of Cubbie Cove. Foul play was never officially ruled out, and his death was ruled a drowning. Rocky Point Pier was just outside of town and beyond the local police's jurisdiction. My friends and I enjoyed the privacy, but we were too scared to stay past sundown. Our parents always warned us to be careful and to never go alone. No one fished off the forbidden public pier, although that was its original purpose. We used the post for the "no swimming" sign as our launching point into the cool brown Pisgah Lake waters. It was a common occurrence to be chased from the pier, and we always told the county sheriffs we would not come back.

The summer of 1994, we rode our bikes to the pier less and less with each passing week. That summer would turn into the first day of the seventh grade before we knew it.

After the Great Depression, the citizens of Swansville raised funds to build a park and a baseball field near Tinker's Creek. Scarborough Memorial Park was named after Preston and Pete Scarborough, the town's hero brothers that never came back from World War I. Pete Scarborough enrolled in the Army after his brother was killed in 1915. Pete gave up his baseball dream and left the local team behind to avenge his brother's death. His body returned in a casket just like his brother. A memorial plaque guarded the entrance to the park. The park had a walking trail, a practice baseball field, game field, and tennis courts. It was located across the street from the only boat launch in Swansville. The park was within walking distance to almost everything in town.

Every spring the town had a lake cleanup day called Green and Clean Day. Green and Clean Day always landed on the opening week-end of the Major League Baseball season. My parents felt obligated to volunteer, so my sister and I were forced to join them. Radios blared the Braves game, and playful arguments ensued over the BBQ lunch and homemade ice cream provided by Frankie Winslow. The early concern was less with the Braves title hopes and more if the season would get canceled due to a work stoppage. Major League Baseball was on thin ice that was starting to crack. A strike seemed inevitable. Our heroes of the Major Leagues and the team owners fought over millions of dollars. When you are twelve years old, you do not need to wipe the greed out of your eyes each day when you roll out of bed. I played the game for free, and I believed I would have if I were in the Major Leagues. I did not understand why a season could be canceled. I felt the innocence of baseball was lost on the Major Leaguers. I understood the importance of the game, but it was still just a game. Baseball was the reason I was accepted by my friends; otherwise, I likely would have been just another outcast.

Winslow's was a bait shop and a convenience store that was located where the water and the road literally met. If the lake water was down, which it typically was, the lakefront bait shop only touched mud. Frankie Winslow's dark-brown eyes must've turned green when the warm fishing weather and baseball season approached. He sold worms, minnows, boiled peanuts, Cheerwines, baseballs, and fishing hooks. We usually sat with our feet dangling just over the shallow water, drinking Cheerwines while we waited for practice. We typically sidled up to the counter to make sure Frankie knew the score of the previous day's games. Frankie had an old chalkboard where he kept the standings of every team from C-Ball to PONY league and his beloved Braves. Each summer the radio broadcast of the Braves games got louder and louder as Frankie's hearing started to fade. Every conversation with the old man featured "What?" about five times. Frankie looked and acted the part of a grandfather. He carried a flyswatter everywhere. His remaining few white hairs peeked out from under a Braves hat that had to be older than my dad. He still called my dad Speedy, a nickname long since forgotten by everyone else.

Our Little League Baseball draft was held the Monday before opening day, but now an expansion draft had pushed it back one week. Our small league had always consisted of only six teams, but the league had grown to seven teams. This year would be different. The seventh team meant we had to reshuffle the deck. The expansion draft was scheduled, and many of us did not know who our teammates would be. Each team had to offer up one twelve-year-old. The new team's coach would get to pick four. Luckily, I was protected by my coach of the previous year. Coach Duckworth spared me the embarrassment. The unprotected players were teased at school, and everyone had an excuse why they were unprotected. My friend Mitch claimed he requested it. He said, "I am sick of being on the Blue Devils and playing for Coach Alex." I believed him, but no one else did.

Frankie's chalkboard would need to be redrawn with the following teams: Mudcats, Yankees, Hornets, Braves, Blue Devils, Red Raiders, and now the Pirates. The redraft, as we called it, would make the league more competitive, or so we thought. The league's most dominant two teams, the Blue Devils and the Braves, would still be our measuring sticks. Our games were played at either Scarborough

Memorial Park or at the Swansville Elementary School field. Practices started the day after the redraft, and our games were only a week away. It felt like we were being pushed into summer, and we still had six weeks left of school.

Ducklings

I started playing baseball when I was four years old. My first coach was Jim Duckworth. Everyone called him Duckworth, and our parents loved him. Everyone in town knew him since he worked the counter at the post office. He taught us the fundamentals, but more importantly, he taught us that baseball was supposed to be fun. The baseball phrase "Ducks on the pond" meant something different to many of us. Coach Duckworth called us his little Ducklings, and our first-year T-Ball team was named the Ducks, despite our jerseys looking like the Pittsburgh Pirates of the 1970s. He constantly shouted, "Ducks on the pond!" along with many other phrases, and I believed he coined them. He was a walking, talking baseball-reference thief. We all knew how to field with our feet, alligator hands, line up our door-knocking knuckles, punch the midget, and many more. I thought these were all his original phrases, until I was much older, when I heard other coaches yelling the same things. He stole everything, and I still viewed him as a genius despite it.

Duckworth had been through T-ball, C-Ball, and Little League before with his eldest son. We were players in his life's second act. Drake had a much older brother that died before Drake turned three years old. Donnie was a basketball star that passed through too quickly. He died at sixteen years old in a tragic hotel fire. Duckworth's dream for Donnie would fall short, just as the reach of the fire truck's ladder. Donnie had been an all-state point guard his sophomore year. Stardom was on his horizon. Duckworth had relentlessly groomed him into a Division 1 college prospect. Donnie and his dad argued constantly over sports, with Donnie usually throwing some type of embarrassing tantrum. Donnie and Duckworth had a love-hate relationship with each other but also with basketball. Duckworth was more of a coach than a father to Donnie. Donnie consumed the game as his father insisted, but his hatred for losing was only matched by Duckworth. Duckworth once stormed the court during a middle school basketball game and threatened a referee. The police had to escort him from the school's gym, and he was banned for one year. The story did not seem true, and many folks could not believe his transformation when coaching Drake.

Duckworth and his first wife's marriage collapsed under the pressure of not having Donnie follow through his sure-to-be-successful junior and senior years. Drake's mother moved away, and Duckworth was left alone to raise their son. Betty Duckworth left town in the middle of the night, and no one knew where the dark-haired beauty had escaped to. She also left Drake her athletic genes. She had been a standout track star, and Donnie and Drake inherited her athleticism. Betty had state records that were still unbroken in the 1,600 meters and 400 meters. Drake and Donnie both had her long legs and dark-olive skin. Drake never mentioned his mother, and he avoided every conversation about his superstar brother.

Duckworth had gray hair and a stubbly gray beard. He had an infectious laugh, and his gregarious nature made people flock to him. He walked with a limp due to knee surgery a decade earlier. He walked like an old cowboy, swinging his stiff right leg. Duckworth eventually married our elementary principal, and Drake later became a big brother to Ashton. Principal Duckworth catered to Ashton's every request. Ashton was Little Miss Swansville, and the two spent the summer on the pageant circuit. We rarely saw Principal Duckworth unless it was a school function. Ashton embarrassed her older brother every chance she got. She was a blond, blue-eyed bundle of energy and was full of personality at five. She and Drake looked nothing alike. Everyone gushed over the young beauty and showered her with compliments. She constantly showed us her new tricks. Drake usually avoided his little sister at all costs. I remember Drake telling me, "Here she comes. Let's disappear."

Duckworth was much older than all our other coaches, although he seemed younger. He was full of energy, and his booming voice welcomed everyone that set foot on the baseball field. He grew old at the same pace we grew up. It happened in the blink of an eye. Duckworth went from running bases and giving jump high fives to pitching batting practice sitting on a bucket. He was not hard on Drake like he was with Donnie. Donnie was forced onto the court, while Drake was encouraged. Duckworth wanted to enjoy everything this time around, while Drake wanted to be the best. Drake had the natural desire Duckworth cultivated in Donnie. Donnie was just a natural talent, whereas Drake had to work for it.

We excelled at baseball because of the fundamentals Duckworth showed us when we were four and five years old. We all still shouted the same batting and fielding cues he taught us before we knew our ABCs. The letter *L* was the first letter I could identify because of Duckworth. When I was asked by my kindergarten teacher to show the class the letter *L*, I stood up and lifted my arm in its shape as Duckworth had shown us one hundred times. The laughter from my classmates was the first of many embarrassing moments.

I believe Duckworth's currency was hearing all his former pupils shout those stolen baseball cues years later, because his teams rarely had winning seasons. Eventually his cues were known league-wide, and every other coach seemed to teach his players using them. Duckworth seemed to know everything about baseball, and he wanted us to consume his knowledge in the event we needed it for future Ducklings. He told our parents and the team after each game, "I love you, and God loves you, and I am proud of each one of you." We believed him.

Duckworth liked having the youngest and least experienced kids on his team; thus, Drake never had team success despite being one of the best players every year. I played on his team the last two years, and I went from marginal player to key contributor. Duckworth developed my skills that had been ignored by other coaches while letting me patrol right field. He woke up my dormant abilities. I began to love the game, and I consumed everything he taught me. Finally, Drake and I would be competitive and have a shot at an elusive championship.

Drake did everything with precision and played the game perfectly. Drake practiced every day, and the baseball field was his sanctuary. He was an artist on the field. Each year that passed, Drake's play became more automatic and the game was effortless. I felt he could play with his eyes closed. He stopped socializing, and he seemed to no longer enjoy the game as each season passed. He rarely stopped in at Winslow's. A Cheerwine with his friends had little value to him; he would rather stay on the diamond. I remember watching him once for twenty minutes practicing on the field alone with no baseball. He mimed it. He and his shadow looked like they were in a delicate ballet that they had trained for their entire lives. Watching him calmed my nerves and made me feel like I was in the presence of Baryshnikov.

The pressure Drake put on himself to be like his older brother made him too serious, and his calm demeanor gave him the look of confidence. He was labeled cocky. Outsiders disliked the quiet boy. Duckworth knew Drake was not born with his older brother's natural abilities. Drake was born with something more. Drake begged his father to stay after every practice so he could take more batting practice or field grounders. Duckworth always obliged. The setting sun signaled the end of practice for him, not a coach's whistle. Drake consumed his father's knowledge in near silence. He rarely even spoke to his dad. Duckworth said enough for the two of them. I began to join the extra practices; thus, Drake and I were dynamic at turning double plays.

Coach Duckworth's mantel was a shrine to his eldest son with trophies and first-place ribbons. A picture of Donnie dunking a basketball in the eighth grade sat over the middle of the fireplace. It served as a reminder to Drake of his brother's dominance. Duckworth never emphasized winning with Drake, but Drake wanted to be his father's second chance. He believed his father deserved it.

Sister's Shadow

I grew up in right field at Scarborough Memorial Park; it is the first place the sun's rays abandon once it starts its descent. The only time I ever led the way was when I was born. My twin sister followed me six minutes later, although she barely survived. She was born with caul covering her head and fluid in her lungs. My mother always says, "I fell in love with her the moment she cried out." Although I was first-born, I was the runt. My parents believed Whitley was born with a halo. She was far more superior in every way. She was tall, beautiful, and athletic. She was the apple of my parents' eyes, and everyone was enchanted with the green-eyed beauty. I spent my youth chasing my sister and watching her fill my parents' scrapbooks.

Whitley's side of the mantel looked similar to Duckworth's shrine to Donnie. Whitley's side was overcrowded with first-place trophies, blue ribbons, and the centerpiece was of Whitley's U10 state championship in soccer. My parents framed the local newspaper highlighting the soccer prodigy. The headline read, "Magic Feet." It would not be the last time she graced the front page of *The Swansville Orator*. Every time we had guests or family over, my father always awkwardly climbed above the television and pulled the frame off the wall for folks to marvel over Whitley. My side of the mantel was only a participation trophy and a trophy for reading two hundred books in the fifth grade. Whitley shone at all times, and even our teachers were enamored with her.

My dad taught Whitley to tell everyone she was a daddy's girl, and my mom taught her to bat her eyes on cue. Strangers would stop to shower her with compliments: "Just look at those beautiful eyes!" I learned very early to let her be the main attraction. I once got lost at the county fair and my mom had difficulty describing me. She could not even recall what color shirt I was wearing. She told the police officer my name was Dustin, which is her brother's name. I sat crying behind a trailer at the petting zoo, hearing people yelling, "Dustin! Dustin!" When I was finally spotted and I was asked what my name was, I told them "Carson Smith," just as my mom ran up, saying, "My baby, my baby!" The search party was confused; they had been searching for a Dustin Smith, not Carson Smith.

Whitley would've never gotten lost, because she was the center of attention. She was lively, and the crowds that circled her made you believe a magician was at the center, putting on a show. She cast a spell on everyone and a shadow over me. I learned how to navigate in the shadows at an early age. I found comfort in the books I began to read.

Whitley's bright-green eyes and perfect smile would torment my friends in the coming years, and she knew it. She looked like she was carved by Michelangelo, and I looked like I was carved from the scraps left over. She knew very early in life how to manipulate our classmates, and she quickly rose to the leader of all the girls and almost all the boys. She feared no one, and she had carried herself with a commanding grace since we were eight years old. She was made for the main stage, and she vanquished anyone trying to steal her spotlight.

We had a late birthday, and we were older than most of our classmates. She had all the advantages of being the oldest and most developed, while I was just a skinny runt. When I was twelve years old, I finally caught up in size despite being nearly a year older. I was awkwardly skinny and tall. The summer of 1994, I finally stopped tripping over my long legs and I finally began to fill out.

My mom and dad worked together at our family real estate company. Home Away from Home Realty was the biggest real estate company in Swansville, but it was also the only real estate company in town. My dad stayed at his office late into the night most evenings. My dad, Mark, and my mom, Emily, were high school sweethearts. The question "Will the Smiths be there?" was common because my parents went everywhere together. My parents missed many of my games because they followed Whitley's soccer team everywhere. Whitley always bemoaned having to attend one of my lowly baseball games. I dreaded the games when I knew Whitley would be in the stands. She somehow was able to draw the attention away from the game.

I became an official Duckling since I usually traveled with the Duckworths. I even chose to ride with Duckworth when my parents were able to attend my game. Duckworth called me Worm, as in *bookworm*, because I always had a book with me. He had a nickname for everyone, and Worm was one of the few that stuck. He took me from a right fielder that was scared of the ball to a fearless second baseman. He taught me how to get on base. I became a leadoff hitter and played the speed game. Duckworth saw that I could run and taught me how to embrace it. I was no longer a colt tripping over my own legs. He helped transform me.

Duckworth always told me I was the best but the ugliest twin. He knew I lacked confidence, because I spent most of my time trying to avoid everyone. I tried to ignore my parents' constant bragging about my sister's accomplishments, but she always dominated the conversation. Duckworth brought me out of my books with his crazy stories. I loved riding to games with Duckworth and Drake. Drake always rode in silence, while Duckworth and I talked the entire trip. I was shy around everyone but him.

Earthquake

It was a scene I remember like it was yesterday. He walked in the classroom and the ground seemed to shake and the lights to flicker. He was a new student. He had a Fresh Prince-like swagger the moment he walked into my math class. His introduction was full of the confidence I lacked. My sister even flinched. He said, "My name is Wyatt Hartley, and I am going to play Major League Baseball." His name was familiar to the teacher, and Mr. Troutman had a look of displeasure. Mr. Troutman assured the new boy, "Math comes first in my class." His family moved around, and Swansville Middle School was his fourth school in six years.

I believe the schools he previously attended were glad he had left, and his classmates were finally able to feel the glow of first place again. He was not much bigger than anyone, but we would learn soon he was stronger and faster than us all. He was more than just a typical twelve-year-old. My sister even saw his greatness, although she acted unimpressed. Whitley's male counterpart had arrived. He was not afraid of anything, and he would eventually seek out challengers.

No one knew it then, but he would slay our giant. Travis Harrison was a marked man, even though he did not know it yet. He was about to teach Travis a lesson everyone had dreamed of teaching him since the first grade. Red ribbons would soon hang in Travis's locker. Travis would need to learn what it felt like not being the champion for the first time in his life, or so I believed. Wyatt moved here just before the redraft. He was given a late-sign-up waiver, and he was assigned to the expansion team. He would be a Pirate or, as everyone called them, a Castaway. He was an earthquake we had no warning of what was about to happen. We never saw him play until it was too late.

When he walked into the cafeteria for the first time, I could tell he was hated. I felt he needed a friend, but honestly, I think I needed him more. The eyes of the entire sixth grade followed him to the seat across from me. Wyatt seemed to enjoy the attention. I knew lunch that day would be interesting. I was not made for the spotlight, and he was bringing it my way. He and I were opposites. He walked up and asked me, "What are you reading?" but before I could answer, "*Fun Facts about Greece*," he started talking. He did not stop. I listened while he spoke, and this would be our dynamic the rest of our lives. He told me outlandish stories, and I knew instantly we would be friends.

He told me he moved due to his father's job but his mother decided to return to Swansville after his father's death. He did not elaborate about his father other than calling his death a tragedy. His father was well-known for all the wrong reasons. I suspect he left to find a place where his name was not associated with nefarious things. Wyatt and his mother moved in with his father's younger brother, Jacob Hartley.

Wyatt's uncle Jacob was the reluctant local legend. Jacob played baseball for two years at North Carolina State University and was drafted in the fourth round by the New York Yankees. Jacob's arm detoured his stardom. He blew out his elbow when he was twenty-two years old, and he lost his fastball. He crashed back down to earth violently, and the pieces of his life were the scattered wreckage. He was still trying to pick up the pieces nearly a decade later. Jacob ran a car-towing and auto body shop. He lived in his mother's run-down old house. He was angry and complained about something or someone all the time. Just driving his tow truck to and from the interstate had to intensify his anger as he passed the once bright-green welcome sign to Swansville, "Home of the 1980 High School State Champion Baseball Team." Jacob wanted everyone to forget what he had been, but over time, his legend had only grown.

My parents, along with everyone else's parents, warned us to stay away from the new boy. His last name alone evoked painful memories for our parents because most of them had heard wild stories of the Hartley brothers. Jacob and Jamie lived a reckless lifestyle back when their names were on the marquee. Their glory days ended far faster than they wanted, and Jacob claimed he was stuck in this boring town. Jamie Hartley was a local troublemaker, but also a great baseball player. The trophy case at the high school had removed his record-breaking home run ball. The school tried to wipe Jamie Hartley from its records as best as it could. He lived in exile after he and Patti eloped one year after the two graduated. Patti was from a rival school about forty miles away, and her upper-middle-class family disapproved of the boy from the Brown Water. Patti and Jamie became outcasts of two separate places.

Patti was a CNA and worked unpredictable hours. Patti Hartley was rarely at our games, and her eyes seemed tired all the time. Patti was the beauty of her town, but she chose to leave and never return. She eventually assimilated to being from the Brown Water, and it seemed like she was originally from Swansville. She moved in with her brother-in-law Jacob for a male role model for Wyatt and for someone to try to tame her wild preteen. It did little good.

Every team was put on notice after Wyatt's first practice. The rumors from the Castaways of what he could do on a baseball field were only surpassed by the truth. Only Ogre, the league's biggest and best hitter, was able to hit a ball in the tennis courts behind the center field fence. Wyatt would clear the courts with an effortless swing. His dark eyes were always squinted, and he seemed to need glasses, but when he stepped in the batter box, they opened wide. He played catcher and was far more superior than anyone our age behind the plate.

Wyatt was a nuisance to all our teachers, but he also might have been a misunderstood genius. I was more shocked than our teachers were at the fact he knew the answers to most their questions. He stayed in detention, and when he was free to roam the halls, trouble seemed to find him quickly. The attention that followed his punishment was his fuel. He bragged about his pink detention slips rather than hide them. He was not scared of detention, and he often bragged that the weather was nicer. He even called the detention teacher Charlie instead of Mr. Younts. It became increasingly clear each week I would go back to dining alone with a book while he sat at the silent lunch table. He inspired my next reading selections as I began to choose biographies on Alexander the Great, Genghis Khan, and Julius Caesar. The days he was not in detention, he ate lunch in silence at what he called his private table. The silent lunch table was a gathering place for all the troublemakers that were not in detention. It was an intimidating place. When he did eat with me, it was as an old friend who had come back from battle. He told me extraordinary stories of why he was always in trouble and the insanity of detention, a place I had never seen.

When Duckworth watched Wyatt take batting practice, it was the first time he was ever speechless. He did not have a clever line to describe what Wyatt could do to a baseball; he just shook his head in disbelief. The league was about to be turned upside down. Wyatt would rival our giant Travis Harrison's trash talk and surpass Drake's and Ogre's abilities at the plate. Wyatt began to call Travis Ruby after he watched Travis dominate against one of the lesser teams. No one knew why. Wyatt would only say, "I'll tell you one day."

The Giant

Most of the league was Travis Harrison's bowling pins, to be set up over and over only to be knocked down time and again. Travis and Wyatt became enemies despite the fact they were a lot alike. Travis was the best pitcher in the league and had been since we were nine years old. It was extremely rare for him to lose. He toyed with everyone while defiantly smiling at his opponents.

Travis made sure everyone knew how many times he had struck them out. His dad, Alex, was his coach, and his mom, Vanessa, was the stat keeper. He had stats on everyone. When I was eleven, I actually put the ball in play for the first time, and Travis pitched an epic fit that would make Donald Duck seem tame. I hit a slow grounder or, as Duckworth called it, a swinging bunt, to third, and I reached on an infield single, bringing my career stats to 1–12, with 11 strikeouts. My next at bat, he threw two fastballs at my head. Duckworth told Coach Alex if he did it again, he'd report his team. Alex laughed then nodded at his son. Travis then made quick work of me with three straight fastballs. My legs were shaking as strike 3 blew by me. Alex smirked at Duckworth as I shamefully went back to the dugout.

Travis was nearly six feet tall by the time we were twelve. He dominated due to his size, but also, he relentlessly worked at getting better. His favorite player was Roger Clemens, and he emulated his every move. Travis was at best an average hitter, but when he pitched, he never lost. The only time I ever finished in first place was when we were teammates at ten. I counted grass blades in right field while he threw a one-hitter in the championship game.

Travis's dad and mom were the league villains, too, but those that sided with them felt like they did no wrong. Alex manipulated the draft each year to his favor and always had a great team. Alex was the president of the boosters' club, and he used his influence for his own benefit many times. Alex was greedy and wins were the only thing that satisfied him. Alex and Vanessa both constantly argued balls and strikes. She would smile and sometimes wave at other parents when her son struck out their kids. If Vanessa befriended you, it was likely she needed something.

Alex was a stressed-out car dealership owner and was a feared boss. I think baseball stressed him even more. He never made it to practice on time. He yelled as soon as he stepped out of the car, and our parents' eyes rolled the minute he arrived. I always wondered, was he planning his tirade while speeding late to practice? Alex did not like to lose at anything, and his intensity made the large man seem colossal. Alex was the only person I ever heard Duckworth say anything bad about. I heard Duckworth say many times, "Alex will live for forever because the devil does not even want him."

Alex forced Travis to stay after every practice and throw another fifty balls. He earned being the best pitcher. He and Alex put in the hard work. Alex would constantly yell two things, "Perfection!" and "What are you doing?" It was common to hear Alex shouting at Travis, "Stop being such a pansy and pop the mitt!" Each year Travis and Alex would argue more despite always winning. They never had enough strikeouts or wins. Alex's postgame speeches were always about the mistakes the team made and how they should be ashamed of themselves. Winning was not enough—he wanted perfection. Travis was a head taller than everyone in the league except Ogre. Travis and Alex only finished out of first place once since we were six years old.

The transition from elementary to middle school was not easy for Travis. He had spent the last few years of elementary school being the alpha dog, but the eighth graders made sure he knew his place. He was not bullied as much as warned. Travis had to keep his ego in check when around the older boys in the middle school. He became increasingly more difficult and disrespectful to those of us in the sixth grade. He constantly fired insults at everyone, and no one ever stood up to him except my sister. Whitley and Travis constantly argued.

She would not tolerate his behavior, and as she put it, "You would be embarrassed to pitch your next game with a black eye." She never followed up on the threat, and Travis just obnoxiously laughed at her.

Ogre

Darren Ogre Winslow was the biggest kid in the league and the best hitter. He led the league in home runs each year. He was a gentle giant, and he rarely spoke. He was already over six feet tall. He nodded at almost every word spoken his way or quietly said, "Yes, sir."

His dad was the most intimidating man you ever saw. Every season, Jack Winslow drove a new jalopy that was full of baseball equipment. He carried a fungo, and he looked like he was on his way to an epic street fight or he had just left one. All your fears subsided as soon as he spoke. Words whistled out of his mouth through his missing front two teeth. When Ogre was nine, he hit a line drive at his dad, knocking out his father's teeth. Jack loved when folks would ask what happened to his teeth, and he told the story while smiling toothlessly.

Jack was the local mechanic, and all his team's baseballs seemed to be covered in grease. Jack was the nephew of Frankie Winslow. Frankie had raised his nephew, and baseball was their passion. Baseball and his son were his life. Jack could take one look at a player and find what he was doing wrong. He would even tell opposing coaches what their players were doing incorrectly. I believe half the league's players were dropping their hands until he corrected them. Duckworth showed us the correct way to play baseball, and Jack fixed our bad habits.

Ogre was bigger and stronger than everyone, and his size and strength allowed him to be the best. He did not need Duckworth's cues. Ogre threw hard but did not have a curveball despite using balls covered in car grease. Ogre seemed scared of the big moment, and he usually was outpitched and outplayed by Travis. Ogre always led the league in home runs, but he never boasted about how many he hit each season. Jack dated and kept every home run ball, and the balls were scattered throughout their messy house. Ogre hit his first over-the-fence home run at eight, and I remember Jack running up and grabbing his son as he crossed home plate. Ogre never even mentioned hitting home runs; we usually found out from the opposing team or the rumblings at Winslow's. He was a menacing figure on the mound, and when he pitched, you lost.

Ogre and Jack cracked the code of beating Alex's team the previous year. The code was to make Ogre mad. He rarely became angry, but Alex had woken something up in Ogre. He pitched with a rage I only saw during last season's championship game. Alex Harrison called Ogre's dad low-rent trash before the championship game due to a dispute. Alex Harrison refused to pay Jack Winslow for his services. Ogre's pale face turned red, and he was unstoppable. He was able to ignore Travis's taunts, and he focused on earning the respect Coach Alex owed his father.

Ogre and Jack lived a simple life, but a fun-loving one. Ogre had free rein of the town, and Jack let him go wherever he wanted. Ogre was always wandering through the streets of Swansville, and everyone in town knew the oversize boy. Ogre and his dad lived beside Jack's shop in the middle of town, and their yard was full of old junk cars. They had an old goat in their backyard named Izzy. Ogre and Jack were generally seen walking to the same two restaurants each night. Jack never cooked, and the boy survived on BBQ from Kermit's restaurant and whatever the special was at the Dixie Grill. Jack was a minicelebrity at the two restaurants, and when he and Ogre entered, everyone loudly greeted the pair. Ogre's mom died during childbirth. The town seemed to be Ogre's adoptive mother. Jack and Ogre were embraced by everyone. Baseball and cars were their lives. Ogre started helping Jack in his shop when he was five years old.

Ogre was usually dirty from head to toe except on game days. He got the nickname Ogre when he was in kindergarten, when our teacher asked the grease-covered boy if he had crawled out from under a bridge. The teacher's assistant said he looked like a little ogre, to the laughter of the entire class. The following day, Travis Harrison brought the book *The Big, Fat, Smelly Ogre* for our teacher to read. I remember laughing, but I have regretted it since.

Ogre seemed hungry all the time despite never missing a meal. He would eat twice as much as any other kid in our class. I forgot my lunch for a field trip in the first grade once, and Ogre shyly told me he had some food to spare. I befriended him when he shared one of his three peanut-butter-and-jelly sandwiches while we were at the North Carolina Zoo. He and I only shared food since he spoke less than I did. Ogre was not just quiet; he was timid, despite everyone being scared of him. We ate in silence while staring at the rhinos.

Truce

On April 30, 1994, I witnessed Wyatt's abilities for the first time. He did not disappoint. We had a makeup game due to a weekday rain-out. Duckworth, Drake, and I would face Wyatt and the Castaways on a Saturday afternoon. My parents agreed to let the new kid in town stay over for the night, but first, he was my opponent.

My parents would miss my game since they had already planned on going to Whitley's soccer match. Whitley had outgrown the Swansville soccer team. She was well-known in the area as the best player, and every travel team begged my parents for her services. She was already soccer royalty. She played for a team out of Charlotte called the Queen City Elite. They contended for the state title each year.

The game was at the field behind Swansville Elementary. No one liked playing at the inferior field. It once served as the high school field fifty years earlier. It was a forgotten place and looked abandoned until the spring. The school's maintenance men only spent one day each spring cutting the grass and weed eating. Each year that passed, the treacherous left field fence boundary grew. The border was marked by yellow "caution" tape that warned the left fielder expanded each year. The maintenance men were responsible for the encroaching left field fence. Time was taking over the old field.

The left field fence was old and dilapidated; if a ball rolled near it, the umpire was forced to give ground rule double. All the left fielder had to do was throw up his hands as the ball approached the old fence. The rule was modeled after the ground rule double rule at Wrigley field, when a ball disappeared in the ivy-covered fence. Everyone had heard the rumor of a kid being impelled by one of its jagged edges. It reminded me of a fortress long past its days of being a stronghold. Years earlier, an overprotective mother pushed for the rule change as a precaution. It was the place inside the park home runs died. Many times a ball was left among the ruins rather than for one to attempt to navigate the rusted aluminum to retrieve it.

The old fence was covered in controversy each season. One year prior, a ground rule double cost Drake a chance at taking down Alex and Travis Harrison. The giant prevailed when Drake was left stranded at second base. Drake would've easily scored and tied the game. Duckworth claimed he had Travis and Coach Alex on the ropes. He still mumbled about the game a year later.

Drake would not start the game since he only had one inning available to pitch. Duckworth was not worried about the Castaways other than Wyatt. He started our second-best pitcher, an eleven-year-old named Leland. Anytime Leland pitched, the game would be close. Leland was chubby, and the only thing slower than his speed to first base was his fastball. He was not a bad pitcher, but he was far from dominant. Most players overswung at his slow fastball, and the game was dominated by ground balls.

The first two Castaways hit ground balls, and our third baseman misplayed them both. Wyatt would bat with no open base except third. Leland could not pitch around all the myths we had heard since Wyatt's arrival just weeks prior. Leland looked back at Drake for reassurance. Drake nodded as if he were a mother telling her child it was okay to get a piece of candy. Wyatt shouted back to one of his teammates as he stepped in the batter's box. He nodded in agreement to the inaudible message. Wyatt hit a mammoth home run on the first pitch he saw. Wyatt trotted by me at second base and said, "Get used to that." I could not think of a clever response before he was gone. Drake backed up to the outfield grass as Wyatt stared at him as he jogged by the quiet shortstop. Wyatt told Drake, "I would be speechless, too, after that bomb." We were already down 3–0 after the top of the first inning. We countered and scored five runs in the bottom half of the inning. After three innings, Drake and I led 7–3.

Wyatt's best teammate was my friend Mitch O'Neal. He made straight As, and all our parents thought he was an amazing kid. No one spoke an ill word of him. Mitch and I had a lot in common. We were both marginal players until we were twelve. Mitch had played in the shadow of a couple of Alex's and Travis's championship teams. He was unprotected during the redraft; otherwise, he would have been in right field for the Blue Devils. He usually batted at the back of the order, but he was given a new baseball life once he left the shadows and played alongside Wyatt.

Wyatt's confidence rubbed off on him, and he began to hit. Wyatt took Mitch under his wing and made him a better baseball player but also gave him the grand tour of detention. Wyatt began to get Mitch involved in his antics. Wyatt showed Mitch how to master the bunt. Mitch wizardly placed bunts perfectly down the line, and he benefited from Wyatt's home runs. Mitch bragged for Wyatt each morning at school.

Mitch spent most of the year playing baseball, basketball, and soccer as a way to let his single mom get a break. Mitch and his younger brother, Mikey, practically raised themselves since their mom, Sherry, worked every part-time job she could find. Mitch and Mikey were both great students despite being left alone most of the time. I stayed at their house one Saturday night, and Mitch made a homemade soup for the three of us. I could not even turn on the stove without being reprimanded.

Their mom, Sherry, cleaned new construction homes by the lake; thus, she missed almost all our weekend tournaments. She recruited Patti Hartley to help her clean. The two moms had a bond, and each hoped their sons would help each other with their weaknesses. Wyatt trusted Mitch, and their unlikely bond paid off for both boys. Wyatt protected Mitch in the same way he protected me. Wyatt resurrected something in Mitch that had been gone for a few years.

Mitch lived in a run-down double-wide trailer on an old dirt road heading toward the lake. His driveway was the unofficial landmark of where Swansville's Brown Water ended and the big water began. Mitch and Mikey were the only two students given the option to choose which middle school they would attend in the fall. Mikey chose Stoney Creek Middle School. Mikey wanted all the things the big-water people were promising. We did not need to convince Mitch to stay behind. Mitch chose Swansville Middle School. He did not want to follow Travis to the shiny, new school.

Mitch O'Neal pitched for only the second time in his career. He did a valiant job, but he could not stop Drake. Drake drove in four runs and even hit his own towering home run. Leland loaded the bases in the top of the fourth with only one out when Wyatt walked to the plate. Duckworth reluctantly did not bring in Drake to face the new kid. I was nervous, and my chest pounded in anticipation of something special. Duckworth brought in Tate Thompson, our third-best pitcher. Duckworth hoped Tate's southpaw delivery could neutralize Wyatt. Duckworth believed we would still score a few more runs if necessary.

Tate warmed up while Wyatt blew bubbles, unconcerned with his next opponent. The midday sun felt like late summer, and everyone was sweating. I stood at second base, conflicted. I wanted to win, but I also wanted everyone to see what my new friend was capable of. Tate shocked everyone and jumped ahead, throwing Wyatt two curveballs before he wasted two more intentional pitches off the plate. Tate hoped Wyatt would chase a pitch out of the strike zone. The count ran 2–2. Wyatt jumped on the third pitch despite it being well out of the strike zone. Wyatt hated walks nearly as much as strikeouts. The pitch sailed over the left fielder's head. The ball headed for the perilous left field fence. Our left fielder threw up his hands to signal the ball was consumed among the high grass surrounding the treacherous fence. Umpire Smelly Kelly shouted, then gave the signal for a ground-rule double. He sent Wyatt back to second base. The game was put in slow motion as everyone returned to the previous base.

The umpire was affectionately known as Smelly Kelly. He was fair and by the book. Almost everyone in town knew him. He worked at the town dump. The story was, Smelly Kelly was valedictorian of his graduating class but his family had no money to send him to college, so he took a job at the dump to save money. A decade later, he was still at the dump, and he was regulated to waving everyone in to just drop off their garbage. Duckworth knew him better than anyone. It was common to see Duckworth chatting the young man up with his arm around him, like he was lecturing him on life. Duckworth once said, "That kid is too damn smart to only sit at the dump all day."

Smelly Kelly stared at Wyatt, waiting for the twelve-year-old to defy his ruling. Wyatt slowly walked back to second base. He made a gesture of disgust, then clapped his hands as if he had just witnessed a performance. The adults and Smelly Kelly began to notice Wyatt's outlandish behavior. The umpire focused on Wyatt's next moves. No one from the Castaways knew to object other than Wyatt. Patti shouted, "What a joke!" and the crowd was silent as Smelly Kelly threatened to throw the single mom out of the game. Wyatt's faced turned red with embarrassment and anger. He would have scored on an inside-the-park home run without a doubt. The Castaways would have had the lead. Wyatt did everything he could think of to distract the pitcher, in hopes of causing a wild pitch. Tate struck out Mitch, then the next batter bounced to Drake to end the inning. The inning and threat were over. The score was 7–5.

The bottom of the fourth was much quicker than anyone anticipated. I bounced out weakly to first base. Drake popped up to the center fielder. The Castaways had a glimmer of hope heading into the fifth. Tate finished off the Castaways easily with three weakly hit ground balls. Drake gobbled them up. We scored another run in the bottom of the inning, giving us a lead of 8–5 heading into the sixth inning.

Duckworth let Tate start the sixth inning. It was a bad idea. Tate was getting tired. Duckworth was trying to groom Tate into something more. The first two batters reached before he inserted Drake. Drake's first pitch sailed over the catcher's head, and both runners advanced. Wyatt unceremoniously stared at Drake, waiting to face one of the league's best pitchers. Wyatt blew a bubble that burst, and the gum remnants stuck to the bill of his helmet. Drake struck at his first batter, but due to a dropped third strike, the bases were now loaded with no outs.

Duckworth called time. He shamefully walked to the mound. He called the infield in to meet him. Drake barely acknowledged his father. Duckworth said, "Do y'all want to win?" and of course we all empathically agreed, "Yes!" Drake's eyes shot up to his father, and he nodded without his father saying a word. Duckworth and Drake were both terrified of what was standing in the batter's box. Wyatt stared down Drake. He was ready to be challenged for the first time since moving to Swansville.

Our catcher stood up to the boos of Patti Hartley and the confused Castaway parents. Wyatt would be walked with the bases loaded. Wyatt was befuddled, and he pointed his bat directly at Duckworth. Smelly Kelly warned Wyatt. Wyatt mockingly laughed at the unheard-of situation. He looked for guidance from his uncle. Jacob stood with his arms crossed, knowing Duckworth's decision was to win the game and not to play the game. Wyatt walked on four pitches and earned his cheapest RBI of the season. Wyatt tried everything he could think of to somehow will the rest of the Castaways into getting one more hit. Wyatt clapped his hands and shouted insults at Drake. He loudly proclaimed, "I am not playing the Red Raiders! Y'all are the cowards!" Our fans shouted back at Wyatt from the bleachers. Wyatt was turning into a villain and a victim at the same time. Smelly Kelly let Wyatt shout insults due to the precarious situation. Drake ignored Wyatt while he struck out the next three batters. We won 8–6, but it did not feel like a win.

Wyatt did not leave the dugout to shake our hands; he nonchalantly just packed up his equipment. Duckworth sought out Wyatt, but Wyatt avoided him. Wyatt shouted as the second game started, "It's not fair!" so loudly his voice squealed. Everyone's attention was drawn to the new kid and his postgame antics. Everyone at the old field took notice of Wyatt, and their negative opinions formed quickly. I was thankful my mom and dad were not at the game. Smelly Kelly delayed the next game to tell Patti she needed to get Wyatt away from the field. His uncle had already disappeared. Duckworth showed Smelly Kelly back to the field as he went to apologize to Wyatt. Wyatt walked away from Duckworth as fast as possible.

Wyatt packed his bag in my grandmother's car. He was still agitated with the fairness of being walked with the base loaded. Wyatt's mom had given up trying to console him. She said, "It's just a game." Wyatt coldly stared at his mother. She must've known it meant more to him, and her eyes rolled up to the bright sun. My grandmother just sat quietly and watched his antics. She had witnessed similar behavior from my sister when rare losses found Whitley.

Whitley was notorious for complaining about her games. In her eyes, the referees were always out to get her. The referees were just as much as her opponent as the other team. Last fall, she was ejected for arguing with the referee. She complained so much on the way home my mom made her walk over a mile in the drizzling rain. My mom warned Whitley to stop grumbling or she could walk the rest of the way. Whitley's response was, "Now everyone thinks I am some type of villain." My mom pulled the car over, then said, "Get out. I'll be the villain today." I said nothing. She did not object, and she walked home. My dad was furious with my mother. My parents loudly argued until my soggy sister walked in the back door. Both my mom and dad hugged her as if she had been missing. Wyatt was nearly throwing the same type of tantrum.

Duckworth finally reached the distraught twelve-year-old and his mother. Duckworth introduced himself to Patti. Patti looked like she was guilty of an atrocity but Duckworth's eyes revealed the real truth. He apologized to them both. I stood and listened as Duckworth told Patti, "Wyatt is not like anything I have ever seen." Duckworth went on to say, "I only walked him to selfishly win, and I am ashamed."

Patti told the old coach, "I understand, but it is the child's game, not the adults'. Don't you know how to just have fun?" She was right, and Duckworth hung his head.

Neither Wyatt nor Patti knew all that Duckworth had taught us and how he had sacrificed winning to teach everyone the game. In my eyes, he was the epitome of integrity. He could do no wrong, but to Wyatt, Duckworth was just another greedy coach. Duckworth knew this season he had a chance at a championship, and if he had pitched to Wyatt, this season's opportunity would have slipped away. Duckworth's opportunities for a championship were fading as Drake was growing up. Wyatt lashed out at Duckworth and called him a coward. Duckworth nodded in agreement as he extended his hand, then Duckworth handed Wyatt the game ball. The old coach and the new kid shook hands as if they were calling a truce.

Duckworth said, "Thank you," as Wyatt replied, "Until we meet again."

Jupiter

Wyatt promised his mother he would check in before the night was over. She hugged him, and we jumped in my grandmother's car. My grandmother did what most grandmothers do: she took us to eat. We stopped at Kermit's and had BBQ sandwiches, then Wyatt and I both ordered milkshakes. My grandmother ate a banana split, and Wyatt helped her finish it off. An outsider would've thought she was his grandmother as the two giggled. Whitley was allergic to bananas, and the smell repulsed me. I left my grandmother and Wyatt at our booth and sat just out of the reach of the smell of bananas. The smell reminded me of Whitley violently puking them up when we were six years old. Neither Whitley nor I ever ate bananas.

My normally reserved grandmother seemed impressed with Wyatt. She was just as intrigued by the new kid in town as I was when I first met him. She asked him about his life, and he answered almost every question with exuberance.

My grandmother asked, "I did not recognize your mom. Is she from Swansville?"

Wyatt explained, "No, but my dad and uncle are."

My grandmother asked, "Who is your dad and uncle?"

Wyatt proudly answered, "Jamie and Jacob Hartley."

The smile on my grandmother's face dropped. She knew of the Hartley boys, and she wasn't prepared for another generation. The bill came just as their conversation began to be awkward.

My grandmother paid the bill, and we left. She stopped at a gas station to fill up. I watched a lone local scavenger dig out empty cans from the dumpster. I had seen him throughout my life, and he always made me feel uneasy. He was a large man with long greasy hair. His hair covered half his face, and when he walked, he only stared at the ground. He wore a camouflage jacket all the time, even in the heat of summer. My grandmother did not seem concerned with him and even gave him a slight nod as she walked by him.

RJ and Ogre walked out to the pumps. RJ laughingly asked, "What in the world happened? Y'all almost lost to the Castaways."

Wyatt shouted, "Y'all might be next!"

The thought of Ogre losing to a team full of rejects made RJ's head snap back in laughter. My grandmother headed our way, and RJ whispered, "Ogre and I will call you later. Stay in town tonight."

Wyatt's eyes dripped with excitement.

RJ was on Ogre and Jack's team. He lived down the street from Ogre. RJ was the middle child, and his two sisters drove him crazy. He walked to Ogre's house daily to escape them. It was not uncommon for RJ to be sitting in Ogre's house, because RJ knew where the secret key was located. RJ just started playing baseball when we were eleven, but his athletic ability gave him a boost to learning a new sport. RJ did it all. He was still a raw talent, but he could play any position. He caught half the time and pitched and played all over the diamond. He was Jack's jack of all trades.

RJ's dad, Coach Ross, was the local high school's football coach. RJ carried a football everywhere he went, and he wore number 16 in honor of his broken hero, Bo Jackson. The day Bo retired, RJ nearly cried, and I assume he did in private. RJ was built like a road construction barrel and could jump over one if he was asked. He did not look like a phenomenal athlete, but he was one. Earlier that fall at a Little League Football game, RJ danced with the cheerleaders during their halftime show. He did somersaults and backflips while wearing his shoulder pads. RJ was everything his dad dreamed of as a football player.

Coach Ross was a no-nonsense guy. He looked like a character in a Dick Tracy novel with his square jaw and good looks. He had the stereotypical deep coach's voice, and he dressed the part. He looked like he ironed his golf shirt every five minutes. He was always wrinkle-free. I assumed his years in the military made him take pride in his appearance. RJ was always in athletic shorts and his father's football team shirt or, more likely, his faded "Bo Knows" shirt. Coach Ross stood with his arms crossed or behind his back just past the dugout. He only spoke when he witnessed what he believed was disrespect or poor sportsmanship. He was very intimidating, and his powerful voice would make us freeze and sheepishly say "Yes, sir" when he shouted our name in displeasure.

RJ was boisterous and constantly chatted on the baseball field and in class. Everyone loved RJ because he was respectful, but he never seemed to stop talking. He could do anything on a baseball field, and he entertained everyone with his odd talents. He always obliged when asked to perform some amazing feat. He once captivated the crowd by balancing a baseball bat on his forehead while juggling three baseballs. RJ's constant talking landed him in detention regularly. He and Wyatt became friends while being locked away in detention together. Coach Ross took notice of the troublemaking new kid. Coach Ross warned RJ not to be guilty by association.

RJ's mom could not be more different from Coach Ross—she always screamed, "Come on, baby, you can do it!" among other embarrassing things. She was loud, and she usually brought snacks and would even give snacks to the opposing team. She went simply by Missy; even RJ called her Missy. Missy was our unofficial mother when our moms were not around. She fed us, made sure we washed our hands, and hugged us when we needed it. Her camera was her weapon, and she required a picture after every game.

My grandmother lived just down the street from RJ and Ogre. When I stayed at her house, I always ended up at Ogre's house. I asked Wyatt if his mom would mind if we stayed at my grandmother's house instead of my house. He said, "Of course not." The day's game was long gone, and now we just went to my room to play some Super Nintendo. Wyatt was terrible at every game. Wyatt had rarely even played a Nintendo, much less a Super Nintendo. He was bored quickly, and he only played for my benefit. He did not like losing at every game, and he kept saying, "This game is so stupid." Eventually, Wyatt asked to go out to play Wiffle ball. I reluctantly agreed. I searched, and I finally found the yellow Wiffle ball bat, but I could not find a ball. I was embarrassed. We went to the backyard to see if we could find a ball. All Wyatt saw was my sister's soccer goal, orange cones for drills, and four soccer balls. Our backyard was her practice facility.

Wyatt and I decided to see if we could score against each other. I set up in goal. I slapped my knees as if I were some sort of expert. Wyatt lined up his first kick with only a few steps for a head start. *Swoosh!* His leg swung through the air, and before I could react, the ball stretched the back of the net. Kick 2 was almost the same, but at least I dived the correct direction as the ball buzzed my fingertips. Wyatt laughed, then said, "This is too easy. I can't believe this is even a sport." His third kick, he decided to kick the ball with his left foot. The results were similar, and the ball blew by again. He was three for three as he trotted back to kick the fourth ball from five feet farther. The grass was his wake as he kicked the ball. The ball sailed over the goal, flying to the back deck of my house.

My sister announced her arrival as she caught the ball, "I am home!" Neither Wyatt nor I cared she was home. She then said, "I won today. How about you?"

I said, "I did," just as Wyatt's words pinned mine down with, "Barely."

Wyatt and I traded positions as Whitley looked on. He manned the goal as I lined up my first shot. I ran hard and fast, but he must've read my eyes, because my last-second maneuver did not fool him. The ball bounced off his hands as he stopped my first attempt. Whitley laughed from her view from the deck above. My next attempt easily flew through the air and reached the back of the net. Again, Whitley laughed at us, and she sarcastically applauded my goal. I lined up my third shot, and Whitley began to float down the back of the steps. My eyes watched her more than the ball, and I kicked the top of the ball and slipped as the ball rolled weakly to Wyatt.

Whitley carried the fourth ball down with her to line up her own shot. She was still in her bloodstained jersey, and her lip was slightly swollen. She played soccer violently, and her cut lip was nothing new to me.

Wyatt asked, "Did you get beat up today or what?"

Whitley responded, "Of course not. The other girl lost the game and the fight."

Whitley pushed me aside to see if she could kick one by my new friend. Wyatt mimicked my early move of slapping my knees. Whitley laughed at him. "Is that supposed to scare me?" She ran toward the ball full speed. Her right leg whipped back, and her legs scissored, and at the last second, her left foot sneaked out from behind. She kicked the ball slowly past Wyatt as he dived to her right. He hopped up, defeated and embarrassed. She pranced back up the deck stairs, holding her hand out as if waiting for a kiss on the ring. He did not ask for a rematch.

My parents came out to tell me to thank my grandmother for taking me to my game.

I asked my dad, "Can we stay with her?"

He excitedly said, "That would be great, as long as Wyatt's mother doesn't mind."

Wyatt assured my parents it would not be an issue, especially since it was walking distance to his house. My dad asked my grandmother, and she, of course, agreed. My mom asked, "What about Whitley?" My parents wanted an evening out, and my grandmother agreed to take all three of us. My dad first insisted Wyatt call and ask his mother. She agreed, just as Wyatt predicted.

Whitley was not happy as she hopped in the front seat of my grandmother's car. We passed the local scavenger again as he was now walking toward the grocery store with a wagon full of tin cans. Ogre and RJ were standing in Ogre's front yard with both Mitch and Dale.

Whitley sighed in dismay. "Great, more boys."

My grandmother assured her, "Don't worry, honey, we gals will find something to do."

Dale was already beginning to be wary of Wyatt, and his eyes did not approve when Wyatt stepped out of my grandmother's car. Dale was the most mature of our bunch. Dale was the second of seven kids. His older sister was autistic, and she was six years older. That Dale's parents, Ronnie and Candice, had their hands full was an understatement. Ronnie did the landscaping of every office and church in town. He was overworked and wore stained green boots. Candice cooked and chased kids along with heading up the PTO.

Dale seemed five years older than us, as he could cook and do laundry, since he was essentially second mate of his family. Dale was more like Coach Ross than RJ. He was a yes-sir type of kid. Duckworth called him Captain because Dale was constantly ordering everyone around. Dale hated it, but everyone frequently answered him with, "Aye, aye, Captain." He tried to make sure everyone did nothing wrong. He was like the good angel on our shoulders, since he always advised us not to do anything stupid. Wyatt despised him. Wyatt assumed Dale was one of the many reasons he found himself in detention. Dale was just responsible and knew how to fly under the radar since his parents were chasing a set of toddler twins, his autistic sister, seven- and nine-year-old girls, and his defiant five-year-old brother.

Ronnie attended most of the games, but he was always late and usually only had at least one of the other Rutledge kids in tow. Dale could drive a zero-turn John Deere mower before he was ten years old. When he was not at school or on a baseball field, he was with his dad. He sat at the counter with all the old men in town when eating lunch at the Dixie Grill. He woke early to spend the day with his dad, and baseball seemed like a nuisance if his dad still had yards to mow.

Dale, Ogre, RJ, and Mitch ran after the car and nearly beat us to my grandmother's house. They all knew my grandmother would offer them some type of treat. She was well-known by all the folks in town for giving out goodies. Everyone called her Granny Kaye. She did not disappoint and gave us all a two-day-old homemade cookie. Whitley and my grandmother went straight to the kitchen, as my grandmother put it, "to cook something up." Mitch was spending the night with Ogre; thus, as long as we could stay out, the six of us had free rein over the streets of Swansville. Wyatt and I dropped our bags in my dad's old room, then ran out the front door. My grandmother shouted, "Just check in by dark!"

We walked back to Ogre's house. RJ said, "You will not believe what Mitch just showed us."

Dale protested, "This has gone far enough."

Mitch said, "Take it easy. It's not a big deal."

Mitch had shown everyone a new trick. Ogre's front yard was not just littered with junk cars but now busted drink bottles. Mitch pulled a bottle of toilet cleaner called the Works from his backpack and a piece of tinfoil from his pocket. He squirted the cleaner, then placed a small piece of tinfoil in an old Pepsi bottle, then he squeezed it. He tossed it about ten feet away. We watched as nothing seemed to happen, until the bottle began to expand. *Boom!* We all jumped. The thunderous explosion even made Ogre's pet goat Izzy faint. We all laughed as Wyatt shouted, "Holy shit!"

Wyatt was still new to town, and hearing the new kid curse in either excitement or fear let us all know he would become one of us before we knew it. We set off a few more bombs, much to Dale's displeasure, before we had to break up for dinner. We made plans to meet after dark, except for Dale. Dale was afraid trouble was in our future, and he warned us, "Do not do anything crazy." Mitch directed me to tell my grandmother we needed to go out around 10:00 p.m. to see Jupiter since it would seem closer to Earth tonight.

Wyatt and I went back to my grandmother's house. She and Whitley were almost finished cooking dinner. My grandmother's pots were old, and the wooden spoons she cooked with made all her meals taste even more delectable. Her pots looked like they had been used before on an open fire. We sat to eat a hearty grandmother meal as I began to ask about going back out. I told my grandmother exactly what Mitch had directed just an hour earlier. She looked skeptical, until Whitley assured her she had learned the same thing in Mrs. Casandra's science class. My grandmother agreed, but only if Whitley could tag along. As she put it, "Ms. Whitley will keep y'all boys out of trouble." I bemoaned but agreed.

My grandmother was fast asleep as the three of us walked out the front door. It felt like we were sneaking out. Whitley carried our only flashlight as we walked down the middle of the street to Ogre's house. Ogre, RJ, and Mitch waited on Ogre's front steps. All three boys had flashlights, while Mitch carried his green book bag. Neither Wyatt nor I had told Whitley anything about the bombs.

RJ asked, "Whitley, are you ready to see one?"

She snobbishly said, "See what?"

Mitch told everyone, "Let's go to Scarborough Park. It will be quiet."

We walked over to Winslow's and threw bombs in the water. Whitley was impatient. "Wow, guys, this is amazing." *Boom!* Brown water and the plastic bottle shrapnel went flying. Whitley was mesmerized. We walked over to the playground and buried a bomb in the sandbox, then sprinted away. Sand went flying as we all laughed.

Whitley said, "Let's get some two liters. I have an idea."

Mitch only had two more small bottles, and we were running low on tinfoil. We decided to sprint to the gas station before it closed to get more supplies. We only had a little over four dollars between us. The value of money was still lost to us. Mitch and Wyatt walked in the store and bought three two-liter Pepsis. Whitley sneaked to the hot dog grill and grabbed a few tinfoil to-go wrappers. She waved, saying, "See ya!" as she walked out, believing she was untouchable. The store clerk locked the door as the three exited at eleven.

Ogre and RJ had to be home by eleven, or Jack would not be happy and he would come looking for the boys. They went home despite Whitley taunting them, "Y'all are scared, the biggest and fastest boys in town. Just go home to bed." Mitch told Ogre he'd just stay with me since he had his bag with him. Ogre and RJ gave us their flashlights. We headed back across town as they went back home.

Mitch told Whitley, "Let's hear your plan."

She said, "I want to make sure anyone that is too afraid goes back to bed." She looked at me and said, "Are you in?"

Wyatt agreed for me. "We are all in." He still had to prove his merit, whereas I was not privy to trouble. Whitley began to detail her plan of going over to the scariest house in Swansville.

On the other side of Scarborough Park stood an old house with a white fence. The white paint was peeling off, and the old tin roof was burgundy with rust. The house looked like it belonged on a post card for Swansville before it succumbed to time. Overgrown trees hid the once-immaculate house. The trees protected it from almost every angle, and the house was assumed abandoned. Everyone had heard the stories of lights being on at the big house and the small building just to the right of the old well. Every Halloween, brave teenagers would see who could walk the farthest down the potholed driveway lined with magnolia trees. Each year the old estate was swallowed more by time.

Whitley told us there was a trash and scrap pile we could reach by climbing the fence. The four of us walked across the lit park to our frightening, dark destination. She directed us to a path through the woods. Warning signs lined the trees in red spray paint: "Stay Away," "Danger," "No Trespassing," then "Turn Back Now." Whitley led the way, with Wyatt following. Mitch and I walked almost side by side—we might as well be holding hands.

We reached what was the back corner of the once-white fence. I whispered, "Whitley, how do you know about this place?"

She silently laughed, then whispered, "I know about lots of things."

The plan was to climb the fence, then set three two-liter Works bombs under the junk piles and tin cans lining the side of the big house. We would throw the two small-bottle bombs in front of the yard as a diversion to escape. Mitch and Whitley mixed up the concoctions for the bottles, but we did not seal the bottles or place the tinfoil in. Mitch warned Whitley she had used too much of the cleaner, and she disagreed. "The bigger bottles need more." Whitley, Mitch, and Wyatt decided to take the two liters while I would set the diversion bombs. Once my diversions were set, I was to flash my light. We all agreed, if something happened, it was everyone for themselves.

Whitley and Wyatt fearlessly climbed the fence. Mitch looked back at me, then whispered, "It will be fine," then he headed over. I kept my flashlight on, as the light of Jupiter or the moon was not strong enough for me to see in the pitch-black night. I aimed it at the ground. The grass was unexpectedly well-kept and short. Mitch set his bomb under what was a pile of tin cans as Wyatt placed his under an old woodpile. I watched as my bombs were last to be placed. I panicked. I had lost my sister. I quickly searched with my flashlight as Wyatt and Mitch openly objected. I shut it off as I saw her shadow. She was putting her bomb inside a trash can on the porch. I threw my two bombs toward the driveway, then flashed my light twice as instructed.

Boom! Wood went flying. Mitch was right: my sister had used too much of the cleaner, and Wyatt's bomb ignited quicker than expected. A light on the small house-like building flickered on. Someone was on the property. Mitch screamed, "Run for it!" A dog began to bark. I headed for the main driveway as Mitch headed for our hidden entrance. I looked over my shoulder for my sister and my new friend, but my frantic pace made it impossible for me to find them. *Boom!* I then heard the rain of tin cans.

The fear in my heart was fueling my feet. I did not see Wyatt as much as I could feel he was running nearby. His shoes hit the grass with a *thump thump* sound. I looked to my left and saw him, then *boom!* A gravelly voice shouted, "Stop, or I'll call the police!"

Wyatt said, "We are out of sight. That's not for us."

He was right; the magnolia trees provided cover. I told Wyatt, "Mitch is long gone."

He looked at me. "I'll head back."

I was too afraid, and I knew if she was captured, I would be of little help.

Wyatt slumped over, then jogged back down the driveway. *Boom!* A diversion bomb exploded. I walked to the edge of the driveway to try to find my sister as Wyatt also searched for her. *Boom!* The last bomb had exploded. I spotted her on the ground, trapped. I shouted in a whisper Whitley's location to Wyatt. Her foot was caught on an old partially fallen clothesline. A large man lumbered off the porch in her direction, carrying a hound. The hound was violently barking, and the shadow-faced man had trouble holding his dog. Whitley's ankle was bleeding from the rusted old clothesline. I did not run away as I watched Wyatt scoop her up and free her from the unintentional trap. He effortlessly ran with her in his arms. Whitley let out a screech, "Ooowwwwhhh!" just as the hound broke free. Wyatt arrived just before the hound, and a chase began. The hound was no match for Wyatt, and they escaped. His long powerful strides left the hound and his caretaker standing at the back of the magnolia driveway. The large shadow retreated back to his small shack, with his hound feverishly barking.

I met Whitley and Wyatt back at Scarborough Park. I could hear police sirens from two directions. Whitley's ankle was no longer bleeding, but her leg as well as Wyatt's arm all the way to his wrist were covered in blood. We decided to sneak back to my grandmother's house as cleverly as possible. We darted between cars and bushes, hoping not to be seen. We ran for cover as two cars rode past. We hid underneath the branches of a magnolia tree in the courtyard of Mount Zion Baptist Church. Whitley limped the entire six blocks. She refused any assistance. When we arrived, Mitch was hiding among my grandmother's azalea bushes. I told him what happened as my heart was still racing.

We did not get to sleep in as expected. Coach Ross woke my grandmother, then she got Wyatt, Mitch, and me up. He detailed bombs being exploded and that RJ admitted we were all involved after Dale confirmed everything. Coach Ross forced us over to Jack's house to clean up the littered bombs. Jack watched all of us clean up the debris, but then he invited us all in for breakfast. RJ followed his disappointed dad home for further punishment.

My dad pulled up with a groggy Whitley. Whitley's face was pale, and I knew the sign meant trouble for me. My dad shouted for me and Wyatt to get in the car. My dad rarely got upset, especially with my sister.

I asked, "What's up?"

He said, "You know what's up. You three are going to apologize."

I said, "For what?"

His chuckle indicated he knew the truth. We did not stop at the park, as I had hoped. My dad pointed over his shoulder, then asked, "Did this new kid put you up to this?" Whitley said no, and that was all the answer he needed.

We drove down the potholed driveway. I shook at what was at the end of the magnolia tree driveway. The place looked different by sunlight. The yard was nearly perfect despite the overgrown flower gardens. This estate was surely the pride of town once upon a time. Standing on the porch of the small shack was the local scavenger and his small red chihuahua. We walked past the garbage on the main house porch; the scattered tin cans and the wood scraps littered the green grass.

My dad introduced us to Cecil Bane. Cecil was a Vietnam veteran. Cecil was from a prominent family in town. While he was away fighting in Vietnam, his father, brother, and mother drowned in a boating accident. When he came back, he had nothing. He lived in the small shack beside his father's big house, and he collected scrap and did odd jobs. My dad was friends with Cecil's younger brother. My dad was one of the few people Cecil would speak to. I am not sure how Cecil knew it was Whitley, Wyatt, and me that set off bombs on his property.

My dad instructed us to pick up everything we had destroyed. My dad left us with Cecil, and he told us he would be back in one hour. Cecil just sat on his porch and held his dog, named Sweetie. She barked the entire time. Cecil pointed out things we had not broken to fix or clean.

Wyatt kept asking, "Are we safe?"

Whitley responded, "Of course. Can we get some water?"

I said nothing.

Cecil showed us the old clothesline and asked us to help put it back up. He said very little other than," help me here." It did not take us long to get it back up. All he needed was another set of hands.

After we finished helping Cecil with the clothesline, he asked if we wanted to come in for some Cheerwine. We all agreed. The small shack house was meticulously kept. The only clutter was a stack of week-old newspapers. He handed Wyatt his hound as he went back to grab Cheerwines. Wyatt let the dog lick all over his face, and he laughed. "This killer terrified me last night."

Cecil looked different in the light of day. He was still large, but he had a kind smile. His long hair hid his cloudy eye and scarred face. An explosion in Vietnam had burned his face, and he was blind in one eye. A Purple Heart was beside a black-and-white photo of his family from when he was a boy.

Cecil came back with our Cheerwines. He thanked us for coming back. Wyatt told him, "Their dad made us."

Cecil looked at Wyatt, then said, "You will always come back. I can tell that about you." He looked at Whitley, then asked, "How is your cut?"

She said, "I'll be fine."

He told her, "Don't neglect it, or it will get worse and you might miss a soccer game."

It was not unusual for someone to mention soccer to Whitley, since she had been on the cover of *The Swansville Orator* a few times, but it was odd the old scavenger obviously knew who she was.

He looked at me and just said, "Are you okay?"

My quivering lip must've shown I was still terrified. I nodded.

Cecil took a deep breath. He stuttered, then he began, "Bombs scare me. That's why I have Sweetie. She keeps me calm."

I tried to apologize at the same time as both Wyatt and Whitley. He shook his head, then rubbed his dog's head. "It's okay, it's okay."

Wyatt stood up and gave the large man a hug. A single tear rolled down Cecil's cheek. I heard my dad's car hitting the potholes and stood up. Cecil grabbed me and Whitley both in for the hug too. The three of us hugged him as he mumbled, "Roads find rewards. Time will stop. Victory is the curse."

Wyatt and Whitley had puzzled looks on their faces. My dad honked the horn, and we ran out.

Wyatt shouted, "See you around, Cecil!"

He smiled and waved.

Regular Season

We hoped for different outcome this season, but it was the same story with the same ending. Wyatt and the Castaways had very little impact on the league due to no pitching. Wyatt was tormented all season. He would get one at bat before the opposing coach strolled to the mound then told the pitcher to intentionally walk him. It made him more defiant, and he began to welcome the boos, and they rolled off him like rain. He confronted parents and was fearless throwing sand at the hostile fans whenever he deemed it necessary. He lost all his games, but he stood one hundred feet tall after each game because he knew he had left it all on the field and you knew deep down you had just escaped another giant.

Drake and I finished third. It was Duckworth's best season. Drake had his best year too. I don't think he struck out once, and he finished tied for second in home runs to Wyatt. Duckworth stopped playing "duck, duck, goose" with us before our games after the second game of the year, when he jumped up, only to drop down with a strained calf. When he was lying on the ground in agony, Drake barely flinched, but my heart was racing and I panicked and shouted to my dad, "Call 9-1-1!" Duckworth laughed and said, "Worm, it's okay, I think I'll live." It was the first time I saw his wrinkles, and I realized he was an old man. While he lay on the ground, grimacing in pain, I wondered what would baseball look like without him. He was unable to pace during our game as he sat on the bench with a bag of ice wrapped around his calf. Duckworth limped for three weeks. Duckworth started growing old before he grew up, and his calf was the first of many injuries. He finished the year pitching batting practice left-handed because, as he put it, he had a rag arm. The fifteen-day disabled list in the majors made more sense to me after the season.

When Travis pitched, it usually meant a quick game. Travis's height and size were magnified when he stood alone on the mound. Coach Alex's genius was strategically keeping Travis available to pitch. It was masterful. Alex would start Jaxon Leonard against the lesser opponent, then Travis would finish up, then Alex would start Travis, allowing Jaxon to finish up. Alex stretched Travis's weekly limit of six innings in what seemed like months. Jaxon usually knocked in half the runs since Travis was just an average hitter. Jaxon was the title character in a straight-to-VHS movie. He was almost a star. Travis received all the accolades. Jaxon blushingly waved off any and all praise as he headed to the shadows.

Jaxon Leonard bounced between his parents and his grandmother when his parents were not trying to make it work. Like RJ, Jaxon could play every position on the diamond. He would go where he was asked with not one shrug. He followed orders. He had been a Duckling too. He was a great athlete and a well-behaved kid, considering his crazy life. The only thing anyone disapproved of him was, Coach Ross hated his long blond hair and he called him mophead. Jaxon was a good pitcher and was a lot like Drake on the field and off. The two were quiet and just played. Jaxon and Drake liked Wyatt because he had come to silence Travis. Jaxon and Travis had been teammates the last three years. Jaxon was afraid everyone had labeled him a villain too. He tried to distance himself from Travis.

Jaxon's dad, Rob, worked for Jacob Hartley and was a lesser legend. He was on the Jacob Hartley-led state championship team, but he was only a sophomore. He tried to shine through Jacob's shadow the following two years, but he never lived up to everyone's high expectations. He lived in the shadows and hid his face under an old hat. Folks in the town always asked, "Whatever happened to Rob Leonard?" He never left, but he stayed out of sight. While Jacob Hartley was out pulling broken-down or wrecked cars off the highway, Rob hid in the garage. Rob watched Jaxon's games from the parking lot. He despised crowds.

Rob attended a small college for about six weeks before he came back for Jaxon's mother, Josie. He was still very athletic and handsome, but his face was always red. The folks in the town viewed Rob as another what-if because everyone expected he would have delivered a state title too. He deemed himself a failure, and he was never able to shake the stigma he put on himself. His star faded just like the blue in his eyes faded. He never got over the fact he gave everything up for Josie. Several years later, I once heard him mumble, "She made me forget about home runs." He knew she was worth it, and she was a what-if for him.

Josie still nearly looked eighteen, and her youthful looks haunted Rob. She always wanted more, but in her eyes, she settled for Rob. She was the prize of the town her whole life. Every eligible bachelor vied for her attention. Her beauty and her bright smile were the object of most men's lust. Josie occasionally left town to venture to the nearby cities with new dreams, and she eventually came back home, then the process started over. She waited tables at Kermit's. The owner, like Rob, always took her back when she returned home. Most of our parents disliked her because she only came around when it was convenient. She never sacrificed for Jaxon. When she did come around, she always made sure everyone saw her and she spoke about everything she did for her son. Rob contrarily never missed a game despite rarely being seen.

Jaxon, like his dad, did not like the crowds or the accolades. He was best suited for being a sidekick. Coach Alex treated Jaxon harshly and constantly yelled at Jaxon despite Jaxon being one of the league's better fielders and hitters. "Jaxon, what are you doing?" was like a chorus of a popular song that Coach Alex sang all the time. Travis and Coach Alex's success was largely due to Jaxon being able to drive in runs, since Ruby swung a bat made of Swiss cheese.

Jaxon was well adjusted because he stayed with his grandmother most of the time. She made it to half the games more as a taxi than a fan. She had lived this life before, and now she was old and tired. Mary Leonard played a key role to all the parents because she knew where all the fields were. Once upon a time, she had spent a summer traveling the state for all-star games. The Duckworth caravan left too early for most parents. Mary Leonard's maps were critical for the parents that did not want to join the Duckworth caravan.

Ogre and RJ had trouble outpitching Travis. The new, seventh team only diluted our records and eliminated our one week with a bye. The chalkboard at Wilson's only changed between who would finish fourth or fifth. The three teams stayed mired in a battle for mediocrity. The 1994 season was the season of the home run, as six players hit more than five, with three hitting nine or more.

Wyatt and the Castaways had a chance to win a game, but he struck out with two runners on. It was the only time I saw him strike out all summer. Anthony Angelo had a herky-jerky sidearm pitching motion that confused batters, but he usually tired quickly. I doubt Duckworth would have let him keep his sidearm pitching motion, but Anthony missed the Duckworth years. I watched in disbelief as Anthony struck out Wyatt. Wyatt smiled, as he did not even attempt to swing at the third strike. Wyatt must've known Anthony was different, because he would later protect him. Wyatt was the first to tell you Anthony had struck him out.

Anthony Angelo was a recent transplant to Swansville. He moved to our small town from Hicksville, New York. He told everyone he had moved to Hicksville, North Carolina. His dad, John Angelo, was a New York City firefighter that took over our small town's fire department just two years earlier. He and Wyatt became friends despite Anthony's dad warning to stay away from the Hartley boy. Anthony was not intimidated of detention or his father, and he joined Wyatt regularly. John grew to respect the defiant baseball phenom after Wyatt stood up for the stuttering runt. John loved North Carolina despite the hatred of his wife, Suzanne, for it. John was a soft-spoken large man. His New York accent and his size made all of us scared of him. Suzanne was loud and rivaled Missy Ross and shouted embarrassing things. Suzanne would scream insults at the umpires. It was comical, and John had no control over his wife. Looking back, we should've been scared of her more than anyone.

John and Suzanne adopted Anthony when he was an infant. Anthony did not look like his giant of a father, nor did he have the dark eyes or hair of his mother. John was injured after a fire and spent two weeks in the hospital. While John was in the burn unit, he would visit the NICU. He met an orphaned baby of drug addicts, Anthony, and decided he needed a better life. John convinced his wife to bring the baby boy home. Eight years later, they moved to Swansville.

Anthony was difficult to control. He was easily distracted, and he talked all the time. His stutter and the number of words coming out of his mouth made him hard to understand. The word *um* was the only thing that slowed him down. Travis was the first to mock him, and even our elementary PE teacher harassed the small boy. I wanted to stand up for him, but I did not want the insults to change directions. The insults did not seem to bother him, but they made those of us witnessing it uncomfortable. John reluctantly never stood up for his bullied son. John believed Anthony needed to stand up for himself, but the insults that most kids would've drowned under had little impact. Anthony seemed to just float by them and rarely even acknowledged the insults.

Midway through the MLB season, the threat of no World Series became a reality. Frankie listened to the radio and complained of two things: a strike and those damn Expos. The Braves' newfound dominance was in jeopardy. I am still unsure what scared him the most. In addition to Frankie's old radio blaring the Braves game, he had a black-and-white TV that seemed to have been fished from the bottom of the lake. The radio broadcast was a few seconds behind the TV, and Frankie would yell at us when he showed emotion, because he said we gave away the suspense. The summer was hotter than usual except to Frankie, and he would say, "Boys, this is nothing. I did not even have ice or a cool place to hang out like this."

There was little suspense during our regular season. The same teams won, and the same players hit home runs. Wyatt only changed the conversation of who was the best player in the league. Ogre and Drake deferred, of course, to Wyatt. Travis demanded he was still the best. Travis's defense was, "Maybe if Wyatt could pitch or if he weren't in last place, he would be in the conversation." Wyatt's response was simple: "I will show you why when we face off."

A Giant Falls

The fifth game of the season was Travis and Wyatt's highly anticipated showdown. Both boys circled the game on the schedule. Frankie even closed his store to watch the showdown. Travis was undefeated, and Wyatt and the Castaways were still looking for their first win. The Castaways improved with each game, and I believed at some point Wyatt would lead them to a victory. Mitch was the Castaways' best pitcher. He struggled most of the time, but he did well for a first-year pitcher. The Castaways' only chance to win was if a team would challenge Wyatt each at bat and a little luck. The stage was set for the worst team and its best hitter against a giant and the best team.

Wyatt stayed out of trouble the entire week at school, and he avoided detention for a record of three days straight. Our teachers all thought he had turned the corner. Proper motivation kept him in the good graces for at least one week. Principal Overstreet was surely lonely without her weekly visit from Wyatt. Wyatt made sure Travis knew something was going to happen at Thursday night's game. Wyatt bragged to my sister and her friends that Thursday night he was going to let everyone know why he had nicknamed our Little League bully Ruby. Wyatt was the only one that called Travis Ruby. The nickname did not stick. Wyatt invited everyone and made sure the news of the invitations reached Travis. My sister was the best art-ist in our grade. Wyatt and Whitley sat together at lunch on Tuesday, Wednesday, and Thursday, working on an art project. She drew, and he colored. Whitley laughed at whatever crazy stories he was telling. It seemed as if a spell was cast. It was the first time I observed her listening to a boy.

I thought very little about this activity until she came home with their art project on Thursday. I knocked on her door, but Ace of Base was blaring from the radio and she did not hear me. When I walked in, she was organizing a collage of pictures and a banner saying, "Click your heels, no place like home." The hairs on my arm stood up, and I had to shake off the cold chills. The pictures consisted of Dorothy from *The Wizard of Oz* with her ruby slippers five times the necessary size, and she had several posters. When she saw me, I expected her to say something, but instead she just said, "If you tell Mom or Dad, I'll kill you." Whitley had chosen sides.

The two boys divided everyone. I think she chose Wyatt because they were a lot alike despite their constant bickering. Travis insulted my sister many times when we were younger, and his insults intensified each year.

I simply asked, "Whitley, what is the plan?"

She said, "I'll tell you only if you go over to the park and help me."

I reluctantly promised. She told me that she and Wyatt had been working on the plan for several weeks. The plan was to put the posters throughout the park. It was obvious to me it would not end well, but I chose sides too. I helped her hang the posters against my better judgment. We even put a poster covering the memorial to the Scarborough Brothers at the park's entrance. The red-and-white gardenias were also hidden by one of their posters. The blooming gardenias warned us that summer had arrived, but we defiantly put posters, hiding them. I kept thinking, *What would Duckworth say?*

Wyatt and Travis's showdown was the six o'clock game, with Drake and me playing after. Travis and Alex showed up to the field, and both were confused with the signs everywhere. Wyatt acted as if he had nothing to do with it. The main banner was not in sight. Jaxon Leonard started the game, and Wyatt promptly hit a two-run home run in the first. The score ballooned to 2–8 by the fourth, and Alex inserted Travis to face the top of the order.

Travis struck out the first two batters. Wyatt did what he always did prior to stepping in the batter's box: he looked back at the dugout and made a comment. Most of the comments were something like,

"I'll be right back. Try not to lose the ball in the sun. Maybe opposite field or maybe not." This time, he stepped in the batter's box and said nothing. Travis threw the first pitch, and Wyatt rested his bat on his shoulder and took strike 1, then he did it again. He stepped out of the batter's box to tie his shoe, and as if on cue, Whitley rolled the "Click your heels, no place like home" banner out. Wyatt stood from tying his shoes. He called out to the dugout, "Ruby better click those heels, because he's going to want to be at home after the next pitch." The pitch was the hardest ball I had ever seen Travis throw. The ball flew over the fence high into the swaying pine trees beyond the right field fence. I immediately looked at Duckworth, and his squinted eyes said more than any words he could've mustered. He was in disbelief of the distance the ball had traveled. Wyatt slowly trotted the bases and, when he touched home plate, in the most obnoxious girly voice, said, "There is no place like home, there is no place like home, there is no place like home." Then he jumped up and clicked his heels.

Umpire Smelly Kelly called the coaches together, then he warned Wyatt. Ogre laughed out loud, and Travis glared at him. Mitch came up, and Travis drilled him in the shoulder. While Mitch squirmed in pain. Travis refused to take a knee, and he simply stared at Wyatt. Two innings later, the game was over, 3–11. Alex refused to shake Wyatt's hand after the game. Travis ran over to rip my sister's banner down. Whitley was grounded for two weeks, and she was forced to apologize. Her apology dripped with sarcasm. "Travis, I am so very sorry if I caused you any embarrassment." She held her head down in an attempt to hide her smile.

Coach Alex responded, "The scoreboard says a lot more than childish banners."

Ruby pointed at the scoreboard, then said, "I am undefeated. What's your record, Carson? I know you lost one game." He was referencing beating me and Drake.

My punishment was one week. It was the first time Whitley seemed to displease my parents, but it would not be the last.

Wyatt had become the alpha dog that day, and he knew as well as Travis. The nickname Ruby stuck that day, and Wyatt was no longer the only one that called our giant Ruby. The story of the home run drifted through school, and a legend was born. The ball was never found, and the distance it traveled only grew each time the story was told. It was hard to feel bad for Ruby; he had made our lives at school and in sports hell. His physical size was matched by his taunts. He always seemed to win at every sport, and he and his father made sure you knew how bad you had lost. Most of us idolized the giant at first, but his taunts began to turn everyone against him.

One is not born the hero or the villain; it takes time, but occasionally it happens in a split second. Ruby had always viewed himself as our hero, and the laughter and the high fives for Wyatt proved him wrong. Ruby's giant ego had turned him into a villain, and he did not know it until Wyatt's home run sailed into the pine trees. He would embrace being the villain just as he had embraced being a false hero. Travis wore the nickname Ruby as a badge of honor. He was glad to be our villain, and the name signified he was special.

Preston Loflin was one of the few that stayed loyal to the slain giant. Preston had benefited from Ruby's dominance a few years prior, and he still idolized him. Among the eleven-year-olds, Preston was the leader, and he tried to learn from Ruby. Preston rarely spoke while at practice, but he was a wild child at school. Rumors of his nonsense reached us, and we were all in disbelief. He hated wearing a shirt. He frequently warmed up with no shirt despite the displeasure of both his parents. He was the first person I knew that took a pill to stay calm.

Preston's team was coached by his dad, Doug. They lived in a big house on the lake, and he was generous with his time and money. Doug's parents had died in a car accident due to faulty equipment, thus his sizable home but modest job. His teams always had the best jerseys and equipment. Doug was the organized drill coach. His practices rarely seemed like a game and more like a carnival, with his players going between carnival booths. Wherever he went, he had a bag of orange cones, jump ropes, and other equipment that seemed out of place. The truck he drove looked like a rolling equipment room. Everything was meticulously placed, and everything had a specific location. Preston had an older brother, Ayden, that looked down on us from his lofty title of coolest kid in the middle school. He sat beside his mom, Angie, at our games in misery all summer. Preston's mom was the outcast of the other moms because she had crossed Missy two years earlier. She was friendly and did not have a mean bone in her body, but she seemed to constantly yell, "Sit down!" to Preston. Angie brought dugout drinks, among other things. Preston chewed a pack of green gum every game and offered us his bright-green gum.

Preston sat with Frankie and Troy to watch his idol, Travis, as he called it, "defend his territory." Preston turned pale and was inconsolable when Wyatt turned Travis into Ruby. Frankie told Preston, "Maybe Travis will get revenge someday."

Troy laughed, then said through a mountain of sarcasm, "Someday may never come."

After the game, Preston approached the giant, then said, "Travis, I think he just got lucky. Next time you'll strike him out for sure."

Ruby barked back, "Call me Ruby! Wyatt lives on luck."

Wyatt force-fed Ruby his own medicine. We all enjoyed the look on Ruby's face that day, but I knew his embarrassment would not stay for long. Ruby changed that day too. The embarrassment became his fuel, and he became more obnoxious and difficult. Wyatt became even more confident, and his ego began to swell. My sister's hatred for Ruby intensified, as did his insults. Ruby taunted Whitley even more, and he constantly embellished stories of Whitley's love for Wyatt. Wyatt became her ally, and he always confronted Ruby when he taunted her. Ruby and Wyatt despised each other, and their relationship would stay fractured for a long time.

Longest Day of the Year

Wyatt and the Castaways were the tournament long shot. They entered the play-in game with confidence. Wyatt believed if they could win the play-in game, the Castaways had a shot at upsetting Drake and me in the second round. I reluctantly went to his game with Duckworth and Drake. I wanted to be home studying for the upcoming seventh-grade math placement exam, but my parents forced me out of my room. They gave me the choice of going to Whitley's soccer game or tagging along with Duckworth.

Wyatt homered in the first inning to give his team a 1–0 lead but the lead would not last long. The Castaways were the worst team for many reasons, but lack of pitching was their doom. Wyatt was helpless behind home plate. Most games, a carousel of base runners crossed home plate, laughing like five-year-olds in front of him. Wyatt was tortured by the image of everyone joyfully blowing his team of misfits out each game. Tonight's playoff would be different, as Curt Christie and the rest of the Hornets gave the Castaways a glimmer of hope.

The Hornets led by two runs in the bottom of the first inning. Curt was not cocky, but he fancied himself the hero, and his stories were usually slightly embellished. If he had climbed a mountain, he would have told you he conquered Mt. Everest. Curt Christie played center field and was a left-handed pitcher. He was an average pitcher, but a great fielder and hitter. He always touted how little he struck out. He would usually say he was the last player in the league each year to strike out, which might or might not have been true. He was also a showman, and his best skill was bowing.

Curt was coached by his stepdad, David Luck. David was Mr. Mom all the way down to the minivan. He even had a sign that said "Mom's Taxi," but he crossed out *mom* and replaced it with *dad*. Kaye Luck had been a single teen mom when David changed her life. His morning cup of coffee was his persistent disguise to see what he called the most resilient person he ever met. She went from high-school-dropout waitress to stay-at-home mom. She played the stay-at-home part at all times. She rarely left the house. I think she was catching up on rest from when she was trying to raise two small children when she was a teenager. She was a beautiful woman, but she had premature wrinkles.

David sold insurance and was an expert at shaking hands. He always called us cool dudes long after we thought it was cool. His minivan and Curt's team's jersey had his logo, "Be Sure, Insure." He was the only adult that I saw wear a tie when not going to church. We all believed Curt was the rich kid. Curt never acted wealthy, but his sister Kaylee did. Kaylee was sixteen months older than her brother. She was an obnoxious brat. Kaylee acted like she was always owed something. She rarely attended our games, and no one missed her.

Curt and David had a bond. They constantly talked WWF wrestling. They loved the drama, and Curt always flexed like Brutus the Beefcake after great plays and pointed at his stepdad. Curt and David looked nothing alike, and when Curt called David Dad, strangers always did a double take. David was chubby with red hair and a bright-red mustache. Curt looked like he lived at the beach with his tanned brown skin. They might have looked different, but the two said the same things and even had the same mannerisms.

Everyone loved Curt and David. David coached Curt's team the last few years despite never having played any sports. David would get coaching advice from Jack Winslow and Duckworth. He was learning the game at a slower pace than we did in T-ball. Curt followed in his stepdad's footsteps and played the team's organizer. He always made sure we chewed the same colored gum.

Wyatt knew tonight's game was his best chance at letting the Castaways feel the euphoria of a win. Mitch had his best game, and the Castaways kept in close. Curt did not want to lose to the worst team in the league. The Hornets wisely walked Wyatt his second at bat. He stole second, then third, and he scored on a slow ground ball to first to tie the game at 4. The score was 6–5 in the sixth inning, and the Castaways had a chance of winning a game. Wyatt was due to bat second. Duckworth said, "Only a fool would pitch to him." He was right. Wyatt slung his bat to the dugout fence and the umpire warned him, and Wyatt waved his hand back at the large man, dismissing any warning. Disgust of walks and losses had taken its toll on Wyatt. He was set to erupt at any moment.

Wyatt stole second on the first pitch. Mitch bounced out to second, and Wyatt advanced to third with two outs. Curt Christie struggled to throw strikes, and Wyatt's lead increased with every pitch. Curt walked the next batter. David Luck called time and had a mound visit with the entire infield. Wyatt began to clap at Curt, hoping to distract him. Smelly Kelly called time and again warned Wyatt. Curt looked in, hoping to get one more out when he threw the ball to third for a rare pickoff attempt. Wyatt sprinted home, and white chalk dust filled the air. The throw home was accurate, and Wyatt tried to dodge the tag as he slid headfirst to the back of home plate. The fifth-grade catcher lunged to tag Wyatt as he was nearly airborne, trying to evade the tag. Smelly Kelly emphatically called Wyatt out. Wyatt stomped on home plate, then shouted, "Safe," at Smelly Kelly. Wyatt was adamant he was not tagged, but Smelly Kelly said, "He got you on the foot." I knew Wyatt would not go quietly, and he continued to have words with Smelly Kelly for the last time of the summer. The game was over.

Smelly Kelly shouted, "Someone get this lunatic off my field!"

I looked for Wyatt's uncle Jacob to put an end to the dramatic scene, but he had already started for his car. Jacob had Wyatt's fire and hatred for losing, but Jacob knew when it is over, it is over. I asked Duckworth, "Do something."

Duckworth stood up and told me and Drake, "Stay put." He walked onto the field and told Smelly Kelly, "Just leave. I'll handle it from here." Duckworth came to Wyatt's rescue again.

Smelly Kelly wagged his finger in Wyatt's face and said, "You have a lot to learn."

Wyatt replied, "I learned not to be a pathetic, smelly umpire."

Duckworth shouted, "Wyatt, let it go!"

Wyatt said, "Duckworth, you just dodged a bullet. I could taste my revenge." Wyatt obnoxiously licked his lips. He and Duckworth both laughed.

The following night, Drake and I played the Hornets. The winner would face Ogre in the semifinals. Drake hit a home run in the first inning, and we never looked back. We cruised to an easy victory. We won by the mercy rule in the fourth inning. Our showdown with Ogre and RJ was set.

My mind was not on the night's game. I would never dare tell Drake. I was not nervous, although I hoped we could pull off a miracle. Tomorrow would be the longest day of the year. I hoped the game would be a distraction, as my thoughts were on the math placement exam. I always had anxiety for our end-of-grade exams and other state tests, but this was something different. If I passed, I would move on to prealgebra and not basic math. Basic math likely meant a classroom full of bullies, and math was my worst subject. If I failed, I would also be in the lower-level science, language arts, and history classes. I wanted to be in the advanced classes despite the fact I would likely no longer have classes with a few of my best friends.

I dressed for the game, but I only thought of tomorrow's test. Tonight, we had a chance to shock the league, but I was worried with prealgebra, not double plays. Drake, Duckworth, and I would get one more shot at beating Ogre. The winner would go on to the championship. Duckworth deserved a championship. He had earned it. It was obvious Duckworth was worried about winning. He paid his dues when we were still climbing the dugout walls during our Duckling years. Jack, on the other hand, had the best chance to take down Ruby and Alex. I was ashamed I thought about stupid school and not tonight's critical game.

Jack started RJ, and he mowed everyone down except Drake. I reached on a dropped third strike, and miraculously Drake drove me in. Ogre homered off Drake in the third inning. After three innings, we were down 3–1. Ogre loomed in the event we would tie or take the lead. Duckworth knew the game was essentially over once Ogre took the mound.

RJ struggled in the fifth inning. We scored one run, and Jack was forced to bring Ogre in to finish the game. Frankie closed his store early and walked over to watch his nephew take the mound in the fifth inning. We were down 3–2 when Ogre was called upon to get the last three outs. We had runners on first and second, with the top of the order due to bat. I was set to face my quiet friend first. Ogre's typically kind gaze was gone, and his eyes turned black. It was a fearful sight.

Ogre made quick work of me. I was no match for three straight fastballs. Ogre tipped his hat after he struck me out. Ogre was one of the few people that knew I worried about tomorrow's test more than driving in the tying run. Drake did not even swing his bat while in the batter's box; he focused solely on Ogre. Ogre and Drake had battled many times. Ogre was victorious half the time, while Drake had bested him the other half. Ogre had to face our best eleven-year-old, Adam, before he and Drake would break their tie.

They would stay tied. Adam weakly bounced back to Ogre. Ogre fired the ball to second to start the game-ending double play. The threat was over. We lost 3–2. Duckworth, Drake, and I shuffled off the field as Coach Alex and Ruby looked on. Another showdown between Ogre and Ruby was set. This year's championship had more at stake, as the winning coach would choose the all-star team.

I shook Ogre and Jack's hands, then I begged my parents to rush home. I did not care if I ate BBQ or a cheese sandwich. I needed to study, and dinner out meant nothing. Whitley mocked me, and she seemed indifferent about tomorrow's test. Whitley's confidence did not spill over to me when she told me it would be easy. She assured me we would both pass the dreaded math monster. She even said, "Ruby and Ogre might pass." She chuckled at the thought.

I studied and practiced every test strategy Mr. Troutman had given me. Whitley loudly played her music in an effort to distract me. She would shout foolish advice and insults, like, "Solve for X, choose your best answer, 2+2=4, dah ta dah!" She openly mocked me. Whitley's best subject was math, and she knew she would pass. I was unable to focus. I scratched my head until flakes of skin fell onto the pages of my math book.

I was tired of her nonsense, and I came up with a plan to silence her. I stopped studying and looked through some old pictures. I finally found the picture of Whitley at Halloween when we were five. She was dressed as an Octopus, and Ruby was dressed as a Roman soldier. My parents had snapped a picture of the two innocently kissing. My parents promised her the picture was destroyed, but my mom told me she had kept the embarrassing photo. I found it.

I swung her door open and shouted, "Shut off your music now!"

She laughed and said, "Try to make me."

We had not been in a physical fight in two years. Whitley had embarrassed me in front of my friends; thus, I had not challenged her since. I pulled the photo from behind my back and said, "Don't make me take this to school." She gasped and lunged for the photograph. I dodged her and grabbed her from behind to put her in a headlock.

She squirmed to free herself until she went limp. She gave up and said, "You win."

I fell asleep with my calculator and the picture on my chest.

The next morning, Whitley demanded to search my book bag and check my pockets. She angrily recounted my victory to my parents. My dad made me swear I would not take the photograph to school. He told me, "Don't embarrass your sister."

I laughed and only said, "It's in a safe place."

The picture was my bookmark for my library book. Neither Whitley nor I had breakfast, as our argument nearly made us late for school.

I checked into homeroom before being assigned my test-taking teacher and classroom. I would head to Mrs. Joplin's room. I was in the same room with Ruby and Wyatt. The two rivals openly joked, and neither was worried with the placement test. Our test administrator was the most menacing teacher in the school. Mrs. Joplin did not tolerate anything. She threatened both Ruby and Wyatt in the first five minutes. She warned everyone just before she handed out the test, "If I believe you are cheating or you are being a distraction, you'll be asked to leave and you will forfeit your test."

Mrs. Joplin read the directions, and she wrote the start time on the chalkboard. She stared directly at both Ruby and Wyatt and said, "You may now begin." The room was flooded with the clicks of the calculator buttons. I was shaking with fear as I opened my test booklet. Sweat began to pour down my forehead and my armpits. Every time I looked up, Mrs. Joplin seemed to be staring directly at me. The test proctor paced the back of the classroom. Her high-heeled shoes loudly tapped the floor. After ninety minutes of torture, Wyatt closed his test booklet and laid his head on his desk. He had given up. I envied him. Wyatt would likely be in basic math next year.

Ruby's eyes searched the room for answers. The walls of the eighth-grade science classroom provided no answers. Mrs. Joplin's classroom walls were covered with oceans and seas describing extinct sea creatures. Mrs. Joplin focused on the giant's eyes. They were wandering. His neck stretched as he looked at my answer sheet. I noticed Ruby had the same color test booklet. My stomach growled, and hunger pangs began to distract me. I was starving and nervous. My fellow classmates looked back at me with every unpleasant echo from my stomach.

Two hours into the three-hour test, Mrs. Joplin sneaked up behind me. It was easy for her since she did not wear the typical shoes of a woman teacher; she wore sneakers, and she did not have the normal click-clop of heels. I felt her staring over my shoulder for what seemed like an eternity. A drop of sweat the size of a quarter released its hold on my brow and fell onto a word problem about a baker. The minute hand on the old industrial clock clicked, and I jumped. I looked over my shoulder at the women's-basketball-coach-turned-teacher, and I brushed the hair off my forehead. My anxiety was winning the battle. The room had grown silent, and only a few of my classmates were still fighting the test.

Mrs. Joplin tapped my shoulder, then she directed the class to close his or her test booklets. I finished bubbling my answer as Mrs. Joplin uncrossed her arms. She had me follow her to the front of the class. I felt I had a trail of sweat and shame following me. She scribbled quickly on the chalkboard the time before asking me to follow her into the hallway. The proctor was given control of the room. Everyone's eyes followed me and my sweat-covered brow.

Principal Overstreet greeted me with, "Carson, are you cheating?"

I stuttered and said, "N-n-n-n-no, ma'am."

Mrs. Joplin then told Principal Overstreet, "His answers were intentionally left out in the open."

I argued, "No, they weren't."

Principal Overstreet peeked in the door and said, "Are you letting Wyatt cheat?"

I said, "He has a different-colored test booklet."

Mrs. Joplin pointed at Ruby and said, "He is letting him."

My face told the truth, and Principal Overstreet knew my aversion for Ruby. I was permitted to finish my test, and Mrs. Joplin restarted the test. I hurried through the last dozen questions.

Principal Overstreet asked Ruby to leave with her, and she allowed him to take his test booklet and answer sheet. Ruby finished the test in the principal's office. I struggled coloring in the bubbles on the answer sheet. My heart pounded, and I felt my pulse in my thumb. I was the last student to finish. I used the entire amount of allotted time. My classmates collectively sighed as we could now finally breath without Mrs. Joplin giving us the evil eye. Mrs. Joplin concluded the test with the familiar words, "Thank you. You have now completed the state of North Carolina's seventh-grade math placement exam." Everyone sat up straight as Mrs. Joplin and the proctor collected our answer sheets.

Our modified class schedule should've sped the day up, but for me it would drag on as I awaited my test scores. Mr. Troutman asked everyone how we thought we did, and I was surprised when Wyatt said, "I aced that test." I shrugged and said, "Just pray for me."

Just before our last period, I ran into Mrs. Joplin in the hallway. She apologized and told me to cover my answers. "Don't feed the bottom feeders, or one day they will expect it." She walked away, and her sneakers loudly squeaked in the empty hallway.

The school day crept to 3:00 p.m., and the test scores would be handed out just before dismissal. I wanted the day to end, but at the same time, I was terrified. Our last-period teacher, Mrs. Cassio, would be charged with delivering the dreaded message. She handed me my envelope with my scores, and I looked at Wyatt, who was grinning. He must've gotten good news. I opened the envelope, and I had scored 97 percent. I would head to prealgebra next fall. Wyatt had failed, and he assured me that was his plan. We both agreed to see each other at tonight's championship game.

Whitley informed me she had scored 99 percent. I was not shocked, but I knew the result of us both passing the exam. We would likely share classes again next year. The school was shrinking. I would need to get accustomed to not being able to avoid my sister.

The Bully Wins

In life, the bully usually wins more times than not. This season would be no different. I attended the championship game with Duckworth and Drake. Duckworth did not smile the entire game. He was always sour when the season ended. He would have to wait longer for an elusive championship. Duckworth had begun to value winning one last championship. Wyatt and Mitch showed up just before the first pitch. The league's best players all started to trickle to the game to see who would be on the all-star team. Troy walked up in flip-flops and sat beside Frankie. Frankie knew Troy since Troy always beached his boat at Winslow's.

Troy lived with his mom in one of the biggest houses on our side of the lake. His house was where the big water started and the Brown Water ended. We all knew Troy before he officially moved. He spent the last three summers at his family's lake house. His mom gave him free rein of the Brown Water. Sylvia moved in to the family lake house after the divorce from Troy's father, Clark. They moved about a year earlier, and he quickly assimilated into detention. Troy's mother spoiled him despite the fact he did not seem too concerned with material things. If he asked for something, Sylvia got it for him. Troy was always impeccably dressed, and he never missed a mirror.

Troy's mouth kept him in trouble. He constantly talked back, and being disrespectful was an everyday occurrence. He was funny but vulgar. His nonsense was never mean-spirited, and it usually ended in a big laugh or a rare lesson learned. He wore number 69, and only few twelve-year-olds had a clue why he wore such an odd number. Every teacher in our school despised the rich kid despite his mom's best efforts to turn him into a quality person. Wyatt said, "If

Troy would shut up for two seconds, he would be tolerable." It was like the pot calling the kettle black. Troy always professed his innocence. Sylvia ran to his defense and usually somehow was able to get his punishment reduced.

They lived in one of the first luxury private communities nearby. They only had six neighbors, and Troy did whatever he wanted. He had all the fun lake toys and a pool. Most folks tolerated Troy just to enjoy his Jet Skis and to ogle over his fifteen-year-old sister, Ella. Going to his house was something everyone desired. Troy never stayed home and spent the majority of his time on the lake.

Ella and Troy could not have been more different. She was very polite and always went out of her way to be nice. Our parents assumed it was just for show. She constantly tried to keep Troy from, as she called it, Troy being Troy. His vulgar language embarrassed her, and she kept her distance. Ella was not spoiled even though the car she was set to drive when she turned sixteen in a year was nicer than most of our parents'. She came to most of our games, and everyone had a hard time not staring at the beauty. She knew she had all of us in the palm of her hands. If she asked someone to do anything, everyone jumped at the chance. Ogre turned red every time he saw her. He was bigger than her boyfriend. Ella's boyfriend, Isaac, drove his convertible Mustang to all our games and flaunted his wealth and his girlfriend. Isaac spent the summer on the big water, and he would later return to Rock Hill, South Carolina. We despised him, and our parents despised Sylvia.

Sylvia had a laissez-faire attitude and let Troy and Ella go and do whatever they wanted. Sylvia allowed Troy to be vulgar. The mother and son spoke to each other like sailors. Sylvia was a beautiful lady that had spent too much time in her tanning bed. She dressed a little too revealing, and the other moms kept their distance. She made sure everyone was uncomfortable, and when we went to her house, she usually made sure we completed some type of menial task, like taking out the garbage or moving furniture.

Troy looked just like his dad, with blond hair and blue eyes. Clark came to almost every game, but he kept his distance from the team and his ex-wife. He owned several jewelry stores across the state.

The Huggins King of Diamond billboards caught the attention of everyone that traversed the state on Highway 85. We were forced to sell doughnuts throughout the season despite the King of Diamonds offering to pay for anything we needed. Clark and Sylvia were treated like outcasts. Sylvia made sure Troy had the best and most expensive equipment. He looked like a baseball equipment model.

Troy was good, although he was not a good fielder. He did not like to get dirty. He played first base during the regular season, but we would be regulated to right field on the all-star team. His bat was valuable, but that was not where his contribution ended. Troy loved to talk and could be fun to be around when he was not cursing, but as Duckworth said, "His name should be Troyable, as in *tolerable*." He liked the attention that was about to head our way.

Troy asked Frankie, "Do you think Ogre and Jack can take them down this year?"

Frankie grumbled, "I sure hope so."

Ruby warmed up before the game, and his shadow stretched across the field. He had an effortless pitching motion, and the catcher's mitt his dad was using popped in rhythm. It was leg kick, grunt, then pop. He was throwing harder than I had ever seen. Across the field, Ogre softly tossed the ball with his dad. Their shadows joined and shaded the parents sitting in lawn chairs along the left field fence.

One year earlier, Ogre outplayed his counterpart, and Jack finally had a championship. Ruby was out for vengeance. Alex had saved Ruby's six innings for the championship, and they would need them all. Ruby threw harder that day, and his control and curveball were perfect. Alex taught Ruby how to throw a slider, and the league had trouble reacting. He and Ogre went pitch for pitch.

Jack was the most animated I had ever seen him. The stakes were not just a championship trophy but the right to coach the all-star team as well. The usually jovial man had grease all over his bald head from rubbing it because of the game's added stress. The usually loud Alex and Vanessa Harrison said little. Nerves silenced them while Ruby dominated.

The first three innings were boring, as neither team reached base. Jaxon hit a double off Ogre for the game's first base runner in the bottom of the fourth. He stole third when Ogre tried to pick him off. Ogre's pickoff attempt floated into center field. Three pitches later, Jaxon scored on a passed ball. Missy shouted, "Don't worry, baby, you'll get it back!"

Ruby mocked RJ for the error. "You can do it, baaaaayyybbbbyyyy!"

RJ struggled at the plate against the obnoxious giant. Ogre would need to somehow get the run back. Ruby intentionally walked Ogre since RJ was struggling. After five innings, the score still remained 1–0. Ogre pitched one hit baseball before being taken out due to a lack of remaining innings. RJ pitched two scoreless innings. In the top of the sixth, Ruby intentionally walked Ogre for the third time. Ogre was not comfortable running bases, and we could all see he wanted to attempt to steal a base. Ogre was slow, but sliding was his biggest weakness. Jack motioned for his son to stay. Ogre could not slide since he was only accustomed to jogging for home runs or stand-up doubles. He was helpless at first base as Ruby struck out the side again. The game ended, and Ogre was left stranded on first base.

Ruby and Alex had bet on Ruby's right arm, and it delivered again. The last week of school, he guaranteed he would win the championship. Duckworth looked just as disappointed as Jack and Ogre did. Ogre did not cry, and he rarely showed any emotion, but he threw his batting gloves to the ground. Ruby had ironically embraced his once-hated nickname, and he told the entire grade, "Rubies look good with gold trophies." Smelly Kelly presented Coach Alex with the league championship trophy before retreating for the shade of the dugout. Once again, Alex and Ruby had the championship trophy for the lobby of the Harrison Toyota.

Coach Alex gave a short speech, then he pulled a piece of paper from his back pocket. He read the names of the all-star team. I was shocked when my name was called fourth. I was honored to be called after Ogre, Ruby, and Drake. I was on the all-star team because of Duckworth. He forced them to put me on the all-star team by threatening that Drake would not play without me. There was a little truth to it, but Drake would've likely still played. I immediately thanked Duckworth. Drake's eyes were filled with excitement despite his typical silence.

Anthony was chosen likely because he was the league's best base runner. John Angelo grabbed his small son and lifted him high in the air as he hugged him. The fire chief had a tear in his eye. Suzanne shouted, "John, put him down before you embarrass him or squeeze the shit out of him!" John waved her off.

Wyatt pointed and said, "Way to go, Yankee!"

Anthony's smile would last for days.

Preston was the only eleven-year-old chosen. Preston's jobs were to be ready to run for the catcher with two outs and to relay the stories of the older kids' adventures to those younger. He told the stories as if he were delivering a sermon each morning while waiting to enter his class. He played the outfield and had a smile of a kid that was just happy to be on the team. I would later watch him secretly touch each of our bats with a wooden cross necklace for good luck. Wyatt did not believe in luck, and he would've confronted Preston if he had known. I kept his secret since he and I would spend most of our summer sitting on the bench together. Preston was the king of the high five despite being ignored and being left with his hand up. His dad, Doug, agreed to be one of Alex's assistants. Doug's job was to wave runners home from third and to agree with everything Alex said.

Troy was chosen, and many of our parents shrugged at the thought of having to see Sylvia all summer. Alex warned Troy, "Any profanity and you are off the team." Frankie punched Troy in the shoulder, then said, "You better listen, bozo." Troy would likely be one of our outfielders. Troy would be our designated unofficial spokesman. An evangelist had nothing on him, and he could make anyone a believer. I grinned at Ogre, knowing Ella would be around too.

Dale was chosen to play in the outfield and to provide the team with extra power. He crushed extra base hits or struck out. It was not uncommon for Dale to strike out three times in a row then have a three-home-run game. His idol was Jose Canseco, and he wore number 33 in his honor. Dale usually led our pregame routine, and he barked orders at everyone. He was our unofficial vocal leader. He would be the first to tell you "Good job" or tell you if you made a mistake. I believe, if Dale had spent more time practicing with someone like Duckworth, he could've been even better.

It was a no-brainer that RJ and Jaxon would make the team. Their versatility would be valuable when shuffling players to new positions. RJ would keep everyone loose on the field and entertain us when we were off. Coach Ross and Missy would be in the stands. I was glad Coach Ross was on our side, because he made me feel safe. I knew, with Coach Ross around, he would keep everyone in line, including the adults. Missy would supply the dugout goodies. Jaxon would give Drake someone to sit with in silence.

Curt Christie was selected for his defense, but we luckily got his showmanship. He bowed to the crowd when his name was called. His stepdad, David Luck, was chosen to be team organizer. David would pass out maps to everyone before the trips to unknown baseball fields across the South. He also made sure we had a place to eat or stay while in the unfamiliar towns.

Everyone was shocked Mitch O'Neal was selected. He was a marginal player, but he had improved immensely over the season. He would have an important role. His job was to bunt and to keep Wyatt under control. He would only excel at one most of the time.

Wyatt's name was called last. Everyone knew he would be on the team or at least be selected. The question was, Would he play for Coach Alex and with Ruby? Wyatt walked up to Alex and awkwardly shook his hand. Alex raised Wyatt's hand and Ruby's hand. It looked as if the two had just won a tag-team wrestling match. Alex announced, "Let's hear it for your 1994 Swansville Little League All-Stars!" The two boys looked at Alex, then each other, before letting loose of Alex's hands.

Jack Wilson reluctantly agreed to be Alex's top assistant coach. I was saddened when Duckworth was not a part of the all-star team's coaching staff, but deep down many of us knew, as well as our coaching staff, he was the real reason we were successful. Fielding with our feet, alligator hands, punching the midget, door-knocking knuckles, and A to C had made us all stars. Jack's grease-covered hand and the clean, car-salesman's hand shook and both agreed to let the past be the past. Alex ended his speech with, "Let me be the first to say it:

these kids can do something special!" The crowd cheered, and in an instant, the league championship seemed insignificant. We had a giant, Ogre, Drake, and Wyatt. The four would ruin any weekend plans and vacations we had the rest of our summer. Baseball unofficially just hijacked the summer.

Big Water

We only had one weekend left before baseball would officially steal our summer, and my parents decided to squeeze in a mini vacation. I was left behind because our first practice was Saturday morning. I begged my parents to let me stay with a friend instead of my grandmother. Luckily, they agreed. I propositioned Drake and Duckworth, but they had family in town for Ashton's next pageant. I asked my parents if I could stay with Wyatt after his uncle agreed. Jacob promised my parents he'd make sure we made it to practice and he would keep us out of trouble. My parents reluctantly agreed.

I was dropped off at Wyatt's house Friday after school. Jacob spoke briefly with my dad. My dad was a few years older than Jacob, but the two men knew each other. They shook hands, and it seemed oddly familiar. Jacob went back to working on a car, and the conversation with my dad did not seem too important. I kissed my mom and told Whitley goodbye as she said, "Can we just leave?" Whitley was unimpressed with Wyatt's house. My dad jumped in the car, then he, my mom, and my sister sped away to Myrtle Beach.

I was lucky. My parents' real estate business was thriving, and I never knew what it was like to not have everything I desired. Wyatt's house was faded. It was gray, not the original white. Broken-down cars littered the driveway. Jacob's tow truck blocked what was not hidden by trees. I felt foreign, and I carefully walked through the soggy yard. Yellow daylilies lined the old porch. I walked up the unfamiliar steps, and the door was ajar. I glanced back at Jacob before entering. I immediately felt welcome, and I entered the rain-cloud-colored house. Wyatt's mother, Patti, grabbed my bags and ushered me back to Wyatt's room.

Wyatt's door creaked as it opened. It served as his warning. He jumped up and hastily covered a puzzle he was putting together. His room was not spectacular in any way, and the only thing that stood out was that his floor was littered with newspapers all folded to the sports pages.

His mom shouted from down the hall, "I am packing sandwiches!"

He answered, "Thanks! And please make a few extra!"

I was puzzled and asked, "Are we going somewhere?"

He shook his head and said, "Just follow my lead."

Patti walked back in the room with four bag lunches. I grabbed two just as he did the same. She looked Wyatt in the eyes, then said, "Promise me y'all will be careful." He agreed, "Of course," and hugged his mom. He threw a few towels and his clothes in my bag, and we walked out of his house.

Wyatt and I walked out to his uncle, and he said, "We are ready."

Jacob said, "For what?"

Wyatt explained we were heading out on Troy's boat to swim on the big water.

Jacob looked at me, and I said, "We can't swim tomorrow because of practice." I was not accustomed to lying, but I was following Wyatt's lead.

Patti ran out and said, "I'll just take them."

Jacob went back to his work, and he seemed annoyed we bothered him in the first place.

Wyatt told his mom we could just walk and not to worry. Patti's head tilted sideways, and she grinned. Wyatt must've understood what this meant, and we got in her car. She asked, "Do you have everything you need?" Wyatt said yes as we pulled up to Rocky Point Pier. I looked at Wyatt as he nodded, letting me know this was his plan.

Wyatt said, "Mom, Troy will pick us up by the water, and I'll call Jacob or you if we need a ride tomorrow morning for practice."

Patti asked, "What time is practice?"

We spoke over each other and told her, "Ah, 10:00 a.m."

She hugged us both and kissed him.

We walked down to the forbidden dock, the ground seeming to shake with every step I took. Wyatt waved his mother off as Troy sped around the corner. Troy was on a Jet Ski with a passengerless tube bouncing in his wake. Wyatt looked at Troy, then threw up his hands in confusion. Wyatt expected a boat, not a single Jet Ski. Troy coasted into the dock as he shouted, "Don't worry, I have it all figured out!" Troy cleared out the extra storage of any safety equipment for our bag. Troy hid everything under some sticks and leaves under the old oak tree near the dock. He only kept his emergency matches in the Jet Ski. He told us his boat would not start but he had a backup plan. He said, "Someone can ride in the tube to my house, and we can grab the other Jet Ski." Wyatt volunteered for the bumpy ride in the tube. We shoved off as Troy directed me to grab his waist. I felt awkward. We all three waved bye to Patti.

We rode on top of the water. The lake looked like glass as we exited Cubbie Cove. The lake was never busy on Friday evenings. Troy talked loudly, and I did not understand anything. I looked over my shoulder the entire trip to his house. Wyatt kept giving me a thumbs-up as we hugged the shoreline to stay away from any of the authorities, as Troy put it. We only passed a few boats en route to Troy's house, as the lake was calm just before the weekenders showed up.

Troy jumped off the Jet Ski, and we coasted ten feet away from his dock. Ella Huggins and her nameless friend sat by the pool. Ella's boyfriend stood on the dock with his hands on his hips. He looked menacing. Wyatt and I stayed in the water. Troy was reluctant to swim to the dock and speak to his sister's boyfriend. He bypassed Isaac and swam to shore. He sprinted into his house while Wyatt and I floated ten feet away from the dock. Wyatt was not intimidated by Isaac, and he even threw up his arm and waved. Sylvia Huggins came down and loudly proclaimed Troy could take out both Jet Skis. Ella was indifferent, but Isaac was not happy. Isaac stared at Troy as he ran down the dock to fire up the newer Jet Ski.

Troy asked Wyatt, "Tie the tube to the dock." Troy directed Wyatt and me to follow him on the older Jet Ski. Wyatt drove as I awkwardly wrapped my arms around his waist. Wyatt squeezed the throttle, and I nearly fell off. The awkwardness gave way to safety, and I squeezed Wyatt's waist with more force. Troy slowed down once we were out of Isaacs's sight, and we had our first big-water rendezvous. Troy told us he'd like to just cruise the lake for a while but he had a special destination in mind. We agreed as two sheriff's boats sped by with their sirens going. Wyatt and I were impressed. Troy was not concerned, but he did watch them until they were out of sight.

The big water was an odd place. My parents and most of the Swansville's locals complained that the big water was just too volatile and unsafe. I believed it was a faraway place even though it was just a short boat ride from town. The water was not dangerous or nearly as choppy as everyone had described. It was a far lonelier place, as the shoreline was not attainable once the safety of the dock was just a spot on the horizon. We cruised the big water as Troy pointed and shouted at everything we passed. Neither Wyatt nor I heard a thing he said.

We kept riding farther and farther away from his dock. We passed the new marina on the other side of the lake. We ducked our heads and went under the last of the low bridges. A sign warned us that if the lake waters rose any more, the bridge would not be passable even for the shallowest of boats. We blindly followed Troy, and he kept waving us forward. We stopped at an island Troy called Golden Island. It was covered in yellow bell bushes. We swam for a few minutes. Troy seemed to be building up confidence.

Wyatt asked Troy, "Where are we going?"

He said, "You'll see when we get there. It is a secret."

Troy paused to listen to the wind before being interrupted by another sheriff's siren. The sheriff was in hot pursuit of a speeding car as it crossed the low bridge. Wyatt said, "It will be dark soon." Troy assured us it was not much farther.

We slowed the Jet Skis down at the mouth of a cove. We floated in near silence. Troy's eyes sharpened just as much as his ears listened. Troy's blue eyes darted from side to side. He was in a trance, but we followed anyway. Wyatt and I finally heard the faint sound of girls giggling, and the echo of music bounced off the water. I was intrigued. Troy motioned for us to be quiet, and he throttled his Jet

Ski in first gear. We followed his lead and slowly ventured farther into the cove. He gave the throttle a burst of gas and then shut off the engine and coasted as he listened. Wyatt did his best to mimic him. The echoes got louder, but we seemed to never get any closer. We passed a marina full of sailboats, and the clanging of the boats in the dock made it difficult to hear the giggles and the music we followed.

Troy stopped, and we drifted to his side. He said, "This is where I lose the trail. These damn sailboats and the water crashing on the rocks cover the bread crumbs." Then he asked me, "Can you still hear it, Carson?" I nodded, and I oddly felt I knew the direction the music was coming from. The sun was beginning to set as I instructed Troy to dock the Jet Skis near the rocks. Troy dead-anchored the Jet Skis, as he called it, and we swam in the direction of the enchanting sound.

Wyatt, Troy, and I climbed up the rocks, and I felt like we were headed for trouble, or possibly Xanadu. The intrigue outweighed the risk. We walked up the shoreline, and every leaf and blade of grass seemed to announce our arrival. I walked on my tiptoes as Wyatt and Troy casually strolled in the direction of the music. We crept farther toward a party we were not invited to. We reached civilization and crossed the road to what was surely a community clubhouse. We climbed up and stood on giant landscaping rocks.

We peeked over the fence, and we saw college girls. Our eyes were instantly drawn to the two topless girls playing twister. We were spotted, and the laughter and music stopped. Shame and embarrassment covered me. A man wearing a hat with the sign for Omega was in charge and shouted, "You're not invited!" then he pointed at security to apprehend us.

Troy said, "Can we be?"

Laughter answered his question, and security headed our direction.

We ran, and Troy shouted, "Well, screw y'all, anyways!"

Security tried to head us off at the road, but Wyatt shouted "Split up!" as the one golf cart chased us down to the water. The golf cart followed Troy as Wyatt and I were chased on foot. My feet bounced on the blacktop road, and I nearly toppled end over end more than once. I heard Troy say, "Just go!"

Wyatt laughingly said, "I will be back," through his heavy breaths.

I made it to the water with a sweating security guard in hot pursuit. I had to navigate the rocks on the shoreline to make it to my sanctuary. I dived in and swam to the Jet Skis. He radioed back, "He made it!" I floated just out of his jurisdiction. Wyatt came down the hill to the water in a full sprint just like I had done, except he had two security officers to outmaneuver. My defeated opponent stood his ground, blocking Wyatt. Wyatt bypassed the rocks and ran down the marina docks. He dived to safety, then he swam to the new Jet Ski.

Wyatt and I sat on top of the idle Jet Skis, discussing if we should leave Troy or see what happened. The sound of giggling girls and the bass of the radio stopped just as the sun finally winked at us before it retreated behind the trees. Wyatt looked at me and said, "They must've caught him. We better just head back." The out-of-breath security guards chuckled at the thought of having captured one of us. Neither Wyatt nor I knew how to get back to Cubbie Cove. We fired up the engines just as a flickering light bounced off the marina boats.

Troy shouted, "Don't leeeeeaaaaavvvveeeee!" He was in a high-speed chase with three other golf carts following him. Troy somehow had stolen a golf cart. He knew he would be safe once he reached the water. The lake was his salvation. The security guards' green lights flashed with the annoying siren of a truck backing up.

Troy slid the golf cart next to the dock, nearly flipping it over in the process. He had to face down my opponent as well as Wyatt's. He was outnumbered. The entrance to the marina was blocked, and Troy hugged the shore of the cove as Wyatt idled in his direction, narrowly avoiding the shoreline rocks. Troy dived into the shallow water to avoid being captured. Wyatt sped to meet him, and Troy swam in his direction. The head security guard dived in after him and snagged his foot at the last moment. He grabbed the shutoff key off Wyatt's wrist, and the Jet Skit fell limp. The other security guards applauded at their victory. Wyatt and Troy struggled to free themselves.

I motored over slowly and frantically thought of what to say. My approach was deliberate. I loudly and clearly asked, "Are you permitted to apprehend someone in the water?"

The soggy security officer replied, "What is it to you, Brown Water?"

I said, "Simple. I doubt my dad, Paul Cox, of Cox and Mitchell, Attorneys-at-Law, would be too pleased." Then I added, "We have a house over on the big water, and I doubt your bosses want my dad to head over here on a Friday night because of your actions."

He stumbled, then said, "Prove it."

I looked at Wyatt and Troy, then said, "Hold tight. I'll be back in ten minutes." I put the throttle down and sped out of the no-wake zone. Wyatt and Troy were released before I made it out of the cove. I had successfully lied again.

We continued the ruse until we felt we were out of sight. We stopped and laughed loudly when we knew the coast was clear. Wyatt said, "Troy, you're my new hero! We just saw real-life boobs because of you."

I said, "But we were nearly caught!"

Then Troy said, "Wow, I'd do it again."

Wyatt proclaimed, "Troy the Kingfish of the Big Water."

We all three laughed, and the cloudy night made the dark lake seem completely black without the moon's light.

Our laughter stopped once we realized we had to navigate the big water in darkness back to Troy's house. Troy always said he could get anywhere on the lake day or night. Now was his chance to prove it. The night air was cold, and the forty-five minutes of a joy ride would not be so pleasurable as we headed back. We followed Troy closely as we motored at half-speed.

The cruise back was not unbearable, until we reached the bridge. We attempted to make it under, and we eventually conceded to the bridge. We were trapped, as the water had risen. The three of us had no way back to the Brown Water. We were trapped on the foreign, other side of the big water. I felt lost at sea. I recommended we find a house with the lights on and knock on the door to use the phone. Neither Troy nor Wyatt agreed, and we decided to play it safe. They both kept saying, "What would your dad, Paul Cox, say?" Troy's idea was to just beach the Jet Skis at Golden Island near the low bridge and spend the night, then call from the campground marina's phone. He said, "The only folks that would look for us are my sister and Isaac." He was right.

Thankfully, Patti had packed two extra lunches that would get us through the night. My overnight bag, along with the extra towels Wyatt packed, were critical for a night under the stars. We slowly floated on the top of the water, and he saw a sheriff's car speed by. Its sirens startled me. We beached the Jet Skis at the small island sixty feet from the unpassable bridge. We set up camp a few feet from the pebble beach. Troy seemed to prefer sleeping under the stars. Troy gathered a few small sticks and leaves, then he started a small fire with his emergency stash of matches in his Jet Ski. The fire was just big enough to knock the chill out of the air, and we talked of the day's nonsense. We laughed the night away. The yellow bell bushes glowed gold, reflecting Troy's fire. Troy looked relaxed as much as I was terrified. The sound of the lake water was my only comfort. I had a hard time falling asleep, and I watched the glowing embers until my eyes shut.

The morning dew and sun woke us along with the hum of fishing boats. Troy told us to hang out until he returned from calling his sister. Troy was gone for nearly an hour, and each fishing boat stopped to check on the stranded Jet Ski. Wyatt and I told everyone we were fine. One of the boats chuckled as they drove off, saying, "Must be Paul Cox's sons." Our exploits were already traveling throughout the big water. Troy returned, and he motioned for us to follow him. We said nothing as we met Isaac and Ella at the nearest public boat launch. Isaac was not happy, and he chastised us. Wyatt mocked him by saying "Yes, sir," after everything Isaac said.

We did not leave the boat launch until after 9:30 a.m. We would miss practice or, at the very least, show up late. Neither Wyatt nor Troy seemed concerned with practice. Baseball only got in the way of Troy's summer on the lake. I knew my parents would find out I missed practice. I thought I blew it, and I assumed I would be kicked off the team. Duckworth would know the truth before anyone. The last practice I missed was when Whitley played for the state U10 championship. Coach Alex would not be pleased. The three of us missed our first all-star team practice.

Coach Alex made examples of Troy, Wyatt, and me for missing our first practice. My parents were upset, but my dad understood the circumstances. My dad was more upset with Jacob and Patti for letting me miss practice. The three of us ran laps at the next practice only after Duckworth talked Alex into letting the team throw water balloons at us. The three of us soggily jogged during practice, reliving every moment of our adventure. Wyatt was impressed with Troy, and both my teammates and I learned a valuable lesson. I learned how to lie.

Villains

Our first tournament was the county tournament. Coach Alex was not worried at all. Ruby and Ogre would surely begin to transform into an unstoppable tandem on the mound. Our first team practice was themed "Perfection starts today." Alex told everyone about North Carolina pitching icon Catfish Hunter and his perfect game in 1968. Wyatt, Troy, and I missed the summer's first speech about perfection. Wyatt said, "I hope the original speech was less intense, because that was too much." Ruby and Jaxon had heard the same theme for several years. It did not seem natural for all of us to be on the field together. We were all accustomed to being rivals, not teammates. We would need to learn to play together. It was awkward playing alongside my rivals, and I deferred to the better players. Wyatt deferred to no one.

Coach Alex did not like chatter while we were on the field. He lost that battle as we all constantly harassed one another except Drake. Drake said nothing as usual, and no one directed their comments his way. He stood at shortstop, ignoring us all. Duckworth watched and paced aimlessly. Coach Ross shook his head at our antics, and he was ready to ignite if we stepped out of line. We bordered being civil and disrespectful, and we let the insults bounce off us while we played.

Alex believed we could breeze through the county tournament and being tournament champions seemed like a forgone conclusion. I had no doubt we would prevail. We played the late game on Friday night. All our parents bemoaned the drive and getting back so late. Missy told everyone, "Y'all settle down. This is not that far." We were playing on the other side of the county, at the brand-new baseball complex. The other end of the county seemed to get all the perks.

Our parents talked about the western part of the county the same way they spoke about the big water. To our parents, they were left behind when folks wanted to move to the city. It was only just over forty-five minutes away. It was far from a big city, but it was three times the size of Swansville.

Ruby only pitched one inning in Friday night's first game of the tournament. Coach Alex wanted to let everyone get an inning, and we wanted to save Ruby for the county championship. Ruby, Ogre, Jaxon, and Drake did not allow a run, and everyone played as we outslugged the weaker kids from the western side of the county. They had a new field, and it was the only thing impressive about their team. We won 11–0.

We played two games on Saturday, and we outscored our opponents 17–1. The one run only came due to three throwing errors on one play. Wyatt started the error by throwing a bunt into right field, and before we knew it, we had given up a four-base error or, as most folks our aged called it, a Little League home run. Our first three games of the county tournament, we scored twenty-eight runs and only gave up one unearned run. Coach Alex was displeased, and he forced us to run for an hour after our game. We ran along the fence while our next victim played to face us in the county championship. Alex shouted "Perfection!" the entire time. Wyatt repeated it each time with a smile on his face, and we all had to hide our laughter. RJ loved to run, and he would stop and do a backflip when we turned around. Perfection or not, we knew we would be hard to beat with Ruby on the mound for Sunday's championship game.

The only thing in our way of being county champions was one of our former teammates and my old friend. He was not as big as Ogre or Ruby, but he had a late birthday like me. Puberty had already tracked him down, and he was bigger than most kids in the league. Holden Stevenson had moved to the other side of the county two years earlier. His dad clashed with Coach Alex, and Coach Alex had won. Alex banished the pair. Elliot Stevenson and Holden left town in an effort to build their own baseball legacy. They fled to the other end of the county. Holden was left-handed, like Ogre, but he had a curveball to match Ruby's. Holden always pitched from the stretch, and he wore his hat at an angle, covering his right eye. When he pitched, all you saw from the batter's box was one menacing big brown eye.

I remembered Holden better than most since his dad and my dad both worked in real estate. Holden and I were friends until he had decided he was too cool for the bookworm I had become. Holden had been a Duckling, and his dad loved Duckworth. He would shout Duckworth lines throughout every game. Facing Holden in the county tournament was like looking back at the past. We had not forgotten him, and we all knew we had to take him down. I was sure Holden would be surprised that I was on the all-star team. Elliot and Holden wanted their revenge against Coach Alex, and fate had given them one chance.

Elliot Stevenson had not been an underdog in a while, and now Coach Alex made sure Ruby was ready to go toe to toe with an old adversary. Coach Alex gave a pregame speech from the top of the bleachers just past the first-base dugout. He wanted to be seen and heard by everyone. His speech was more like a sermon, and he raised his voice for all to hear. He spoke of dominance, and he referenced going for the jugular. Elliot Stevenson saw the display from his dugout. He looked disgusted. Holden warmed up near his dad, and the two glanced over every time Alex enthusiastically emphasized the word *dominate*. Alex finished his sermon with, "Today we show no mercy!" and he pounded his hand into his right palm, then jumped down. Coach Alex's teams normally shouted "Perfection!" as a group prior to the game, but today we would break it down by saying "Dominate!"

Holden gave us a one-eyed stare and started throwing heat. He was an intimidating figure on the mound, and we would need to learn to ignore our opponents' giants and monsters if we wanted to play baseball all summer. Holden pitching from the stretch threw off our timing, and his fastball jumped out of his hand. Wyatt even struggled and hit a soft grounder to third. The sight of Wyatt struggling to catch up to Holden's fastball made the rest of the team feel intimidated except for Drake. Drake hit a home run and gave us an early lead.

Ruby struck out the first two batters, then he walked one before he faced the one-eyed stare of his rival. Holden was not scared of our giant, and he jogged the bases a moment after stepping into the batter's box. We trailed for the first time. Holden pointed and smiled at his dad when he crossed home plate. His dad looked at the shiny, new scoreboard. It flashed 2–1, and his chest poked out at the thought of taking down his rival. Holden and Elliot's revenge would not last long. Holden's second time through the lineup did not go as he or his dad had hoped. They would not get their revenge. The father and son would have to settle for being royalty only on the western side of the county. Ogre and Wyatt hit home runs, and our time-trailing only lasted a short time. Our dugout seemed like a party, as everyone was giving jump high fives and congratulating one another after they scored.

Coach Alex grinned from ear to ear as we cruised to the win. Holden gave up four home runs, and Ruby even connected for a rare home run. Elliott had to shake Coach Alex's hand after the game and congratulate the man who had run him out of town. Holden was good, but he was not as good Ruby. Coach Alex condescendingly told Elliot, "I wish Holden would've been a part of our team, because we could always use one more pitcher." We won 10–2.

Alex chose Ruby as the tournament MVP, and he made a spectacle at the awards ceremony by grabbing the microphone and addressing the crowd. The rest of the county turned us into villains while listening to Coach Alex's overly arrogant speech about us dominating the tournament. He told the crowd, "It will take a special team with special kids to take us down." He rambled on about playing to near perfection and we should have not even given up one run. No one clapped when he finally stopped speaking. Duckworth looked like he could not get away fast enough. Alex acted as we would leave in triumph, but Coach Ross, Duckworth, and Jack Wilson hung their heads in shame as we victoriously loaded up to head back to the Brown Water of Swansville.

Rocky Point Pier

Our first practice after our dominance of the county tournament, Coach Alex made us feel like we squeaked by our opponents. He never mentioned we outscored our opponents 38–3. His mantra was *perfection*. It was at this practice that I knew he would preach the same sermon on perfection all summer. He would do his best to convert the nonbelievers. Every ground ball misplayed resulted in ten push-ups for the entire team. Jaxon and Ruby were accustomed to push-ups, and this punishment was second nature. They dropped to the ground as soon as someone committed an error. Coach Alex coached by discipline accompanied by punishment. He did enjoy celebrations, but they were short-lived. We never even took batting practice for the two-hour-long practice. His message: "Throwing errors will cost you a game."

After practice, Wyatt asked Duckworth to stay and pitch batting practice, but he declined. Duckworth had promised not to interfere with the team. He was reduced to being a parent and a fan. Duckworth's eyes told a different story. He said, "How about a group of y'all go down to Rocky Point Pier and play dock derby?"

Wyatt was perplexed, then asked Drake, "Is this why you are so good, swimming at the lake?"

Drake grinned as I said, "Wyatt, I'll explain. Let's all go."

Drake rarely did anything outside of practice or play a game other than playing the game he and his father invented.

Duckworth offered to drive, then assured our parents we would all be fine at the old forbidden pier. Dale, Anthony, Wyatt, Ogre, RJ, Drake, and I piled in Duckworth's Blazer. Ruby shouted at the group, "When I am finished, maybe I'll catch up!" Ruby still had to finish his pitching routine. His practice ended when his dad felt Ruby had thrown ten perfect pitches. Duckworth dropped us off and handed Drake a skinny yellow Wiffle ball bat. It was not particularly odd of Duckworth to have the bat with him. Drake and I played this game many times after a long day of practice. It was one of the few things Drake seemed to enjoy. The only difference was, Duckworth would not be pitching the pebbles. Duckworth waved and said, "I'll be back in two hours."

The game was simple. Each batter was given a chance to hit ten pebbles while balancing on an old pier piling. The pitcher treaded water or stood on his toes to toss the tiny pebbles. Pitching was the hardest part of the game and the most critical. The distance of the pebble did not matter, but staying on the piling and making contact was the key. I assumed Drake would dominate as he and his dad had played this game many times. Duckworth usually pitched, and without him, I assumed his position. Ogre, of course, agreed to keep score since he would sit on the edge of the dock.

When we arrived, Cecil's shopping cart full of cans was just to the left of the entrance of the old dock. Wyatt carefully pushed it aside. The group was shocked Wyatt took such special care of the old shopping cart. In an effort to deflect the attention off why Wyatt would be so concerned with Cecil's shopping cart, I made the comment, "Guess we will look pretty goofy swimming in our baseball pants."

Dale laughed, then said, "Are we even allowed to be here?"

I responded to impress Wyatt, "Does it really matter?"

Wyatt angrily said, "Then go home, Captain." Wyatt then asked, "Drake, how does this work?"

Drake responded, "Explain the rules, Carson."

I told him, "Two rounds, most hits out of ten wins. You get two passes, and if you fall off, you give up your remaining chances."

Wyatt agreed to go first for a practice round. We all agreed, if you'd never played, then you would get five practice pitches. Only Wyatt and Dale had never played. We all collected pebbles, and I set up to pitch. Pitching was not easy since I would be treading water and bouncing off the bottom, which was just under six feet deep.

The practice round went as expected, with Wyatt claiming, "Carson, can you throw a pitch I can hit?" He continued to claim I was a terrible pitcher, and he asked if Ogre would replace me. Ogre refused and stayed onshore. Drake went seven for ten. RJ finished round 1 in second place with five for ten. Dale and Wyatt all were only able to connect and hit three pebbles. Wyatt was disgusted, proclaiming, "This game is stupid." Anthony hit four out of nine before erratically swinging for a bad pitch. He plunged into the Brown Water, and he barely made a splash with his dive into the Brown Water. Wyatt complained I was favoring Drake. "Guess you're going to make sure he wins." I shook my head in disagreement.

Drake's second round, he struggled. It was the worst round he ever had. He only hit two before falling off the pilings. Everyone had an opportunity to beat Drake at his own game. RJ and Dale both struggled in the second round. They only hit four for ten. I wished I had chosen to bat. I had never beaten Drake, and I usually hit at least five per round. Anthony surprised everyone hitting five for ten in his second round. He did a swan dive off into the lake. When he resurfaced, he pumped his fist. Wyatt would need to hit six out of ten to beat Drake.

Wyatt's eyes looked different as I fired the first pebble. The yellow Wiffle ball bat made a sound like thunder. Wyatt boomed a pebble to the other side of the lake. Leaves rustled, and the pebble did not sink back to the warm waters of Cubbie Cove. Five of the first eight pebbles I threw, he deposited to the other side of the cove. He only needed two more hits to become the new king of dock derby.

Honk! Coach Alex and Ruby pulled into Rocky Point Pier just as I released my ninth pebble to Wyatt. He let it pass, and he stood exposed on top of the old piling. Coach Alex shouted, "Travis, I'll be back in hour!" Ruby strutted toward the dock. Ogre was the only one of us that had a chance to stop Ruby. Ruby grabbed Cecil's cart, pushed it into the lake. He loudly proclaimed, "A little more trash for the Brown Water!" Wyatt carefully climbed off the pier piling, then swam to shore. I followed. I knew what might happen next.

All of Cecil's cans were floating on top of the water. I screamed, "Anthony, Dale, help clean this up!"

Wyatt went straight for Ruby. Wyatt shouted, "Get the hell out of here!" Ruby stood his ground and waited for Wyatt. I crawled up the shoreline and grabbed Wyatt by his wrist to hold him back. He jerked away.

Dale screamed, "Is it worth it?"

I frantically tried to settle Wyatt down. I failed. Wyatt confronted the larger boy. Wyatt was not intimidated, and he stood on his tiptoes. The two rivals looked ready to fight until Drake shouted, "Stop! Y'all better not! I'll quit right now!"

Ogre quietly said, "Me too."

Wyatt and Ruby knew they needed each other, but any chance at winning something special, they needed to have Ogre and Drake. The fight ended with the threats of the two quietest boys and no punches.

Ruby retreated, and he went to sit by the road, alone, to wait for his father. Anthony and Dale were already picking up the cans floating in the water. Drake came down to help, and he walked the shoreline alone, searching for more. RJ and Ogre were working on pulling cans out of the on-site trash can. Wyatt and I searched for Cecil to apologize. We never found him, but we collected a few more cans.

Wyatt asked, "Do you think they would have quit?"

I answered, "Drake would never abandon us."

I heard the faint sound of Duckworth's horn, and I said, "That's our ride."

We both sprinted Duckworth's way.

Watermelons

The qualifier round was played about an hour and a half away. We would not get a hotel room unless we could advance past the next round. We were motivated by the dream of staying in a hotel with all our friends, and I looked forward to seeing Troy's sister more. Ella Russell was about three years older than us. She was the first girl that made me forget about baseball, or anything else, for that matter. She and Troy were exact opposites. Ella behaved with class and dignity. She walked like a person of high standing and gave the impression she was some type of royalty. She carried herself in a way we all loved. We loved everything about her except for two things: she ignored us, and her boyfriend Isaac. Isaac looked like a villain from a 1980s movie. His hair was perfectly quaffed, and his white shoes were spotless. He was definitely not someone that was mistaken for a person from the Brown Water of Swansville.

My parents were able to attend the qualifier, and my sister joined them. If I remember correctly, it was the first game she attended since the "Ruby Slippers" game. The ride to the game with my parents was awkward, and I barely spoke. I assumed Duckworth talked the whole drive, with no one laughing or answering his questions, to keep a conversation going. Drake would have drifted away within minutes of the drive. Whitley sat and listened to her own music with her headphones and barely looked up. She did not want to spend her weekend watching me and her rival, Ruby, play baseball. My parents, of course, sang beach music the entire trip while I read Ty Cobb's novel *My Life in Baseball*. I would later find out the book was not an accurate depiction of Major League Baseball's first superstar. He was different behind closed doors, and many hated him. I felt betrayed by the legendary player. Life would teach me it was more common than I ever wanted to believe.

When we arrived for the qualifier in the small town of Biscoe, the town was having its annual watermelon festival. The streets of the small town were flooded. David Luck helped Coach Alex round everyone up as we were forced to park several blocks from the baseball field due to the festival traffic. We had to walk through the middle of the festival, and our eyes lit up at the sight of the carnival-like games. We begged our parents to let us play. Coach Alex barked at us, "It is time to start thinking about baseball and quit worrying with games of chance!" Jaxon ignored Alex's decree and stopped to play a football-throwing game. RJ, Coach Ross, Wyatt, and I stopped and watched, much to the displeasure of Alex. Jaxon put on a throwing display and easily won the top price of a giant stuffed Simba from *The Lion King*. Coach Alex noticed almost half the group had stopped to watch, then shouted, "What are you doing?" as he summoned the group. Jaxon gave his prize to Missy.

Coach Alex stood on the bricks surrounding a flower bed full of sunflowers to address the team. The sunflowers stood tall behind him as he spoke, and he seemed ten feet tall as he addressed the team. My parents and my sister stood at the back of the crowd, looking in the direction of the events and booths for the festival. Coach Alex's pregame speech was simple and short. He of course talked about perfection and giving 110 percent. He altered his speech: "It is time to focus and play baseball, and the festival games can wait." He closed with, "We should cruise through this tournament like we did the county tournament." He pointed at Wyatt, then said, "The field is small, and I will not be satisfied unless you finish the weekend a minimum of four home runs." Wyatt acted as if Alex were pointing at me. He slapped me on my shoulder, then said, "You can do it, big guy." The rest of the team laughed at the thought of me ever hitting a home run. Alex pointed at Ruby and Ogre and said, "Be unstoppable." Ruby said, "Yes, sir," pounded his chest, then took a glance over at my sister. She was unimpressed. Ogre said nothing and only stared at the ground.

After the speech, I asked Coach Alex, "Will you play me in the first game? I doubt my parents will make the second game."

His response was exactly what I expected: "Hopefully, we will get an early lead and you can play mop-up duty."

My parents seemed more concerned with the watermelon festival than my games. Whitley did not seem to care either. My mind drifted somewhere else too. I tried to sneak looks at Troy's sister, and I could not get her off my mind. Her blond hair and beautiful eyes were my constant distraction. I knew I had no chance with her, but my daydreams were of me being a hero and she running on the field to give me what would be my first kiss. It would be hard to be a hero from the dugout.

The first game, we would face the host team from Biscoe. They would be our only challenge of the weekend. Their starting pitcher was most likely their second-best pitcher, and we started Drake. Drake singled in the first, and Wyatt hit a mammoth home run and trotted the base slower than normal and had a defiant smile. Immediately after touching home plate, he was booed. The team from Biscoe had a fan that was the president of the bank that built the field. He was a midget named Louie Longwood, and he never stopped harassing Wyatt after his home run. Wyatt and Drake were the only two to get a hit as the rest of the team saw two things, a small field and my sister. Everyone wanted to impress her with their own home run.

The first inning ended tied at 2–2. Little Man, as Wyatt called him, was beginning to get under Wyatt's skin. He purposely missed a ball during warm-ups between innings, and he threw dirt at him. The crowd exploded. The umpire had to settle everyone down, especially Louie. The host team replaced their pitcher with their biggest and best kid; although he was no giant, he pitched like one. Wyatt led off the top of the third inning and was promptly hit by the first pitch on his wrist. He threw his bat, then pointed at the pitcher, and before we knew it, he was ejected.

Wyatt did not leave easily. The crowd booed and taunted the phenom. He took his time leaving, and he yelled back insults. He told Ogre, "Go step on the little man." The first-base umpire attempted to escort him off the field as best as he could. The opposing coach shouted at the umpire, "Get this jerk off the field!" Wyatt resisted even more. Coach Alex argued with the home plate umpire and even had words with the Biscoe team's coach. He insisted the pitcher should be ejected too. Duckworth looked ready to run onto the field as he stood and shouted to Alex, "Don't let them get away with this atrocity!"

The two rivals agreed on something for once.

Louie shouted, "Sit down, old man!"

Duckworth lost his composure, then headed toward the field. David Luck had to get between Duckworth and the field to restrain him. Missy and Vanessa attempted to keep the old coach calm. Duckworth was so mad he turned pink and his green shirt made the old coach look like a watermelon. Surely, the Biscoe fans saw Duckworth as the crazy old coach. His hair was a mess as he threw off his hat. He looked disheveled, and he looked the part of the crazy, obsessed coach he had once been.

Louie called the umpire by his first name. "Karl, this has gone on long enough. Get this delinquent off my field, now!"

The umpire told Coach Alex, "If you cannot control your players and fans, you will be forced to forfeit. Get him off the field now or go home!"

Alex gave up trying to get their pitcher ejected, then attempted to assist in getting the angry phenom off the field. Wyatt told Alex, "Stay away, Coach," as he angrily walked toward the exit. Coach Ross shouted, "Get over here now!" from just beyond the dugout. Wyatt exited slowly. Coach Ross grabbed Wyatt forcefully and began to walk him off the field. Wyatt struggled to free himself from Coach Ross, but he was no match for the strong coach. Wyatt continued to lob insults at the crowd as Coach Ross led him away. Wyatt's squinty eyes were wide-open, and his face was red. The pain in his wrist must've fueled his anger. I had never seen him so uncontrollable.

Wyatt threw his jersey back on the field. I saw my sister casually take her headphones off and walk toward him. She intercepted Coach Ross and Wyatt about halfway up the bleachers. Whitley began to walk with Wyatt and Coach Ross. Coach Ross eventually pulled back as he realized Whitley could somehow calm Wyatt.

When they reached the entrance, I watched her whisper something to Wyatt, and he smiled, then he immediately stopped his tantrum. I asked her the next day how she calmed him. She did not answer the question and just smiled. We continued to play while Whitley and Wyatt roamed the streets of the watermelon festival.

Wyatt's Uncle Jacob and Rob Leonard stepped out of the shadows. They usually kept their distance from the chaos, but for the first time, they headed to sit in the bleachers. After Wyatt exited the park, the two former high school baseball stars quietly went to sit behind the little man. They recognized him from the games when he taunted them when they passed through on their way to the state title. Jacob's and Rob's shadows loomed over the little man, and he looked over his shoulder to see who would dare invade his space. The banker recognized them, and he stuttered when he said, "I-I-I-I r-r-remember you two. You…you were on t-t-t-the n-n-nineteen e-e-eighty state ch-ch-championship t-t-t-team." Both men nodded, and Jacob said, "I would hate for the crowd here today at your new field to witness a catastrophe because of you." The little man quivered as Jacob menacingly stretched his once-potent right arm. Louie had no escape route, so he quietly sat back down as sweat poured from his brow.

Wyatt did not even think of the game once they exited the park. He did not even bother finding out the score. Wyatt entered and won the watermelon-eating contest. The prize was a hat that looked like watermelon. He wore the ridiculous hat with pride as he roamed the festival with no self-awareness. Whitley and Wyatt learned the line dance the watermelon crawl. Whitley finished third in a greased watermelon race, and her prize was a watermelon pendant. My sister never seemed to have any fun, but she told the story of the day at the festival with an exuberance I had only seen when she helped Wyatt turn Travis Harrison into Ruby.

Our bats came back to life once Whitley was not in the stands. Ogre and Troy both hit home runs, and I watched Ella chase her brother's home run ball down. Ella's queenlike elegance was gone as she shoved an eight-year-old girl to retrieve the ball. I never took my eyes off her. Her cheeks were red, and her perfectly combed blond hair was tangled. The little man said nothing as Jacob and Rob sat behind him. Coach Alex let Ruby finish the game out of spite. Duckworth approved of the decision, as Ruby struck out the last six batters in a row. Duckworth was embarrassed of his behavior, and now he sat politely in the stands, saying nothing. We won 8–2. The Biscoe team did not come out to shake our hands. Coach Alex huddled us up at home plate just in front of the little man. We chanted, "Swansville! Swansville!" much to the chagrin of the host team and of the little man.

After the game, Coach Alex shocked everyone when he apologized for his actions during the controversy. He made it clear Wyatt's behavior would not go unpunished. Duckworth told the group, "Coach Alex was protecting his players, and we should be proud of him," then he apologized for his own actions. Our parents gave Alex and Duckworth a soft clap. Just as the awkward postgame speech was ending, Wyatt and Whitley walked up. We all laughed at the watermelon hat Wyatt was wearing. Wyatt walked up and stood by Coach Alex, then he looked over at my sister. She gave him a little nod. Wyatt told the team, "I deserve consequences for my actions, and I will sit out tomorrow's games." Our parents were shocked that Wyatt showed this type of integrity. He was on their side now, and everyone wanted him to play. It seemed our parents now valued winning more than integrity. It was hard to take him seriously since he was wearing one of my sister's old soccer jerseys and the comical, watermelon-shaped hat. Coach Alex thanked Wyatt for being a man and told him he'd think about his punishment.

We held our heads high as we walked through the festival to our cars. The festival games no longer excited us as walked triumphantly through the streets of downtown Biscoe. We all went to our rides, and the mood made me think it was about to rain despite the ninety-degree temperature. Wyatt told me, "I wish you had made it in the game," then he showed me his injured wrist. It was still swollen, and the seams of the baseball were imprinted on his wrist. I knew it was not a simple injury. He said, "I do not think I will be able to swing a bat for a few days, or throw a ball. I'll wake up early to test it out." He swore me to secrecy. I was beginning to have too many secrets with him.

My parents picked up Wyatt the next day. When he opened the door to my mom's minivan, he used his left hand. His right wrist was still swollen, and it looked double the size of his left. My sister did not bring her headphones with her for the hour-and-a-half ride.

My dad asked him immediately, "How does your wrist feel?"

Wyatt only said, "A little sore," as he rubbed it. He sat beside me, then asked me, "What are you reading today?" He saw the name Ty Cobb and answered his own question with, "I've heard of him."

My sister interrupted our conversation by asking Wyatt, "Would you play today?"

He answered with, "No. My actions yesterday deserve consequences."

It was a lie. He could hardly move his wrist.

Before our first game, Coach Alex told everyone he had decided not to let Wyatt play either of today's games. We sighed and belly-ached over the decision, but I knew the real reason. Wyatt stood up and told everyone he was fine with the decision. In the short time Wyatt had been in our lives, he had become the difference maker and our leader. I remember thinking, without him, we were a normal group of twelve-year-olds. He made us special. I felt bulletproof when he was around.

Coach Alex wrapped up his speech by saying, "Today we keep our heads down and only play baseball," then he tossed the ball to Ogre and said, "It's up to you, big fella."

The first team we played was a team from Randolph County. Their starting pitcher looked like if he stood sideways, he would disappear. He was nicknamed Danimal due to the length of his hair and the first appearance of a mustache. He was lanky and tall. He was no match for us. Ogre and Drake hit back-to-back home runs in the first inning, and we never looked back. Danimal whimpered back to the dugout and did not return to the mound after three innings. We did not make a sound the entire game, and the Randolph County team never stopped with their chatter. Ogre cruised through the first four innings before being replaced by Anthony. I finished the game at second base for an uneventful two innings. I walked in my only at bat. Ella and Isaac had already left to check out the watermelon festival, and she never saw me get off the bench. My parents were listening to live music at the festival and missed my two innings too. We won 9–1. Ogre hit two home runs and struck out nine and did not allow a run.

Game 2 on Saturday was not much different from game 1. Jaxon pitched, and Drake led the way at the plate. We were already up 8–1 by the third inning. Coach Alex was confident and began to move players around, and he started to unload the bench. I finished the game up at third base as Drake moved to center field, positions neither of us had ever played. I watched Ella eating cotton candy while I tried to focus on the batter. The game was called in the fifth inning due to the mercy rule. We were up 14–1. I felt like the Castaways could have beaten the team from Moore County.

The qualifier championship was set for the next afternoon. Wyatt called my house about ten minutes before we left and told me, "I am sick. I can't play today." I begged him, but he was adamant.

I asked, "Is your wrist the real issue?"

He took a long pause, then said, "No. I have been on the toilet all morning." He chuckled as he said it. He told me he had called Coach Alex. Alex believed we'd be fine without him.

I knew as soon as I arrived everyone would want more details than Wyatt had given me. No one would be satisfied with me telling them Wyatt had diarrhea. It would be the first of many times I had to answer questions about him.

Coach Alex told the team of Wyatt's absence. He was confident, and Wyatt's absence did not make him nervous about the game. We all had learned to rely on Wyatt for more than home runs. Wyatt's confidence rubbed off on all of us, and today we would need to look to Ruby. Ruby would need to lead us again, and of course, he was up for the challenge. Ruby led with arrogance, and it would have to work one more time.

Ruby pitched and was nearly unhittable. The opposing team's best player was a chubby kid named Big Deal Davy. He was their giant, but he was no giant. He strutted to the plate with the crowd and the dugout stomping and clapping. Stomp, stomp, clap. Ruby looked back at Drake and Jaxon in disbelief that someone would dare taunt him. Ruby fired a fastball to silence the crowd, then Big Deal Davy swung and the ball flew over the center field fence. The crowd and the dugout erupted, singing, "We will, we will rock you! We will, we will rock you!" It would be the last time of the summer. They enjoyed the moment, but Ruby did not let it last long and he pitched a gem. He finished with nine strikeouts.

Big Deal Davy pitched but proved not to be more than a side-show for us. He was half the size of Ruby, and he pitched to his size. He and their fans were shocked when almost everyone on our team got a hit against him. Dale hit a home run, and Troy nearly hit for the cycle. Drake was typical Drake, and he reached base four times and scored four runs. Jaxon finished the team out of Chatham County with ease, and we won 11–3. We would head to the sectionals in a week, and we needed Wyatt's wrist to heal. I did not believe we could continue winning on arrogance. We needed confidence again.

Where I Belong

The last month of the school year, Mitch and I, along with two seventh graders, won the county geography bee. The two seventh graders were the outcasts of their grade. We all qualified for the regional bee in Raleigh. The timing could not have been worse. Neither Mitch nor I ever imagined being on the all-star team. Our summer priorities changed, and now the geography bee meant very little to us both. Contrarily, the geography bee would be the pinnacle of the rising eighth-grade outcasts' summer.

Mitch and I had morning geography bee practice and evening baseball practice on Monday and Tuesday. He and I agreed not to tell our teammates of our upcoming competition. It would've only drawn laughs from boys that only valued base hits and strikeouts. The first round of the geography bee was held on a Wednesday, and if we won, we would advance to the state competition on Friday afternoon. We were more concerned with sitting the bench for the sectionals in the country town of Hopewell than heading to the North Carolina coastal town of Wilmington.

The rising eighth graders bounced off the walls with excitement at each practice. Mitch and I were annoyed with their early-morning exuberance. Chloe and James both talked of the potential of competing for the state championship held in Wilmington. James seemed obsessed with visiting the battleship in Wilmington. Chloe asked Mrs. Henry, "Can we visit Johnnie Mercer's Pier?" I had visited both places the previous summer. A trip back to Wilmington was worthless to me since neither place was too spectacular in my opinion. Chloe's pale skin and dark dresses would draw second looks at the beach. Winning the regional was their opportunity to escape the

Brown Water for a couple of days. Mrs. Henry also planned her vacation around the four of us getting her to Wilmington a day earlier.

Our plan of secrecy was breached as someone on the team found out about our competition. I told no one of the nerdy competition, and I assumed my sister let my secret out. Mitch and I were harassed at practice Tuesday night. Ruby chuckled. "Geography bee is better suited for you two brainiacs." RJ was not much nicer, as he could not believe anyone would agree to a school activity once the school year was over. Coach Alex added, "Don't worry, you guys. We can win without you." Wyatt interrupted Coach Alex's next sentence with, "At least we will not go down this summer as the dumbest all-star team." The dugout ribbing ended, and we took the field. Insults would fly our way occasionally, but I learned long ago to ignore the castigators.

Practice ended, and everyone wished us luck. Wyatt secretly told me, "You're the glue. We can't win without you." My heart raced with the added pressure of Wyatt saying he needed me. I did not stay after practice with Drake. I had to leave first thing in the morning to win a trip to the coast. Mitch stayed at my house, and my dad would take us to school at six in the morning. Whitley asked, "Are y'all going to win or what?" Mitch and I looked at each other and simultaneously said, "Of course." Neither Mitch nor I decided to cram for the competition, as our teammates suggested. We stayed up late playing Super Nintendo.

My dad woke us up late. He had slept in the recliner and did not hear his alarm clock. Mitch and I had to rush to get ready. I did not even comb my hair, and I threw on my all-star baseball hat. Mitch dressed in an old Aerosmith T-shirt and cutoff blue jeans. Mrs. Henry was unhappy with our appearance, and she scolded us. "You're representing Swansville. Would Coach Alex let you two look like ragamuffins?" We shamefully said no. My dad apologized and tried to take the blame, but Mrs. Henry did not allow it. She told my dad, "They are old enough now to get out of bed without their mommies and daddies." Chloe and James snickered, as they were both dressed in their Sunday's best.

We left ten minutes late, and Mrs. Henry complained we might miss the registration and be disqualified. I would not have been disappointed with that outcome. Mrs. Henry's mood was sour, and she complained all morning. Her husband drove as she asked us question after question for the nearly three-hour ride. Chloe and James gave each other high fives, treating us as outcast. Mitch seemed to relish being an outcast. I wanted to be accepted by everyone, especially Mrs. Henry. She would likely be my seventh-grade social studies teacher. She had a reputation of being tough, and I thought she would not forget how things would unfold in Raleigh.

We stopped for lunch about thirty miles from Raleigh. Mrs. Henry barely let us swallow our food as she pounded us with questions. Mr. Henry bought our lunches and even got us all an ice cream sundae, much to the dismay of his wife. She indignantly looked at him, then said, "Dillon, they've not won anything yet." Mitch and I looked at her in disbelief. She looked at her husband and chuckled, as if it was a planned statement, not a reaction. Mrs. Henry tried to cover her tracks by telling us, "If we win, we will eat a steak dinner on the way back to Swansville. How does that sound?" Chloe's and James's eyes lit up with excitement. Mr. Henry said nothing as he drove to the chorus of geography bee questions. The last thirty miles were the toughest. If we missed a question, she would slap her forehead in disgust. She did not give us a pep talk but rather told us the importance of showing how intelligent people were in Swansville.

The first round was a breeze. It was an open format, and anyone on the team could answer. Chloe and James's diligence studying during the drive paid off. Mitch only answered two questions, and he drew the ire of Mrs. Henry when he missed a question that she declared was simple. I was one-for-one, as I did not want to miss a question and draw the frustrated stare of Mrs. Henry. James had a full grasp of landmarks throughout the state and the state park where each was located. We finished round 1 in second place. The head-to-head competition terrified me. I would have to answer more than one question going forward.

We had a brief break before our second-round matchup. Mrs. Henry said nothing positive about our first-round performance other than "Congrats, y'all are headed to the semifinals!" She scolded Mitch again, "Guess you wanted to embarrass your school today. I'll remember how you presented yourself and Swansville next fall." Mitch did not seem concerned with her threat. After our pleasant conversation with our future teacher, Mitch and I found a table far away from our teammates. We sat with four girls from Forsyth County. The four girls looked like they were from the same family. Each had strawberry-red hair, and freckles dotted their rosy cheeks. They shared their snacks with us, and we chatted until Mrs. Henry shouted our names across the lobby. Mitch and I yawned, and the girls laughed. They tried to get us to stay longer, but we eventually left and headed back to our future teacher. I guess the lack of sleep made me lethargic, and my feet were heavy as I stumbled across the lobby. Mitch rubbed his eyes, then said, "Let's get this over with."

The semifinal round was a head-to-head. We would have to face off the same four girls from Forsyth County. I felt like I needed a nap. Mitch's mouth and head tipped back with each yawn. He looked like a lion with no roar. Mrs. Henry clenched her teeth and fist. Her eyes were zeroed in on Mitch. I tried to disguise my yawns with unconvincing cough. Despite my energy, I answered the first five questions. Mitch did little and did not even buzz in. He was ready to go home after being scolded. We defeated the Forsyth County girls despite Mitch's indifference.

The final round consisted of a group answer, then a lightning round, where everyone on the team would have to answer. Neither Mitch nor I could benefit from Chloe's and James's knowledge. We would be exposed. Our next opponent did not have to wake before dawn, and they looked well rested. Chapel Hill-Carrboro City Schools had a short drive over to Raleigh. They looked refreshed and professional, unlike us.

Uncharacteristically, Mitch snapped out of his funk and began to contribute. He provided answers for over half of the first-round questions. Mrs. Henry was shocked as Mitch led us to a first-round lead. I was terrified of the lightning round. I could not answer under pressure, and I struggled, thinking on my feet. I was not a fast thinker. If we could hold our two-point lead, then we would head to Wilmington on Friday instead of the sectionals.

Chloe and James did not miss a question in the lightning round. Mitch stumbled twice, but they were both honest mistakes. Mrs. Henry wiped the nerves off her forehead. I missed an early question, opening the door for the Chapel Hill-Carrboro City Schools. We were down one point, with thirty seconds remaining. I silently prayed and hoped I would not be the last Swansville Middle School student to answer. Of course, when you're twelve, things don't go your way, and the last question found me.

My struggle was not with the question. Wyatt told me I was the glue, and I believed him. I felt needed for something other than my brain. I was accepted by the more popular boys and the better baseball players on the all-star team. My newfound confidence on the diamond made me feel important. I had the choice to let my friends down or the baleful staring of Mrs. Henry and Swansville Middle School. Wilmington did not sound like fun with Mrs. Henry as the chaperone; however, I did not want to let my school down. If we won, then I would definitely get my name on the front page of *The Swansville Orator*, and maybe my side of the mantel would draw second looks. Winning rarely found me in my life, and I had it within my grasp, but now I valued friendships and my social status more than a championship medal.

The clock struck zero, and I was forced to answer. "Ithaca is located in what European country?"

I lifted my hat and wiped my brow as the clock ran out, and I answered, "Italy." The *ehhhrr ehhhrr* punched my ticket to the sectionals and not Wilmington. The answer was Greece. I would not get my name on the front page, and I would have to live with the shame of losing a championship due to a baseball game. Mrs. Henry's glare told me she would have me in her sights next year. Mitch and I both slept the entire ride home despite the wails of Chloe and James.

Nowhere Lights

After winning the county tournament, we had our first tournament where we would get to stay in a hotel. After three intense practices with Coach Alex telling us one mistake would end our summer, we hit the road. Coach Alex was so confident he recommended our parents book our hotel rooms for the entire weekend. His coaching philosophy was to yell and repetition. His practices never ended or started on time. We took infield for an hour, then we hit for whatever time he deemed necessary. He was the strictest with Ruby. Ruby had a specific routine, and sometimes he seemed to practice on his own. Ruby listened to his father but argued with his coach. Alex would yell until he could barely talk, and his dip would always end up choking him at least once. I could see why his teams were always the best; he religiously shouted, "It's all about perfection!" His message on perfection had fallen on my deaf ears when he was my coach, but now the words resonated with me.

The tournament was an eight-team showdown that was almost three hours away. I never heard of the small town, but the closer we got, the farther away it seemed. It was just far enough for us to get hotel rooms. We would sleep three or four to a room in most cases. The upcoming hotel-high jinx would be one of our perks of the summer. Hopewell was a town a new highway had bypassed. The old route became obsolete. The vacationers now did not need to ride through the small town. The main road through town was littered with abandoned firework stands and fruit stands. Cows seemed to dominate the population more than people. We passed a Hardee's, and I assumed we were getting close, but the David Luck-led caravan drove for another twenty-five minutes. The curvy road passed the ruins of two hosiery mills.

We finally reached a caution light with what looked like the town's own Winslow's. The gas pumps were no longer operating, and the place looked like it belonged on *The Andy Griffith Show*. An old lady and, surely, her granddaughter ran the store. The bell announcing our arrival made them both jump to their feet. It seemed we were the first customers of the day. The old lady wore a 1986 Mets World Series shirt. She did not greet us with a typical Southern accent but rather welcomed us with, "Come on in, yous guys." I chuckled, but I held my composure, in hopes of not embarrassing myself in front of the striking, dark-haired teenage beauty. She said nothing, but her sharp aquarium-blue eyes watched us load up on bubble gum. Wyatt noticed the anxiety the girl caused, and he loudly proclaimed, "I sure hope the rest of this town is as pretty as it is in here." He elbowed me as he said it, and my face turned red, then I tried to hide from her gaze behind the bread aisle. I lost control of my senses, and I ran out of the store as quickly as possible. The old lady shouted in her raspy voice, "He looked like a spooked deer!" Wyatt and the no-name girl both laughed.

We drove through a light rain for the last fifteen minutes to the secluded baseball fields. It drizzled most of the day in Hopewell. The clouds parted, and we were set to play at six o'clock. I remember thinking, if we won, I would spend every weekend with Duckworth. Duckworth rarely turned on the radio, and he talked nonstop during car rides. The prospect of hearing his wild stories excited me. Once the rain stopped, Duckworth rolled down the windows, then said, "It feels like baseball out." The air was thick, and the sweet smell made me lick my lips.

The baseball fields were just past the post office and a Family Dollar. The baseball field was directly behind Hopewell Elementary. The school once served as the town's high school, but all that was left of it now was just the elementary school. Honeysuckle bushes lined the side of the two-story school building. It looked one hundred years old and abandoned despite the schoolchildren's good-luck posters in the windows. The school and the town were thirty minutes from civilization. Duckworth said, "The local folks got lost every day because every road looks alike and the cows give bad directions." I snorted at his corny joke then I embarrassingly looked around.

A gravel road led behind the school's old green gym to what seemed like the only thing in town that time had not forgotten. The small town looked like progress had skipped it, except the immaculate baseball fields. New lights were recently installed on the main Hopewell field. The top of both dugouts had faded red Coke logos painted on them. The baseball complex had batting cages and a concession stand. It was more like a general store for baseball than a place to grab snacks. It had everything from snacks to bats and batting gloves. Two teenage boys worked the store. It had a small kitchen, and they sold plain hamburgers and fries. The two main fields were flanked by a practice field that had cow pasture over the right field fence. The cow's moos filled the night air.

The Hopewell all-stars had won the state tournament three years earlier, and this year's team was full of their younger brothers and hope. They were our first opponent of the weekend, and we started slow. Ruby and Ogre did not know how to lose, and Wyatt hated it even more despite the fact he learned to lose all spring. Coach Alex's warning of mistakes must've hit a nerve with Drake. Drake made two uncharacteristic errors that led to four runs in the first inning. Drake looked like he wanted to fly away when Coach Alex shouted, "Drake, what are you doing?" Drake sat quietly each inning, believing he had ended our all-star season before it really started. Drake struck out in his first and only at bat. Coach Alex tried to revive the baseball savant, but he grew frustrated with Drake. He assumed the boy was indifferent. Alex did not understand how a boy could play a game and never smile. Alex took Drake out of the game, and I was inserted at second base, with Jaxon moving over to shortstop. It was odd being at second base without Drake beside me. I felt lonely and out of place. I looked over at Drake, and his emotions never changed. He blankly stared at the scoreboard.

Ruby pitched a great game, but the four unearned runs turned up his volume in the dugout. The giant never gave up that many runs, and he was unfamiliar with losing. He stomped around the dugout, saying, "Pick me up, fellas."

Alex said, "It is time for perfection," at least fifty times.

Jaxon sat with Drake, and the two looked like statues. Jaxon was amazing, and he drove in two runs. When we reached the top of the fifth, we were still down 4–2. We squeaked out a third run to close the gap on a Dale Rutledge sacrifice fly ball. We entered the sixth inning down 4–3. I was due to bat third.

I started to feel sick, and my stomach turned just like I had exited a roller coaster. The idea of making the last out terrified me. Wyatt played despite his ailing wrist. He now seemed mortal. Wyatt could see my confidence drifting away, and he simply said, "Take a deep breath and just try to make contact. That's all you can do." The pat on the back that followed was not his style, and I think he was trying to tell me it would be okay if we lost. I believed I had somehow absorbed some of his amazing abilities. My shoulders rolled back, and I held my head high. My upcoming at bat terrified me, but now with Wyatt's reassurance, I believed, for the first time in my life, I could do anything. I now regretted running out of the old store and not having the courage then to, at the very least, make eye contact with the beautiful girl.

I came up with two outs, and in attempt to shake my nerves, I took one last deep breath. My nose filled again with the sweet smell of honeysuckle bushes. Wyatt nodded at me from the on-deck circle. My sister had been the hero her whole life, and now it was time to see if I had hero's blood too. I stopped shaking and stepped into the batter's box. The pitcher must've forgotten I was a benchwarmer, because he threw me three straight curveballs. I had no chance against his fastball. One curveball hung up just enough for me to poke a soft line drive to right field. The right fielder misplayed the ball. Coach Ross yelled, "Dig, dig, dig!" in his booming coach's voice. The last thing I heard was Duckworth yelling, "Run, Worm!" and I started for second. My helmet bounced off just as I made the turn for third. The perfectly groomed outfield grass allowed my lazy line drive to skip to the fence. By the time the right fielder reached the ball, my legs were tingling as I approached third base. The right fielder slipped on the grass but managed to make a perfect throw to the cutoff man. Doug Loflin uncharacteristically held up the stop sign. Alex shouted, "Stop!" But it was too late. Doug was a blur in a baseball uniform as I headed for home. My feet bounced off the infield dirt, and each push off the ground made me feel like I was flying.

I could not hear a thing. I had lost all my senses. I saw Wyatt frantically waving for me to slide to the back corner of the plate. I slid headfirst and tasted the brittle brown dirt. I felt blood slowly dripping from a cut on my elbow onto home plate. When the buzzing in my ears stopped, the first thing I heard was the scoreboard loudly clicking from a three to a four. The score was tied at 4–4. I glanced in the crowd to see if Ella had seen my hero moment. She had her back turned while she chatted with the two boys at the concession stand. Our summer was not over yet.

The Hopewell head coach adamantly disagreed and protested the call. Wyatt brushed me off, and he squeezed me until I was unable to breathe. The dugout waited with their palms up for high fives. Drake did not acknowledge anything. I smiled and tried to play off being the hero. Ruby rubbed my head as I walked by him. The unfamiliar feeling made me seem more awkward than ever. Our parents and the Hopewell fans shouted, "Safe and out!" at one another until the umpire finally gained control. Vanessa Harrison just kept saying, "Let's move on and live with the call." Suzanne Angelo was loud and intimidating as she began to argue with the Hopewell coach. "Sit down, chump!" she screamed. The crowd booed her and gave the umpires the thumb-down sign.

The new lights flickered on for the first time when Wyatt stepped to the plate. The rural school field looked different when the lights were on. The bright lights cast a shadow on the crowd, and the game became the focus. Our parents faded under the lights, and their shouts floated into the night sky like ashes over a fire. Wyatt was made for the lights. He learned to lose during the regular season, but now he was going to teach us how to never give up. He hit a ball at the same right fielder that gave us new life. The right fielder nearly made a diving catch of the jam-shot base hit. Wyatt stole second with ease on the first pitch. He took another big lead off second, and he dashed toward third base. The catcher popped up in anticipation and made a perfect throw. Wyatt slid headfirst, and the umpire emphatically called him safe. The crowd again disagreed with the call, and the game was delayed again. The Swansville fans collectively gasped when Wyatt's wrist jammed into third base. He shook the pain out of his wrist, then rubbed dirt on it. Ogre loomed large in the batter's box. He was walked on four pitches. The Hopewell coaches never stopped screaming, and they seemed unwilling to cope with what the future held. The cries of the Hopewell fans once again filled the field. RJ came up and faked a bunt. Their third baseman nearly stumbled charging the fake. The next pitch, RJ bunted the ball toward first base. Missy screamed "Go, go, go, go, baby!" just as the throw sailed high and the Hopewell first baseman's foot left the base. The umpire's dramatic safe call enraged the fans for a third time in the inning. Wyatt scored. We led 5–4. Jaxon struck out to end the inning, but the damage was already done.

The bottom half of the sixth inning almost did not happen as the adults from both teams yelled insults at one another. The host fans did not let up on the umpires. Both of the gray-mustached men had given up their weekend to be insulted by the parents of preteens. Their eyes told me they were ready to flee. Ruby stood on the mound, softly tossing the ball to Wyatt, while the umpires had to have the Hopewell head coach escorted off the field. The lone police officer only escorted him to the corner of the green gym, where his presence looked over both teams and the umpires from atop the small hill. The Hopewell Little League king had been exiled, and all he could do was yell from afar. His shouts died before they reached the first-base dugout. He stood with his arms crossed, seeing into his baseball future. Next summer, a new king would try to bring the crowds back to the forgotten town.

Ruby made quick work of the first batter, and I made a diving stop to quell a potential rally. My throw bounced, and the crowd argued again that Ogre did not catch the ball. The argument did not last this time, and summer was on the horizon for the citizens of Hopewell. It was the first game I felt like I had contributed. I wished the feeling had stayed, and I envied those that felt that way every game. Wyatt seemed to intentionally drop the third strike on the last batter just so he could tag the beleaguered batter for the last out of the game. It was over, and Drake still looked like he carried the weight of the world. I rushed off the field to line up for the postgame handshake. We had won, and our summer would last another game.

The Hopewell parents shouted at the umpire, while the disappointed kids' heads dropped in silence. The defiant king spoke, as he had secretly rejoined the team. He was still complaining about how the umpires gave us the game. He claimed, "Boys, y'all were cheated out of your baseball destiny this summer." We never got to shake the Hopewell team's hands, since their coach did not stop berating the umpires. The final score was 5–4, and the scoreboard operator quickly turned off the lights and the scoreboard. The field in the middle of nowhere was pitch-black, and it was difficult navigating our way through the unfamiliar setting. The crowd was stunned, and they came one out away from keeping those lights on for another game.

I remember seeing parents' and kids' eyes fill with tears. We shuffled back to our cars in the darkness, and the complaints of "That's not fair" echoed in the parking lot. I knew baseball meant more to these people, because I did not see that type of disappointment in another team's eyes all summer. Their summer dream ended under a perfect field with brand-new lights surrounded by more cows than people. Tomorrow the kids could go swimming or sleep late and not think of baseball. Winning at baseball was the town's chance to be important again and not a forgotten dot on the map. The people and field in the middle of nowhere reminded me of Swansville. I assumed they would all go back to their jobs and forget about baseball until next spring, but this loss would stay with them.

The car ride back to the hotel seemed short despite the fact it was thirty minutes away. Duckworth jokingly said, "I should call you Lightning instead of Worm." So for one night, I was Lightning and not Worm. Lightning never stuck, and my triumphant moment did not last long either. I sulked because Ella had missed it. My hero moment would soon be forgotten. History books would never know I once was a hero.

Coach Alex summoned us for a team meeting as soon as we all arrived at the hotel. He said, "We were lucky, and each team would be tougher. And thankfully, Ruby—I mean Travis—bent but never broke and that we needed to shake the nerves off and be ready tomorrow at noon." After the brief speech, we excitedly ran to our rooms. Coach Alex and Coach Ross yelled, "Get some rest!" at the same time. I bounced to our room.

Alex asked Drake and Duckworth to stay. Wyatt stayed and hid out of sight to spy. He later told me Alex said Drake needed to commit to the team and to focus. He wanted perfection, and he would not tolerate a player not looking him in the eyes when he spoke to him. Duckworth turned red, and we all could hear the two men shouting. Drake silently sat on the sidewalk. Alex asked Drake, "Can you give me 100 percent tomorrow and strive for perfection?" Drake only said, "Yes, sir." Duckworth had been like Alex, and winning once was more important than the game. Drake valued winning just as much as Alex did, but he hid his desire to win quietly. Duckworth believed baseball was meant to teach us life lessons, and Alex believed winning was life's number 1 lesson to learn. Drake stayed in his father's room instead of the room with me, Wyatt, and Jaxon. We barely slept, as I wanted my hero's moment to last as long as I could.

We cruised through the rest of the tournament while torturing the hotel staff with our shenanigans. We stayed up late each night and sneaked out past curfew just for the thrill of saying we did it. Drake did not say another word all weekend, and he roomed with his father rather than stay up late with his friends. He did not make another error, and he scored nine runs over the remaining games the rest of the weekend. Ogre dominated the next two games at the plate, and the third game, he was unhittable. Jaxon and Ruby wrapped up the sectional championship with another pitching gem. Wyatt's ailing wrist began to improve, and his dominance returned. He hit two towering home runs that scattered the cows in their pasture. The Hopewell king seemed to favor our phenom, and he never missed one of Wyatt's at bats. He sought Wyatt out and told him, "You better hit your knees and thank the man upstairs." Wyatt shook his hand, then said, "I know."

Camping Magic

Our parents realized this summer would be different far sooner than we did. Our weekends and spare time were spent worrying with baseball. Some of our parents agreed to let a few of us go camping during the middle of the week. Jack Wilson told our parents he would keep an eye on us and he would make sure nothing happened to us. He loaned us an old tent, and he helped arrange the trip. The Wednesday before Father's Day, Ogre, Wyatt, Troy, Mitch, and I decided the logical spot was Rocky Point Pier. We wanted to see if we had the courage to make it through the night at the spooky place. Drake declined to tag along despite his father's urging.

When we arrived to pick up Wyatt, he opened the front door and waved me inside. I ran in just as my mom shouted, "Just hurry!" Whitley's eyes rolled. She and my mom were going shopping and staying in Charlotte for the night. I stopped at the door, then turned to my mom and held up my hand to indicate I would only be five minutes. Wyatt was barely packed, and he scrambled to throw everything in his backpack. He was talking through breaths, and I barely understood him. The excitement of staying out all night made the words fly out of his mouth at an uncontrollable pace.

Jacob entered his bedroom, then said, "I have something for you to take for protection." Jacob handed Wyatt a wooden Louisville Slugger. Jacob warned us that drunk high school boys might be out and to only use it if necessary. Jacob said, "This bat is not for hitting rocks. It is special."

Wyatt asked, "Where did you get this?"

Jacob responded, "I will tell you when we are alone."

Wyatt objected, "Go ahead. We can trust Carson."

I nodded in agreement.

Jacob said, "Don't repeat anything I say." Wyatt assured his uncle by miming he was locking his lips and throwing away the key. Jacob told us, "It was your father's bat. He played Minor League Baseball for two seasons in Asheville."

Wyatt's eyes lit up at the fact his father had played professional baseball. He was speechless. Wyatt began to swing the heavy wooden bat. I asked Jacob, "So the stories my dad tell me are true?"

Jacob said, "Yes."

I reluctantly asked, "Was he as good as you?"

Jacob hung his head, then said, "No. He was better than everyone. He made my fastball disappear many times."

I asked, "What happened?"

Jacob said, "I will tell you the whole story one day, but he made too many wrong decisions, then he chose to come back for her." He motioned to Patti's room.

The bottom of the bat had Wyatt's initials, WDH. Wyatt said, "The *D* is for David, my grandfather's name." He handed me his new prize possession. Wyatt encouraged me to swing the heavy wooden bat. I did my best as I struggled to swing it.

My mom or more likely my sister honked the horn. I handed Wyatt back his father's bat. We ran out to the car, and he said, "Can you believe my dad played pro baseball?" I was impressed, but the stories my dad told me let me believe it was possible. Jamie Hartley was the talk of the town before Jacob took over being known Swansville's best.

We met everyone at Frankie's, then we hopped in the back of Jack's truck. We bought supplies from Frankie. Frankie told us to be careful and to not do anything stupid. He said, "I would hate to read something bad about you boys in next week's paper." Frankie poked Troy in the chest. "That means you too, hotshot." The plan was to fish and eat junk food and sit by a fire.

Wyatt showed everyone his new bat as we bounced down the road in the back of Jack's beat-up old pickup truck that he called Goldie. The truck was not golden but covered in rust. Mitch asked, "Where did you get it?" Wyatt's eyes glanced my way as he said, "My uncle gave it to me." Wyatt went on to say it was for our protection and he was the only one allowed to use it. He was the only one that could swing it with any force, anyhow.

We hiked up a couple hundred feet from the pier and found a spot about forty feet from the shoreline. We cleared out a spot, and we struggled putting up the tent. Beer cans littered the shoreline nearby, as this was an obvious place for high schoolers to hang out. It was starting to get dark when we decided to collect firewood. Troy brought matches, and Ogre had some old *Auto Trader* magazines to help get a fire started. Ogre and Wyatt struggled to get a fire going. I learned that most twelve-year-olds do not know how to start a campfire. Troy took over the duties of lighting the fire, and he carefully stacked the magazines and the small pieces of wood. He seemed to have the magic touch.

We roasted hot dogs and ate chips. Wyatt caught a fish, and he had thoughts of cooking the hand-size green brim. Ogre would not allow it. Wyatt did everything he could to get under Ogre's thick skin. Wyatt insinuated Ogre had a secret girlfriend and he likely kept her under his bed. Wyatt laughingly said, "Ogre kidnapped a redheaded girl." We all knew which girl he referenced. Kandi Edwards went to stay with her grandmother in Ohio each summer. Ogre turned red when Wyatt mentioned the dainty redhead. Ogre and Kandi had speech classes together since they were in the first grade. She was his protector, despite the fact Ogre was five times her size. Kandi struggled with her *L*, and she replaced it with *TH*. Kandi grew up just outside of town, in an old, run-down trailer at the back of a long dirt road. Her driveway marked the unofficially beginning of the Brown Water. Kandi's four older brothers made her tough, and she always stood up for herself and others. Ogre only shook his head at the constant harassing. He did not have confidence or the words to get into a battle with Wyatt. Wyatt's laughter echoed off the nearby lake, and it seemed both he and the full moon were laughing together.

I had never stayed up that late near the lake before, and I began to feel afraid. I did my best to hide my fear. The wind blowing down from the big water made a howl, and the leaves shook. I felt like we were being watched and someone was lurking just out of sight.

Wyatt walked down to the water to piss, and he ran back frantically. He said, "I saw a light across the lake at the island at the mouth of Cubbie Cove." His voice did not tremble, but I could tell he was anxious. We all walked down, with Ogre and Wyatt leading the way. Wyatt carried his new bat as the rest of us carried rocks except Mitch. Mitch carried a long Maglite.

We walked as one, and each step was like a quiet march down to the shoreline. One of us stepped on a stick that snapped, and we all jumped but Wyatt. He angrily shouted, "Hush! This is serious!" We did our best to stay quiet in effort not to upset Wyatt as he led us down to the shoreline. We kept our flashlights off and let the moon guide the way. The only thing we saw were empty Coors Light cans and the remnants of small bonfires after we reached the shoreline. We all stood perfectly still, and no one said a word as we stared at the island, waiting for the dim light to return. It never did.

My father had searched the island when Ben Lee Chapel went missing three years earlier. My dad described the island, "It was beautiful despite the trash and empty, washed-up worm containers. It was peaceful, and I was relaxed listening to the lake's waves crash the untouched shoreline's rocks. The island was just out of reach of any developers." Troy said, "That island is treacherous due to the sandbars on each side." He went on to describe Isaac getting their Pontoon trapped last fall when the lake was down. Troy had named the island Sandy Pass.

Wyatt swore he saw a light, and he even described the light in great detail. He said, "It looked like a flashlight aiming down at the ground, as if someone was looking for something they had dropped. It was dim."

Ogre asked, "Are you sure you saw something and it wasn't just the moon shining down?"

Wyatt told him, "Do I look like the kind of guy that doesn't know the moon from his own ass?"

Ogre shamefully apologized.

Mitch told Wyatt, "It is not Ogre's fault the light is gone."

Wyatt told everyone, "Shut your mouths and look for the light."

No one ever saw Wyatt's light. And he did not seem embarrassed, as I expected.

I wondered if someone occasionally still searched for Bee Lee, but I was too scared to even mention the idea. Mitch second-guessed his friend as Wyatt's words began to fly out of his mouth. Wyatt seemed uneasy. I knew Wyatt the best, and I knew that when the RPMs on his sentences sped up, he was nervous or upset. I believed he had seen a light, and he must've felt foolish when no one else saw it. We all walked back to our campsite, and the ground was unsteady as the breeze off the lake rustled the leaves in the small oak trees dotting the shoreline.

We sat by the fire, and Troy added more wood. We discussed if we should leave or plan for an attack. Ogre did not believe Wyatt's story, and he was not amused or afraid. It took a lot to frazzle the man-child. Wyatt jokingly told everyone, "Ogre was so scary that even the dark was afraid of him." I said nothing. Wyatt walked back down to the shoreline, carrying his father's bat, to check for the light one more time. I secretly followed him. He grabbed a few rocks and threw them toward the island. He clenched the bat, then swung at the night air. Neither he nor I saw the mysterious light.

Wyatt came back to the campsite, then apologized, "Maybe I was mistaken, because there is still nothing there."

Troy said, "Let's just move our camp by the shoreline. Someone can keep a lookout, plus the breeze off the lake is prefect this time of year."

So at midnight, Troy talked us into moving the tent. We decided to try to carry it without taking it down. The old tent collapsed. Troy convinced everyone to use the bottom tarp and just sleep out under the stars. He said, "You'll thank me one day." Ogre transported the fire as best he could, and we collected a few more pieces of brush and broken limbs. The fire nearly went out, but Troy saved it just in time.

Our new, makeshift campsite on the shoreline was much nicer and seemed perfect, until Mitch pulled out a Ouija board. The creepy howl off the lake just intensified, and the small fire added to the unsettling ambiance. The planchette was lost, so Mitch had replaced it with the end of a broken spatula. We asked the typical questions, and it seemed Wyatt was driving the makeshift planchette. He constantly kept asking, "Are you moving it? I'm not moving it." Our first set of questions were based on baseball, such as, "Would Ogre hit a home run next game?" "Would Mitch ever get to play?" and many more. Ogre only played along because every time he said he was tired of the nonsense, Wyatt claimed Ogre was afraid. I asked the only question that mattered to me. "Would Ella fall in love with anyone on the team?" Shockingly, it answered yes. Troy scoffed, but he smiled at the question about his older sister. Ogre turned red as Mitch told him, "There you go, big fella."

Ogre eventually wanted to see if he could get Wyatt riled up, and he asked, "Spirit, spirit, is Wyatt in love?"

The planchette spelled out the word *green*. We were all confused by the answer, and Mitch asked, "Spirit, spirit, tell us your name." The spatula pointed to the letters "EELNEB" just as the fire started to fade. Ogre was running out of *AutoTraders*, and he stoked the fire with the last remaining pages. I secretly shivered, and I tried to hide the goose bumps on my arm. Wyatt began to talk a lot and make jokes at all our expenses, but we continued.

Ogre asked EELNEB, "Should we be afraid?" and the answer was, "Pain." Ogre asked, "Who will feel pain?" The spatula pointed at WDH. Wyatt laughed, and the spatula sped to the word *yes*.

Mitch asked, "Will anyone be harmed tonight?" and the answer was no. Mitch then asked EELNEB, "Why Wyatt?" and the answer was more confusing. It said, "Magic." The fire began to fade, and Wyatt asked another question. "What causes the pain?" and the answer was *heart*. He asked one last question, "When?" and the answer was "Time." Then EELNEB repeated it again. The last branch fell over, and the fire died. We all jumped and pulled our hands off the broken spatula. Wyatt laughed it off, then he began to mock everyone and even EELNEB. Wyatt's voice cracked as he said, "No one or nothing can hurt me," as he clenched his father's bat.

We all laid our sleeping bags on the tarp, and we slept under the stars and the full moon. We quietly chatted until we finally fell asleep one by one. Wyatt and I sat up, and we watched for the light on the island. He said, "It was a dim light, and it was like someone was looking for something."

I told him, "Maybe they found it."

He said, "I sure hope so. Searching for something can be maddening."

It was rare for him to say things like this, because he hid his emotions. Wyatt was usually easy to read. He wanted to be normal and not the hero he was destined to be. He asked, "Why do you think EELNEB was after me?"

I had no answer, but I told him, "You must be special, and you need to learn to overcome people wanting to see you fail."

He simply said, "Thank you," then closed his eyes.

The bright, early sun rose and pointed at us all. We all jumped up as the morning sun's heat woke us. I had never seen the sun rise of the lake over the lake, it was magnificent. We packed up everything. Wyatt instructed, "Grab a few cans on the way out. We can leave them for Cecil." No one had a watch, but we all knew it was early. Wyatt immediately and quietly asked me if I was moving the spatula, and I answered no. Then he said, "Was it real, then?"

I told him, "I don't think so."

We walked back to town since we were up before Jack was scheduled to pick us up. Our walk was short, and the conversation was only on baseball. We called Jack from Frankie's, and we all went home to rest up for our afternoon practice. We had to get ready for the district tournament.

Medals

I did not see my dad on Father's Day weekend until it was over. My sister had soccer tournament in Boone, and she would be the best player on the field while I would cheer from the dugout. Whitley usually was the priority when we both had games. My parents and Whitley left on Thursday, before the weekend tournament, so they could go enjoy the mountain town. I stayed with Drake. We headed to Jacksonville, North Carolina, for the district tournament. Each weekend was a step closer to the Little League World Series. The longer the summer lasted on baseball fields, the closer we got to Williamsport.

Coach Ross had an old military friend give us a tour of the Marine base in Jacksonville, North Carolina. Sergeant Michaels was the epitome of a hero. His large neck held his head high. His voice was not as booming as Coach Ross's, but he spoke clearly and his deep voice demanded our attention. He proudly showed us all his Silver Star medal and let us all touch it. He even gave us a motivational speech on commitment and sacrifice.

Coach Alex was not happy with Sergeant Michaels's speech. Coach Alex liked to be the headliner. He never missed an opportunity to talk. Coach Alex rudely shrugged while Sergeant Michaels eloquently spoke of commitment and sacrifice. His speech was short, and it cut like a summer breeze. We all felt it, and many of us had goose bumps. Sergeant Michaels gave a few examples of commitment and sacrifice, but he did not give the full account. He left out the details of what made him the hero. He finished with, "When you commit to something, you must sacrifice to fulfill that commitment."

Missy interrupted him while staring directly at Coach Alex. "Boys, this man saved lives, and he took shrapnel in the neck." Her voice quivered, and her tone was not of happiness but of anger. Coach Ross mimed pushing his hands to the ground to quiet his wife. She shook her head as Coach Ross nodded sideways at his friend. The unspoken message was received by Sergeant Michaels.

Drake stared at Sergeant Michaels, then shockingly asked, "Why are there pink flowers lining the entrance to the barracks?"

Sergeant Michaels said, "Years ago, one of the men planted them, and they've been here ever since."

The question was odd, and I remember thinking Drake was more concerned with pink carnations than the inspiring speech on commitment and sacrifice. Drake had already sacrificed, and the speech meant little to him. He had lived it already. Drake had committed to greatness by worrying more with home runs and winning. He sacrificed his last few innocent years of childhood before puberty made us all crazy.

Sergeant Michaels ended with, "Good luck this weekend." Wyatt's eyes unceremoniously rolled my direction. We all clapped, and RJ hugged his father's friend. The hug obviously meant more to RJ than Sergeant Michaels. RJ held him tight. Sergeant Michaels did not embrace RJ with both arms, his right arm instead dangling at his side. Missy joined the embrace, then pried her son away. Coach Ross looked away to likely hide his own tears.

We played the district tournament a week after the county tournament. The shadows of Ogre and Ruby from the mound must've scared every team, because they all seemed to cower in fear when the nearly six-foot Ruby and the six-foot Ogre took the mound. I observed opposing coaches watching the two oversize preteens warm up. The look on their faces gave me confidence the district tournament would not be much different from our previous tournaments. Ruby and Wyatt must've felt the same way, as the two rivals' confidence poured out of their mouths with every word.

Friday's game was a shutout. Ruby, Jaxon, and Anthony combined to strike out ten. Dale and Curt both had three RBIs, and Wyatt hit a home run in the first inning. He was walked the next two at bats, but the impending win kept his anger at bay. Coach Alex started his best nine, and he did not sub in the first game in effort to win big and to intimidate the other teams. I sat idle with Mitch and just enjoyed being on the team. Coach Alex shouted, "Now that was a perfect inning!" after the third inning. He boisterously clapped as the team ran in to get ready to bat. Wyatt even gave Coach Alex an unexpected high five.

Ruby and Wyatt must've been reading each other's minds, because the two were perfectly in sync. The rivals looked like best friends when Ruby was pitching. Ruby had toyed with all of us, and now he had a partner helping him do it to strangers. They both talked trash. Wyatt warned the opposing batters, and Ruby delivered his message. The displeasure we had for Ruby during the regular season disappeared, as we now were cheering his antics. My sister would have been appalled. While she was out scoring four goals a game, I sat on the bench and cheered her adversary. We won 11–1.

Game 2 was the same story with different actors. Ogre replaced Ruby and pitched the majority of the game, with Jaxon finishing it. Curt and Troy both had two RBIs each, and Drake hit a three-run home run. I even reached base and scored. When I looked in the stands for my parents after I crossed home plate, I only saw Duckworth giving me a thumbs-up sign. I smiled and nodded at him.

After the 13–0 win, the team from Fayetteville protested the game. They wanted Ogre's birth certificate. David Luck had anticipated something like this, and he had brought every document he could get his hands on for every player, especially our giant and Ogre. He had birth certificates, report cards, proof of address, and doctors' notes, to name a few. After the Little League official verified Ogre was a man-child, we headed to the hotel. We were already in the district championship. We would be back tomorrow.

It was at this moment we began to realize we had a lot of baseball left to play this summer. We played the returning district champions from Wilmington, and they showed up on a bright-blue bus with one giant. He was every bit as big as Ogre, and there were rumors that he had hit a ball four hundred feet. Their giant was no match for Wyatt and Ogre. He challenged them both each at bat. Wyatt crushed a solo opposite-field home run while Ogre pulled his own solo moon shot down the line. The plan was to start Drake and bring in Ruby if we had any trouble. He did not struggle.

Drake quietly dominated. He was always the most focused player on the team, but he seemed to be in a more intense zone than normal. He struck out the first ten consecutive batters with ease. The Wilmington coach looked more like a mesmerized fan than the opposing coach. He knew he was watching something special. The Wilmington team averaged eight runs a game, and they could not figure out the quiet pitcher. Their fans did everything but boo Drake when he walked off the field between innings. He ignored them. They mistook his quietness for cockiness like most of our opponents.

Wyatt knew Drake was in a zone. Wyatt said, "Drake's eyes looked black and not brown." Drake's intensity was felt throughout the dugout, and our usual chatter was almost silenced. Drake, per usual, sat at the end of the dugout in silence, but now he secretly rubbed a pink carnation petal. Drake hit a home run in the fourth that seemed to rival the towering shots of Ogre and Wyatt. When he stepped on home plate, he looked at the scoreboard. It was full of zeros for the Wilmington team. Drake was pitching a no-hitter. After Drake's mammoth home run, we led 9–0 with six outs to go. Drake took the mound, and he did not throw a warm-up pitch. He and Wyatt just tossed the ball back and forth. The casual warm-up gave Drake the appearance of arrogance, while Wyatt was just trying to keep him calm. When the first batter came up, Wyatt simply just pointed out to Drake. Wyatt had given up calling pitches. Drake was in control. Drake struck out the first two batters. He made an amazing play on an attempted bunt. He bounced off the mound and threw the runner out from his knees. We were three outs from winning the district, and Drake was on his way to a perfect game.

Alex asked Drake, "Do you want to continue or let Ruby finish?"

Drake nodded. "I'll finish."

By the sixth inning, Duckworth had moved to the fence beside the dugout. The crowd was silent when the Wilmington team came to bat. Drake needed three more outs. Drake's face and emotion never changed. I believe he was smiling on the inside while my stomach was full of butterflies. It was the best pitching performance I had ever seen from him.

Drake's arm was surely aching, but he never let on, and Wyatt let Drake control the final inning. It was Drake's game. The first batter showed bunt, and Drake bounced off the mound quickly despite the ball rolling foul. Drake's next pitch was inside, and the batter jumped back, knowing he would not have the opportunity to surprise the fielding savant with another bunt. Drake threw a fastball low and away to retire the first out of the inning. The second batter of the inning was a chubby backup catcher hoping to use Ruthian swing to give his team a glimmer of hope. Drake's first curveball bounced in the dirt, and the large boy pounded his bat on the plate. His second curveball fooled the batter, and he swung out of control for strike 1. Drake was unimpressed, and he threw two straight fastballs. The first fastball was called a strike, and the count was one ball and two strikes. The crowd began to sense the outcome. Drake clenched his teeth and threw his second fastball, and the Ruthian swing stopped in midair. The check swing gave the backup catcher one more chance. Drake snatched the ball out of the air in displeasure as his dad yelled, "Come on, Blue!" Drake walked around the pitcher's mound to calm himself. Duckworth shouted, "Keep your composure, son!" Drake straddled the pitching rubber and stared in as Wyatt motioned for Drake to throw whatever he wanted. Drake fired another pitch. The batter curled backward and gave it his ferocious swing just as Drake's change-up floated to Wyatt's mitt.

The Swansville fans knew it would be over soon, and our summer would continue. The last out of the inning sheepishly walked to the plate, and he looked like the last man in line for the hangman's noose. He must've known his summer on baseball fields would be ending soon. Drake was ready to finish the game, and his ailing arm was throbbing. He called Wyatt to the mound to give his arm a short break. Wyatt later told me he told Drake, "It doesn't matter if you finish or not." Drake responded, "Of course it does," as he nodded in his father's direction. Wyatt told him to relax before he jogged back to his place behind home plate. Drake fired in a fastball. The hard sound of an aluminum baseball bat echoed as the ball curved fouls down the right field line. Drake bounced a curveball before he decided it was time just to throw the old number 1. He finished the batter by painting the corner with two perfect fastballs. I wondered to myself, Would he have rather been at the geography bee or on the bench?

It was over, and we were district champions. Drake had struck out thirteen of the eighteen outs and hit a home run. He was named MVP of the tournament. He reluctantly walked up in front of the crowd to receive his MVP medal. He did not allow them to place it around his neck. He grabbed it and hurried away. He retreated before Missy could get a picture. Drake always deflected any cheers and accolades. They were somehow his weakness. The shower of cheers from our fans along with the coaches from the team from Wilmington rained down on him. He was uncomfortable, and he tried to disappear as quickly as possible.

After the game, the Wilmington coach came over, then said, "I have never seen a team so competitive. I expect you to play baseball all summer." His giant did not seem so menacing when standing next to his dad.

Alex said, "I feel the same way." He did not say it with his usual bravado but a man that now believed the narrative he had created. Alex must have realized how humble he sounded, then he quickly changed his tune. He then told the opposing coach, "Drake was our third-best pitcher, and my son would've dominated too." Duckworth heard this exchange, and he followed the Wilmington coach to apologize for Alex's conceited remark. Duckworth never wanted an opposing team to think we were arrogant. His label was beginning to stick, but Duckworth tried to change our narrative. He took pride in sportsmanship, and he knew what it was like to lose to Alex.

We were district champs on Father's Day. Drake gave his district MVP medal to his dad, and he awkwardly hugged his father. The hug was foreign to Duckworth, and it looked like a hug between strangers, not the embrace of a father and son. Drake knew he had pitched a monumental game, and he wanted his father to bask in his accomplishment. We piled in Duckworth's Blazer, and we headed back to the Brown Water of Swansville.

Duckworth's Blazer had a picture of Donnie hanging from his rearview mirror, and the picture seemed to dance from the air conditioner. I often saw Drake solemnly staring at the dancing picture. The ride back from Jacksonville was full of Duckworth telling funny stories about his job at the post office, and he always told us stories of those first few years of T-ball. I laughed despite having heard the same stories many times. Duckworth asked Drake some questions in effort to have his son open up and join our conversation, but Drake never did. Drake's brown eyes were always somewhere else, and his father's questions brought him back. Duckworth put the MVP medal on his key chain.

The Hole in the Wall

Father's Day was in our rearview mirror. Summer was nearly half over, and the July 4 holiday was just a few short weeks away. Pisgah Lake and Swansville would be overflowing with people any day now. Swansville held an annual catfish and bass tournament the last Friday in June. Boats from all over the state would be launching at Winslow's in a few days. Normally, Jack and Ogre would spend the weekend helping out Frankie at the bait shop, but this year they would be on a baseball field.

We would spend the weekend playing baseball, and we would miss the weigh-ins Sunday morning. We decided to try our luck and catch a trophy before every fisherman in the state showed up. Ogre, Wyatt, Troy, and I would take Troy's undersize boat out on the Brown Water. The boat would be too small for us all, but we would pile on it anyway. We would take turns fishing with Captain Troy. He always wore a foolish-looking fishing hat, and he insisted on being called Captain. Troy cared little about catching a fish but just wanted to spend the day on the water. Troy enjoyed leisure more than anyone.

My parents dropped off Wyatt and me at Ogre's house. We loaded up a makeshift cart with fishing rods and other supplies. The three of us headed to Winslow's. It was overcast when we left Ogre's house, but the sun eventually came out. The sun's rays were visible, and it was easy to tell it would be a hot day. The temperature was expected to be in the upper nineties. Wyatt tied his shirt around his head, then pulled the cart as Ogre and I pushed it from behind. We crossed the desert of Swansville to get to Winslow's. The normally short walk took over twenty minutes due to the rickety old cart. We stopped as we reached Scarborough Park to catch our breath. Wyatt, out of nowhere, loudly shouted, "Hell no! I'll throw him off the boat." Ogre and I were puzzled, until Wyatt pointed to Winslow's. We finished pushing the cart, and our journey in the excruciating heat ended. Wyatt grumbled as we approached a smiling Ruby and Curt standing on the dock at Winslow's.

Troy had invited Ruby and Curt to fish without telling us. Curt was not the cause for concern. Curt immediately approached Wyatt to settle him down and to talk him into not causing any trouble with his rival. Wyatt and Curt's conversation was loud, and Wyatt's arms indicated he would remain unhappy. Ogre was disgusted, but he said nothing. Ruby loudly stated, "Let's all just have fun and fish." I knew at some point we would have confrontation. Ruby and Wyatt only looked like allies when they were on the baseball field. I hoped a day out on the Brown Water could somehow mend the two baseball stars.

Ogre would fish from the shoreline per usual, but the rest of us would spend time with Troy on the boat. We would go out two at a time with our captain, while two of us would stay and fish with Ogre. Ruby started telling a story of how he and his dad had caught a forty-five-pound catfish using cocktail shrimp. Curt said, "I hope y'all know what you're doing, because I don't know how to fish." Ruby assured him he'd show him the ropes and Curt would be fine. Ruby and Curt were dressed like expert fisherman, and Ruby even had a one-hundred-dollar fishing rod.

The five of us went in to visit the more-than-usual-irritable Frankie while we waited for Troy to pick us up. Frankie was prepping for the tournament and was chaotically stocking shelves. No one could even get his attention as the Braves game loudly blared. The store was like a cave the weekend of the tournament due to Frankie stocking every nook and cranny. It was difficult to walk up and down the aisles. Fishing gear flooded the store, and Frankie put all his base- ball inventory away for the weekend. We bought worms with Ruby's cash. Frankie gave Ogre an old cooler for us to use. Frankie said, "Fill it up. I don't want to buy groceries next week." He chuckled as he said it. Jack told everyone to wear a life jacket and that the lake could be dangerous if you were acting like a bunch of fools. We all promised. Frankie shouted, "Don't let that rich boy do anything stupid!" as we walked out of the bait shop.

Troy came flying into the dock, and the prop on the boat spit a little mud, as the lake water was already down about two feet deep. Ogre was the first to board the small boat, and we piled in after him. We did not have enough room for Ogre's cooler, so we just carried our Gatorades in our laps. We shoved off, with Troy pushing the boat through the shallow water as Wyatt steered. Ogre clenched a life jacket, and his knees shook. Once the water depth was over four feet, Troy jumped in, and brown water poured over the side. The small boat was not ready for the weight of six nearly teenage boys, especially two the size of grown men.

Troy immediately began cursing all the extra folks on the lake. He was well-known by the locals for always being on the water. He waved at every boat and made comments like, "There is stinky Nick" or "Oh god, I hope Rutherford doesn't try to find me later." I wondered if all these old men interacted with a twelve-year-old. I went to the park for extra practice when I had free time while Troy cruised the lake aimlessly. What Troy only had to do was check in with his sister every few hours. She usually stayed by their pool. Summer to Troy was baseball and boats. The lake was his best friend.

Troy knew every inch of the lake, and he made sure everyone knew it. He had odd little nicknames for his favorite spots. He said he regularly caught crappie at a place called the Bull's Eye; another of his favorite spots was back of the Alligator Island. Troy said, "Guys, I am taking you all to my favorite spot on the lake." We bounced on the water in Troy's fishing boat for about twenty minutes until he abruptly pulled back on the throttle. We coasted on top of the water. The lake was like glass, and his boat was the cause of its disturbance. We drifted for fifteen feet, then he slowly crept the throttle back up to allow us to drift into a secluded cove he called the Hole in the Wall.

I asked Troy, "Why do you call it the Hole in the Wall?"

He said, "The entrance to this cove looks like someone punched a hole in a wall." He was right. The shoreline was unbroken except at this spot. He pulled out a lake map, and it nearly blew off. He showed us our location on it, and the Hole in the Wall did not exist. Troy had somehow found a place off the map. It did not even feel like we were on the lake. We could hear the buzz of boats, but we could not see them. The cove was sheltered from the big water. Ogre would be able to touch the bottom in every spot of the shallow cove. Troy beached the boat on a pebble shoreline, and Ogre quickly jumped off.

The plan was to fish in the shallow water of the Hole in the Wall and catch small bait fish. Ogre helped Ruby bait his $100 fishing rod with a worm. Ogre wiped the dirt from the container of worms on Ruby's swimsuit, much to his displeasure. Ruby angrily said, "Damn, this is my favorite pair." Curt caught the first keeper of our bait fish and flexed and said, "Time to slay some fish." Troy only watched and floated around the cove. I caught a hand-size bait fish, and Curt continued his hot streak and he reeled in two more. Our bucket was full of bait fish in a matter of minutes.

Wyatt, Troy, and I were the first to shove off in search of an elusive trophy fish. We left Ogre standing on the shoreline with Ruby and Curt. The two large boys' shadows stretched the length of the cove, and the place was dark despite the midday sun. Curt waved and chuckled. Ruby shouted as we exited the cove, "I will try to find a honey hole while you are gone!" He wanted to sound like a fisherman.

Troy took us over by the dam to fish by way of the big water. It was an ominous spot, and only a few boats would even fish the area. A lumber company had recently taken all the mature trees. The shoreline was an eerie wasteland, and every buzzard was easily spotted. Troy recycled his uncle's stories and told us, "I heard the dam had catfish as big as Volkswagens." Troy did not even bother to watch his fishing pole. After he cast out his line, he grabbed a life jacket and floated around with it between his legs. It looked as if he were standing on the bottom.

Wyatt barely spoke as he kept telling Troy to hush every five minutes. Troy's boat did not have a canopy to block the sun, so eventually Wyatt and I jumped in the deep, dark water to cool off. The water near the dam was almost black, and it seemed much cooler than the brown water I had swam in my entire life. I watched our lines as we floated around. Troy rambled on about the new school and how he'd miss those of us left in Swansville. He said, "I am not ready for it to be an us-versus-them town." The water seemed to calm him, and he made sense while floating around.

"Holy crap!" I pointed. "There is an eagle!" I ogled the majestic bird, but Troy was unimpressed. He did not even turn to look as the eagle swooped down to grab a fish. It was one of the most amazing moments of my summer.

Troy said, "His nest is at the mouth of the river." He pointed in the direction of the lake's highest peak. Troy called the mini mountain King's Crown.

Wyatt asked Troy, "How can you catch a fish being so loud?"

Troy shrugged and let a cackle. "Guess I'm a natural."

Troy confidently told us we would not catch anything just as Wyatt's line popped. We all frantically swam to the boat to reel in our trophy. The fish fought for a good ten minutes before it must've run out of energy. Wyatt pulled the catfish next to the boat. It had to be at least thirty pounds. Wyatt's borrowed fishing rod was not strong enough to pull it in the boat since Troy had forgotten a net. Wyatt grabbed his sweat-drenched shirt in an effort to aid his struggle of pulling the fish onto the boat. The line snapped, then the reel turned into a bird's nest. The trophy fish slowly dived back underwater. It had survived three twelve-year-olds. Wyatt screamed in agony, "Ughhhhhh!"

I said, "That was an amazing fish," just as Troy said, "Dive deep, big fella."

Troy looked at Wyatt and said, "Who gives a shit, anyway?" and he started the boat. We sped back to the Hole in the Wall. The free air-conditioning, as Troy called it, gave me goose bumps after I had been in the cool black dam water. Wyatt complained and was openly disgusted with Troy. Troy ignored Wyatt's incessant whining. Wyatt loudly said, "Who will believe I caught a fish big enough to win the tournament, because you can't even bring a damn net?"

Troy had the boat drift in the same way, and I asked him, "Why drift in?"

He responded, "There is a big sandbar at the mouth of the Hole in the Wall, and that is why no one bothers to go in." He explained, "That is why I love it. My sister or Isaac can't find me." Troy had found a hiding place.

Ruby and Ogre were fishing on opposite sides of the cove as Curt swam around. Troy asked, "Any luck?" Ruby and Ogre glared at each other as Curt spoke up. "These two big dummies can't get along, so I separated them." He said it while laughing. Ruby shouted, "I am trying to catch a bass, and Ogre keeps following my line!" Ogre just shook his head. Troy sat on the beached boat and told Ruby, Curt, and an uninterested Ogre of how close we were to pulling in a monster. Ruby questioned everything, and Wyatt just kept telling Ruby, "Go catch a fish, then come talk to me."

Ruby responded, "If we were hungry, we'd starve eating your bounty."

Wyatt replied, "I hope you can cast a fishing rod better than you swing a bat."

Ruby shook his head, then he reminded the group who was the league champs.

The last thing I wanted to happen was for a fight to break-out. Curt kept making jokes to try to ease the tension between the three boys. Curt used his best, loudest, and deepest voice and said, "In the blue corner, the biggest and quietest kid in school, Oggggrrreeeee! And in the red corner, the reigning champion, Rrrrrrrubbbbbbbbyyyyyyy!" Then he followed up with, "He is the neeeeeewwwwww kid, Wyatt Hartley." No one was impressed, but Troy and I laughed with Curt.

Ruby's $100 fishing rod popped, and a fight started with a fish. Ruby was not a fisherman, but he had finally hooked a bass. Ogre ran to his side of the cove to assist the novice in reeling in a trophy. Curt and Troy floated around the water. Eventually, Curt and Troy floated over as the fight continued on. Troy kept trying to determine the size of the bass. He said, "It's a fighter, and that can only mean one thing." The fish's head popped up occasionally, but it would dive back down into the shallow cove water. It splashed and jerked until Ruby handed his fishing rod over to Ogre. Ogre fought the fish until he had no choice but to have Wyatt join the battle. Troy confidently floated over on his life jacket. He seemed unimpressed and talked casually the entire time. Eventually, Curt said, "Give me a chance!" Curt wasted no time and pulled the fish to shore within minutes. He did not even need a net. The monster bass was not much bigger than our Gatorade bottles that now littered the shoreline.

Troy laughed, then said, "It took y'all over twenty-five minutes to reel in this tiny thing." Ogre grinned and shook his head.

Wyatt said, "My monster catfish would've eaten this little fella."

Ruby said, "What fish? I've not seen this monster fish yet." He pointed at the small bass and said, "At least I have proof." We all agreed to release the fish back out on the big water in the event it was trapped in the small cove due to the sandbar. Troy told us all his uncle always said, "The big fish are lazy, and they can't keep the fight up, but the little fish desires to one day be the big fish, and they have still more left to fight for."

Troy, Curt, and Ruby cruised out of the cove to release the bass. We swam around for a few more hours before deciding to head back to town. We loaded up the boat, and Ogre demanded we not leave any trash on the shoreline. As we were cleaning up, I noticed an area where a campfire had been, and I asked Troy, "Do you come out here at night?" He said that he did and showed us where he sometimes would sleep. He told me, "Sometimes I just want to stay away from the house." I was shocked to learn the richest kid we knew sometimes slept under the stars like a hobo. We jumped back in the boat, then cruised back to the brown water and Winslow's.

Troy docked the boat and helped us unload everything. Frankie came out, then said, "Where is today's trophy?" Curt immediately went into the story, and his hands told half of it. His version sounded like he had just spent the day with Captain Ahab. Troy hushed Curt when he started to give away Troy's secret spot. Frankie more than likely knew where the Hole in the Wall was, but Troy needed a place to hide. Frankie went back into the store to finish preparing for the onslaught of fishermen coming to town. We finished unpacking Troy's boat. Curt went inside to call his dad for a ride home.

Troy was set to motor off when he decided to go inside to grab a Cheerwine for his cruise back home. Ogre, Wyatt, and I said our goodbyes, and we started to push the cart off the side bridge. Isaac pulled up in his convertible Mustang, slinging rocks in the parking lot. He and Ella hopped out of the fire-red car. Isaac forcefully grabbed Ella's hand and pulled her in our direction. Troy stepped out of the bait shop and whispered to himself, "Oh, shit, I am in trouble now." Troy had forgotten, as always, to check in, and his mother sent his nemesis after him. Troy did not have the look of fear but the look of someone wanting to make sure his friends did not see him get chastised by someone only a few years older.

Isaac started toward Troy and shouted, "Big surprise, moron! I had to hunt you down again!" Troy motioned to his sister to get Isaac to let him be. Isaac angrily pointed at Troy, then said, "Don't ask her to come to your rescue, you little shit!"

Troy tried to beg his sister's boyfriend, "Isaac, I swear it will not happen again."

Isaac laughed. "I think I have heard that before." He poked his chest out and headed for Troy. Ella tried to hold Isaac back, but he jerked her arm and she nearly fell.

I shouted, "Watch it, jerk!"

He glanced my way, but he was focused on Troy. Isaac stomped in our direction, with Troy's sister pleading with him, "It's not a big deal. Who cares, anyway?"

Isaac just said, "Yes, Ella, it is. He seems to ruin my day every weekend."

Troy looked back at us all, then said, "See why I hide?" It was evident our carefree friend did not live the lifestyle we all had imagined.

Oddly, Ruby tried to intervene. Ruby was bigger than Isaac, but his voice cracked when he tried to sound tough as he said, "Isaac, what's up? You need to chill out."

Isaac shouted, "Shut your mouth!" He never took his eyes off Troy.

Troy was frozen, and he began to stammer in an effort to convince Isaac to leave. His words failed, and the sixteen-year-old boy headed his way.

I looked back at Ruby, and the giant's shadow stretching across the dock suddenly filled me with confidence. I had the two biggest boys and the toughest boy I knew on my side, so I foolishly decided to confront the sixteen-year-old boy as he walked up the side bridge to Winslow's. I stepped in the center of his path, but he was unimpressed. Isaac yelled, "Stay out of this, string bean!" I unsuccessfully tried to block his way, and he pushed me into the shallow water. Ruby embarrassingly cowered away and let Isaac pass by. Wyatt stood idle, as if he were in some type of trance. Ogre stepped in front to block the smaller sixteen-year-old boy.

Isaac told Ogre, "Move."

Then Ogre menacingly said, "Leave my uncle's store now."

Isaac stopped, as if to think it over, then he shouted, "Troy, I've wasted my day trying to find your little ass!"

At that moment, Curt came flying from nowhere and screeched, "Eeeeyaaaa!" and he double-fisted-hit the older boy in the shoulder. Isaac tossed Curt to the side. Curt slid across the wooden dock, then grabbed his knee as a nail had punctured his skin. The blood trickling through Curt's fingers must have awoken Wyatt from his trance.

Wyatt walked next to Ogre as Ogre turned to Troy and said, "Stay back."

Isaac grabbed Ogre's shoulder in an attempt to move him. It was a mistake. Ogre turned and punched Isaac in the nose. His nose burst, and blood poured from his nose like champagne at a celebration. Wyatt pushed Isaac over Curt's outstretched leg. The villain stumbled off the dock into the muddy brown water. Ella screamed, "Please, please stop!" Isaac landed just a few feet away from me as I was attempting to get up. Isaac grabbed me and threatened me until Ruby bounded off the dock onto him. Ruby held Isaac down as I pulled myself up. Curt and Wyatt ran to Ogre's side. They stood shoulder to shoulder, threateningly staring down the older boy. I felt safe as I looked up at the three menacing figures. Isaac understood the message: he would have to take all five of us. Ruby freed him. Isaac trampled back to shore through the muddy water.

Frankie finally came out to see what all the commotion was about. Curt joyfully said, "Darren just taught that boy a lesson." It was odd hearing someone call Ogre by his real name.

Frankie yelled, "Leave and never come back!"

Isaac left a trail of blood to his car from the back of the Brown Water to the parking lot. He sped off after cleaning himself up with a towel from his trunk. I shouted, "Ella, we are sorry!"

Troy said, "I will be sorry if I don't beat them home."

Frankie knew if Ogre had to punch someone, it was warranted. Ogre's face was red with shame, and Frankie hugged his nephew.

We all looked at Troy for an explanation. Troy hurriedly said while preparing his boat, "When I don't check in, my mom worries and she sends Isaac and Ella after me. Isaac believes he is my father. My father is not a bully. I must've let time get away from me while we were fishing." He went on to tell everyone he was sorry.

I assured him, "You have nothing to apologize for."

He thanked us. "Maybe we can do it again sometime, with less blood and guts."

The dock was unsteady as Troy sped away. I watched him disappear out of the cove.

Frankie looked on, then whispered under his breath, "That boy needs to slow the hell down."

David Luck pulled in just as Troy was out of view. He looked puzzled, and he threw up his hands, looking for an explanation. Frankie waved him home so no explanation would be needed.

Ruby shook Ogre's hand, then said, "Slayer of men."

Curt flexed and said, "Then I am the slayer of fish."

Ogre said nothing as usual, and his anxiety of the event was written all over his face. Wyatt, Ogre, and I pushed the fishing cart back to Ogre's house. Cars stared at me, as I was covered in blood and mud. I looked like I had lost a battle. Jack only laughed when we told him what happened.

Queen City

The state tournament was historically played in Raleigh, but the Queen City of Charlotte would be the host city this year. Charlotte just built a brand-new baseball complex, and the mayor wanted to showcase the new facility. Eight teams would vie for the opportunity to represent the state of North Carolina. We were the closest to Charlotte, and the town would be in our weekend caravan. Josie Leonard joined the caravan and acted as if she had spent the summer following Jaxon to baseball fields all over the state. Sylvia, Missy, and Vanessa all bemoaned Josie's sudden interest. Josie had not paid her dues all summer, and the other moms spent the weekends looking after Jaxon. The whispers of Williamsport were now open conversation among our parents. The Williamsport fantasy was within reach.

Coach Alex gathered the team and our parents for a short team meeting. He told us, "We need to represent Swansville in a positive way." Someone from the Biscoe team had called and complained, "The team from Swansville is a bunch of classless bullies, and their fans are no better." We laughed it off at first to try to hide our shame. Only Ruby and Alex had the stain of being classless bullies, and they had adapted it over time. They had grown accustomed to the feeling. We were branded in an instant. Ogre, Drake, and I were baptized by an anonymous letter and by the words floating out of Coach Alex's lips. It was surprisingly exciting to be viewed the villain for once and not the underdog. We embraced it. Coach Alex said, "We will need to be perfect, because we have accomplished more than any Swansville all-star team, and I intend on accomplishing more."

Ruby shouted, "Villains from Swansville!"

We all cheered and gave one another high fives. Our smiles united us.

The first team we played was the Robeson County team. The team from Robeson County was made up of mostly Lumbee Indians. Coach Alex started Ruby based on the rumor that they were a great hitting team. The rumor was true. Ruby struggled in the first inning, gave up three runs. Ruby gave up hit after hit, which was a rarity. He was frazzled. It was one of the few times he did not have his usual look of arrogance. It eventually came back in the second inning, and he squashed them with ease. Wyatt and RJ both homered in the first inning, and Ogre and Jaxon reached on singles. After one inning, the score was 5–3. Ruby settled down and cruised through the next three innings. Our bats were never silent, nor were Wyatt and Ruby. The two enemies were perfect allies when staring at adversity. Troy and Dale both homered. The Swansville fans stayed on their feet for each batter.

Ogre entered the game, and we were leading 9–3. Ogre gave up one run in the fifth inning. The Robeson County team still trailed 9–4. Coach Alex let me, Anthony, and Mitch all get an at bat. I bounced out to the pitcher, and Anthony and Mitch both struck out. Ogre finished off the Robeson County team in the sixth with three straight strikeouts, and we won the game 10–4.

We all stayed and watched the next game to see the fabled girl pitcher from Ashe County. We laughed, and no one was concerned if we could get hit against a girl. She quickly mowed down her opponents for one inning. Her father wanted to save her innings in the event she was needed for the championship game. We barely watched as we all made comments about her. We did everything but heckle the beauty. It seemed unlikely anyone could stop us, much less a girl. The Ashe County boys and one girl easily won 9–1. We loaded up, only to return the following day to face off against the Halifax County team.

The Halifax County team would not be a match for us. Becca Gorgan and the Ashe County team looked on as they had dominated the early game. She drove in three runs and closed the game out on the mound to lead her team to the state final. She loomed if we could get past the Halifax County team. Drake gave up a run in the first inning, and Jaxon hit a three-run home run in the first inning. We never relinquished the lead. After three innings, we led 5–1. Drake gave up a solo home run, then he walked two batters. Coach Alex did not waste time, and he brought in Ogre to get us out of trouble. The threat was over. Ogre got the next six outs with no problems, and Ogre and Wyatt both homered and the score ballooned to 8–2. Jaxon pitched a perfect sixth inning, with his mom cheering like he had just finished off the 1927 Yankees. Missy stood on the bleachers to outcheer his mother. "Way to go, baby!" she shouted over and over.

Ogre would start the championship game against the most peculiar opposing starting pitcher of the summer. Becca Gorgan was not your typical pitcher or your typical twelve-year-old. Becca was raised in the shadows of the North Carolina mountains. Becca's mother died when she was five years old, and her father had raised her like a boy. Becca's beauty was only matched by her athletic abilities. She played football and basketball. The western part of the state had experienced her dominance in person, and the rumors slowly had reached the Piedmont. The girl pitcher was a celebrity. Roy Gorgan had turned his daughter into one of the most terrifying pitchers in the state.

She looked out of place among her teammates. She was the tallest player on the team, and she carried herself with DiMaggio-like grace. The girl from the mountains was surrounded by wily twelve-year-old mountain boys. They were loud, and they looked like they had more fun on the field than any of our previous opponents. Their jerseys were covered in grass and dirt stains. Becca did not seem to have fun unless she was striking someone out. Baseball was not a game to her but a struggle in which she did everything necessary to prover herself a worthy opponent.

Becca was not just tall, but she was also breathtakingly beautiful. I felt like I was looking at Ashe County's version of Whitley. I would have struggled being her teammate. Becca's one green eye and one blue eye sunk into her freckled baby face. I was mesmerized, and only Ella Russell distracted me the same way. When I looked at Becca, I quickly looked away, for the fear of being caught staring. She

146

could freeze you with one simple look. She was the most intimidating pitcher I had seen, but not for the same reasons.

Becca's father, Roy, yelled, "You can do it, Big B!" when she was on the mound. Becca's eyes rolled each time he shouted the nickname, but it garnered respect. She had a sidearm delivery that was effortless. The ball jumped out of her hand like an arrow from a bow. Becca's fastball was feared, but her gravity-defying sinker ball made her nearly impossible to hit. Any joke about playing a girl disappeared once you stepped in the batter's box. She would coldly stare each batter down, and at that moment, she did not have the look of a victim but a villain. Becca distracted the batter when she blinked her long eyelashes just before her different-colored eyes rolled back in her head. The ball sped past the batter, and it was like the opposing hitter was turned to stone by the mountain beauty.

Becca retired the first eight batters with ease. She had five strikeouts and three weak grounders. Preston was not fazed by Becca's stare, and he hit a sinker over the right field fence. Preston was not known for home runs, and it was only the second one he had hit all summer. He somehow had broken Becca's curse over all of us. Preston's feet did not seem to touch the ground as he trotted the bases. The score was 1–0 after three innings. Ogre had to get three more outs before handing the ball over to Jaxon. Ruby was scheduled to close the game out.

The top of the fourth inning, Ogre walked two in a row and Becca doubled in two runs to give the Ashe County team a 1–2 lead. Becca's teammates began to taunt Ogre. She tried to quiet the mountain boys, but they persisted. They mocked his size and his big head with taunts like, "Melon head" and "Fee fie foe fum big and dumb." Ogre looked down before delivering his next fastball, and when he looked up, his eyes betrayed him. Rage filled his eyes, not tears. Ogre did not like to be teased, and the mountain boys had angered him. The next three batters did not stand a chance. Ogre angrily struck each of them out. He walked off the field with a menacing look. He looked every bit the giant that other teams feared.

Becca was able to get Wyatt to weakly ground out. Wyatt was hitless against her. The rare hitless day kept Wyatt unusually quiet.

Ogre said nothing as he walked to the plate. Becca stared him down, and Ogre sheepishly smiled. It was a look I had never seen from my large friend. He was happy, and the look on his face told me he knew something no one else did. Ogre was not affected when Becca blinked her eyes before firing a fastball. The ball bounced in the parking lot just behind the scoreboard. It was the slowest Ogre ever trotted the bases after a home run. He wanted to enjoy it, and he was booed for the first time in his life.

The score was tied 2–2. Jaxon walked, and Ruby weakly bounced to third, but he reached on a throwing error. The Ashe County fans began to chant, "Becca, Becca!" Dale had no chance, as he did not even swing at the three fastballs down the middle. She walked Troy to load the bases. Preston ignored the mountain beauty's stare, and he promptly hit a double into the right center field gap. Preston had cleared the bases, giving us a 5–2 lead. Becca's head dropped, and her father replaced her. She exited the game with tears in her eyes and only her father's arm around her for comfort. He sensed the impending doom without his best pitcher. He did not want her on the mound when it was over. RJ lined out to shortstop to end the inning.

Jaxon took the mound to get the next three outs. Becca's replacement led off the inning, and Jaxon promptly struck him out. The inning was uneventful. Jaxon walked one, but a double play ended the inning. Drake and Wyatt hit back-to-back doubles, and our lead was now 6–2. Roy Gorgan was forced to change pitchers again, and his daughter sat in the dugout with her hat covering her crying eyes. Preston drove in two more runs before the inning was over, and our lead was 8–2. Coach Alex did not sub in Ruby to close the game out. He let Jaxon get the last three outs of the state tournament. Josie Leonard stood on the top bleacher, loudly cheering for her son as he closed out another game. Missy let her enjoy it.

Coach Alex personally shook Becca's hand after the game and told her no other pitcher held us in check like she had done. Alex told her, "Don't hang your head, sweetie."

Jack whispered to her, "When you look in the mirror, just know the best pitcher in the state is looking back at you." He hugged her and wished her luck. She looked up and blinked her green and blue eyes as tears rolled down her cheek. She whispered, "Thank you," and dropped her head to hide any remaining tears. I shook her hand, and neither of us made eye contact. I was embarrassed. Roy Gorgan wished us good luck, and he told Ogre, "Ignore the taunts. It's just a shortcut to thinking."

Coach Alex gave a postgame speech and presented the game ball to Preston. Coach Alex said, "Today's game ball is for the only eleven-year-old on the team. Preston cracked the code on hitting the unhittable Becca Gorgan." Our parents openly cheered, and Preston's grin was not that of a baseball player but of a kid that had earned respect from the "older boys." He asked us all, "Please sign my ball. I will never forget today's game." We obliged, and everyone gave Preston a much-earned high five.

Coach Alex finished the joyful moment with, "Next weekend, we will drive to Greenville, South Carolina."

We were now more than just the kids from the Brown Water; we were the boys from North Carolina.

Cursed Ground

Road construction was completed before Christmas, and now the new four lanes connecting Swansville to the highway brought a new gas station. The new gas station was set to start construction, and the lot was cleared. Concrete would be poured in the coming week. The new gas station would welcome everyone off the highway to Swansville. It would accommodate boats and even had a bait shop. Winslow's customers would not have to drive all the way to the back of Cubbie Cove to get minnows and other fishing supplies. The gas station and bait shop was named Swansville Gas and Tackle. A sign announcing the future mega gas station had been up for nearly a year.

Frankie openly complained about his future rival. He grumbled, "Guess it's time for me to retire." Everyone objected, and we told him the locals would stay loyal. Ogre called me. "We must do something to save Winslow's," he said. I told Ogre, "I'll come up with something." My corrupted twelve-year-old brain came up with the idea of placing a curse on the ground of the construction site. I asked my mom if Wyatt and I could stay at my grandmother's house, and of course she agreed. She warned us, "No blowing up bombs this time." I called Wyatt to invite him over. He of course always had permission to stay with me. I told him the plan, and he chuckled. Whitley overheard me tell Wyatt. She said, "You fools have no idea how to curse anything." She cackled at the idea, then waved her hand. "Nonsense," she decreed. I hushed her, then disagreed. "You'll see." I told him we would be at his house in ten minutes.

Wyatt and I walked over to Ogre's house. He and RJ were in the front yard, throwing a football. The plan was, Mitch would come to town and stay with Jaxon at his grandmother's house. We would all sneak out and ride our bikes to the construction site. The two-mile bike ride would not be pleasant, especially after ten. It would definitely seem a little eerie. I told everyone to bring something that was bad luck. We would burn, then bury the ashes of our cursed items.

The clock struck ten, and my grandmother was fast asleep on the couch. Wyatt and I carefully sneaked out the creaky back door. We put on our backpacks, and Wyatt brought his father's bat, as he put it, "just in case." We rode our bikes over to Ogre's. Ogre, RJ, Jaxon, and Mitch waited at the stop sign a block away from Ogre's house. I had matches, and we all brought a snack and a drink. The ride out to the new gas station was a slight incline; thus, I underestimated how long it would take to ride out. The ride back would be much easier, and we would be able to essentially coast back. We laughed and chatted mostly about the seventh grade. Mitch said, "I sure hope Mrs. Henry mellows out before school starts." He looked at me then said, "Thank God we did not win. Otherwise, we would have been stuck with the hag for the weekend."

We reached the construction site, and we walked onto the forbidden future home of Swansville Gas and Tackle. The "Danger" and "No Trespassing" signs warned us to turn back. We ignored them. Our bags of cursed goods did not give me confidence, but walking step for step with my friends did. My first step was full of trepidation as I scouted a site to burn our cursed collection. We all agreed we would explain why our item was cursed.

I started a fire with newspapers and sticks. I did my best to use the strategy Troy used earlier in the summer. I continually had to stoke the fire, and Wyatt poked it with the handle of his father's bat. Mitch pulled out a championship trophy. The trophy was only two years old. He broke the trophy, then dropped it in the fire. Mitch explained, "I earned this trophy while watching Ruby strike everyone out. I do not want anything to do with the Harrisons." Jaxon had the same trophy. He gave Mitch a high five, then put his arm around his former teammate, then Mitch began to stomp. He was in a half-squat, and he only stomped with his left foot. Mitch's elbow and knee seemed to nearly touch. The flicker of the fire transformed Mitch as he stomped. His shadow stretched high into the surrounding trees. He looked like some sort of wild beast, not the weakling he had always been.

Jaxon opened his bag and pulled out a cracked mirror. It was a lady's makeup mirror. Jaxon stated, "Break a mirror, seven years' bad luck." He dropped it in the flames, and it shattered. Mitch's stomp was rhythmic. *Stomp stomp.* Then he wailed at the moon, "Ooooooooyyyyyyaaaaa!" Jaxon glanced over and grinned at Mitch's antics. He joined his former teammate in the ritual. Jaxon gave his own shout to the cursed gods, "Byyyyyyyyyayyyaa!"

RJ angrily said, "This jerk ruined the greatest football player's career!" We all knew he was refereeing to his broken idol Bo Jackson. RJ threw a football card of Cincinnati Bengal Kevin Walker. RJ spit on the card as it was being consumed by flames. RJ then let out his own beast-like shout, "Eeeeeeyyyyyeeeeeeaaaaa!" Jaxon and Mitch joined with their own night wails. I warned everyone to be quiet, and I pointed at the "Danger: Do Not Enter" sign. Their eyes were glassed over, and they paid no attention to my warning. The three boys were arm in arm, stomping.

Ogre opened a brown paper bag and threw in goat hair, and the fire instantly began to smell. The nauseating smell choked us as the hairs made a sound like a fuse set to go off. We all coughed before Mitch's "Ooooooooyyyyyaaaaa," Jaxon's "Byyyyyyyyyayyyaa," and finally, RJ's "Eeeeeeyyyyyeeeeeaaaaa." Ogre said, "Duckworth told me goats are good for curses. I took his word for it." The smell was unbearable. Ogre turned red and looked at his feet, and they, too, joined the *stomp stomp* of the night. All three were in some type of primordial trance. Now Ogre bellowed out, "Uggggghhhhaaa!" The *stomp stomp* continued.

It was my turn. I explained to the *stomp stomp* rhythm and the beastly howls of my four friends, "Y'all are going to think I am crazy, but salting a field makes the soil never able to bear fruit or prosper."

Wyatt loudly laughed. "Leave it to you to give us a history lesson."

I poured salt onto the flames. The flames flickered and nearly went out. I told Wyatt to hurry before the fire turned to ashes. I only had a few more newspapers. Mitch grabbed me, and I joined the trancelike stomp. The earth vibrated under my feet with each *stomp stomp*. I shouted after the other four's chorus, "Wyyyyaaaawyyyyaaaa!" Our cursed *stomp stomp* echoed across the forbidden site.

Wyatt pulled a book from his bag. It was *The Catcher in the Rye*. I asked, "Why is that a curse?" We all five howled. He said, "I am not sure, but my mother told me it was forbidden. She told me to never open it." Mitch objected to burning a book. I tried to reason with Wyatt, but to no avail. He threw the book in the flames. It opened upon impact, and an enveloped was exposed from the novel's pages. Wyatt quickly grabbed it just before the letter was consumed by the remaining flames. Wyatt refused to open it. The envelope was addressed to Sweet P. He tucked it in his bag.

I added the remaining *Swansville Orator*'s last pages to the fire, and along with the burning book, the fire grew higher. The six of us were surely an odd sight, stomping and wailing beside a cursed fire. Wyatt did not have our enthusiasm, but he played along. He screamed, "Rrrrrrooooooaaaarrrrraaaw!" His howl seemed real, more like a lion than a twelve-year-old's silliness. He joined the *stomp stomp* too. His shout scared whatever birds were in the surrounding pine trees. The mass departure of birds screeching as they flew away startled the group, and we stopped. We oddly looked at one another. Everyone had the look of shame as we all knew our antics were just that of children, not that of boys nearing our teenage years. The last ten minutes seemed to have happened in a flash.

No one ever spoke of the curse or the *stomp stomp* dance. We all agreed to finish our snacks and our drinks by the fire. The cursed fire began to die out just after eleven thirty. RJ began to entertain the group with his impressions. He stood up and performed one of the songs from the movie *CB4*. I had no idea what he was doing, but Ogre laughed uncontrollably. He surely had seen the performance before. Ogre rarely, if ever, became animated, but the *stomp stomp* and RJ's nonsense must have rattled something loose inside the oversize boy. Ogre's smile that night was worth the long bike ride out.

During RJ's silliness, Wyatt pulled the letter from his bag. He silently read it as our burning curse began to turn to ashes. Wyatt hid his face with the letter. Shadows danced on the back of it. I asked him, "What does it say?" He handed it to me and said "Promise." I agreed. It was a goodbye letter to Patti Hartley from Wyatt's dad. Jamie Hartley was alive but locked away.

Dear Sweet P,

This will be my final letter. I deserve my punishment. The innocent man I drunkenly crashed into deserved his life. I am truly sorry, and I wish I had not let that bottle suck the courage and integrity out of me. His family deserved better. The jury was unjust when they gave me only thirty years in prison. I am thankful it gave me a chance to repent. I have come to terms with my punishment, but you should know I am reborn again within these walls, thanks to our Lord and Savior.

I wish I had not spotted you wearing that green dress. Your life would have been extravagant, and you would not be reading letters from a prisoner but rather wearing elegant gowns in ballrooms of the wealthy. You are the greatest thing to ever happen to me, and I am likely the worst thing to happen to your life. The best day of my life was when I skipped that meaningless state championship game to spend it with you. Home runs meant nothing to me once you told me you loved me. I remember your eyes matching the blue of the horizon as we drove in your father's car back down the mountain. That vision alone gives me peace inside my lonely cell. I smile when I close my eyes because of you.

Tell Wyatt I love him, and tell him I died in a wreck. The man I was needed to die. He doesn't need to worry with me. I would only bring him bad luck. He will make his own legacy, and my name would only slow down his rise. Go back to Swansville. The boy needs a Hartley to warn him of my past mistakes and, at times, shield him from the pain. Tell Jacob to make him whatever he wants but make sure he becomes a man, not a coward like me. He can be anything—a cook, a businessman, or a ballplayer. He can be anything in Swansville, and the people there will embrace you and him. The Brown Water will baptize you both. He will become strong, and you will feel strong again too. He will rise without the shackles I would've placed on him.

When I put my head to my pillow each night, I will think of your blue eyes and I will be free. You need to be free again too.

Forever yours,
Jamie

After I read the letter, I was shocked. Wyatt refused to make eye contact. The moon and the light of the dying fire provided cover if his eyes were filling with tears. I told everyone to head back. Wyatt and I would stay and put out the fire. The other four agreed, and they quickly mounted their bikes. Mitch shouted as he rode off, "For the Brown Water!"

Wyatt and I covered the ashes, and he barely spoke. I asked, "Are you going to do anything?"

He responded, "What can I do?"

I did not have an answer.

The cool night air made the ride back to town nice. Wyatt and I chatted about everything except the letter and baseball. He asked, "What in the hell was RJ doing tonight?"

My answer, "No clue, but Ogre sure loved it." Neither he nor I had ever seen Ogre so animated.

Wyatt said, "I bet he'll apologize for it tomorrow."

Time would prove that Wyatt was correct. Ogre told me first thing, "Sorry I lost control laughing." I assured him it was not a problem.

Wyatt and I approached Swansville just after midnight, and the town was silent as we rode in. The only thing I could hear was the click of the caution light by Kermit's. We sneaked back in my grandmother's house through the creaky back door.

Once in bed, I whispered, "Your secret is safe with me."

He responded, "I know."

Secrets would begin to define our friendship.

Heights

The east regional was played in Greenville, South Carolina. When we arrived in the David Luck caravan, he took the team straight to see the Shoeless Joe Jackson statue. The statue was impressive, but I wondered why he deserved a statue after being kicked out of baseball. I knew of Shoeless Joe Jackson thanks to the movie *Field of Dreams*. The movie portrayed Joe Jackson as a pawn that did not deserve his punishment. My father explained, "The truth is likely a combination of the facts and the lies. There is more to his story than we will ever know."

David unsuccessfully tried to tell a motivational story using Joe Jackson's life. He explained, "You are all like Shoeless Joe, because you came from humble beginnings." The speech fell on deaf ears since the man giving it was one of the richest people we all knew. He then warned us, "Do not do anything that would get us kicked out of the tournament or embarrass our town." His final statement was, "We are from Swansville, and we need to set an example and be upstanding citizens all weekend." His words floated like babbles that no one older than six years old would have thought sounded inspirational. I remember looking at all the guys and thinking we were far from upstanding, and as if on cue, Ruby said, "Enough with the history lesson. Let's hit the pool!"

Thursday night was one to remember. The pool had a rare high dive. It was time to show off and to overcome fears. Ella Russell sat and watched and giggled at the upcoming show. Anthony's high-dive routine was mesmerizing. Anthony's small frame allowed him to contort into what seemed like unhealthy positions, then at the last second, he would come out straight as fungo, and *bloop*, he was under the water.

Wyatt Hartley was scared of two things: his uncle Jacob and heights. We spent the entire night talking Wyatt into jumping off the high dive. It was a comical affair. His routines involved shouting, "I am a soldier!" at himself, then he would cower back in fear. Wyatt would make outlandish statements that he had jumped off a high dive before and his swimming trunks came off and he did not want everyone to see his shiny butt. He tried to hide behind the laughter in an effort to not seem afraid. He seemed mortal.

Ogre sat sheepishly silent, hoping not to be spotted. Everyone knew Ogre hated water. When Ogre was four years old, he jumped off the dock at his uncle's store and he misjudged the water's depth. He went under and was out of sight in an instant. A regular at Winslow's jumped off his moving boat to save the oversize boy. Ogre was underwater for more than two minutes. He was blue when he was retrieved from the bottom of Cubbie Cove. Jack frantically called for help, and fate intervened as two out-of-town firemen just happened to be walking into Winslow's to buy nightcrawlers. The two men performed CPR on Ogre, and when he gasped for air, Jack grabbed his son and squeezed more murky brown water from his son's lungs. *The Swansville Orator*'s headline the following week was, "Tragedy Avoided as Strangers Save Toddler." Ogre never spoke of his near-death experience, but that was the day everyone in town was introduced to Darren Winslow.

After over an hour, Ruby Harrison shamed his enemy into jumping. Ruby walked out on the board with Wyatt. Wyatt's legs looked like an earthquake had hit him. Ruby called, "You dainty flower!" then they both jumped. One had a look of fear, while the other smiled the entire way down. It was the one and only time Ruby seemed to have the upper hand against his rival. Ruby felt he had re-established himself as our leader. Wyatt's fear of heights stayed at the pool in Greenville, South Carolina. He had conquered his fears.

Ruby's arrogance from the pool carried over into our first game the next day. We played a team from Charlottesville, Virginia. Ruby was dominant. Their pitcher struggled to get anyone out in the first inning, and we took an early lead 5–0. Jaxon led the way at the plate, hitting a home run before he was sent to the bench. He, Wyatt, and Ruby watched the last two innings from my view in the dugout. It was a rare sight to see those three on the bench. Ruby and Wyatt made comments loud enough for everyone to hear. The two rivals seemed to like each other. I even finished the game up at second base. My diving stop to end the game reminded me of the only time that summer I felt like I was a part of the team. We won 11–1. The kids from Virginia did not like the antics of Wyatt and Ruby from the bench. The Virginia boys and their parents began to spread the word to the other eliminated teams to cheer against the North Carolina team.

Our second game of the day, the bleachers were full of kids and parents that had turned the "humble beginnings" team from North Carolina into the arrogant villains. The role suited Ruby and Wyatt perfectly, and they embraced it. Drake did not like the crowd's hateful gaze, and it was the biggest crowd to date. He was alone on the mound and felt the heat of their stares. His calm demeanor gave the eliminated kids a target. Drake did not like the main stage or being the villain. He wanted everyone to like him or, at the very least, not to notice him. Drake had heard the stories of his brother's arrogance and his father's desire to not only win but to embarrass their opponents as well. He was not his brother, and his father's metamorphosis seemed complete.

Drake sat silently in the dugout per usual, but it was different this time. The anxiety he hid was pouring out from under his cap. He struggled early to throw strikes, then he settled down, but he uncharacteristically did not hit. He did not look comfortable batting. He could hear the insults and taunts from the eliminated players. He could not block it out. He could not retreat, and Coach Alex was forced to let Ogre finish the game on the mound. Thankfully, Ogre and Wyatt each drove in three runs each. We narrowly won 8–6. Drake reluctantly left the dugout to shake hands with our opponent. The optics were, the conceited pitcher was too good to shake the hands with a team that frazzled him. Wyatt and Troy tried their best to attract the negative attention with postgame antics of pretending to admire Wyatt's long home run. It was one of our closest games of the summer, but our postgame behavior said differently.

Coach Alex chastised our performance. He spoke more with his hands than ever before. He told us we were far from perfect. Ruby clapped at his father's words, only to draw his father's stare. He told Wyatt, "Kid, one day you will run out of luck."

Wyatt replied, "I hope for your sake it is not anytime soon."

Coach Alex finished his postgame speech by telling us, "It will only get more difficult, and it is time we start taking our opponents more seriously."

Ogre was scheduled to start the semifinals, but he only had four of his permitted six innings; thus, we would need someone else to step up. The plan was to start Jaxon in an effort to save Ruby's innings for the championship. The first inning, Jaxon breezed through the chanting Tennessee team. They had a chant for everything and at all times. It felt like we were at a pep rally, and the crowd had only grown since yesterday. Now every parent and player from the eliminated teams cheered against us.

Jaxon ignored the crowd, but he could not tune out chants of "RBI! RRBBI! RBI!" and the whispered chant of "Batter, batter, swing, batter, batter," and many more. The second inning went on so long they had to recycle their chants. After two innings, it was 2–5. We were aided by the errors the Tennessee team made. The rumor was, they could hit and they had two good pitchers, but the scoreboard usually had more *E*s than what was in Tennessee.

Ogre pitched the last three innings, and he stopped the scoring and the RBI chants. He gave up nothing. The silent giant had silenced the hostile crowd. He threw fastball after fastball, and they did not even have a chance. Coach Alex's previous game's postgame speech seemed like a lie, as we easily won 11–6 behind Troy and Wyatt's three-run home runs. We were onto the regional championship against the boys from the Sunshine State. Wyatt and Ruby had brought a bath of boos to us, and we needed to wash it off tonight.

Brown Water Is Thicker than Blood

David Luck took the team out for pizza at Game Time Pizza after we won three straight games to advance to the regional championship. It was a twelve-year-old's dream pizza and arcade games. We all ate like animals in an attempt to maximize our time in the arcade. We made a team decision to combine all our tickets in an effort to try to win a giant Donald Duck to become our unofficial mascot. Drake found the basketball top-shot game and never left, and the tickets flowed. The rest of us bounced between games except me.

I sat in the corner and tried to finish a book on Alexander the Great, but the game room proved to be too loud. Arcade games were not my forte. I was easily distracted as my eyes followed Ella Russell's every move. She attempted to win her own prize in the claw machine. I wanted to walk up and say hello, but my confidence from earlier in the summer had fizzled out, and now I lacked the courage to speak to her. I eventually wandered over to play Skee-Ball with Mitch. He and I said little as we played. We took turns taking glances at Ella until she gave up on the claw machine.

Just as we were about to leave, Ruby grabbed Mitch's tickets and held them high above his head. He was showing off for Ella. The look of disappointment on his face asked me to help him retrieve them. Mitch and I looked like fools trying to jump for his earnings. Wyatt walked over and grabbed Ruby by his left hand and kicked his feet out from under him. It happened fast. The giant tumbled to the floor, but on his way down, he attempted to grab a nearby coin changer. He cut his right hand's index finger on its corner. Blood dripped from his finger while tickets rained down.

The laughter that filled the game room instantly turned into shouts. Tomorrow's regional game became very interesting in those twenty seconds of chaos. Ruby was set to pitch, and Ogre only had one inning available. Drake was already maxed out on innings. The jubilation that entered the pizza place was replaced with shouts from Vanessa and Alex Harrison. Vanessa grabbed Wyatt, then yelled in his face, "Look at what you've done!" Wyatt jerked away just as Alex told him, "Get back here, young man." Wyatt acted as if he did not hear him as he walked to the other side of the room. Mitch and I shamefully picked up the bloody tickets. Missy examined Ruby's hand and just shook her head as a waitress helped her wrap the wound in a pizza restaurant bandage. The cut was hidden, but the bandage still dripped with blood.

I was speechless. Baseball had become our lives for the last few months, and with Ruby's injury, I did not see how we would manage another win, especially if Wyatt was thrown off the team. Jaxon Leonard looked like he had seen a ghost. His face was pale, and it was obvious he was not ready if he was asked to pitch tomorrow. Ogre also knew without Wyatt in the game, his at bats would be crucial. Neither Jaxon nor Ogre seemed ready to lead us to Williamsport. Over the summer, we had learned to let Wyatt lead us. Drake, Ogre, and Jaxon were more suited for sidekicks, not heroes. Wyatt sat on the concrete outside the door to the restaurant, contemplating what he had just done. He was not the type to apologize. Troy tried to ease the tension of the room by doing a Donald Duck impersonation, but no one laughed and the restaurant was funeral-home quiet with only a few whispers.

Duckworth, Alex, Jack, David, and Coach Ross had a meeting in the parking lot. I watched and tried to make out what was being said despite the Donald Duck being thrown around. Ruby sat injured in a booth with his mother. Ruby shouted across the room at Mitch, "Thanks a lot, Brown Water!" Vanessa tried to calm her son. His tears were not from the pain of the cut but from the realization he might not be able to pitch tomorrow. Alex talked with his hands, and his face was bright red. He looked like he was being swarmed by bees. Duckworth did a lot of talking and was displeased with Alex. Coach Ross believed both boys needed discipline and should not play.

Coach Ross gave an example of eight years earlier, when he had to bench his starting tailback in the playoffs and the team lost. Everyone in Swansville knew the story of Amon Townsend. He was blamed for not bringing Swansville a football championship, but now he was one of Coach Ross's most trusted assistants. Duckworth said, "If we do not take this opportunity to teach these kids that this type of behavior is unacceptable, we may not get another chance." Alex reluctantly agreed, and now our regional championship was in jeopardy along with a shot at the Little League World Series. The trip to Williamsport was the topic of our conversations most of the summer. Our two best players were now benched for the only game left in our way. When you are twelve years old, nothing should be this important, but winning the Little League World Series was our new obsession. Coach Ross ended the meeting, then all the men shook hands and walked to their cars. It was a scene straight out of a Mafia movie. They walked to their cars like criminals heading different directions to throw off the authorities.

Wyatt walked up to me, then whispered, "I would do it again." No one knew the consequences other than me. Wyatt defiantly smiled. He had taken down our giant for a second time. He did it for all the right reasons, but his temper was starting to control his actions.

I asked him, "Do you think we can win tomorrow?"

He answered, "Of course. We are a team. Y'all are not the Castaways." Wyatt knew he was unlikely to play.

Mitch placed his hand on Wyatt's shoulder, then apologized. "You did not need to come to my rescue. I have learned to tolerate Ruby."

Wyatt stood tall and confident and softly told Mitch, "Don't let bullies push you around. You have it in you to fight back too."

Mitch knew history would never blame Ruby or Wyatt. Mitch understood as we would age, he would be the boy that somehow instigated the fight that cost us our chance at Williamsport.

Our parents grounded us the rest of the night. They all agreed with the coaches that everyone needed to go to their rooms and go straight to bed. Drake asked his father if he could stay in the room with me, Wyatt, and Ogre. Duckworth was shocked, and he, of course, agreed. He hugged Drake tighter than usual, and Drake gave his dad a reassuring pat on the back. It looked more like two old friends hugging at a funeral rather than a father and son.

Drake immediately turned the television to ESPN. The ESPN anchor and Keith Hernandez debated whether baseball was dying in America as they discussed the surely impending strike. Ogre said, "It is alive and well. Turn the damn channel!" And he angrily threw a hotel pen at the television. Drake obliged, and he started flipping through the channels. It was obvious Drake never watched much television, as he nomadically searched the channels, waiting for the commercial to end before seeing what lay on the next channel. It was frustrating to both Ogre and Wyatt. The two did not have cable television, and the slow search was maddening. Ogre oddly said, "Drake, just find something." He tossed the remote to Ogre and walked across the room.

Wyatt unceremoniously asked Drake, "Why don't you ever talk or have fun?"

Drake stopped before entering the bathroom, then he took a deep breath and glanced over at me for validation. I nodded, although I did not know what he was about to say. He must've thought I always knew. Drake eloquently, and seemingly practiced, said, "My brother was loud and cocky. God gave him special abilities, and in the blink of an eye, God took him away. His life was unfairly cut short, and God took him away to punish my father, so I figured I would stay quiet, in hopes of not drawing God's attention or wrath. My father deserves to be a champion. He is running out of chances."

Wyatt walked over to Drake and put his hand on his shoulder, then said, "Let's make a myth for Duckworth." Neither Ogre nor I said a word, and the silence was thick as the two baseball savants had their moment.

The buzz from the hotel room's air-conditioning was the only sound, until Coach Ross banged on the door and said, "Lights-out."

Lies

Ruby was warming up when we arrived at the field. His hand had a makeshift bandage. He and his father hoped it would hold. Wyatt was still benched. Wyatt's eyes opened wide in anger. His face was red and looked like a balloon ready to pop. I knew Wyatt would not handle being sentenced to the bench, especially under the new circumstances of his rival having evaded any consequences. He looked back just as Coach Ross called Alex Harrison over with his deep football voice. Alex waved him off and shouted back at the intimidating man, "It's my decision, not yours!" RJ looked up at his dad as if his dad would take him home. Coach Ross told the group of players that walked in near him, "Boys, life is not always fair, but it's never the right time to do the wrong thing." Jack mumbled under his breath, "That son of bitch."

Our normal playful warm-ups took on an ominous feel. I felt like we were waiting for a storm to pass. Our conversations were uncomfortable and seemed scripted while we quietly threw the ball back and forth. The lonely sound of a glove's popping was odd. Drake shocked everyone and said, "It's just another game. We've done it all summer." Then he clapped his hands. He sounded like his dad, and I hoped it had worked on the others, but I was still shaking.

The team from Atlanta had their own giant. Paul Hamilton had many nicknames, and everyone affectionately called him Hambone, Hammy, or most frequently, Pork Chop. He was large in every possible meaning of the word. His head was larger than most adults'. His belly peeked out of his uniform, which was at least one size too small. He was their best pitcher, but he had four innings available. He was better known for hitting and his smile. He hit singles or home runs.

The smile on his face was his enemy. He did not intimidate like most boys his size, because he smiled from ear to ear all the time. His pleasant demeanor and good sportsmanship were his weaknesses. When he was not pitching, he played first base, and he always told the opposing players, "Good hit," or some other encouraging comment.

Our giant slayer paced the dugout while the rest of the team was on the field. Wyatt barely took a breath between sentences as he berated Coach Alex in every way possible. This went on for the first three innings. Coach Alex barely acknowledged the taunts, and I think Wyatt had prepared his clever, nasty comments the night before, possibly with Rob Leonard's and his uncle's help. Most of the comments seemed to target Coach Alex when he was younger, which included, "No wonder Vanessa can keep stats, because that was your job in high school, "Bragging about your stats while playing junior varsity as an upperclassman must've made your dad proud," and "You know as much about baseball as George Steinbrenner." I sat in silence while Dale and Mitch tried every angle to get Wyatt to shut up. Wyatt turned on Dale a few times. He told him, "If you were not such a mama's boy, maybe Travis would have learned a lesson by now." When Coach Alex heard this, his ears turned gumball purple. He was beginning to take the bait.

The cut in Ruby's hand started to bleed, and by the bottom of the second, we were losing 1–0. Hambone hit a solo home run in the second inning. Ogre only had one eligible inning to pitch, and without Drake, we were in trouble. Alex left Ruby in as long as he could before the pain and the umpire would not allow him to continue. The baseball was beginning to be covered with blood. The Atlanta coach asked the umpire to check the bloodstained ball. Coach Alex knew Ruby was running out of time, but he angrily protested the opposing coach's request. The umpire inspected both Ruby's hand and the ball, then he forced Coach Alex to remove his son. Ruby argued, "I am okay," but the umpire objected. Coach Alex tried every trick in the book to convince the umpire to let Ruby stay on the mound. RJ was inserted with two runners on and one out. Both runners scored, and we were in trouble. Ruby and Wyatt were on the bench together when the top of the fourth inning started.

Wyatt continue to make comments at Coach Alex. His taunts intensified. Coach Alex and Ruby started defending every remark. Alex must have lost track of what was happening, because RJ had walked two straights and the bases were loaded with no outs. RJ was struggling. The ever-calm Coach Ross stormed in our dugout and grabbed both Ruby and Wyatt by their jerseys and slammed them against the dugout walls. I cowered in fear in the corner of the dugout. Alex stood in disbelief, and he knew not to intervene. Coach Ross told them, "Shut your mouths!" then he looked directly at Wyatt and menacingly said, "Take your punishment and stop talking. You did the crime, now be a man and do the time."

Wyatt slowly closed his eyes and said, "Yes, sir, and I just want to win."

Ruby said nothing while avoiding eye contact.

Coach Ross walked out of our dugout after tucking in his shirt and looked at Coach Alex in disgust. Coach Alex told Coach Ross, "I hope that works."

Wyatt sat and said nothing for the next two innings. Ruby paced the dugout in anger, and he clapped his hands and pointed at the field as the Atlanta Hambone crossed home plate for his second home run. The Atlanta fans cheered, "Pork Chop, Pork Chop!" He smiled and waved to the crowd. Ruby wanted everyone in the dugout to believe he would not have allowed the home run. We were down 4–0, and time began to speed up. Our summer was slipping away. He began to say if we lost, it was Wyatt's fault for injuring him. He began asking himself questions, then he would answer, "What did you do this summer, Travis? Well, I almost went to Williamsport and won a championship." Wyatt sat quietly in the dugout. He watched his nemesis openly taunt him, but he bit his tongue. Ruby's antics did not stop despite everyone telling him to sit down and close his mouth. He argued back, "I am in the dugout because of him, and I will say what I want." Our childhood bully believed he was in control again.

While Ruby caused tension in the dugout, Ogre came to our rescue. Ogre had saved the day many times before, but today's game was different. Ogre's two-run home run in the bottom of the fourth inning got us back in the game. No one gave him a high five as he entered the dugout. The entire team could tell he was angry, and no one wanted to upset him even more. Ogre had cut the lead in half. It was 4–2. Ogre banged his fist on the bench while shouting, "Let's go!" We were down to the last six outs of our summer. RJ was pulled from the mound and sent behind home plate while Missy shouted, "Good job, baby!" Jaxon Leonard got us through the fifth, but barely. He left the bases loaded with their giant on deck. Drake made a diving stop to end the inning. Drake hit a two-run home run in the bottom of the fifth. The score was tied at four. Troy shouted, "That is what I am talking about!" as Drake trotted in from home plate. He and Curt tried to ease the tension with cheers. It did not work.

When Ogre walked to the mound, the boys from Atlanta stared, and they could obviously sense impending doom. His stride was different, and he was more menacing than ever. He was bigger than their giant, and they all knew that a boy Ogre's size would be nearly impossible to hit. Ogre faced Pork Chop first. Pork Chop did not look like a giant when facing Ogre. Ogre struck him out on four fastballs. The next two batters did not even swing as they both struck out, looking.

While Ogre was striking out the side on fewer than twelve pitches, Wyatt quietly walked up to Coach Alex and whispered an apology. It was a foreign act, and he looked back at me. I had never heard him say he was sorry before, but I would hear him beg for forgiveness in the coming years. Per his usual bravado, Wyatt said just loud enough for Coach Ross to hear, "Give me one swing and I'll win this game for you." Alex glanced over at Coach Ross, and Coach Ross gave a very subtle nod. Coach Alex simply said, "Get a helmet." Wyatt wasted no time, and he led the inning off with a home run. Just like that, we were the East Coast regional champions and we would head to Williamsport, Pennsylvania, in seven days. Our coaches did the wrong thing at the right time.

After the postgame handshake, Coach Alex gave the shortest speech of the summer. He spoke of staying perfect, but no one paid any attention. Everyone was ready to head home. All the adults associated with the team attempted to hide their shame, but it slowly dripped off their once-confident smiles. We victoriously retreated to our rides back to the Brown Water. Goose bumps covered my arms in anticipation of Williamsport.

Old Heroes

Williamsport was no longer just a fictional destination or a fantasy we dreamed about. It was a real place, and we were headed to the fabled Williamsport fields. We still had one more tournament to win, and it was the biggest and our last. Most of the next few days would be spent planning for the trip to Williamsport. Additional practices at this point were of little use. If we did not know how to play by now, it was too late. Coach Alex gave us a few days off. I suspected it was to allow Ruby's hand to heal and to keep Ruby and Wyatt away from each other. Summer was limping to an end, and our classmates prepared for the first day of school.

Coach Alex called for one last practice three days before our final baseball journey of the summer. The practice was held at the high school field, and it was not even a practice. We had a glorified exhibition with our parents and a few of the high school players. The field was enormous compared to Scarborough Memorial Park. Wyatt and Ogre would not be able to jog the bases. Ogre may even be forced to slide. The exhibition game was fun and lighthearted. I watched my dad awkwardly race the bases after a base hit from the best player on the Swansville High School team. I cringed as he awkwardly slid into home plate without a throw. My dad's smile as he searched the bleachers embarrassed both my mom and sister. Coach Alex, Duckworth, and Jack served as umpires. A playful argument ensued at the end of the game, and the three umpires ejected one another.

The game was uneventful other than Jacob Hartley taking the mound. The high school players all desired to stand in the batter's box against the onetime face of Swansville High School baseball.

They had heard the rumors of his dominance and now wanted to see the real thing, or at least what was left. The crowd clamored to see him pitch again too. Jacob refused at first to participate, but he eventually gave in to their desires. He emerged from the dugout wearing a Swansville Red Raider hat. He slowly walked to the mound to a sound only which he was familiar. The crowd whispered, "Hartley, Hartley," in cadence of each step. The crowd was in a trance. They were instantly back to the 1980 championship season. The whispered chant of his name was like a forgotten song that came on the radio, and now everyone remembered the words. The familiar chant gave him confidence and a forgotten strength. The walk was natural despite the time in between. The old path he had worn was now covered in grass. He looked at his feet, and with each step his head began to rise. He stood on the mound, and he looked comfortable as the setting sun shone down. The fans erupted as if Mick Jagger had returned for an encore. Once upon a time, he was the king of this field and our small town. The crowd was silent as he threw his first warm-up pitch. The pop of the mitt echoed, and our parents smiled like teenagers. Jacob Hartley had turned back the clock for a few moments.

Jacob quickly struck out the five current Swansville High School baseball players. They had heard stories of Jacob's fastball, but the stories were tame compared to the real thing. *The Swansville Orator* had affectionately proclaimed it the Hartley Heater. The murmur from the crowd was, the only player that could hit Jacob's fastball was Jaxon Leonard. Jaxon refused to step in the batter's box despite everyone's request. He was safe in the shadows, and he elected to stay there. He claimed his shoulder was injured. Josie begged him, but she, too, failed. Jacob Hartley spoke to me as he walked off the field. "Guess I still have a little magic left." I was starstruck despite getting to know him over the course of the summer. He had just given truth to all the myths I had grown up hearing about. I smiled at him in disbelief of the ease of the game he had abandoned.

After the game, Duckworth spoke and told everyone the town had planned a pep rally. Tomorrow afternoon, the town would have BBQ and a pep rally at Scarborough Memorial Park. The high school band was scheduled to perform, and Mayor Neal had waived the no-fireworks ordinance in the town limits. Wyatt asked Duckworth, "Why are we having a pep rally? We've not won anything yet." Coach Alex mockingly gave Wyatt a standing ovation. Duckworth laughed. "A preparty, then."

The pep rally was hosted by Duckworth. Oversize baseball cards of the team with fake stats decorated the park. Four months prior, the town had cleaned the park along with the littered shoreline. Now both the shoreline and the park were full of trash again. The worry of Green and Clean Day was fulfilled when Major League Baseball was halted by a strike a week prior. The Montreal Expos, Matt Williams, and Ken Griffey Jr. would not have a chance at baseball immortality. The clock ran out on their baseball season. The Expos would never recover, and a World Series would stay in Canada. Injuries and Father Time would keep Matt Williams and Ken Griffey Jr. from ever threatening Roger Maris's home run record again. The redraft was a forgotten event, and our regular season was just a distant memory.

We had little time over the summer to even think of the baseball strike, since our summer was one baseball game after another. Ogre was the only one of us that ever mentioned it. I suppose it was due to hearing Frankie constantly complain about it. Ogre was intrigued by Ken Griffey Jr.'s effortless swing. Ogre complained we were cheated out of seeing something special due to old men's greed. Jack, Ogre, and Frankie did not blame the players as much as they did the owners.

Greed had taken away the World Series. My dad always allowed me to stay up late and watch the World Series. It was one of the few times he and I bonded. Baseball was our connection. The previous year, he and I nearly became Phillies fans. My dad loved the rough and tough group from Philadelphia. We were heartbroken when Joe Carter hit the series' clinching home run. Mitch Williams crouched on the mound as Joe trotted the bases in triumph. I identified with Mitch Williams more than the jubilant Blue Jays. Of course my sister cheered for the Blue Jays to be contrary.

The baseball cards lining the fence reminded me of when Travis transformed into Ruby. Ruby's card had all his stats and no mention of his nickname. The epic moment seemed like it happened a lifetime ago. Ruby's transformation from leader to follower was not easy, and his nickname signified the moment he was no longer invincible. He deserved the recognition that was headed our way as much as anyone did. He pitched us to Williamsport just as much as Wyatt's bat did.

Everyone in Swansville attended. Every business and restaurant in town closed for the event. Principal Overstreet was scheduled to speak, as well as the mayor. The pep rally was not scheduled until after we all ate. Frankie provided homemade ice cream. The hit-and-miss engine ice cream maker was the highlight of the day. While we ate BBQ, the citizens of Swansville came to wish us luck. A photo stand was set up for folks to take pictures underneath a sign reading, "Swansville 1994 All Stars Little League World Series Bound." Children under five looked at us all like we were celebrities or big leaguers.

The parade of folks wishing us luck began to slow down, then we mingled with the crowd. I learned how to shake hands that day. Drake and I sat on a picnic table, finishing off our ice cream, prior to the ceremony. A lady approached, wearing a faded yellow gardening hat. It was evident the olive-skinned woman did not want to be recognized. She approached us with her head down. It was Betty Duckworth. Betty's eyes met Drake's, and his usually calm demeanor changed, as if he had seen a ghost. Drake instantly looked anxious. Duckworth was too busy chatting with everyone to notice his ex-wife had returned. Drake had not seen his mother in over five years.

Betty's eyes asked forgiveness as she said, "Hey, there, kiddo." The mother and son embraced, and heartache was squeezed from them both. I did not know what to do. I doubt Duckworth would have allowed the reunion, but Drake needed a hug from his mother. I stood in front of their embrace to block Duckworth's view. I felt like I was betraying him. Neither Betty nor Drake said anything. It was the first time I ever saw Drake cry, and it would be the last.

Drake walked over to Winslow's to use the restroom and to hide his red eyes. Betty asked me, "Does Jim still act like the mayor of the Brown Water?"

I was shocked that she spoke to me, and it was odd hearing anyone call Duckworth Jim. I replied, "He's not the mayor, he's the king."

She turned her back to the crowd of folks, hoping to stay camouflaged. We chatted for five minutes, waiting for Drake to return. She asked, "Is Drake's father still obsessed with sports?"

I answered, "Thankfully, he still is."

She was not happy with my answer, but I did not care. My loyalty was with Duckworth.

I nervously looked over my shoulder and saw Drake walking back from Winslow's. I was running out of things to say just as Wyatt bounced into the conversation, asking, "Carson, is this another one of your adoring fans?"

She laughingly said, "Of course, I'm his biggest fan."

Before the words hit my ears, Duckworth walked up and interrupted our conversation. He asked, "Betty, now you decide to show up."

The tall striking woman shriveled up, and she knew she needed to leave. Drake almost reached his mother, but his father's stare froze him and he stopped five feet away. Duckworth called Drake over, and he shamefully walked to his father's side. Wyatt was confused, and I motioned for him to follow me.

I looked back at Drake as his mother knelt down to hug her son one last time. Drake stared at his father and barely hugged his mother back. She took off her hat and kissed him on the cheek. The soft embrace signaled it was time to leave her twelve-year-old son again. Father and son both stared as she walked away. She followed her own shadow back out of Scarborough Memorial Park. Drake looked like he wanted to fly away to wherever his mother was headed. Duckworth tightly held his son by the shoulder.

Betty Duckworth was gone, and I doubted I would ever see her again. She and Duckworth seemed like an odd pair. It never made sense how and why the two had married; they were exact opposites. Betty left Duckworth after Donnie's death, because she knew it would be difficult to watch Duckworth raise another son. The tragedy that took Donnie away too soon was less tragic for her than watching Duckworth struggle through life with another son.

Moments later, Duckworth climbed up our makeshift stage and began the ceremonies. He introduced everyone and called us by some goofy nickname. Ogre drew the most cheers. Everyone in town knew and loved him. His heroics at the regional championship were known by everyone. The cheers did not bounce off of him for the first time, and he even smiled for a brief second. Wyatt was still unknown to almost everyone, but his last name resonated with the cheering fans. Duckworth introduced Coach Alex last, and the crowd only politely clapped. Coach Alex gave his usually speech about perfection and said, "These boys can put Swansville on the map!" The crowd cheered.

The unfamiliar faces in the crowd of people made me nervous. I tried to hide behind Ruby and Wyatt. Drake found the end of the stage the best place to hide, and he looked ready to jump off the stage at any moment. I found my sister and even saw Josie Leonard. Rob Leonard was not in attendance, nor was Jacob Hartley. My parents stood proud alongside Curt and Kaye Christie. Principle Overstreet spoke briefly and wished us all good luck. Mayor Neal gave a speech. He made sure the crowd gave us another ovation. He stumbled through the closing statement. "Thank you all for attending and supporting our troops—I mean these boys." The red-faced mayor had secretly celebrated with a few sips of whiskey. The crowd heckled and laughed at the chubby man. It felt like we were being sent off to a war and many of us would not return.

We walked off the stage just as the fireworks began. The sun had barely set. The sky's glow was purple from both the fireworks and the setting sun. Wyatt threw up his hand, waving at a distant figure. Drake looked out to the dark horizon, searching for his own distant figure, but she was already long gone.

Wyatt grinned and asked, "Who was that woman from earlier?"

I shushed him, then whispered, "I'll tell you later."

Wyatt was staying the night with me since my parents had decided to leave a day before the caravan to Williamsport. Duckworth wished us safe travels, then said, "I'll see you in Williamsport."

We drove by Wyatt's house after the pep rally, and he grabbed his bags. His mother and Jacob were coming up in three days. They would miss the first game. He hugged his mother. Patti Hartley did not want to let her son go. My dad assured her, "He will be fine." He walked off the porch, and his mother watched us pull out of the driveway. He waved at her one last time as she blew him a kiss.

My sister, Wyatt, and I played cards late into the night. The three of us could not sleep. My parents insisted on leaving early the next morning to take the scenic route. My parents wanted to visit Lynchburg, Virginia. Whitley was the first to fall asleep. Wyatt asked about Drake's mom. He assumed Principal Duckworth was Drake's mother and that was why he was so well behaved. Wyatt was shocked when I told him about Drake's older brother, Donnie. Wyatt asked, "Have you told anyone about what we found out about my dad?"

I said, "No one. Does anyone else know?"

The letter we read earlier in the summer seemed like a lifetime ago. His eyes rolled back into his head as he said no, but I believed it was a lie. "Should I ever ask my mom about it?" Wyatt asked.

I did not know what to say.

Wyatt's eyes filled with tears, but they never let go. I knew his family secret, that his dad was not dead but in prison. It was the first of many secrets he and I would have in the upcoming years. We sat in silence until we both fell asleep.

Detour

Our journey began at dawn. The sun and the moon were both barely out. The dark-blue morning sky was fading and giving way to the sun's morning rays. My eyes were barely open when we left the house. Wyatt insisted he needed to stop once more at his house. He had left his bat. He called his mother to let her know we were stopping by the house. She did not answer, and he left a message on the answering machine. The porch light was off. Wyatt quietly walked up, and he found a brown bag on the porch. Wyatt picked it up and looked confused. The light came on as Jacob opened the door to hand him his bat. Jacob said something to him, and Wyatt agreed, then they shook hands.

Wyatt bounced back in the van, disturbing Whitley. He said, "Can't believe I almost forgot my bat." Whitley sighed, then put a pillow over her head. Before his most recent heroics, he acted strong, but now he felt strong. Confidence began to drip from his every pore. He was comfortable with my family, and he began to seem like my brother.

I asked Wyatt, "What's in the brown bag?"

"Let's find out," he replied as he excitedly peeked in the bag. He pulled out a small canning jar full of muddy brown water. The brown bag had a note. It said, "A little Brown Water to make you feel at home," signed CB.

My dad chuckled. "A little bit of home is coming with us."

Wyatt and I discussed what to do with the jar of Lake Pisgah water. We decided to pour it out on the field. My dad agreed. He said, "It will make Williamsport your home field."

Whitley and my mom both angrily told us, "Please just shut up. We are trying to sleep!"

Wyatt and I whispered about our plans once he reached Williamsport. Whitley would occasionally groan or giggle as she listened. Wyatt and I finally began to succumb to our lack of sleep. Whitley stretched out in the back seat as Wyatt and I slept sitting up.

Everyone was asleep except my mom when I woke up a few hours later. She listened to country music and lip-sang the lyrics. I startled her when I asked, "Where are we?"

She said, "Just a few more hours."

The scenic route was slow and tedious as we meandered over hills and through valleys. We passed the ruins of an old house, and my mother decided to turn back as she said, "Let's stop and stretch our legs." The chimney still stood, and what was left of the old house's porch was lined with yellow daylilies. We walked behind the house, and I spotted an old well overtaken with vines. I decided it was a perfect place to pee before we got back on the road. A hillside cornfield was its backyard, and the house was flanked by a barn that was barely standing. A golden horse, a painted horse, and their sidekick, a brown donkey, were content standing under the field's lone tree. My mom sighed, then said, "This place reminds me of my grandmother's house. You would've loved it. It was full of places to hide and just sit and read a book." I never saw my mom with a book, and when she mentioned reading, I was surprised. Maybe she and I were more alike than I thought.

She was at peace as she and I walked around the vacant property. She took deep breaths to breathe in the country air. I felt a million miles away from Swansville. We followed a trail down a small hill, and we found a creek, and the trickling water over the rocks sounded like distant church bells. She reached down and cupped her hands and took a drink of the clear water. I did the same as my mom said, "I bet this water makes it to the river that fills Pisgah Lake." I did not believe her, and I knew the crystal clear water would never make it to the brown water of Pisgah Lake, but the thought was nice. All roads, rivers, and creeks seemed like they led to Swansville in my mom's eyes. She grabbed me by the shoulder, and we headed back to the van. She picked a wildflower. The sun shone off her dark sunglasses, and my mom's blond hair was brighter than ever with the red petunia behind her ear.

We reached the van, and I was surprised no one was awake. My dad was loudly snoring in the front passenger seat. My mom had left the van running in an effort to allow everyone to stay asleep.

Wyatt groggily asked, "Where were you?"

I answered, "Drinking clear brown water." Then I said, "Go back to sleep."

He climbed in the back seat and pushed Whitley to make more room, and he slept on the opposite window of my sister.

We finally reached a road that was not so treacherous, and my mom was able to hit cruise control. My mom turned off the radio, and the hum of the tires was the only sound. My mom hated silence, and she started asking me questions. She wanted to know where I wanted to go to college. I had no clue, but I told her I wanted to go far away. She asked why. I replied, "Surely, there are more adventures away from Swansville."

She chuckled. "I used to think the same thing." She began asking about my perfect vacation and what I would do if I had a million dollars, along with other goofy things. She asked me, "Who is your crush?"

I turned red as I told her, "No one," then she began to name my classmates. The conversation embarrassed me, and it ended when I ignored her to watch a train run parallel to the highway.

I was not ready to discuss my life's hidden details with my mom. I was no longer a child bragging about having more than one girl-friend to the chuckles of my parents. My mom and sister seemed like the same person at many times throughout my life, and Whitley and I usually were at each other's throats. I was afraid if I answered her questions, she would tell my sister and I would become the punch-line to one of their many inside jokes. My mom seemed more concerned with the trip to Williamsport for the adventure of leaving Swansville, not the upcoming baseball games. She did not value the same things I did.

We crossed over a bridge, and the train was below on another bridge. I imagined the old bridge was once below, too, and at times the road would have been impassable when the waters raged. I lost the train in the next set of small mountains, and we never crossed the railroad track. We reached Lynchburg, and now we were halfway to Williamsport.

I woke up both Wyatt and Whitley. I shouted, "We are here!"

They both looked at me, and their eyes said, "Big deal."

Neither Wyatt nor Whitley were excited about being in Lynchburg. Whitley wanted to get to Williamsport as quickly as possible for an unexplainable reason. Whitley's summer heroics happened weeks prior. She was able to tag along and watch us attempt to become heroes. She liked the attention, and following us to Williamsport allowed her to feel the spotlight for a few more weeks. She and I, along with our teammates, had traversed the Southeast just to head to the fabled fields of Williamsport. A detour through Lynchburg just delayed the inevitable.

The Barracks

The Little League World Series provided barracks for each team. We were assigned the barracks with the team from Venezuela. The Venezuela team was one of the international pool favorites. Almost all the boys from Venezuela sat on their bunks, playing Game Boys. Wyatt and I were the first to check in and introduced ourselves. The language barrier was not too difficult, as most of the Venezuelan kids could speak broken English.

The rest of our team was a few hours away, so Wyatt and I played a game with our barrack mates. We set up an obstacle course inside the barracks. It was more like a maze than an obstacle course. We took turns guiding a blindfolded boy around in our own language. We had to jump an invisible river, walk a balance board, backpedal between a row of bats, avoid a rogue baseball being rolled by the onlookers, among other things. The distracting part was the blaring Venezuelan music. The finish line was the bonus. The finish line was a piñata shaped like a bull. We were given two blindfolded swings.

Wyatt and I both tried to best the obstacle course for a swing at the piñata, but we failed on our first two attempts. We struggled understanding our roommates, and neither Wyatt nor I had a chance to bust the piñata. Wyatt gave directions to the best player on the Venezuelan team. Diego Torres seemed uninterested in the game until no one finished and busted the piñata. His teammates stopped dancing and loudly singing to watch Diego attempt the feat. The music was shut off after Diego gave the unofficial team a dirty look. It was obvious who was in charge. Diego reached the end with Wyatt's guidance, then he swung and cracked the bull-shaped piñata. A fracas ensued as Diego stood proudly as his teammates, Wyatt, and I scrambled for candy. The mazelike obstacle was no match for Diego.

The rest of Swansville's finest rolled in after Wyatt and I, along with our barrack mates, finished our pizza dinner. We dined with the Venezuelan boys and their coaches. They detailed their journey to the Little World Series. Almost all the stories painted Diego as the hero. Diego said little while his teammates told stories of his dominance. He looked like a gambler holding a winning hand as he sat and listened to his teammates tell story after story of how he had led them to Williamsport.

Tonight would be the last of the nonregimented week at Williamsport. Everything was meticulously planned for all of us going forward. David Luck had every meal and activity planned around all the activities of the Little League World Series. We were supposed to be all business from this point on. Our summer full of excitement and laughter would need to be replaced with seriousness. Neither Ruby nor Coach Alex liked the setup of sharing our sleeping quarters. The rest of the team eagerly bounced around the barracks, claiming their bunks. Drake grabbed the top bunk beside me. Wyatt and I had already scouted everything out, and we chose the best two bunks. Wyatt slept on the bottom, and I excitedly had the top bunk. We chose the bunks in the back corner.

The Venezuelan team had pregame warm-ups at ten thirty in the morning. They had to play Japan at noon. Their coach told Coach Alex we must let his team get plenty of rest. Coach Alex agreed and told the room, "Y'all can't soar with eagles if y'all are out with owls." He warned us any shenanigans could result in sitting the bench. Nine meant lights-out and Game Boys off. I knew I would not be able to sleep; thankfully, Wyatt had plans.

Shortly after ten, Wyatt kicked the bottom of my bed. I hung my head down, then asked, "What do you want?" I had been asleep for at least thirty minutes.

Wyatt answered, "We've got to mark our territory."

I knew exactly what he meant. We somehow had to sneak out to pour the brown water on the main field. The ritual seemed silly, but it was critical. We had to sneak by the Venezuelan team's coach to accomplish our mission without getting apprehended.

Wyatt stood up but crouched and whispered, "Do you have any ideas?" I was nervous, and the thought of being caught terrified me. Risking being kicked off the team at this point was foolish. I slowly had become a risk-taker over the course of the long summer, but I was out of ideas. Drake must've heard Wyatt and me talking, as he sat up to listen. I was surprised when Drake offered up a plan.

Drake's plan for us to sneak a small mason jar out to the main field seemed like a fool's errand, but Wyatt insisted. Wyatt told Drake what he wanted to do, and Drake was immediately ready to assist. Drake thought for a minute. He whispered the detailed plan, and now Mitch was awake. He was in on the ruse too. Wyatt and I had chosen the bunk farthest from the exit, and now we had to distract the barrack's lone security.

Drake sneaked over and woke both RJ and Ogre. I heard Ogre laugh quietly. Drake shouted, "A mouse!" Ogre and RJ started a ruckus, and within a minute, the lights were on. Everyone not involved in the plan squealed. Spanish and English expletives filled the room. Ruby jumped on the top bunk. "This place is covered in filth!" Drake's plan was working. RJ and Mitch both shouted, "There it goes!" and they both jumped back onto their beds. They pointed to the corner of the barracks. Coach Torres went to investigate. Wyatt and I sneaked right out the front door, but to our surprise, Drake followed.

Drake, Wyatt, and I sprinted to the main field. The cool evening grass tickled my toes, and I frantically ran like an escaped prisoner. I was nervous when we jumped the fence. Wyatt asked Drake, "Where is a good spot?"

Drake answered, "Let's pour some on the mound and behind the plate."

Wyatt nodded. Wyatt poured some of the brown water at home plate, and Drake rubbed it in the freshly groomed dirt. Wyatt handed Drake the remaining brown water to pour on the pitcher's mound. Drake refused to baptize the pitcher's mound, and I did the honors.

All three of us trotted to the bases by the moon's light. Drake sighed as he crossed home plate. My bare feet were sore as I stomped on home plate. I knew I'd never feel the euphoria of a home run, but the cool summer night's trot would have to fulfill my baseball home run fantasy. Wyatt jogged home just like he had done all summer. Drake and I both gave him a high five. Drake said, "Can you believe we made it here and it is almost over?"

I am not sure which he was more excited over.

The lights were back off at our barracks as we slowly walked back. Wyatt asked Drake, "What's your plan now?"

Drake shrugged and looked at me. I didn't have an answer. We had not thought of trying to sneak back in. Wyatt said, "Can we get RJ or Mitch to create another diversion?"

Drake said, "That's our only chance."

We tapped on the windows just outside of RJ and Ogre's bunk. Both boys were sound asleep, but Dale heard us. We whispered, "Let us in." Dale refused at first. Wyatt said, "Do it now, Captain." Drake pleaded too. Dale sneaked past Coach Torres and opened the door. We all four sprinted back to our bunks.

I barely slept the rest of the night. I heard every sound. Wyatt tossed and turned all night too. He talked in his sleep a few times, and I woke him from his bad dreams by simply telling him, "It is okay." Tomorrow was important to all of us, but Wyatt knew the pressure would be on him more than the rest of us.

Coach Torres complained to Coach Alex about the previous night's commotion. We thankfully would not play for one more day. Things did not go well for the Venezuelan team. The Japanese team was dominant, and rumors of their excellence were well documented. Diego was hitless against the dominant pitching. Diego usually dominated the game at the plate and on the mound. The Japanese team hit everything he threw. The Venezuelan team only had one base runner. The Japanese team made quick work of our barrack mates. They lost 8–0. Coach Torres blamed the ugly loss on the lack of sleep and a mouse. They did not socialize with us much after their loss. They had traveled across a continent for their summer to suddenly end. They would be regulated to cheerleaders for the rest of the weekend.

Redneck

We won our first game against the team from Corpus Christi with ease. Drake started and pitched the first three innings. Drake did not allow a run. Ruby and Ogre both pitched an inning each, then Jaxon finished the team off from Texas. Wyatt had two doubles and hit a line drive home run. The fans sitting on the hill on the other side of the left field fence were forced to jump out of the way of the rocket shot. Jaxon and RJ both scored two runs each. We won 9–2. Our first game of the Little League World Series seemed too easy. We bounced around the fields at Williamsport with a new level of confidence.

Our first real challenge of the Unite States pool was against the team out of Staten Island, New York. Coach Alex made sure Anthony started at the request of his parents. Anthony led off and singled before stealing two bases. He scored on a double by Drake. John Angelo did not sit down the first three innings. Anthony struck out his second at bat, then he was removed to a standing ovation. John wore a New York Yankees hat and proudly cheered for his son. The ESPN cameras found him and assumed he was cheering for the team out of Staten Island. The cameras followed him down to the Swansville dugout to congratulate his son. John poked in his head in the dugout as his adopted son ran up, then hugged the large man.

The team out of New York was coached by brothers. Each had a son on the team. Kerby and Ollie openly argued with each other. Kerby barked at the home plate umpire, and Ollie kept telling his older brother, "Just shut your mouth!" Kerby's son Ty was their best player and pitcher. Kerby reminded me of Coach Alex, but far harsher. Ollie's son Oscar patrolled right field. Ollie constantly shifted players by motioning with his hand and shouting, "Move, move, one more step!" Their intensity boiled over into their players as they shouted at each other throughout the game.

Ty was a chubby kid. He was built like Ogre, but much shorter. When Ty did not get a favorable call from the umpire, he showed his displeasure by snapping the ball out of the air then stomping back to the pitcher's mound. Ruby would've fit right in with this team. Each time they looked disgusted or Kerby argued a call, Wyatt would joyfully shout, "Great call, Blue! You're the man!" The home plate umpire was not amused with Wyatt or the New York team.

Wyatt walked in his first at bat and was left stranded on second. We led after two innings 2–1. Ogre gave up a home run in the first inning to their third basemen. He bowed when he crossed home plate, then told Wyatt, "Piece of cake, country boy." He jogged back to the dugout. The New Yorkers began to taunt Wyatt with chants of, "Redneck, redneck!" Wyatt shockingly said nothing. He told me, "Winning an argument with these fools would be like being the tallest midget."

Wyatt shouted to Mitch as he stepped in the batter's box, "I'll let my bat talk for me today! It has lots to say!"

Wyatt hit a line drive on the first pitch, and the ball struck Kerby in the knee. The park echoed, "Oooouuuuuwwwwccccccchhhh!" then Kerby began to cry. Wyatt sprinted to first base, and Drake headed for second. The trash-talking third basemen ran to retrieve the ball to try to throw Wyatt out. The ball sailed over the leaping first basemen as he tripped over the base when he landed. He had rolled his ankle. Wyatt and Drake sprinted for more bases. The right fielder hurried to get the ball as Drake rounded third to easily score. Wyatt did not stop at third, and he ran with his head down. A cloud of dirt followed him to home plate. The throw home beat Wyatt by two steps, but he did not care as he intentionally collided with the catcher. The catcher dropped the ball, and Wyatt defiantly stepped on home plate as the catcher writhed in pain, holding his ribs. Wyatt knew he was out, and he would receive a warning. He wanted the crowd chanting "Redneck!" at him to understand he was much more than a simple country boy from North Carolina. Wyatt was of course called out for not sliding, but he did not care. He grinningly strutted back to the dugout. Coach Alex, along with both Kerby and Ollie, rushed to attend to the injured three boys. The first baseman would stay in the game. Ty was carried off, and his catcher walked off, holding his ribs. The New York fans demanded Wyatt be ejected. He proudly stood on the dugout steps, looking upon the injured boys.

The game resumed, and we took the field, leading 3–1. Ogre breezed through the next two innings. The New Yorkers taunted Ogre, but their taunts fell on deaf ears. We scored four more runs against their relief pitcher. We led 7–1 going into the top of the sixth inning. Jaxon would close the game, and I was inserted to play second. My dad waved from the stands like a teenage girl. My sister rolled her eyes just as the TV cameras showed his exuberance of his son being a last-inning replacement. The ESPN reporter approached my dad for a late-game interview.

The reporter asked both my dad and sister, "How do you like Williamsport?"

Whitley smiled at the camera, then sarcastically said, "It is beautiful. It is a pleasure to watch my brother and his friends play."

My dad answered and pointed at my sister, "What she said," as he chuckled.

The reporter than asked Whitley, "I heard you are quite the little soccer star too. How do you prepare for big games?"

Whitley answered, "I try to focus on one thing at a time and not get too wrapped up in the moment."

The reporter told my dad, "You must be proud. You and your wife must have good genes."

My mom waved at the camera as the game went to commercial.

After the game, we shook the defeated and injured New Yorkers' hands. No one spoke as we told them, "Good game." Kerby and Ollie congratulated Coach Alex, then said, "You should kick that boy off your team." Coach Alex told them, "I will address it how I see fit." Wyatt obnoxiously laughed, and Ruby joined in. Kerby and Ollie barked at the two boys, "Show some class!" Wyatt and Ruby laughed and pointed at the scoreboard. The New York fans left in the stands began to boo. Coach Alex gave a short speech as the boos continued.

He said, "It is every team for itself. We were nearly perfect. Wyatt, let this be your warning: no more poor sportsmanship." Wyatt nodded and seemed to take the warning seriously. We breezed through pool play, and we were headed for a showdown.

A Monster

Our opponent for the United States championship could not have been any different from us or any farther away without leaving the continental United States. The blond and blue-eyed boys always seemed to smile, and they never bickered. The Long Beach, California, team was accustomed to playing for the United States title. They had won the United States title three out of the last five years. The team was even coached on how to interview and how to conduct themselves while on television. The California boys seemed like professionals, and they even taught us how to eat sunflower seeds like a pro.

Coach Sammy Gibson had coached the Long Beach, California, team for the last decade, and he was well-known in Williamsport. He reminded me of Jack Wilson but was stern like Coach Alex. He carried himself similar to Coach Ross. He was polished from his bald head down to his spotless white baseball shoes. He seemed like a senator in a baseball uniform. He was always shaking hands with someone. He knew baseball, but more importantly, he knew how to relate to the kids. I remember him clapping a lot and shouting Duckworth-like praise to his team. He did not have to speak to get his point across. His team knew what mistake they had made just by how he looked at them. He was the perfect mix of a coach.

Sammy Gibson's youngest son was his pride and joy. He was a six-foot-two-inch colossal monster named Duke. Duke looked like he was molded by the baseball gods with the sole purpose of destroying everything in his path. He was named after his grandfather's favorite player, Duke Snider, and he lived up to the name. He hit monstrous home runs. He was also a dominant pitcher. Duke had only given up three hits while in Williamsport. Duke was so big that once he was at a waterpark, the zipline he was on stopped midway over the alligator pond. The national news covered his rescue, and the man-child got his first taste of stardom when he was ten years old. Duke was the first player that Ruby and Ogre looked up to. Wyatt licked his chops, and he said, "Another giant to topple." But he was no giant; Duke was a monster, and he would not go down easily.

Duke Gibson would not start the game since he only had four innings available to pitch. We had two innings to do some damage at the plate and to keep the opposing monster from hitting a home run. We scratched one run across in the first inning when RJ drove Drake in from second with a double. They wisely pitched around Wyatt. Wyatt's reputation had made its was way around Williamsport. He was already feared. Alex told Ruby to do the same against Duke, but Ruby stubbornly challenged the California monster in the first inning. The ball looked like it was fired from a cannon as it reached the high grass of the home run hill in center field. We were down 2 to 1 when Duke stepped on the mound to start the third inning. After the home run, Ruby matched Duke pitch for pitch. Ruby had learned his lesson and never threw the California monster another strike.

RJ led off with a bunt single to start the fourth. He then stole second base, and the catcher's throw flew into center, allowing RJ to reach third base. The California monster started to look vulnerable. Curt hit a sacrifice fly ball to tie the game. Duke Gibson was a lot like Ruby; neither boy had ever really had to experience difficulty on the baseball field.

The game was tied when Dale Rutledge stepped in the batter's box against the intimidating California monster. Duke threw Dale a fastball, and Dale swung late. Our chances of scoring another run on Duke were slim. Duke threw two balls in the dirt, and the count ran two and one. Troy shouted, "You can do it, Captain!" Duke's next fastball spun so fast all I saw was a red dot heading for the catcher's mitt. *Boom!* Dale Rutledge shocked everyone when he hit a mammoth home run. His home run rivaled those of Wyatt and Ogre. Duke seemed confused that someone could get on base, much less hit a home run against him. The monster stomped the mound in anger. Sammy Gibson walked to the mound to comfort his son and to settle him down. Rage filled the monster's eyes while he seemed to ignore his father's advice. The bright blue-eyed California boys began to show concern for the first time. We had 3–2 lead after the fifth. Ruby's curveball started to hang, and the California team rallied and tied the game with a walk and three straight hits.

Alex was forced to take our giant out and insert Ogre into a tie game with bases loaded and no outs. Ogre came in throwing fire, but more importantly, he had a late breaking curveball. There was something different about Ogre, and he easily struck out the first two batters. Ogre rarely felt like a hero, but today the confidence he never showed peeked out for the second time all summer. I believe it was the first time in Ogre's life he was able to feel smaller than his opponent. He viewed himself as an underdog for the first time. The big lefty had to face Duke Gibson with nowhere to put the monster. Ogre challenged the California monster with a first-pitch fastball. Duke shook his head just as the umpire called strike 1. Duke banged his bat against the plate to let Ogre know he was not intimidated of his fastball. Ogre grunted when he released his next fastball, and the crowd went instantly silent and admired Duke's mammoth foul ball. It was the hardest-hit ball I had ever seen, but Duke had pulled it foul. Ogre threw a curveball that froze the monster as he struck him out and the bases were left full. Duke was just as surprised as the fans in the crowd that someone had struck him out. The only thing larger than the California monster was his reputation. We showered Ogre with high fives, and he was set to lead off the sixth inning.

Duke Gibson had steam coming out of his ears, and his blue eyes were now red with rage. Only Ruby pitched with that type of fire in his eyes. Duke reached back nearly to second base and threw a ball as hard as he could at Ogre. Ogre took the fastball in the back and fell to the ground. Ogre fell over in slow motion, and I could tell he was wounded. Ogre slowly stood back up, then he walked to first base without showing any pain. Jack tried to run out to check on his son. Ogre just threw up his hands, motioning Jack to stay. Alex asked Ogre if he needed a replacement, and Ogre shouted back, "I am fine!" as he stood on first base.

RJ pushed a bunt to third base in an attempt to get Ogre in scoring position. The catcher tried to get Ogre at second, and again his throw sailed center field. Ogre popped up and lumbered toward third. His feet seemed to echo with each step. I could hear his footsteps, *thump thump*, as he headed for third. Ogre rarely had to run at full speed because he hit home runs and stand-up doubles. The crowd was quiet as both teams had a lot riding on the throw and upcoming slide. Ogre slid just under the tag, but the sound of the gentle boy's scream and bone popping stopped the game. Ogre could not motion for his dad to stay as Jack was already on the field. We all took a knee, and we sat for ten minutes as paramedics put an air cast on Ogre's ankle. My quiet friend was in agonizing pain as he shouted, "I just want to play baseball!" His summer on the diamond ended at third base in Williamsport. He was the potential winning run.

The delay ended, and everyone was allowed a short warm-up. We had runners on second and third with no outs. I was inserted to run for Ogre, and I had sixty feet that seemed uphill to score the winning run against the California monster. I could taste being a national champion. Curt Christie was intentionally walked to load the bases. Dale Rutledge struck out on four pitches. Mitch O'Neal was inserted to pinch hit for Troy. As soon as I saw Mitch, I knew the plan. Alex relayed the signs to everyone. Mitch was set to squeeze bunt on the second pitch. Mitch and I were the last two boys picked for the all-star game, and we were the critical players to attempt to win the game to send us to the championship game. Duckworth shouted, "We need you now, Lightning!" Just as Mitch walked to the plate, Wyatt shouted, "Your batting gloves, Mitch!" Wyatt ran them out to him, then assured him, "Take a deep breath and pretend you are back at Scarborough Park."

I looked in the dugout, and Drake stood by the fence for the first time all summer. Duckworth paced and tried to look away. Duke stood tall on the mound, and the monster looked more menacing when facing the second-smallest player on our team. Shadows began to creep onto the field. The first pitch was a fastball strike. The monster's reach looked like it touched second again when he threw his second pitch. I took off at the same time as the third basemen, and we ran step for step with each other. Duke and the first basemen crashed too. Mitch's bunt was terrible, and the ball slightly popped up for what normally would've been an easy out. The monster had crashed toward home plate too early, and now he had to put on the brakes to dive back for the terrible bunt. I slid past the catcher without a throw, and the ball tipped the monster's glove as it landed just out of his reach. The California monster lay defeated on the ground as loose grass showered down. The crowd bellowed and erupted in cheers as we had won.

We slayed the California monster, but we lost Ogre. Ogre was headed to the hospital, and now no one knew who would pitch in tomorrow's championship game. Ruby, Wyatt, Ogre, and Drake made us invincible, but without Ogre, we seemed mortal. Tomorrow's championship game against the dominant Japanese team already seemed impossible, and without one of our titans, we would need a miracle. I was afraid our last game of the summer would end in disappointment without having Ogre on the mound. We were national champions, and we would be the next United States team to attempt to break the eleven-year drought of a Little League World Championship. Japan had won two straight titles, and they had won four of the last six. The Japanese team was set to defend its title, and their ace had three innings available to pitch.

The MLB strike and the absence of a World Series put the spotlight on our championship game. The game against Japan was pushed back, and for the first time in history of the Little League World Series, the championship game would be played in prime time, under the lights of Williamsport. Our scheduled starting pitcher was on his way to the hospital. Ruby had only one inning to face the potent Japanese hitters.

Secret

After the win, Alex looked like he had seen a ghost. He was at a loss for words. He walked with his head down, trying to find answers. We were all shocked and saddened. We had made it to the championship game, and instead of cheers and laughter, we were all nearly silent. We played baseball all summer, and now at the end of the long summer, our opportunity for greatness was slipping away. We sacrificed days at the lake, sleepovers, and our summer vacations. Tomorrow's championship game meant something more to us all now. An outcome less than winning would not be fair for everything we had all sacrificed during our summer. Swansville seemed farther away than ever. Weeks prior, the dream of Williamsport seemed impossible, much less an opportunity to win the Little League World Series. Coach Alex made us believers before we actually believed we could accomplish our lofty goal.

The championship game was going to be complicated. Ogre was hurt, and our giant only had one inning available to pitch. Drake and Jaxon both only had two innings available to pitch. Coach Alex's plan for pitching us to a Little League World Series collapsed when Ogre's ankle broke. It did not seem fair that we made it this far only to be cheated at our best chance of winning. Coach Alex's postgame bravado was gone, and his speech was somber. He told us, "I will come up with a plan. We made it this far, and we could win despite Ogre being unable to pitch. Now is the time to believe in ourselves and one another." I believed, without Ogre, winning would be a monumental task.

Just then, Wyatt stood up and looked at Duckworth, saying, "Duckworth, tell them what I can do."

Duckworth was speechless and only mumbled. Drake spoke up in his father's place. He stood up and spoke clearly, as if he was going to give a sermon to nonbelievers. "Wyatt is the best pitcher I have ever seen." Then he sat back down. Alex's eyes found me for confirmation. I simply nodded in agreement.

Jacob Hartley stepped from the back row of our parents. He menacingly shook his head no at Wyatt. Jacob only watched our games from afar with no interest in having an impact on the team with his baseball knowledge. Wyatt and his uncle had a nonverbal argument in front of us all, with both shaking their heads and Wyatt waving his hands. Jacob told the group Wyatt would be unavailable to pitch. Wyatt began to protest his uncle, and everyone began to speak. The loud rumble of our group upset Coach Ross, as he loudly said, "Everyone, close your mouths!" Then he added, "We have a hurt young man, and all of you want to argue about a game."

Alex was unafraid of Coach Ross, and he defiantly disagreed. He said, "Not just a game, the championship game, the biggest game of our lives." Alex wanted to know if Wyatt could really pitch.

Earlier in the summer, when we were out of school for Memorial Day, Drake called and asked, "Do you want to go hit a couple of buckets of balls?" This was not an unusual request, and I agreed, as I always did. I invited Wyatt without consulting Drake. Wyatt always liked to hit, and Drake always felt he needed additional practice. The three of us took a bucket of balls and Gatorades and went to the field. Drake had a routine, and Wyatt interrupted it. Wyatt pitched to Drake as I was set to shag balls. Wyatt softly threw a few balls to Drake, and he crushed them into the left field gap. Wyatt asked Drake, "Can I actually pitch a few?" Drake, of course, agreed. I could tell he was puzzled with the catcher's request. Drake did not hit another ball. Wyatt's fastball had a gear neither Drake nor I had ever seen. Drake swung and swung, and he was either late on the fastball or he foolishly missed curveballs. The best catcher and hitter in the league was also secretly the best pitcher. The memory from earlier in the summer made me feel guilty as I had recapped the day for my teammates.

Wyatt made Drake and I swear to his secret. Duckworth had seen the pitching display from Winslow's. Wyatt told us, "My uncle refuses to let me pitch." Jacob did not want Wyatt to risk an injury as he did over ten years earlier. Wyatt said, "Jacob says everyone would fall in love with my arm and I would never leave the mound." Jacob would've been right. If Wyatt had pitched during the regular season, he and the Castaways would have won the championship. History would have been altered.

Everyone was shocked that Drake had told the team that Wyatt was a dominant pitcher. Alex asked Wyatt, Jacob, and Duckworth to stay for a postgame meeting. Curt Christie led a rare prayer, and we prayed for Ogre's ankle to heal quickly. I think most of us prayed for a miracle for Saturday's championship game. Our miracle sat beside me, wearing number 13. After we said, "Amen," we all were eager to know the outcome of the pending conversation.

Whitley and I watched and listened as best as we could, just out of sight. Alex led the conversation off by asking Duckworth, "Was it true?"

Duckworth said, "Yes, but I understood Jacob's request." Duckworth added, "I swore to those boys I would not say anything after watching from the parking lot that day." Duckworth remembered the former town superstar and how everyone said he was a "can't miss" prospect. Duckworth remembered Jacob autographing baseballs at sixteen, and he even had one of the forgotten memorabilia in his attic. Jacob told Duckworth that was a long time ago and he had hoped everyone had forgotten about him. Duckworth knew the green Welcome sign reminded everyone daily and that the Hartley Heater had put Swansville baseball on the map. The man with the most baseball knowledge had kept a valuable secret. Alex was upset that he had no idea he had another dominant arm. Duckworth advised Alex, "You have to respect Jacob's wishes and to not let the boy make the decision against his uncle's request." Alex nodded in disappointment.

Jacob said very little as Wyatt incoherently protested. I never saw Wyatt ever plea this strongly against our teachers as they were sending him to detention. Wyatt's plea started to turn to anger, and he became uncontrollable. His faced turned bright red as tears began to slowly fill his eyes. He shouted, "It's not fair!" over and over. Coach Ross joined the meeting to calm Wyatt down, but he failed, as Wyatt's anger finally began to turn to tears. Coach Ross eventually escorted a defiant Wyatt from the meeting. Coach Ross told Wyatt, "Your uncle only wants what is best for you," but Wyatt disagreed by saying, "What's best for me is to win tomorrow."

My sister and I continued to eavesdrop from afar. Wyatt's pleas fell on deaf ears. Wyatt let out a shriek that seemed to silence the regular cacophony of the baseball barracks. The night was silent. Wyatt ran off as the four men could only watch. My sister and I followed the phenom as he ran to the dugout to cry. I had never seen him cry like this, and I believed that he would want to cry alone. I was correct. I was one of his many disciples, and I wanted to take away his pain. He wanted to be left alone. Whitley and I arrived to his uncontrollable sobs echoing in the dugout. He roared at us to leave just as I peeked my head in the dugout.

Whitley floated down the steps without any trepidation. She was not scared or intimidated. I watched her walk over to him, and I was unsure of how he would respond. She simply whispered something in his ear and sat beside him, putting her hand on his wrist. I reluctantly stayed. I sat in silence on the dugout steps.

A light drizzle started as his sobs became a whimper. I felt she had somehow tamed a wild beast. Awkwardness and the smell of sunflower seeds drifted my way. We sat in silence until Duckworth found us and said, "It is time to go and get some rest." Duckworth escorted us back to the barracks in silence. Duckworth and Whitley walked up the hill toward the parking lot in the rain. Wyatt and I watched until she disappeared from the horizon.

Calm before the Storm

It did not feel like summer the night before the Little League World Series championship game. The rain brought in the cooler weather. Back in Swansville, my classmates were already in school. RJ was absent from football practice, and the middle school football coach was clamoring for his superstar to return. The crisp wind blew, and I felt like I was sitting on the big water as a storm approached. The trees swayed as the howling wind whispered to me. It was ominous, and I felt like I was on unsteady ground. I listened to the wind whisper long into a nervously sleepless night. I knew the only time I would set foot on the diamond would be during warm-ups and the postgame handshake. I had never been that nervous in my life. I understood why Broadway actors have understudies.

Whitley and my parents stayed at a nearby hotel, and my sister would be able to drift off to sleep watching reruns. I wondered if Whitley was ever nervous before her championship games. She was in so many I assumed she was accustomed to the feeling. The blue ribbons and trophies on our mantel proved she was born for the big moment. Whitley's name in the paper had become common for my parents, and her scrapbook was starting to burst at the seams. Fortune had rarely shone down on me, and I learned most of my baseball and life lessons looking up from the bottom. I was buried by the losses and the insults from my longtime adversaries and class bullies. The opportunity to place a championship trophy beside one of Whitley's many trophies excited and terrified me.

Wyatt had only been in our lives for less than six months, but it seemed he had been here forever. Every story and adventure in my life now involved him. I stayed in the shallows until his confidence pulled me into deeper waters. He had not assimilated to our group of friends, but he had taken control. Drake, Ogre, and the others all looked to him for his leadership and his heroics. He delivered every time he was called upon. He was something different to us all, but we all needed him. He could magically cloak all our weaknesses. He made me feel invincible when I was with him. When he was nearby, I felt like nothing could stop us. He spoke up for Ogre, and he pulled the unwanted attention from Drake. Tomorrow the eyes of the United States would be on all of us and especially Wyatt. I could tell he understood the magnitude of it all.

I was unable to sleep that night, and I silently watched Wyatt pace the floor of our barracks. Wyatt was quiet, and his eyes thankfully never looked my way. He carried his father's bat over his shoulder. He looked like he was on night patrol of our barracks as he marched back and forth. Wherever he was, I did not want to be the one that pulled him back. He seemed calm, but I could tell a storm was brewing. Tomorrow's game brought the biggest and brightest spotlight his direction. The spotlight had followed him since the moment he arrived in Swansville, but this was the country's spotlight, not the spotlight from a town where a lake stopped at a dead-end road. The way he paced and the way he looked reminded me of Drake before every game. It was difficult not to feel unsteady. The normally jovial catcher was preparing for foes of the likes none of us had ever encountered. Watching him pace eventually calmed my nervousness, and the ground stopped shaking with each step. I fell asleep to the sound of his footsteps.

The Japanese team looked like warriors that were poised to invade. They did everything with precision, and errors were their enemy. They did not speak when warming up or playing. Drake would've fit right in with our opponent. Someone had sucked the joy from the game for these boys. The game was a joyless job. I assumed they had trained for this moment their entire lives, and many generations knew the feeling. Winning was everything. They did not fly across the world to lose.

They woke up every morning at the same time, and they even dressed at the same pace. They ate the same food, and they never smiled. We loudly joked and enjoyed every moment. They looked on in displeasure at our nonsense. Baseball was serious business to them. The Japanese fans seemed to even clap on cue. The once-in-a-lifetime trip to the Little League World Series in Williamsport was expected, and failure would not be tolerated. They had been here too many times, and the perfectly groomed fields did not impress them.

The Japanese players looked like they were built in a factory for baseball. The factory's sole purpose was Little League World Series titles. My twelve-year-old brain saw them being trained to be samurai monks, not baseball players. They were the first team that did not seem to have even one weakness. They were defending their title, and they looked to win a third straight. They were all the same size, except for a set of twin brothers. Ryoto and Ryuu did not look up to Ogre, as the twins were taller than our man-child.

The twins were mythical, and I felt they should not have existed. I believed Ryuu and Ryoto were only something you read about. The entire time we were in Williamsport, everyone heard rumors of their dominance. Strikeouts were their fuel. The rumors seemed to come from a faraway land, since the Japanese team and the twins were rarely seen at anything other than Little League World Series functions. They were not made in a baseball factory. The baseball gods created them, and their sole purpose was to dominate. They were not giants or monsters; they were something much more frightening. Their path to the Little League World Series was littered with twelve-year-olds that had met their demise at the feet of the oversize twin brothers. They could win the game in warm-ups, much like Ogre and Ruby had done earlier in the summer. I knew we were in trouble when Ruby reported that the rumors were true.

Ryuu was the Japanese team's catcher and second-best pitcher. He was a slightly better hitter than his brother. He reminded me of Wyatt when he was batting. His body was calm, and at the last second, he flicked his bat at the ball as if a tail had whipped around his body. Ryuu was a menacing figure when standing in the batter's box. He and his brother looked like they could reach on first base in one giant step. Their lineup was formidable with the twins batting back-to-back. There was no way around them, and the warriors protected their colossal teammates. Ryuu threw harder than his left-handed brother. He had a direct, over-the-top delivery that made the ball look like it was somehow shot out of his mouth. His pitching delivery was similar to the California monster's. He was hittable, but just barely. He had one inning available for the championship game.

Their father was the Japanese team's coach, and he had been so for the last decade. He and Sammy Gibson had faced each other several times, with the Japanese team always prevailing. He intended on retiring after this season, and much like the California coach, he was a fixture. He was strict, and if one of his many warriors made a mistake, he simply subbed in a nameless replacement. He had five sons, and his twins were his last baseball phenoms. All three of the twins' older brothers had won the Little World Series. He only respected wins, and he was the only coach that desired dominance more than Coach Alex. As much as Coach Alex was despised, he seemed tame compared to Coach Matsui. He valued dominance, and a simple mistake unleashed his wrath.

Ryoto was the most dominant pitcher in the tournament. He toyed with the international pool teams. He burned down every team's best hitter with ease. He was brash and cocky. The California monster was the only other pitcher that even compared. Ryoto was left-handed, and he had a similar herky-jerky pitching motion as Anthony Angelo. The ball jumped from his hand much like it did from Becca Gorgan, but only faster. He confused batters as the ball sped past you. Left-handed batters had no chance, as his fastball looked like it would hit you, then it would fade across the plate as one foolishly swung too late. It seemed he could take the first baseman's hat off as he threw the baseball. He was a twelve-year-old version of Randy Johnson. No one had even put the ball in play against him in the tournament. He simply nodded at his victims after easily dispatching them. He turned the batter into ashes, and they were gone in a puff of smoke. He was to his country what Ruby was to Swansville. The only way to reach base was to hope for a walk. Ryoto had given up six free passes and zero runs. He was brought in to pitch the international semifinal to save his father's last chance at returning to Japan as a conquering hero. Ryoto had three innings available to pitch, and we had no idea who would even start for us.

Spotlight

Coach Alex gathered the team first thing in the morning and told us to enjoy the day. He did not want us worrying about baseball, but he knew we all still would. The final game of the summer intimated him. He had dreamed of the moment all summer, but somewhere deep down he did not think his giant of a son and Ogre and Wyatt could make his impossible dream a reality. The game was moved to prime time on Saturday night. It would be the first championship played under lights at Williamsport. We were scheduled to start at 7:00 p.m. It would be a long day. I knew Drake would retreat to the same place in his head. Coach Alex told us the plan was to start Drake and use his three innings, then figure it out from there. Drake looked like he had seen a ghost at our morning meeting. Ruby had one inning available. Coach Alex ordered us to meet at 5:00 p.m. to dress as a team. Wyatt usually mocked or made jokes at Coach Alex during his speeches, but today he was silent. Coach Alex even looked puzzled. He approached Wyatt, and the two briefly chatted.

We had eight hours to kill. We needed a distraction, and I tried to organize something for us to do. Dale and Curt had the idea to go watch a movie. Instead of going to a theater, David Luck rented a banquet room at a hotel. He had a television and a VCR brought in. We decided to watch *The Sandlot*. Wyatt begged for something other than baseball. The movie was a good idea as it took a big chunk of the day. Wyatt fell asleep within ten minutes. Ruby uncharacteristically talked through the entire movie. He claimed he'd one day be the first to reach the Major Leagues. Drake went with his father and did not watch the movie. The odd pair went to a local park to shoot

204

basketball. Duckworth needed to keep Drake's mind off baseball. He knew his son would not think of baseball while shooting jump shots.

Wyatt joined my family for lunch. My parents took us to Legends Steakhouse. My dad told us, "Order whatever you all want. Today you eat like kings!" Wyatt thanked my dad and only ordered a bacon cheeseburger despite my dad urging him to order lobster or a steak. Whitley and I both ordered shrimp cocktails to go along with our steaks. I was uncomfortable being the family attraction, and I deferred to my sister. I asked her about her last soccer match of the summer, knowing she would not be able to resist telling the table of her three goals. She lost, but those details were left out of her story. I loved watching Whitley talk with her hands, telling everyone how she could kick a soccer ball. Wyatt was unimpressed and interrupted her, asking her the outcome of the game. He knew she had lost in the state semifinals, but he asked anyway. Whitley turned on Wyatt and asked, "Have you won yet?" She chuckled, then said, "Oh yeah, you have Ruby on your team now." Wyatt clenched his teeth, and he did not offer a rebuttal. My dad sensed the direction of the conversation and deferred to my mom.

My mom interrupted the conversation and began to ask us all embarrassing questions. We ignored her. She was relentless and probed us, "Who is your crush, Whitley?"

My sister ignored her and pretended not to even hear her.

Wyatt told my mom, "Ask Carson about Ella."

I turned red and told Wyatt, "Come on, that is all I need."

My mom said, "Stay away from those big-water people. They are all trouble."

Our food arrived just in time as I began to sweat the comments and questions. My dad said the blessing and prayed for Ogre to heal quickly, and he closed the prayer with, "Lord, please be with these boys today in triumph and in defeat. Amen."

Wyatt repeated, "Amen," then we feasted.

The team met at 5:00 p.m. and dressed in our USA uniforms. I was not nervous, for some reason. Deep down I knew I would not play. Wyatt and Ruby argued as we dressed. It was playful, and the room was light. Coach Alex continually had to tell Wyatt to close his mouth. Wyatt had more energy than ever, and he ignored our coach. Wyatt usually talked and provoked everyone, but today he was ten times worse. He was excited, and his nervous anxiety made us, especially me, now more nervous. We gave one another high fives to try to ease the tension of the room. We were about to play on national television again, but tonight's game was different. It was the end of something that started when the spring nights were still cool and baseball was what we did to keep us busy while the school year slowly marched to its end. I did not feel like a child any longer. We grew up that summer and soon mirrors would betray us and our childlike faces would be gone.

Ogre sat with his crutches and grinningly stared at the two rivals. Ogre knew that Wyatt and Ruby deep down understood that they were better together. Ogre called Wyatt and Ruby over, and the three boys shared an awkward moment. Ogre told them, "Our summer would be decided one way or another. Just play it." After today, it would be a long time before the pitcher and catcher would share a dugout.

Coach Alex gave us one last speech. All our parents were present as he told us about perfection for the one hundredth time, but something was different in his voice. He was humble for the first time, and he did not have his usual forcefulness. It was the calmest he was all summer. I felt like he had just returned from somewhere crying alone, and now he was asked to address us. The summer had caught up with him too. He knew it was over after tonight, and tomorrow he would return to Swansville either a hero or a failure. The thought of baseball ending for the year had made his sails sag, but whether he liked it or not, he had guided our ship to the championship.

Coach Alex thanked all our parents and the other adults that had supported us all summer. He apologized for stealing their summer. He asked Duckworth to come up. Alex then asked everyone that had been a Duckling to stand up. Everyone was a Duckling at one time or another except Ruby, Wyatt, Ogre, and Anthony. I stood next to Duckworth, and I hugged him. I told him I loved him. Duckworth's eyes were filled with tears as Coach Alex thanked the old coach for teaching us how to play baseball the correct way.

Alex pulled out an extra game jersey with "Duckworth" across the back. He asked Duckworth, "Would you hit ground balls during warm-ups?" Duckworth politely declined and said, "It's your team." Duckworth and Alex shook hands and gave each other a hug as if congratulating an opponent after a loss. Alex's voice cracked as he closed with, "Regardless of the outcome, this has been the perfect summer."

Preston started the chant, "USA, USA!" and we ran to the dugout to prepare for our pregame warm-ups.

Drake stayed behind and did not run to the dugout. He stopped Coach Alex from running with us, and he told him, "Start Ruby. He can get us through the first inning and past the twins."

Coach Alex asked him, "Can you give me the next three innings?"

Drake nodded and said, "Yes, sir. They will be perfect."

Coach Alex ran on the field, and the first thing he had to do was rethink his pitching strategy. The plan now was to start Ruby and let him lead us past the feared twins. Drake would pitch the next three innings, and Jaxon would come in for the last two innings.

We all went to our normal positions, and we started to take ground balls. The first ball was hit to Drake, and Wyatt obnoxiously yelled, "Field with your feet!" Everyone laughed, and Drake grinned at Wyatt. Wyatt pointed at the baseball artist. We all chatted and made off-putting comments and insults at one another in an effort to keep everyone loose. RJ caught a fly ball, and Ruby shouted, "RJ knows baseball!" Coach Ross joined and yelled at Jaxon, "Make a play, mophead!" We all made Duckworth comments as we took ground balls. Ruby and Wyatt openly taunted each other. The strategy worked for now, and our nervousness magically floated out of Williamsport. Outsiders must've thought we did not like one another with all our insane comments. We had spent the summer together, and tonight's game would be our last.

We were introduced, and we all were able to wave at the ESPN camera. A short fact was under our name as the television flashed each one of us across the screen to everyone watching. My fact said, "My nickname is Lightning." It is a mystery who edited my original note to the ESPN crew, but I assume it was either Wyatt or Duckworth. The intended fact was, "My favorite book is Ty Cobb's *My Life in Baseball*." Wyatt's fact read, "I do not believe in luck." Troy winked at the camera, and Curt flexed. Drake did not acknowledge the camera as he stoically stared off in the distance. Ogre received the loudest cheers as he walked out on crutches to the first-base line. The national anthem finished, and I suddenly felt ten feet tall. I was bursting with pride as I went to sit on the bench.

Ruby and Wyatt walked out of the dugout together for warm-ups for the last time. The two rivals did not speak, but they had an unspoken alliance to take down the twin phenoms in the first inning. Ruby struck out the first batter in his typical Ruby fashion. Ryoto stepped to the plate and calmly stared Ruby down. Ruby's first pitch was a curveball that Ryoto sent down the right field line, and it hooked foul at the last second. Ryoto would not be intimidated. Ruby bounced two curveballs in the dirt, and the count was 2–1. Ruby's fastball was no match for Ryoto as he deposited into the center field grass for a home run. The Japanese team led 1–0. Ryoto emphatically stomped on home plate as he stared at Wyatt. Wyatt smiled, as he also knew the rare feeling of hitting a home run off Ruby.

Ryuu confidently strolled to the plate after his brother's home run. The first pitch Ruby threw nearly hit Ryuu, and the Japanese fans collectively gasped as one of their stars hit the ground. Ruby's second pitch was a strike low and away. The count was 1–1 when Ruby threw another ball high and tight, and the boy had to dust himself off for a second time. Ruby's next pitch curved just under Ryuu's bat for strike 2. Ruby struck out the phenom as he watched another fastball paint the outside corner. Coach Matsui objected and began to shout at the umpires.

After surviving one of the Japanese supertwins, Ruby took a deep breath. He and Wyatt had a brief mound visit. Wyatt rubbed the ball down. He looked like a catcher from the turn of the century when he handed the ball back to his rival. The two boys had conversation that resulted in Wyatt and Ruby tapping gloves. The national television cameras caught everything. I believe Wyatt apologized to his rival for the world to see.

Wyatt squatted behind home plate and flashed Ruby the next sign. Ruby nodded, and the two rivals became one. Ruby struck the next fastball in the Japanese cleanup batter's back. The Japanese fans said nothing, but they all glared at Wyatt and Ruby. The crowd knew the pitch was not off target. The next warrior hit a line drive right back at Ruby, and somehow he saved his own life and made the catch. If Ruby's glove did not block the ball, Ruby would have taken the screaming line drive off his head. The score was 1–0.

The Japanese team started Ryuu. RJ started the game with a bunt to surprise the baseball warriors, and he was effortlessly thrown out at first base. It was the first time the ball was faster than RJ. Drake followed with an opposite-field double, and the crowd erupted. Wyatt stepped to the plate, and for the first time all summer, he did not turn and make a comment to the on-deck batter. I did not know if he was nervous or he was that focused. The first pitch he saw, he swung wildly and fell to the ground as Ryuu fooled him with changeup. Ryuu menacingly stared down Wyatt. Wyatt looked confused, and the next pitch he lined just over the reach of Ryoto at first base. Drake scored just as Wyatt was thrown trying for an ill-advised double. Ryuu finished Jaxon off with ease, and the inning was over. The sold-out Williamsport fans looked at the scoreboard tied at 1–1.

Drake ran out to the pitcher's mound to start the second inning. He stood there alone for a moment, waiting for Wyatt to come warm him up. Wyatt had a broken strap on his shin guards that needed to be replaced. Coach Alex sent me to warm up Drake while Wyatt finished putting on his catcher's gear. I did not say anything to Drake, and he threw four fastballs before Wyatt returned to squat behind home plate. I casually ran off the field, and I scanned the crowd for a familiar face. I only saw Duckworth sitting behind the dugout. My sister stood just out of my view of the catcher behind the dugout, and my parents were grabbing cotton candy. My parents had missed my only action of the game.

Drake promised Coach Alex he would give him perfection and backed up his promise in the second inning. He struck out the first three batters he faced. Drake had to face the dreaded twins in the third inning. He wisely did not throw a ball even remotely close, and he walked them both. Drake induced an easy ground ball to Jaxon to end the inning. After three innings, the score was still 1–1.

The pressure Drake put on himself to be the best was nothing to playing on national television. He had that same look in his eyes he had on Father's Day. After each inning, he went to sit in the same quiet corner of the dugout. He stared at the field in silence. I do not believe he felt the shower of cheers each inning as he masterfully dominated the Japanese team.

We had two innings to score more runs before Ryoto was scheduled to take the mound in the fourth inning. The next inning, Coach Matsui brought in one of his warriors, and he survived without giving up any runs despite Troy reaching third base with one out and walking Preston. The third inning would be different. RJ reached on a single, then Drake singled to have runners on the corners with one out. Coach Matsui brought in his third pitcher of the game to face Wyatt. Wyatt was intentionally walked, and the USA fans loudly booed. Jaxon singled up the middle to drive in RJ, but a perfect throw stopped Drake from scoring. We had the lead 2–1. Troy walked before Dale hit the loudest out I had ever seen. The crowd was on its feet as one of the baseball warriors jumped up and robbed a home run. No one tagged up as the cutoff man was Ryoto, and he would have thrown anyone out. It did not matter. Ruby struck out on three pitches to end the inning.

Drake took the mound for his last inning of the summer. We needed to preserve our lead before Ryoto entered the game. Drake struck out the first two batters before walking two in a row.

Coach Alex visited Drake on the mound along with Wyatt. Alex asked, "Are you tired?"

Drake shook his head and said, "I will keep my word and get you one more out."

Drake masterfully struck out his last batter by painting the corner with three straight fastballs. The Japanese baseball warrior did not even swing his bat.

Ryoto slowly walked to the mound despite his large steps. Ryuu and Ryoto seemed as one as the pitcher and catcher began to warm up. Before every pitch, Ryoto took a deep breath, and he exhaled, and it looked like he was breathing fire. Curt was due to lead off, and he was terror-stricken. Curt crouched his stance to shrink his strike zone. This strategy worked, and he walked on five pitches without swinging his bat. Preston tried the same thing, and Ryoto threw a fastball that hit Preston in the ribs. Preston went down in agony, and his screams echoed under the lights. Preston was just another casualty of the Japanese pitcher. He did not even take a knee while Preston screamed in agony. Preston exited the game, and Mitch was subbed in to run and play left field. Ryoto had sent a message: he would destroy anyone that crouched for a base on balls. RJ wildly swung at the first three pitches, and he ran back to the dugout. He looked like he was running from something terrifying. Drake struck out, and he retreated back to his corner of the dugout. Wyatt oddly looked in the crowd, and it was obvious he was searching for someone. Ryoto's first pitch nearly decapitated Wyatt. He backed off the plate, and Ryoto threw him a changeup low and away. Wyatt did not move as the umpire emphatically called strike 1. Wyatt swung at the next two pitches, and he was late. Wyatt's rare strikeout sent shivers down my spine. The inning was over, and we still had the lead despite three straight strikeouts.

Jaxon was asked to get the last six outs of our summer. Ogre patted Jaxon on the back and told him, "You can do it!" Jaxon retired the first batter, but then he had to face the twins. He walked Ryoto, much to the displeasure of the Japanese fans. Jaxon looked to do the same when Ryuu flicked his bat at a pitch nowhere near the strike zone. The ball landed in the crowd behind the right field fence. Jaxon's head dropped, and Wyatt walked to the mound and shouted, "Who cares? Let's get the next guy!" The score was 3–2. We were losing, and it was getting late. Drake made two diving plays in a row for the next two outs, and we had to figure out how to get one more run.

Ryoto continued his dominance in the fifth inning by first striking out an emotionally wounded Jaxon, then Troy. We all hoped Dale's swing-for-the-fences magic would tie the game, but he was easily sent back to the dugout after Ryoto threw him three straight changeups. The ground shook as the twins walked off the field. Ryuu and Ryoto looked as one as they disappeared into the dugout. I do not know how my teammates were able to continue playing. I could not control my nerves, and I was openly shaking.

Jaxon did not look like he wanted to pitch as he slowly walked to the mound with his head down. Ruby handed him the ball and said, "You got this." Our giant rarely encouraged any of his teammates, and I could tell Ruby knew Jaxon would not have the confidence to get three more outs. Jaxon walked the first batter, and the next warrior doubled. Coach Alex directed Jaxon to walk the next batter to load the bases in an effort to get a force-out at home. Jaxon pulled his hat down, hoping the world would not see the face of the boy that lost the Little League World Series. Wyatt shouted something at Coach Alex before the next batter stepped in the batter's box. The next batter hit a ball to Drake, and he made an amazing diving stop, but he would not be able to get the runner at home plate. Coach Alex called the team to the mound. The score was 4–2 and no outs.

Coach Alex was not a coach at that moment but a boy willing to do anything to win. He told the team, "Boys, we have nothing to lose." He looked at Wyatt and said, "Show me what you can do."

Wyatt's cheeks turned red, and he said, "Did he say yes?"

Alex nodded and acknowledged the plan was cleared with Wyatt's uncle. The bases were loaded, and Wyatt would make his pitching debut surrounded by Japanese warriors on live television. RJ sprinted to the dugout to put on the catcher's gear.

Wyatt quickly took off his catcher's gear as RJ hurriedly put it on. RJ was talking faster than he could run. He asked Wyatt, "What signs do you use?"

Wyatt told RJ, "Calm down, and everything will be fine."

I believed him, because I had seen how foolish he had made Drake look several months earlier. Wyatt looked odd on the mound, and I could tell the place felt foreign. He was dirty, and he did not have the shine of a pitcher.

The bases were loaded, and Wyatt had to get three outs. His uncle casually stood next to the side of the dugout. The first Japanese warrior came to the plate, and Wyatt's first fastball sailed over RJ's head and the ball violently bounced off the backstop. Thankfully, the runners were unable to advance. Coach Alex's decision to put Wyatt on the mound looked like a desperate attempt to win. Wyatt looked at his uncle, and Jacob motioned with his hands to settle down. Wyatt took a deep breath, and he looked behind the dugout again. The next fastball surprised everyone except me and Drake. The Japanese warrior looked on in disbelief as the ball went over the outside corner for a strike. Our parents began to believe as Vanessa Harrison shouted to the crowd, "You can do it! Just pop the mitt!" Missy echoed, "You got it, baby!" Wyatt threw two more fastballs, and the warrior disgracefully ran to the dugout to hide. The Swansville fans had faith in a Hartley again.

Ryoto only needed to put the ball in play to drive in more runs. Ryoto smiled at Wyatt. Wyatt's body looked like it was about to explode as he grunted with each pitch. Ryoto missed badly on Wyatt's curveball. Wyatt fired the ball at Ryoto's head, and again the ball bounced off the backstop. RJ was able to hold the runners, and no one advanced. Ryoto dusted himself off and shouted something back at his dad. Coach Matsui shouted back, and Ryoto stepped back in the batter's box. Wyatt reached back and fired a fastball by Ryoto. Ryoto rarely struck out, and he was in disbelief. He shamefully walked back to the dugout after swinging at Wyatt's next fastball.

Ryuu was not impressed with Wyatt either. Ryuu never struck out, and he was the most feared batter in the tournament. Wyatt had experience taking down giants, monsters, and other foes all summer, but never from the pitcher's mound. Ryuu was bigger and scarier than them all. Wyatt's fastball did not intimidate him, and he promptly fouled one off as the crowd gasped as the ball went far but wide of the foul pole. Coach Matsui shouted at his son and the bases full of warriors. Ryuu stomped as he stepped in the batter's box, and the dugout vibrated. Wyatt threw a curveball that just missed the outside corner. Wyatt threw up his hands, questioning the call. The umpire warned Wyatt. Wyatt shrugged in displeasure. Coach Alex shouted, "Garbage!" and drew the umpire's attention away from Wyatt. Coach Alex called time, then visited Wyatt on the mound.

Coach Alex did not bring RJ or the infield to the mound. I have no idea what the two spoke about, but they both openly laughed. The count was 1–1 when Wyatt threw a ball at Ryuu's head. One of the biggest kids in the tournament ducked and stood up, then laughed at Wyatt while shouting something to his brother in the dugout. Ryuu fouled off two of Wyatt's curveballs. Wyatt missed badly with a curveball in the dirt, and again RJ held the runners with his catlike reflexes as he backhanded the ball out of the dirt. The count was full. Wyatt was sweating, but his smile made him glow. Ryuu looked like he was ready to finish things off. Wyatt reached down and picked up a handful of dirt and rubbed it on his wrist. He had not done it before, and I was confused. Maybe there was some magic in the dirt that Wyatt, Drake, and I poured the brown water on. Wyatt's next fastball was faster than anything anyone did all summer. Ryuu went down on strikes just like his brother. Wyatt had saved the day again.

Wyatt's pitching debut was exactly as I had imagined. Drake Duckworth could hit anyone, but not Wyatt. His fastball was special. Wyatt had made Drake look foolish earlier in the summer, and if Drake could not hit him, then no one could. We trailed 2–4, and only three outs remained of our summer. I foolishly believed I could hear the faint sound of a ticking clock, and I waited for church bells to send everyone home. We needed more magic to score on the Japanese ace pitcher. I quietly began to pray. Wyatt was due to bat sixth.

Everyone entered the dugout excited, but the task of scoring two more runs seemed monumental. I shouted, "Great job, guys! We can do it!"

Ruby answered, "Go back to praying, Worm. We need it!"

Ryoto looked in our dugout during warm-ups and grinned, showing his teeth. He obviously had seen teams with the same dejected look during his journey to Williamsport.

Ruby led off the inning, and he walked to the plate with fear. Ryoto put a ball in the back of Ruby with his hardest fastball. It happened fast, but Ruby fell to the ground in slow motion. Ruby held back the tears, then waved off his dad, but Coach Alex ran to check on his son. Alex barked at the grinning Coach Matsui. Ruby looked ready to attack Ryoto as he glared from first base. Ryoto effortlessly struck out Curt. We were down to two outs.

Mitch looked in the dugout, then said, "Pray I can get on."

Coach Alex called Mitch back to the dugout and told him, "Do your best, son. That's all we can do now."

Drake bounced out of his seat and shook the fence, then barked at Alex and Mitch, "We need more than your best. We need perfection!" Drake angrily nodded at Alex and continued, "We made it here on perfection, not prayers, not luck or our best. It was perfection. This summer is not perfect, but it can be."

Ogre joined in. "Give them perfection, Mitch."

Alex grinned back at the two quiet boys.

Drake finished with, "Don't waste our summer not being perfect."

We all began to whisper, "Perfect, perfect." Our silent chant had my heart racing as Mitch stepped to the plate.

Mitch swung late at the first two pitches. He was clearly overmatched. The whispered chant continued, "Perfect, perfect." Mitch called time, then asked for Wyatt's bat. Mitch rubbed down the unfamiliar and much heavier bat. Ryoto threw a curveball just as Mitch surprised everyone with a two-strike bunt. Mitch raced for first as Ryuu fired to get Ruby at second base. The ball was late, and the giant slid in safe in the nick of time. He gave Ogre a thumbs-up. Some giants can slide. Mitch had broken the spell of getting a hit against Ryoto. The tying run was on first base. RJ tried to bunt on Ryoto, and this time the warriors were ready and they threw Ruby out at third base. Ruby walked off the field for the last time. He did not stop talking and motioning to the crowd to make some noise and to get on their feet. Ruby joined the chant, "Perfect, perfect!" The stadium seemed to be shaking when Drake stepped in the batter's box. He was calm. Big moments did not scare Drake, and his expression never changed. Ryoto got ahead of Drake 1–2 as Drake missed on two curveballs. The chant was now getting louder, "Perfect, perfect!" Wyatt was on one knee as he watched every pitch. Drake was the only player other than Wyatt I believed could hit Ryoto. Ryoto fired a fastball, and Drake hit a single up the middle. Mitch was held at third. Ogre banged his fist against the dugout seat as the chant, "Perfect, perfect!" grew even louder.

The showdown between Wyatt and Ryoto was set. Wyatt stood up from one knee, and he walked to the plate. He glanced back at the dugout for the final time of the summer. Wyatt stepped to the plate. He did not look like he was facing anything more than just another pitcher. He had planned for this moment all summer. He drew his bat from his hip and pointed it at Ryoto. The first pitch sailed high and inside; Wyatt went to the ground as the ball just missed his head. I looked in the stands and saw Duckworth and my parents, and they now chanted, "Perfect, perfect." Wyatt again pointed his bat in the direction of the Japanese pitcher. It looked like he was not playing baseball but preparing for battle. Wyatt fouled off the next two pitches, and we had only one strike left of the summer. Ryoto fired another pitch at Wyatt's head, and he ducked just in time. Wyatt stood back up, then he looked over his shoulder at the fans standing in the stadium. Everyone was chanting, "Perfect, perfect!" The stadium was in some type of trance. Only those of us that heard Drake's proclamation understood the true meaning. Wyatt bent over and grabbed a handful of dirt, then rubbed it again on his wrist. He took a deep breath and slowly closed his eyes, as if someone was whispering something to him. The count was two balls and two strikes. Wyatt's toes were almost on the plate.

Ryoto's eyes were red as he stared Wyatt down. Ryoto let go of the ball. The ball had flames chasing it as it flew through the air toward his twin brother's mitt. I closed my eyes as tightly as possible and kept chanting, "Perfect, perfect." The crowd erupted, and my ears popped and the stadium was silent. I felt safe as I had drifted to the same place where Drake always retreated. I was scared to open my eyes.

Ogre pulled me back, and he simply said, "He did it!"

I opened my eyes to see Wyatt slowly trotting to second base. It was so loud the ground vibrated, and I was disoriented. I was told the ball flew higher than the lights and it did not even have a shadow as it sailed over the center field fence. The fans on the hill ran to retrieve the ball that went over everyone's head.

Ryoto ran to Ryuu, and the twins embraced. They slowly fell to the ground, and they looked like one body with two heads. They sobbed as the rest of their teammates ran to the dugout for safety. The twins had failed their father. They were unable to protect the baseball kingdom their father had built.

Wyatt crossed home plate, then buried his face in his hands to hide his tears. His tears were for his future, not for the epic moment. He must've known he was no longer the new kid from Swansville but the hero to the country. Wyatt's life would never be the same again. He was Wyatt to us, but now he was Wyatt to the country. Everyone knew his name. We mobbed him as he crossed the plate. My teeth vibrated because of the noise. It wasn't just the fans in Williamsport; it was a nation of baseball fans cheering for us. We all had tears of joy in our eyes.

Ruby said, "Let's carry Wyatt off the field!"

Wyatt quickly objected. He did not want to be carried off the field as a hero, but he wanted to lead us off as a conqueror. We marched in unison behind him as he headed for the dugout.

The ESPN reporter approached Wyatt on live television as he led us off the field. Drake and I hid in the back. The reporter asked, "Wyatt, you just hit an iconic home run. It must feel magical."

Wyatt smiled and said, "It is what every boy dreams about. I can't believe the team got here."

We cheered in the background as the reporter said, "You guys just won the Little League World Series, and you snapped the United States championship drought."

No one replied as we all cheered as one.

Coach Alex stoically sat on the dugout steps. He was melancholy and was in disbelief. The shock of the moment was too much for him. Ruby looked at his dad and shouted, "What are you doing? Don't miss this perfect moment!" Coach Alex ran to join us while wiping the tears away.

The ESPN reporter congratulated him. "You are the first USA team to win the Little League World Series in a decade."

Alex said, "These boys sacrificed everything for an opportunity to be perfect, and they deserve to enjoy it." Then he rushed toward the team.

Our parents and siblings ran onto the field to celebrate. Fathers and mothers embraced their sons. Our parents cried more than we did. They deserved the moment just as much as we did. They had sacrificed their summer to be baseball vagabonds. They traveled to places they did not know existed, only to end up in Williamsport, Pennsylvania.

My parents hugged me, and my dad lifted me up. It was odd finishing as a champion. Whitley hugged me, too, but the awkwardness of our approaching teenage years made it one of our last. I interrupted Drake and Duckworth's celebration, and I thanked them both. Duckworth squeezed me tight and whispered, "You're not a Duckling anymore." Drake was the only one of our teammates that did not shed a tear. Duckworth's eyes were full with tears. Drake's estranged mother did not come on the field, and she sneaked away. It was the last time I ever saw Betty Duckworth. Ogre stood on the pitcher's mound with his dad, and the two wondered, Would Ogre have been able to take down the Japanese team? Ruby and Wyatt shook hands before Ruby pulled Wyatt in for a hug. He lifted Wyatt off the ground, and they both laughed. I assumed they ended their summer with an insult to each other. Troy's parents, Ella, and Isaac crowded around him. I sneaked in one last summer gaze at his sister. Jacob Hartley and Coach Alex chatted and shook hands. The two men looked like they had struck a deal. Jacob Hartley understood the euphoria of winning it all, but he knew life's disappointment more. Patti had brought Wyatt to Swansville, and she stood proud as she hugged her son while tears of joy ran down her cheeks.

Wyatt was the center of attention. Everyone wanted to congratulate him. Coach Ross shook his hand, while Missy loudly hugged him, saying, "Baby, you did it!" Reporters began to congregate near Wyatt. My parents and I showered him with compliments. I hugged and thanked him but not just for his homerun. Whitley stood by and was unimpressed. She spent more time on baseball fields than soccer fields this summer. Tomorrow Wyatt would have his picture on the front page of *USA Today*. He was a national icon in an instant, and I had missed it. I could even feel the heat of the spotlight headed his way. A rumor that *The Late Show with David Letterman* wanted him as a guest would prove to be true. The spotlight was getting brighter.

Cooperstown

My parents volunteered to take Wyatt to New York. My mom always talked about wanting to go to New York City, and Wyatt's upcoming appearance on *The Late Show* gave her an excuse to fulfill one of her life's dreams. Patti and Jacob had to go back to their lives on Monday. I begged my parents to stop in Cooperstown so we could visit the Baseball Hall of Fame. The plan was to leave tomorrow, then stop in Cooperstown for one day, then head over to New York. Wyatt, Whitley, and I still had a few more days left of summer.

Saturday night after the game was amazing. We celebrated with pizza and ice cream. David Luck made sure the night was special. He rented out a hotel banquet room. David and Missy arranged everything. They intended on celebrating even if we lost. A giant baseball card with our faces lined the walls. Each card had our stats along with an action photo. Missy had snapped a photo of me and Wyatt hugging after I slid headfirst earlier in the summer. The back of the card contained a short writeup about each of us. My profile detailed my calm demeanor. I fooled everyone all summer, since I was a nervous wreck for most of our games. The highlight of the evening was when all our parents and team joined to sing "Take Me Out to the Ball Game." Duckworth of course did his best Harry Caray impersonation as he sang.

Coach Alex fought through tears to give us one last speech. He thanked our parents and ended his speech with, "The summer was perfect. I'll see you all when we get back to Swansville." He would be going back to a different Swansville. He and Ruby and a few others would be going to the new school on the other side of Cubbie Cove. The party began to settle down, and the mood was sober. We said our goodbyes and took our baseball cards. Tomorrow morning the caravan would head back to Swansville, and I would head to Cooperstown with Wyatt.

Cooperstown would never be this close again, and thankfully my parents agreed to take us on our way to New York City. The trip would take around four hours. Whitley begged my parents to let her go back with the caravan, but they forced her to go. Wyatt and I sat in the middle row of the van, while Whitley sat in the back row and pouted. She had had her fill of baseball, and she was ready to start the seventh grade. She was a long way from the place where everyone knew her name.

The ride to Cooperstown was uneventful as my parents sang to the radio. It reminded me of our family trips to Myrtle Beach, where we would all excitedly sing for the entire car ride. Wyatt and I took turns playing my Game Boy as Whitley either slept or listened to her headphones. We stopped for lunch in an area called the Valley. My sister wanted to grab fast food and stay on the road, but my mom called the shots and we stopped in Athens, Pennsylvania. My mom wanted to explore the town and eat somewhere local. We parked at the small downtown park, and we created our own shortcut and walked through a flower garden. The fall flowers were ready to bloom. The orange and dark-red chrysanthemums were the first flowers to start to show their autumn colors. My mom peeked in all store windows. The townspeople stared back at her. We walked for a few blocks before stopping at a small café.

My mom pushed two tables together as the locals rolled their eyes at her. She took over the place and acted as if we were at Kermit's. Old men sat at the counter, reading the paper, unaware that the boy on the front page was in their presence. My sister bought a *USA Today* to read what the world was saying about the boy sitting across from her. She quietly read, then she burst into laughter and looked at me. She pointed to my name in the paper, and it read "Chuck Smith," not "Carson Smith." I tried to laugh it off, but my mom gave away my disappointment when she said, "Don't worry, honey, we all know it was you." History was written for Chuck Smith, not Carson Smith, and I feared one day I would have trouble explaining I was on the team that broke the Little League World Series drought for the United States.

I excused myself and found the bathroom. I tried to cry alone, and I asked my dad to leave when he came to check on me. He left as I requested, and I began to cry out loud. I clenched my fist, and I thought about punching the wall. "No one will ever know it was me!" I shouted at the back of the bathroom stall door. I openly sobbed with my hands over my eyes.

My isolation did not last long, as an old man with dark glasses walked in. He asked, "What is wrong?"

I told him, "It is unfair that I, Carson Smith, contributed and I sacrificed my summer to be a sidekick whose name was misspelled." I told him how our summer unfolded in less than five minutes. I felt foolish as I recapped everything so quickly. It no longer seemed important. The stranger surely did not care about baseball and my summer as I did.

The old man said, "Would you do it all over again knowing that the history books may not acknowledge you?"

I said yes, then he patted my shoulder and walked out.

I stood in front of the mirror and looked at myself. I did not recognize the boy staring back with red eyes. My shoulders no longer sagged, and I stood tall. My transformation was far from complete, but I could feel the outer layer peeling off for the first time. The pimples peeking through my cheeks were not a concern. Carson Smith was a champion. I leaned in closer to the mirror, and I spoke directly to the boy looking back at me. "You are a champion!" My smile swelled with pride. My pep talk to myself worked, and I began to believe I was important. My name was misspelled, and history would likely forget about me, but those that I held in high esteem knew I warmed up Drake Duckworth between innings at the Little League World Series.

I regained my composure, and I exited the bathroom. Wyatt was throwing the newspaper in the garbage. Wyatt said, "Carson, you look different."

I told him, "I am different. From now on, Carson Smith is not hanging his head."

Wyatt laughed. "Carson Smith, Little League World Series champion." He put his arm over my shoulder, and we walked back to the table. We did not speak of my outburst again.

We left Athens, but not before I saw the same old man walking in the park with a service dog. He did not see me wave at him as we rode by. The hotel was not much farther, and our journey to Cooperstown was nearly complete. My mom drove the rest of the way, and my dad slept. Whitley asked Wyatt, "What are you going to wear on *Letterman*?"

He shrugged and said, "No idea."

My mom gasped and said, "I'll get you something."

We arrived at the hotel just after two in the afternoon. Whitley, Wyatt, and I explored the Holiday Inn, but we only found brochures. I grabbed a Hall of Fame brochure, and we went back to our room.

My parents booked adjoining rooms. Wyatt and I shared one room, with my parents and sister sharing the other. We unpacked, then fell down on the bed to watch TV. I turned it to ESPN just as they finished showing highlights of our game. Wyatt insisted we watch something else. He fell asleep as I roamed the channels.

My mom entered our room, then instructed me, "Wake him up."

I tapped him on the shoulder, and he jumped up. "What now?" he asked.

My mom wanted to take him shopping. Whitley and my dad stayed behind to swim. She requested my mom buy something to entertain us. We went to the nearest outlet, and she dressed the baseball hero for his national appearance. She grabbed a Magic 8-Ball for my sister's entertainment. My mom told the cashier who Wyatt was as she checked out. She said, "Have you heard about the kid that hit the game-winning home run in the Little World Series championship game?" Then she pointed and said, "This his him." Wyatt shook the unimpressed college girl's hand, then grabbed his new outfit.

After dinner, Whitley came in our room and we watched TV. We played cards and chatted. Whitley began to mock Wyatt and me by asking her Magic 8-Ball absurd questions. She asked the Magic 8-Ball, "Will Carson ever have enough courage to talk to a girl?"

She then laughed uncontrollably when it answered, "Outcome not likely." Wyatt told her to stop, but she asked one more question. "Is Wyatt as good as he thinks?" It answered, "Can't predict now."

Wyatt told Whitley, "That is a kid's toy," then he went on to tell Whitley about EELNEB.

She did not believe it and claimed, "It is foolishness to believe in something so absurd." She tossed the Magic 8-Ball in the trash, then said, "It is nonsense, anyways, and not real magic."

My parents shouted from their room for Whitley to come and get in the bed. Wyatt and I started a card game of War that went on for about twenty minutes when he heard a quiet knock on the door. It was Whitley. She said, "I can't sleep. Can I just hang out?" We both agreed.

Wyatt and I decided to start a new game of War, and we included my sister. I muted the TV as it played a rerun of *In the Heat of the Night*. Whitley said, "I am not ready to go back to school." She did not want the summer to end either. She told us she was glad she missed the start of school. Whitley said, "During the summer, the only person I have to impress is Mom," as she pointed at me. I believe she secretly enjoyed the attention the baseball team was getting. Wyatt asked Whitley about her soccer teams. She said she did not want to talk about it. He tried to cheer her up, but she remembered Wyatt taunting her over her season-ending loss. She dreaded the idea of having to go back to put on a perfect smile.

I was eliminated from our game, and the two continued. Whitley began to harass Wyatt. Wyatt fired back at her insults, and the two began to argue about everything. Whitley questioned Wyatt's intelligence since he was always in detention; she felt he was able to cheat. I intervened and told her to shut her mouth or go back to her room. She stopped, and the two continued their game in silence.

It was after eleven a clock when my mom knocked on the door. She asked, "Whitley, what in the hell do you think you are doing?"

Whitley respond with her usual eye roll, then said, "Oh god, Mom, we are just playing cards."

My mom looked at both Wyatt and me in disgust. She grabbed Whitley by her arm and said, "Okay, young lady, time for bed." She snapped at us and demanded we go to sleep. I apologized and turned off the TV.

Wyatt and I fell asleep shortly after my mom's episode.

The next morning, we headed to the Hall of Fame after breakfast. It was not busy, and the tourist season was over in Cooperstown. It seemed we were the only people interested in the museum. The Major League Baseball strike had detoured the normal tourist away from Cooperstown. Baseball fans now were clamoring for the NFL, as baseball had become an afterthought until Wyatt brought it back. Whitley stayed by my dad's side as Wyatt and I bounced from exhibit to exhibit. Wyatt wanted to see the newest inductees' information. He was enamored with the newly elected Reggie Jackson and asked my mom to take his picture in front of his Hall of Fame bust. I had my picture taken in front of Ty Cobb's and Babe Ruth's busts.

Just before we exited the Hall of Fame, Wyatt asked, "Who do you think I am most like, Cobb, Ruth, Mantle, or Williams?"

I did not know how to answer, and I told him, "I don't know." He demanded an answer, and I said, "You're all of them to me. You're ruthless like Cobb, and you'll do anything to win. You are like Ted Williams because you crave the title of the best. You play the game with a smile and exuberance like Mantle. You're Ruth because baseball is easy for you and there is nothing you can't do on a baseball field. We all envy you because you can do special things on a baseball field."

He thanked me, then said, "I just want to be me."

A New Name

We woke up, then headed for New York City. My dad stopped and grabbed coffee, and we ate fast-food biscuits. We had an over five-hour trip ahead of us; thus, we all tried to sleep. My dad drove the entire trip. My mom barely spoke, and she gazed at the passing cars. The night before, I heard shouting from their room and Whitley crying. She sat in the back and said nothing as well. It felt like we were heading to a funeral and not New York City.

Wyatt, my dad, and I decided to play the baseball name game. The game went on long enough for both my mom and Whitley to fall asleep. My dad asked Wyatt, "How will you describe the moment?" Wyatt was puzzled and said nothing, then my dad said, "You're going to be asked to tell the story for a long time."

Wyatt said, "I am not sure. How would you describe it?"

My dad advised Wyatt to close his eyes and imagine the moment as if he were in the stands, watching. Wyatt asked my advice, and I told him, "I missed it because I had my eyes closed."

We all three laughed, until my mom said, "Huuuuusssssshhhhh." We were barely able to contain our laughter since no one dared wake her.

Whitley woke up, and we stopped the conversation. We drove for a while longer, and my dad asked us typical dad questions. He wanted to know our favorite subject, our favorite song, our favorite movie, our favorite baseball player, and our opinions on the new school. We all agreed the new school would suck. Whitley was excited Ruby would be gone.

We stopped one last time just outside of New York City, and the skyline was now within our view. The skyscrapers blocked the horizon, and the sun was on the back side of the buildings. Shadows surely covered the sidewalks, and the citizens must've walked in darkness most of the time. Swansville seemed like it could fit inside one city block. We were a long way from the safe waters of Cubbie Cove.

We checked in to a massive hotel that looked like it was built two hundred years ago. The front desk treated us like royalty. The bellhops addressed Wyatt and me as Mr. Hartley and Mr. Smith. The bellhops carried our bags as my sister, Wyatt, and I gazed upon the first-class hotel. We meandered in the lobby while we waited for my parents. We went straight to the brochure rack, and we all three grabbed one of each attraction. The three of us rode the elevator to the top floor, and we looked down on the biggest city in the world.

We did not have adjoining rooms, but instead we would share a suite on the eleventh floor. My dad opened the door to our room, and on the counter were three gift baskets and a dozen roses for my sister and my mom from *The David Letterman Show*. Each basket contained a shirt and a signed letter. My mother and father were suddenly back on speaking terms, and all was fine. Wyatt called his mother and excitedly described the room. My dad and mom looked over the instructions on getting to and from the theater for *The Late Show*. We ordered room service, and we ate our dinner in our pajamas. My dad and mom shared a bottle of wine while sitting by the window overlooking the traffic below.

We all went to bed early. Wyatt and I lay in our beds, chatting about our summer. Whitley joined us, and she sat on the floor at the foot of Wyatt's bed. We whispered for over an hour, and the mood was lugubrious. Wyatt's appearance tomorrow seemed to mark the unofficial end to our summer. The following day, we would head back to the Brown Water and our lives would go back to normal. Whitley fell asleep on the floor. Wyatt carried Whitley to her bed as I led the way to her room.

Room service brought up a feast for our morning breakfast. My parents only drank coffee and ate toast. They were sluggish, and Whitley, Wyatt, and I bounced around with excitement. My parents both kept telling us, "Please settle down." We quickly showered and dressed for *The Late Show*. A limousine drove us to the theater, and we had the privilege of experiencing New York City traffic. It took us twenty minutes to drive six blocks. The big city excited my mother, and she spoke of booking an actual vacation next summer, not just a two-day trip.

Wyatt was approached the moment he set foot in the theater. He was ushered away, and my family cluelessly stood idle while we waited for our instructions. Wyatt had very little time for his rehearsal before going on live. He was introduced to David Letterman, and I saw the boy and the talk show host shake hands. A man with a microphone in his ear took us to Wyatt's dressing room and asked if we would prefer to watch the show from backstage or from the audience. Whitley and I agreed to stay backstage, but our parents wanted to sit in the audience.

Whitley and I waited in the dressing room for Wyatt to finish his rehearsal. I paced while waiting for his arrival. The musical guest stopped in to say hello to the baseball hero. Whitley and I had them sign our *Late Show* shirts. Pearl Jam was scheduled to sing their hit song "Go" after Wyatt's interview.

Wyatt returned, and David Letterman poked his head through the door to say hello. My parents had front-row seats for Wyatt's national coronation. Wyatt was speaking a mile a minute. He was nervous despite his denial. He was confident, and he told us he had his story ready. He said the reason he was nervous was the actor Gary Sinus told him that Letterman was bad about surprising his guest with an unrehearsed question.

We played cards to try to distract Wyatt, but he kept asking, "What do you think he will ask?" We could hear Pearl Jam strumming their guitars through the wall. Whitley looked at Wyatt and asked, "Do you want their autograph?" He nodded. We walked to their door, and she knocked on the door. Eddie Vedder opened the door. He immediately asked us to come in. Before Whitley could ask them for their autograph, Eddie Vedder asked for Wyatt's. Wyatt and the band traded autographs. We heard a knock on Wyatt's dressing room door, and the stagehand said, "Five minutes." We said goodbye to the band and left.

Wyatt began to rapidly talk again. I told him, "It will be okay," then asked him to settle down.

He said, "Easy for you to say, Worm." He used my Duckworth nickname, and I felt like a lesser person. He paced the green room and rubbed his eyes.

Whitley told him, "Stop, or it will look like you've been crying."

Wyatt did not look like a boy about to be showered in applause by a national audience, but a boy headed to a guillotine. The stage-hand stuck his head through the door and said, "You are up, slugger." His eyes were full of consternation as he walked out of the room. Whitley grabbed him by his wrist and pulled him close, and she whispered something in his ear. A coy smile came over him, and he followed the stagehand to face the world for the first time.

"Our next guest is the hero of the Little League World Series. Please welcome Wyatt 'Home Run' Hartley!" David Letterman gave Wyatt a nickname that he would never be able to shake. Wyatt wore a gray shirt and blue jeans. My mom wanted him to look casual but confident. He awkwardly waved to unfamiliar fans as he walked across the stage before taking a seat.

Dave Letterman asked Wyatt, "So I heard you've had a pretty exciting summer."

Wyatt responded, "Yes." He looked intimidated, but I knew he would gain his composure and answer each question thought-fully. Wyatt told the crowd, "I was able to live every Little Leaguer's dream."

Letterman said, "A lot of baseball fans feel like you have given the greedy professionals and team owners something to think about as they negotiate for next season."

It was just the beginning of Wyatt being portrayed as the kid who would help save baseball.

Letterman pulled out a *USA Today* with Wyatt on the front page, then asked, "Did you ever think you'd be on front page of the *USA Today*? And will you sign it?"

Wyatt responded, "No and no. The article, recapping every-thing, incorrectly called one of our key teammates Chuck and not his name, Carson."

Letterman and the audience were speechless from the stubborn twelve-year-old's comments.

Wyatt said, "Carson is backstage, and he deserves to be recognized properly. He came through when we needed him most."

David Letterman summoned me to the stage, and the spotlight followed me to the chair beside my best friend. Whitley looked at me and shook her head. Wyatt explained to the audience and everyone watching at home that he and I practically went everywhere with each other since the baseball season began. Wyatt looked directly at the camera then said, "Friendships are what I will remember most about this summer and not the home run."

They played the clip of Wyatt's home run, and he looked uncomfortable watching himself. His face was pale, and his normally defiant smile was gone.

Letterman then asked Wyatt, "How did you feel when jogging the bases, knowing the entire country was watching?"

Wyatt sighed and said, "It was unbelievable, and I thought about how quickly the summer had gone by and tomorrow morning it would be over. I jogged slower than normal, hoping to safeguard our summer from the pending autumn."

Letterman responded, "You heard it here. This kid ended summer."

The crowd jokingly booed. Wyatt thanked the crowd and *The Late Show* for allowing him to extend his summer another week. Wyatt smiled, then said, "I hope I don't have a mountain of homework to make up for when I start school." The audience gave him a standing ovation, and we bowed as the show went to commercial break.

We sat backstage and listened to Pearl Jam. I was still nervous, and I was still openly shaking. Wyatt put his arm over my shoulder and squeezed. I stopped shaking for a moment. Wyatt's shoulders were back, and his chest poked out. He was famous, and he knew it. Whitley said very little, and she seemed upset with me. I asked, "Are you okay?" She answered, "Of course," but she sat with her arms crossed. Wyatt had pulled me onstage so I could feel like a hero for a few moments, but I envied him. The gods had given me a brain, but they gave Wyatt a bat that clapped thunder. His bat was more valued than my brain. Wyatt had a talent that would always be revered. He respected it, but he also took it for granted because it was so easy.

My mom and dad joined us backstage and told us, "Y'all were great." My mom was in a hurry and wanted to leave. She was in New York City, but she had little time to explore.

My parents took us to the Empire State Building after we left *The Late Show*. Wyatt, Whitley, and I looked over the city, and I felt like we were on top of the world. Whitley was impressed, too, despite her comment: "Why does it even matter?"

Wyatt laughed as he said, "I can see why King Kong came here. It is astonishing to look over a place you love."

Our New York City excursion was short but impactful.

The following morning, we left and headed back to a Swansville. Wyatt and I slept nearly the entire way as my parents took turns driving us home. We did not stop as my parents drove straight through the night. I woke up, then rubbed my eyes, but the clock was still blurry. I was disoriented, and the minivan was completely silent. I asked my dad, "Where are we?"

His voice sounded gray as he raspingly said, "Almost home."

Our summer was spent in cars almost as much as it was on baseball fields. We were driving home under the cover of darkness to no fanfare. I felt like we were sneaking back home after breaking curfew. My dad whispered, "Go back to sleep." The hum of the van's tires made it difficult to drift back to sleep. I looked over my shoulder to see Wyatt and Whitley sleeping back-to-back. The strength of the other made them sleep comfortably in the world's most uncomfortable minivan.

We reached the Brown Water in the early morning hours. Wyatt stayed at our house until the exhausting eighteen-hour trip's effects wore off. We dropped him off at his house after five, and I told him, "See you tomorrow at school." He smiled, then gave us a propitious wave.

Wyatt's mother met him on the steps of the gray house and hugged him.

Home

School started for everyone on August 22. The team's first day of school was ten days later. Wyatt and I started the Tuesday after Labor Day, a few days after the rest of the team, due to the trip to New York. Summer seemed like it was finally over, although it flashed by. School and our lives would never be the same. Our classes would no longer be overcrowded, and now friends, rivals, and teammates were separated.

Troy, Curt, Dale, Preston, and Anthony would follow Ruby into the shiny, new halls of Stoney Creek Middle School. Their arrival was announced over the intercom their first day back. They were all welcomed as heroes. They became our rivals the moment they entered school. Ruby would be back on top, but his reign would be at another school. Stoney Creek Middle School started with only the sixth and seventh grade; thus, Ruby was not just at the top of the seventh grade, but he would also be in command of the school for two years.

The new school held a pep rally the first Friday our teammates were back, and their principal even invited the rest of the team. Principal Overstreet denied the request, and we were captive between the old walls of Swansville Middle School. The new school's gym was jam-packed with both students and parents. The pep rally began with the Stoney Creek principal announcing to the cheering crowd, "Your 1994 Little League World Series champions!" The school hung its first banner in the gym, claiming the Little League World Series title. A picture and profile of our new rivals hung just below the shiny, new scoreboard paid for by Harrison Toyota.

Coach Alex led what was left of the team out of the locker room to cheers as confetti showered down on them. Coach Alex was the first to speak, and his first statement was, "This is our championship. These boys and Travis brought this championship to all of you." The student body erupted, and Coach Alex took a long pause to inhale in the cheers. His lungs filled with triumph, and he began his victory speech. Coach Alex, per usual, spoke of perfection and how this was the perfect place and time. He rambled on to no one's surprise. Ruby even rolled his eyes at his father's barely tolerable boasting. Coach Alex's arrogance was not only accepted but also promoted at the new school. The Stoney Creek Middle School staff and parents looked down on those of us at Swansville Middle School. We were now second-class citizens to our wealthier neighbors.

Ruby addressed the crowd after his father. He did not say too much, as he had learned from his long-winded father. Ruby spoke clearly and told the crowd of how *he* was the hero. He had become a false idol to his new classmates, but the cheering crowd was not in stands. They needed a hero to hang on to, and he would be it. His dad applauded, and they both must've forgotten who had hit the home run. I am sure Ruby deep down knew why and how we had won. Ruby was not a follower, and now he was set to lead again. Ruby had always been our leader, until the day Wyatt walked into our second-period math class. He was a good leader, despite his shortcomings. Ruby would now be leading the Stoney Creek Black Knights and not the Swansville Red Raiders.

After the pep rally, the school had an ice cream social to celebrate. The ice cream was provided by Alex and Vanessa Harrison. She was the school's first PTO president, and the new school's registers were filled by Harrison Toyota dollars. Ruby and our teammates were treated like kings. While the ice cream social was taking place, they were interviewed by their fellow classmates. They would be on the front page of the first issue of *The Knight Times*, the new school's newspaper.

Troy answered most of the silly questions with even sillier answers. A sixth-grade girl asked, "What is Wyatt like?" Troy answered, "Like me, just not as awesome." Wyatt was a mystery to some of these kids, and Troy never elaborated when asked questions about the phenom. Another student asked Ruby, "Do you think you could've struck out Wyatt?" and he confidently lied, "I can strike out anyone, and I did once." Ruby did not want to answer questions about Wyatt, and in his eyes, he was more important. Preston gladly told every detail he could remember, and Curt made sure everyone knew of their heroic moments.

Stoney Creek Middle School would feed the new high school that was set to open in two years. Ruby would ultimately become the first star for the high school Black Knights. He was up to the challenge, and he became our biggest adversary. He would be the school's first giant. Ruby, Ogre, and Wyatt would battle one another for the next six years. Everything at Stoney Creek Middle School was shiny and new, while those of us that were still Red Raiders would need to appreciate the beauty of an old school with its creaky wooden floors. Our trophy case did not recognize our accomplishment. We were the Castaways now.

I nervously walked back into Swansville Middle School two weeks after the first official day. I felt like a new student, and Wyatt looked like he owned the old place. Less than a year ago, Wyatt was the new kid in class, but now he was known not only school-wide but across the United States as well. He was credited with keeping baseball alive while MLB was on strike. MLB would need another savior soon. Thankfully, a Cub and a Cardinal would come to the rescue. *The Swansville Orator* would have an entire issue dedicated to our summer hitting the newsstands next Wednesday, and we all assumed Wyatt would be its focus. Everyone in school wanted to talk to him except those of us that had spent the summer watching his transformation.

Ogre struggled down the hallway on crutches, and Wyatt helped carry his books. The two would be late for first period for different reasons. Wyatt was openly cheered, and high fives and hugs would make him late for every class. Ogre and Wyatt had four of our six classes together that year, and the man-child and the phenom began to become close friends. Ogre needed Wyatt's confidence and voice just as I once did. I would hardly see either of them at school. I needed to rely on the lessons I learned from him and begin to apply them right away. Unfortunately, I had my sister in every class, and she took over as I knew she would. It was the first time since the second grade she and I shared the same teachers. It was easy for Whitley to be in charge without Ruby or Wyatt to challenge her. She would go back to ignoring every boy and being loved by all our teachers. It would be a long year living in her shadow.

Just after the tardy bell rang for first period, Principal Overstreet loudly announced Wyatt's arrival on the intercom, disrupting the entire school. She said, "I'd like to have everyone's attention and let everyone know that Little League World Series hero and MVP Wyatt Hartley has returned." Wyatt had not even made it to class yet. Principal Overstreet and Wyatt had spent the last few months of the previous school year as adversaries, but now she openly championed him. I wondered who felt more awkward when she praised him that first day back. The halls were flooded with cheers from each classroom after the announcement. The entire school and country were enamored with him. He would need to learn to adjust to constant adoration.

We did not have a pep rally or an ice cream social. Principal Overstreet was tough and no-nonsense; however, she came over the intercom in sixth period and asked for all the school's televisions to be turned on in ten minutes. The gym, band, and shop classes were directed to report to the media center. At 2:35, all of Swansville Middle School's televisions tuned in to watch Wyatt's big moment and a few of the moments that led up to his coronation. The entire school was silent. It was eerie; it was as if we were about to witness a tragedy.

A short video showed some newspaper clippings as well as candid pictures of the team. Missy never left her house without her camera, and she had secretly snapped pictures all summer. I grinned from ear to ear as a picture of the day I transformed into Lightning flashed across the screen. My teeth were clenched and my eyes squinted as I slid through the dirt confetti that day. I looked around, hoping my classmates knew it was me. My moment seemed a lifetime ago. Whitley focused on the television, as if she had not witnessed most of the summer in person. I looked over at Drake when a photo of him standing stoically on the mound was on the screen. He was uninterested, and he did not even look at the television as he doodled. Pictures of our former teammates seemed out of place. They had left, and now they were our enemy. The slideshow of our summer went by too quickly. I was unsatisfied; the video missed so much.

The video of the newspaper clippings and the pictures finished, then the ESPN video began. It was not the first time Wyatt had to watch his home run, nor would it be his last. The ESPN clip started with Wyatt striking out the side before he strolled to the plate. The ESPN announcer magnified the moment as Wyatt stepped in the batter's box. I remembered watching it from the dugout, and I oddly became nervous again even though I now knew the outcome. My heart began to race. I remember feeling like time stopped when the ball left the Japanese pitcher's hand. The video was in slow motion until the ball jumped off Wyatt's bat. The angle of the camera as the ball sailed over the fence showed Ruby standing next to me on the dugout steps. The school erupted in cheers, and the halls were flooded despite the dismissal bell not having rung. The old school seemed to shake, as if it were an earthquake. I ran into the hallway, looking for Wyatt and my teammates. He was nowhere to be found.

Wyatt stayed behind and helped Ogre. He knew everyone wanted to see him. Everyone was not his concern. Ogre had given Wyatt an excuse for staying behind. His epic home run had just early dismissed Swansville Middle School, and no teacher or Principal Overstreet seemed to care. Everyone grows up wanting a hero moment, and Wyatt got his when he was twelve years old for all the world to see. Drake did not get up from his desk when the mayhem started. He waited for the dismissal bell. I ran through the halls, looking for my friends, and I only found Mitch, and for a moment I wished Ruby were there to bow for us all. The dismissal bell finally rang after the five minutes of chaos. The halls were clear except for Wyatt and Ogre as the two headed for the bus parking lot. Ogre limped, and Wyatt walked slowly, disguising his anxiety by carrying Ogre's books. All seven school buses left the parking lot chanting, "Home Run Hartley!"

Cheers and accolades would follow Wyatt from that moment forward.

Last Dance

Our remaining years in middle school raced by, and in the blink of an eye, we were set to play our last middle school baseball game. We did not look the same, as hairs began to poke out one by one on our chins. Everyone had forgotten or they did not seem to care of our Little League World Series heroics. A few of us remained friends, but our connection kept all of us close. We always acknowledged one another when passing in the hallways. Wyatt struggled our last year of middle school. He was still the most dominant boy in our grade, but he never seemed to fulfil all the expectations. The spotlight was on my sister more than ever, and she was the darling of the entire school. Wyatt became more defiant, and detention became his home.

The middle school championship baseball game conflicted with our last middle school dance. Friday, May 13, seemed fitting for those of us still relying on luck with eighth-grade girls. We had less than one month before school was out, and our last dance as kings of the school was more important to most of us than a baseball game. Winning another conference championship and the conference tournament compared very little to our Little League World Series title. Almost everything after it seemed insignificant. We only lost one game the previous season, and it was a fluke. We were undefeated, and the championship was a forgone conclusion despite our best player being suspended.

The school policy was, if any student athlete was suspended from school, then he or she would also be suspended from the next game. Principal Overstreet was more than ready for Wyatt to move on to high school. Wyatt had been a thorn in her side for the last two years. The principal and the student battled frequently, but she had a soft spot for the baseball player. Wyatt was suspended earlier in the week for nearly fighting. He was apprehended holding a new student by the throat.

Amos Campbell was kicked out of Stoney Creek Middle School, and his sentence was the Brown Water. Swansville Middle School become a dumping ground for the unwanted troublemakers from the other side of Cubbie Cove. Troy warned everyone that Amos would be a problem. Troy said, "Amos personified the big water, and Pisgah Lake was still not big enough for him." Amos had failed a grade and was a year older than nearly everyone. He was not bigger than anyone despite his age. His parents objected of Amos being exiled to being a lowly Red Raider. Alex and Vanessa Harrison did not like Amos. The Harrisons were the catalysts in exiling Amos after he and Ruby were caught setting fire to a trash can. Amos would not be around for long, as his parents decided to move back to the big city once the school year ended. Neither Swansville nor Stoney Creek was good enough for the Campbells.

Amos openly taunted everyone as the poor brown-water people. He would spit out water from the school's water fountains as he said, "Oh god, another roach came out with the brown water." He was instantly hated. Wyatt tried to ignore the smaller older boy, but it was impossible. Amos was the exact opposite of Wyatt. Wyatt had embraced the Brown Water, and when someone openly disgraced the town he loved, they were in his crosshairs. Amos did not care who Wyatt had been, much less who he had become in the year or so since.

Amos started an argument with Kandi Frederick. The tenacious redhead would not back down from Amos's insults. She stood up for the Red Raiders and Swansville. She was not intimidated by anyone. Amos mocked her speech until Ogre exited the locker room. Ogre ran to her side, but he was not a fighter. Amos was not scared of Ogre. He must've known Ogre would not even consider throwing a punch. I, too, was a coward and watched as Amos told Ogre, "I bet you wish your brain filled out your giant skull." Ogre tried to calm Kandi. She threatened to hurt Amos. "At theast he doesn't have thit for thrains, and Th'll knock what you have out." Amos cackled at how Kandi spoke. Wyatt ran and grabbed Amos by the throat and held him against the gym wall. Coach Cass exited the locker room and immediately saw Wyatt holding the smaller new kid by the throat. Kandi begged Coach Cass to spare Wyatt. Her pleas were ignored.

Wyatt and Amos were ushered to Principal Overstreet's office. Amos asked the principal, "Does everyone bully the new kid at this school?" Amos even painted a picture of Wyatt telling the class to lie for him. Amos had discounted any testimony from Kandi or Ogre. It was not unusual for Kandi to be in the center of some drama. She thrived in it. Wyatt said nothing except, "He's been here a week, and he's caused problems with everyone." Principal Overstreet asked me what I saw, and I corroborated Ogre and Kandi's story. It did little good when Amos's mother threatened a lawsuit. She said, "That bully might have damaged my son's vocal cords." Amos ultimately was not suspended, and Wyatt was given a two-day suspension. He missed the semifinal baseball game, and he was not permitted to play in the championship. Principal Overstreet let Wyatt ride the bus, but he was not even allowed to dress out for the game.

Wyatt did not want to even attend the championship. Ogre told him, "You stood up for us. You're our champion. We can't do it without you there." Wyatt agreed to attend. Ogre started and dominated our former rival, the East Uwharrie Dragons. Ruby and the Black Knights were anointed our new rivals despite being handily beaten each game. Drake led us at the plate, driving in four runs. We won with ease 9–1. Wyatt sat silently in the dugout.

The bus ride home from our games was usually one of the perks. Coach Asher always played music, and we stopped at a McDonald's. East Uwharrie hosted the conference tournament. East Uwharrie was over forty-five minutes away, and it would be tough for us to get back to the dance with any time to spare. Coach Asher insisted we stop for fast food on the way back. We all begged him not to stop. RJ pleaded and said, "Let's just get the food to go." Coach Asher defied everyone. Wyatt did not care if we made it to the dance since he was not permitted to attend. He sided with Coach Asher, and he ignored our boos.

Coach Asher agreed to let us order and eat on the bus if he could get five volunteers to help clean the bus. Drake volunteered, then the rest of us agreed that three seventh graders would stay along with Wyatt to help clean. Wyatt said, "No way! I've paid my penance today." Ogre raised his hand to take Wyatt's place. I felt guilty for not volunteering, but I wanted to walk into the dance a champion.

The dance would be over at ten, and if we were lucky, we would get just over an hour. We entered through the bus parking lot doors, and we strutted in like we were celebrities. I carried the championship trophy in, and I expected to be swarmed like a rock star. I was wrong, as no one even noticed our triumphant entrance. Two of the reasons we had the championship were on the bus, cleaning. Wyatt walked through the doors, trying to hide from Principal Overstreet. She approached the team to congratulate us on our accomplishment and to make sure Wyatt did not try to sneak in to the dance. Wyatt broke away from the group almost immediately, and he walked sorrowfully to the pay phone. He called his uncle to pick him up. He exited the commons area and sat alone on the curb in front of the school doors.

The first person I saw was Whitley. She was slow-dancing with Amos as the song "Wonderwall" finished the last chorus. She had her head on his shoulder, and our eyes met. She looked guilty, but she grinned anyway. I searched the dance floor for my crush, and she, too, was dancing with another boy. I had hoped if I carried the trophy into the dance, I would be validated for being a part of another winning team. Sadly, no one seemed to care of our baseball accomplishments anymore, especially fourteen-year-old girls.

Revenge

Our sophomore year, I played shortstop and batted third for the junior varsity. I shone, but no one was there to see it. I led the freshman and those unable to make the varsity team. I almost gave up baseball as a tenth grader since I was left behind, as all my friends moved up to varsity. Wyatt and Ogre played varsity baseball as a freshman. Wyatt assimilated to the varsity team and the upperclassman way of life with ease. He was immediately accepted, and his brashness was encouraged. He was invited to all the upperclassman parties, and for a year he was a ghost at my house. Ogre still wanted to play on the same team with those of us left on the junior varsity, and he struggled to adjust being the biggest but the youngest. He was by far the biggest kid on the team as a freshman, but his size mattered little to the juniors and seniors he looked up to. It was the last time, I believe, Wyatt was not the true leader of the Swansville Red Raiders.

Ruby was the leader of the Stoney Creek Black Knights. The Black Knights stayed in the cellar of our conference in every sport. They were at a disadvantage due to the school only having a freshman class and sophomore class. Each year the school added another class of students, but Ruby and our old teammates were the upperclassman at all times. Our sophomore year was their first year of varsity sports. They were the whipping boys of the conference in every sport. I felt sad for them because they were always overmatched from the beginning. I knew the feeling well.

Our sophomore year, Wyatt began to seize control of the leadership of the varsity baseball team despite the best efforts of the only senior, Johnny Stevens. Johnny was the last link to a team that had a deep playoff run three years earlier. He had been the backup catcher and left fielder on the team that lost in the state semifinals. Johnny was good, and he would brag about his freshman year if the opportunity arose. Johnny and Wyatt clashed. Johnny looked and acted the exact opposite of Wyatt. Johnny was fair-skinned, and the sun seemed to be his enemy. He hid from the sun in his catcher's gear. He hit for a high average and only had one varsity home run. He was a vocal leader, whereas Wyatt did not seem to take the game seriously. He seemed to give a speech after each inning. He annoyed more than just Wyatt with his constant "Ra Ra" speeches. Johnny worked hard to be the baseball player he was, whereas Wyatt was born with natural abilities. Wyatt was Johnny's backup catcher even though Wyatt was far superior behind home plate. Johnny even wore Wyatt's number 13. Coach Charles always sided with his only senior, and the team had terrible chemistry.

Johnny did not like Wyatt. Johnny cared about winning more than anyone on the team, and he constantly referenced the team from his freshman year. Johnny would challenge the five sophomores on the team and even seemed ready to fight. Drake, Jaxon, Ogre, and RJ never entertained him. Wyatt, on the other hand, would go toe to toe with the smaller Johnny Stevens. Johnny would look up at Wyatt's chin and turn his knuckles outward as if he was ready to swing at any moment. Wyatt laughed him off and would tell him it was just a game. Johnny played baseball as if his next meal depended on it. The only thing the two had in common was the two argued and fought with the umpires constantly.

Ogre was the team's best pitcher. He was still a special talent on the mound, but the growing pains he felt as a freshman stunted his growing confidence. He towered over everyone in school. Ogre's bat had been dormant for a year, but there were glimpses of his home run abilities returning. Ogre was nervous at the plate and on the mound. Johnny tried to talk the oversize boy up, but it did little good. Jack sat in the crowd with Duckworth, trying to figure out how to get him to hit again. Home runs were rare, but a year later, he found his stroke and confidence began to return.

Wyatt was the designated hitter and the occasional left fielder. He rarely got to squat behind home plate. Wyatt had catcher's legs, and his catcher's eyes struggled to pick up fly balls. Wyatt struggled in the outfield, but not at the plate. Wyatt hit a school-record nine home runs a year after hitting four as a freshman. The crowds came out to the varsity baseball games, and the school brought in additional bleachers for fans to watch the young prodigy chase the school record. Flashbacks to the summer when we were twelve were everywhere, and *The Swansville Orator* took notice of the baseball team. Wyatt's stardom was once again upon us with no end in sight. My sister's dominance on the soccer field was the only thing that challenged Wyatt for front-page supremacy.

Coach Alex and Ruby struggled with coping up with the losses. Ruby argued with his dad more than ever, and it only intensified with each loss. The pair had rarely lost when we played baseball as kids, and neither knew how to be the underdog. Coach Alex's remedy was to get special coaching to help his giant of a son. Coach Alex reached out to an ex-major leaguer to help Ruby. Ruby's private tutor was at best a mediocre former major league middle reliever and semi-con artist named Curtis Watts. Curtis bounced around the majors for six seasons but came back to his hometown of Charlotte. He drifted up to Swansville when his hometown figured out he was just a lowly con artist. Curtis opened up batting cages around Charlotte and offered private instructions. He took the money for his private lessons, but his unqualified assistants taught the hitting and pitching lessons. The paying customers wanted the ex-big leaguer to coach their kids, not batting cage attendants. They paid big money for it, but they were duped. The pamphlet's fine print stated Curtis Watts might be unavailable for the nonrefundable lessons.

Curtis found Coach Alex and Ruby. Coach Alex desired for Ruby to dominate again, and Curtis desired cash. Curtis gladly took the cash while teaching Ruby how to pitch like a big leaguer. Curtis's wallet expanded as Ruby's pitching knowledge did; Curtis taught Ruby the unwritten rules of the mound. Ruby learned how to doctor a baseball and how to play mind games with batters. Ruby stopped growing in the tenth grade, and Curtis took aim on the brain of a shrinking giant. Ruby knew how to throw hard and how to paint the corners with breaking balls, but he did not know how to get into the batter's head.

Ruby was the player stuck between good and great. The things that had made him good would prevent him from being great. Ruby stopped growing at sixteen, and he had to use the fundamentals his dad had taught him when he was a foot taller than everyone except Ogre. Ruby's lifelong dream was to pitch for the Yankees, and each year that passed, he became more hittable. Curtis Watts came to help Ruby at the perfect moment. Ruby needed the nefarious lessons to regain his dominance. I doubted he would ever make it to the major leagues, and I felt sorry for him at times. One day his boasting would catch up to him.

We played the Black Knights twice during the regular season. Ruby only pitched five of the twelve innings, but it did not matter, as we cruised to easy victories. Wyatt was four-for-four against Ruby. Wyatt had driven in five runs when Ruby was on the mound as he still owned the giant. The Swansville Red Raiders finished first in the conference behind Johnny, Ogre, and Wyatt. The town began to look forward to another long playoff run. Red Raider mascot logos were in the windows of every business and restaurant in town again.

The conference playoffs were hosted by Stoney Creek High School since this was their first full season with a brand-new base-ball field. The shiny, new school had everything. Time had faded Swansville High School more each passing year. We were all jealous of the shiny, new school, and it was hard not to blame our classmates that fled like refugees to a place that seemed destined for the future. The school had just installed lights prior to the conference playoffs. We were the top seed; thus, we had the opportunity to feast on the lowly Black Knights.

Ruby did not start the game, and Wyatt and company jumped out to an early lead. I sat in the bleachers and felt like a foreigner while cheering my classmates. Johnny Stevens shouted in the dugout, "Let's ride the donkey-donkey!" referencing a once-popular song. It had become the team anthem when they were winning. I assumed Johnny had learned it during his freshman year. The sophomore stars did not need motivation as they wanted to reclaim the title the Black

Knights had claimed when they stole our Little League World Series championship. The Red Raiders led 4–2 going into the top of the fourth. Ruby uncharacteristically hit a two-run home run to tie the game. The Swansville crowd was stunned just as the black clouds rolled in. We struggled to put the ball in play as Ruby was inserted in to pitch.

The rumor was, Ruby did not start due to an elbow injury. His elbow seemed fine as he mowed us down for two innings. His arrogant smile was still there after years of losing. The sky opened up just as the sixth inning began. The umpires held off calling the game, and the game went on while the new baseball field's lights clicked on. Ogre took the mound to shut the Black Knights down. Troy stepped in against Ogre. Ogre's would-be curveball hung up, and Troy sent a ball into the rainy night's sky. Wyatt lost it in the lights and the rain, and it fell to the ground without a play. Troy strutted to third base and later scored on a passed ball. Johnny shouted at Ogre as if it were his mistake. The Black Knights had the lead. The rain continued, and the umpires just wanted to get the game over. The rest of the inning went as Coach Charles had planned, and Ogre sat them down in order with little effort.

Ruby had a hard time gripping the ball just as Ogre had. The field looked like the bottom of a barn, with divots and mud everywhere. Drake and Jaxon reached on walks just after Ruby struck out the leadoff batter. Duckworth and Jack looked on, as they could see the coming drama between the two Little League rivals approaching. A rainy showdown was on the horizon. Neither Ruby nor Wyatt looked ready for it as the rain diluted the moment.

Wyatt stepped in the batter's box, and the bleachers rattled with thunder just as lightning struck the right field fence. The remaining crowd ran for cover. Both teams waited in the rain for the storm to pass. It never did. The playoff game would be postponed until the next afternoon, and the Black Knights only needed to get two more outs to have the school's biggest upset. A 4:30 p.m. showdown was scheduled to finish the bottom half of the sixth inning. It had been four years since the two rivals had a scheduled showdown of this magnitude.

The big-water fans from Stoney Creek and the Swansville Brown Water fans would have their shortest but most attended game. The animosity between the two schools existed from the first bell of Stoney Creek High School, but the rivalry was really born with less than half of an inning of baseball. The Swansville Red Raiders had clenched a state playoff berth, and the Stoney Creek Black Knights needed to win the conference tournament to have chance to even qualify. The Black Knights had to pull off a miracle. The Black Knights' miracle showed up wearing his iconic ruby-red baseball slippers. It had been several years since our Little League giant was transformed from Travis to Ruby. Travis embraced the nickname, and Ruby was all anyone except his mother and father called him.

The crowd attending a two-out game was enormous. I felt like something bad was about to happen. The air was thick, and the ground breathed steam. The sunflowers that welcomed everyone to Stoney Creek High School were still bent over from the weight of previous day's rain. My sister even attended the game. She and I sat together just behind the first-base dugout. She had missed the previous day's game while she was scoring three goals to lead the Red Raiders girls' soccer team to the conference championship. Whitley even went to chat with her old rival, Ruby, before the first pitch. I remember seeing her laugh at his evidently funny joke. It was awkward seeing her having a conversation with her childhood nemesis. I did not believe I was the only person to witness her brief encounter.

The new stadium whispered of "Home Run Hartley, Home Run Hartley" as the Swansville crowd readied to erupt with cheers as the ex-child prodigy stepped to the plate. Everyone in attendance expected to see another epic home run. Wyatt had grown tired off the chant, but it was beginning to be an echo in his life. I sat in the stands with my head down. I could not watch. He did not need a home run; he needed a single, and the game would be tied. I was just as nervous that day as I was the day of the Little League World Series game. It was the feeling of impending doom. Wyatt looked in the bleachers as he always did before stepping in the batter's box. Whitley looked on as I hid my face in my sweating palms.

Ruby did not seem to be looking at his catcher's signs but rather looking at his new pitching coach, Curtis Watts. Curtis and his dad stood just behind home plate. Ruby shook off his catcher's signs multiple times before stepping off the mound. Wyatt did not step out of the batter's box. Ruby stepped off the mound to regroup and stared down his rival. His eyes were red with aggression, and it was the same look I saw after he nearly decapitated me after my first infield single against him several years earlier.

Coach Alex shouted, "Perfection!" just as Ruby released his first pitch. Ruby's first pitch seemed to scream as it flew through the air. The pitch was high and tight, and Wyatt barely dodged the fastball headed for his right wrist. Wyatt moved the bat just in time to unintentionally foul off the near-ninety-mile-per-hour fastball. Ruby looked for Curtis again and ignored his catcher. Ruby's next pitch was in the exact same place, but Wyatt dropped to the ground to dodged the next pitch. Ruby was in control when the catcher threw the baseball back. Wyatt was rattled. He stood up and wipe off the wet dirt.

The count was one and one when Ruby threw a backdoor curveball over for a strike. I saw Wyatt flinch, and it was one of the few times he looked uncomfortable at the plate. Neither Wyatt nor half the fans agreed with the low and away pitch. Wyatt crowded the plate in anticipation for another pitch away. Ruby nearly hit Wyatt again. The two exchanged words, and the umpire intervened to settle everyone down. The familiar sound of boos floated down from every direction, and I had no idea of whom they were aimed at, Wyatt or Ruby. The two rivals knew boos as well as they did cheers of adoration. Ruby let loose another fastball aimed at Wyatt's head. Wyatt was nearly hit again, and the count ran to three balls and two strikes. Wyatt looked like he had been dragged through the mud as the damp batter's box left its mark.

Everyone was on their feet as the two sophomore baseball stars went toe to toe in front of everyone. The "Home Run Hartley" murmur was now a full-on chant. Ruby's next pitch hung over the plate, and Wyatt's bat sent it high into the sky but for a foul. The loud strike did not faze Ruby as he glared at his rival. I could barely watch, and my sister held her hands together as if in prayer. She was smiling when the ball left Ruby's fingertips. Ruby's next fastball was low and away, and the umpire emphatically called strike 3. Wyatt was in disbelief, and he questioned the umpire's strike zone. He had struck out with his bat sitting on his shoulder for strike 3. He rarely struck out, and he never went quietly back to the dugout. Cheers and boos erupted like confetti shot out of a party popper. Vanessa Harrison's cheers were the loudest. Coach Alex and Curtis smugly looked on in validation. Ruby pumped his fist as Wyatt entered the dugout.

Ruby stood tall after striking Wyatt out, but he still needed to finish off Johnny Stevens to preserve the win. The senior was not ready to give up. I knew it was over, and I hurried for the exit. My sister stayed to watch the remaining drama unfold. I begged her to leave with me, but she refused. She almost grinningly said, "I need to see this." I did not want to be around for the aftermath. I knew Wyatt would be uncontrollable. The crowd began to leave after Wyatt struck out, and they, too, assumed no heroes were left for the Swansville Red Raiders. Everyone was right. Johnny fouled off three balls before Ruby finished him off. The senior was no match for the sophomore giant.

Coach Charles and Wyatt argued after the game for all the remaining crowd to see. Wyatt fired insults in the direction of the umpire too. Wyatt narrowly escaped being ejected by the umpire after the game was over. Wyatt stayed in the dugout during the post-game handshakes, and Coach Alex arrogantly stared him down from the winning dugout. Coach Charles referenced this game the next several weeks as Johnny, Wyatt, and Ogre kept baseball on the tips of everyone's tongues with a deep playoff run. Coach Charles tried to convey the lesson of not overlooking an opponent to Wyatt. The lesson fell on deaf ears. We lost in the quarterfinals of the state playoffs, but the crystal ball for our baseball team indicated we had a bright future ahead of us.

The Stoney Creek Black Knights had upset the Swansville Red Raiders. Ruby hung around the field long after the game to bask in his own glory. Coach Alex and Curtis Watts somehow had taken down Wyatt. Ruby and the Black Knights lost the next game, and their season was over. Ruby had his revenge. The two rivals would battle for two more years, and Wyatt dominated Ruby from that game on.

Broken Spotlights

Wyatt was pushed back onto the main stage our junior year. After five years, he returned to being a star as if he had never left the night sky. The words *top prospect* began to describe him. The town had baseball fever again because of Wyatt and Ogre. Wyatt pushed my sister off the front page of our local paper. She was leading our high school soccer team for the third year and was on a collision course for a second straight state title. Wyatt was chasing records. Soccer success seemed inevitable, while another elusive baseball championship was becoming more attainable.

Wyatt was on a record home run pace. The previous summer, Sammy Sosa and Mark McGwire had reignited the lost love of baseball with their own record paces. Wyatt was closing the gap on the state record for home runs in a season. Every college in the country began to pursue the phenom. The previous season, he had broken the school and county record. Ogre pitched us deep into the state playoffs. Ogre was a rising star, but Wyatt's star shone brighter and higher. We were early favorites to win the state championship. Jacob and Rob Leonard came to every game but said nothing. Rob no longer watched from his car, and he stepped out of the shadows. The two had felt the magic when Jacob led the way two decades prior, and now the magic was drawing them back. Jacob and Rob were a side attraction at each game, as many of the locals wanted to shake their hands. The comments of Jacob's fastball and Rob's sweet swing floated aimlessly into the warm summer night sky.

The local papers seemed to mention Wyatt's heroics from when we were twelve in every article. Headlines like "Return of a Legend Home Run Hartley," "Once a Hero, Always a Hero," and simply "Home Run King" were frequent. When he was interviewed, he always deflected the attention to the team. He spoke about Ogre's and Jaxon's impact the most. I felt betrayed, but I understood. I was just a role player, and no one cared. Ogre, Jaxon, and the rest of us were footnotes in all the articles. Occasionally, an article would reference Ruby and the Black Knights, but Wyatt's success sold papers, not Ruby's losses. Wyatt tied the state record when he had a two-home run game in the second round of the state playoffs. The same weekend, Whitley scored four goals against a soccer powerhouse on her way to the state championship. *The Swansville Orator*'s headline featured a picture of Wyatt touching home plate from when he was twelve next to the similar image of him five years later. We marched to the semifinals behind Ogre's and Jaxon's pitching and Wyatt's bat.

The second weekend of May, things dramatically changed.

Whitley's soccer team had not lost a game in over a year, and only the game's stats made the back pages of the paper. Wyatt stole the town's attention from Whitley, and she began to become more difficult and she resented everyone. She complained nightly about her success and how no one even cared. Whitley angrily told our mom, "These stupid people don't even know how good the soccer team is because of Mr. Home Run Hartley," then she angrily slammed her door. Whitley would stay locked in her room with her radio blaring to hide her frustrated shouts into her pillow. The next morning, she had taken down the framed "Magic Feet" article, against my father's wishes. The bare spot on the wall made the room seem empty. Eventually, my dad replaced it with Whitley's winning county fair painting of field of tulips.

We all dressed at my house and laughed at the absurdity of the upcoming night. Ogre never seemed to fit into any clothing, and tonight was no different. His pants were always tight, and I always thought they were about to bust. Clothing companies did not have an Ogre size. Wyatt made sure Ogre knew it by acting as if a button popped off and hit him in the eye. Over the years, Ogre developed a rebuttal, and he unapologetically said, "Go jump off a bridge." Wyatt always told him to stay under it. The two had become good friends, and the pitcher and catcher balanced each other. Wyatt awkwardly dressed for our big night. He was more hyper than ever. Words flew out of his mouth at a speed I had not seen since his appearance on *The Late Show*. Wyatt said, "I never get nervous," but when the pace of his words burst out like this, I knew it was a lie. We tied our shoes and tucked in our shirts to head out. My mom burst in to the room to take one last picture of "the men" before we left. We poked our chest out and smiled, then Wyatt insisted we take one more. He ran out to Ogre's Bronco and grabbed his father's bat. Wyatt held the bat over his shoulder, Ogre put on a pair of my father's aviators, and I flexed, squatting in front of my two friends.

The ride was short, and I remember feeling like we were kings. We walked arm in arm with our dates as we entered Branbury Country Club. Yellow and dark-red canna lilies were meticulously placed along the steps of the entrance. Wyatt and his date looked like they floated in, while Ogre and I squeamishly walked steps behind. Ogre was six feet, eight inches tall, and I was six feet, three inches tall, but the smaller Wyatt towered over us. He seemed to have magical glow around him. Wyatt grabbed a purple tulip from a flowerpot on the front porch of the country club and had his date pin it to his collar.

We took our prom photos as a group and then with just our dates. Wyatt's bow tie matched his date's green dress, and the two looked like models. Ogre reluctantly stepped on the dance floor once while my date forced me to dance all night. I looked like I was tripping over wires, and I wished I could dance like Wyatt. I envied his every move and how he carried himself. He danced the night away, and his cheeks were red and his shirt was untucked when he was crowned the prom prince. My sister, of course, was named princess. Wyatt and Whitley awkwardly danced, and their crowns glowed green. In a year, Wyatt and my sister assumed they'd be king and queen, and bigger crowns were headed their way.

We walked out of the country club, and I looked at Wyatt and said, "Your carriage awaits, Your Highness." He laughed it off as if he had heard it before. We all piled into the shiny white limousine. We had one hour left before we would be booted out and we would be back in our old teenage cars. We had the driver take us first by Scarborough Memorial Park, then over to Rocky Point Pier. I'd not been back at night in a long time. We did not stay long, but for the first time ever, I was not afraid of the eerie place. Wyatt was the only one to get out of the limousine. The yellow light by the forbidden dock guided him down to the water. He walked over to the shoreline, picked up a pebble, and threw it as far as he could in the direction of the island, and the pebble met the water at the moon's reflection. He jumped back in, then said, "Let's get the night started." He ordered the driver to take us home by saying, "Home, good sir, before one of these two turns back into a toad."

Mitch O'Neal had invited everyone to a party at his house. Wyatt and Ogre never had a curfew, and they planned on staying out all night. Whitley and I now had to convince our parents to let us go. It would be unlikely either of our parents would allow us to stay out, especially if alcohol was involved. My date and Ogre's date demanded to go home and not to stay out partying. We dropped Wyatt off with Ogre, and the two made plans to pick up Whitley and me. Whitley told Wyatt and Ogre that if her lamp was on in her room, she would need to sneak out. Whitley's sales pitch to our parents did no good. My mother no longer fell for her tricks. My parents promised next year that they would be more flexible. Whitley and I would be locked away for the night.

My sister would not stay locked away for long. She turned on her lamp and ignited the signal. Just after midnight, I heard her window creak open. I walked across the hall and peeked in just as she was climbing into Wyatt's arms. He could effortlessly scale our garage and jump to our second story, then expertly crawl along the roof's edge to my sister's room. I reluctantly followed them out of the window. I knew we would be caught and a hefty price would be paid the next morning. I did not like to break the rules, and I felt like an outlaw. My justification was, my parents always took it easy on us when we broke the rules together. I needed to keep an eye on my sister. Ogre, as usual, agreed to drive Wyatt. Wyatt was reckless and would at times drive after drinking too many beers. Ogre protected his catcher and kept his friend safe.

We jumped in Ogre's black Bronco, which he had named Black Stallion. It was far from being a stallion, and it coughed black smoke all over town. Wyatt already seemed drunk. He denied it, but when he drank, his squinty eyes opened wide and rolled. He was talking a lot about being a legend when he was twelve and how he was about to do it again. Neither Ogre, my sister, nor I wanted to hear about it. Everyone had read about him in the newspaper since February. Whitley angrily told him, "Who cares about the Little League World Series anymore?" Whitley's accolades took a back seat to all his home runs. Wyatt knew she was jealous of his stardom in our small town. He would often provoke her, and arguments would ensue.

Mitch's party was low-key, with just a few people, mostly stoners. Mitch had a different group of friends, but he and Wyatt were still close. Wyatt was his connection to the baseball guys, and he was Wyatt's connection to people that did not care about sports. Mitch no longer played sports, but he could play any instrument. Mitch and Wyatt made an odd pair when they were together. Mitch had turned into a hippie. Mitch's hair was now long, and he wore a faded blue bandanna at all times. It was a regular occurrence for Mitch to play the guitar while Wyatt sang. Mitch was strumming the guitar when we walked in. Wyatt sat beside him, and as if on cue, Wyatt began to sing the chorus to "Comfortably Numb." Wyatt sang with his eyes closed, and he seemed relaxed. Ogre, Whitley, and I stood awkwardly among a few of the stoners while they passed around a joint and swayed to the music.

The song ended, and Wyatt instantly opened his eyes. He was back from the calm place the song had sent him to. Wyatt boisterously said, "Anyone want to go shot for shot with the champ?" No one dared to agree to his challenge. Wyatt liked to win, but when he lost, he transformed into an uncontrollable beast. Mitch warned everyone not to engage. "We all know you are the champ, and there is no need to prove it again." Wyatt scowled at Mitch, then he looked at me and pointed as he said, "Worm, you've read about moments like this. Now, step up." He called out everyone in the room by name and said they were scared. He was almost right. One person wasn't, and she stepped up to him and simply said, "Let's go." The stoners collectively gasped that someone would dare agree to his challenge.

My sister had only had a few beers in her life, and now she accepted a challenge from a belligerent drunk. Wyatt grabbed a fifth of cheap tequila and slammed two shot glasses on the table, then said, "A challenger." The two went shot for shot, and my sister's green eyes rolled back in her head as she downed each shot. Wyatt laughed at my sister after each shot. The stoners began to choose sides, and the room began to chant her name. Wyatt's eyes turned red when the room was filled with "Whitley, Whitley!" He did not like being the villain, and it had been a long time since someone else was the hero. Most of kids at the party did not value home runs, and to them he was just an obnoxious bully. A stoner named Nate shouted, "You can do it, Whitley!" as she downed her ninth shot. I said nothing as I slowly drank my first beer.

The empty bottle surprised everyone as the two rivals had downed an entire fifth of cheap tequila. It was deemed a draw, and no winner was crowned. Wyatt persisted that my sister took smaller shots or not as many. He did not want to share the title of champion, especially with Whitley. He defiantly growled at everyone and protested the ruling. The stoners went back to smoking weed and sipping on beers. His legs started to wobble when he walked, and he looked like he would fall at any moment. Whitley was not in any better shape as she caught herself from falling.

Wyatt and Whitley began to openly argue, which was a normal occurrence I had witnessed many times. I had played referee and judge over the course of my friendship with Wyatt. Wyatt had retreated back to my room over the years after she put him in his place. Whitley drunkenly stumbled through her defense as Wyatt only mocked her. Words only trickled from his mouth like blood from a fighter's lip. He had no place to retreat, and she started tearing him down with every insult she could muster. Everyone at the party knew not to intervene as the two clashed. I knew how it would end, and it would not be pretty. I tried to step in before she embarrassed him. He turned red as Whitley exposed his secrets.

Whitley grabbed Wyatt by his wrist, then pulled him close and whispered something to him. Wyatt's head dropped in shame. He wisely stopped arguing and let her win. She had brought him to tears before, and he wisely would not allow it tonight. He was full of a lethal dose of alcohol, but his pride was at stake and he did not want to lose any more of it. He was not willing to lose to her twice in one night. She was the only person he would obey. She waved her hand in his face and told him to sit down. He sat on the end of the couch as if under a spell. Wyatt sat quietly on the couch, and he began to look like he would fall asleep. I apologized to Mitch and everyone for his behavior as well as my sister's. They had all seen Wyatt be a drunken, inconsiderate fool, but not my sister. She had taken down their bully. She was celebrated, and she kept drinking. Whitley was the life of the dying party.

Things started to settle down, and the party was wrapping up. Ogre and I had the dilemma of getting my drunk sister back in her room without waking my parents. I asked Mitch, "Do you have any bright ideas for getting my sister back in her room?"

He answered, "Just stay out all night if you know you are already going to be in trouble." Mitch's advice made sense, but I knew the punishment would be far worse if we did not make it home.

Ogre said, "I'll try to get her on the roof if you could get her across it."

We decided to attempt it.

Just then, Wyatt jumped up from his semislumber, then crawled over to us, saying, "Don't leave me."

Whitley and Wyatt were a royally drunken mess.

Ogre carried Wyatt and I carried my sister to the Black Stallion. When we got to my house, Wyatt thankfully insisted on helping get Whitley back in her room. She was semiconscious, and the two walked arm in arm to the side of the garage. They stumbled and looked like they were on a boat dock, swaying under the waves. Ogre was too big to attempt the acrobatic maneuvers of getting a drunk girl to her second-story window, and I was not strong enough. Wyatt could effortlessly perform the delicate balancing act even with my sister over his shoulder. He looked like he had performed the difficult feat one hundred times. He opened the window with one arm and gently laid her inside. Whitley's head popped up, and she whispered something to him and they both laughed. She fell back inside, and he slipped. Wyatt lost his footing, and he slid down the shingles. He caught himself on the gutter, and he dangled over my parents' rhododendrons. I ran over to catch him, but I was not fast enough and he came crashing down.

Ogre and I helped him up, and he seemed fine, other than saying his wrist hurt. I sneaked back into the house, and Ogre took Wyatt home with him. He had to care for our intoxicated friend, and I had to check on my sister. I checked on Whitley, and she was on the floor at the window, completely asleep. I put her in her bed, then went to crash in my own bed. When I entered her room, a note hung on her door warning us for tomorrow morning's conversation. Whitley's note was long and concluded with the words "You're not above punishment." My letter simply said, "You too."

The punishment Whitley and I received was typical. No car for three weeks. Three weeks is a long time when you're seventeen. I called Ogre at noon and got no answer. I had no ride and a sister that was a demon in the mornings, and now it was intensified by the lingering smell of tequila. Sunday was a day I usually spent at the park with Drake, and now that was not an option.

Ogre pulled in my driveway just after two in the afternoon. I asked my mom, "Can I go see what he needs?"

She responded, "Hurry."

Ogre usually walked with his head down, but today he looked right at me and shook his head. The first words from his mouth were, "The state record is safe." He then explained that Wyatt had broken his wrist. Ogre would have to carry us to the state championship.

The task was too big, and four days later, we lost in the semifinals. Jaxon and Ogre tried to carry the offense in Wyatt's absence. Wyatt could only play cheerleader. He sulked in the dugout and kept his head down. Ogre was not a hero, but he gave a valiant effort. After the loss, I heard for the first time the excuse "If we only had Drake." He had been gone for a year. I felt like a fraud because I took his number after he left. I could not do what he could, and our fans and I both knew it.

The Swansville Orator's headline read, "Wait until Next Year," with a picture of the injured phenom in a cast. My sister completed her undefeated soccer season as she led our school to its second straight state championship. She and Wyatt were both named all-state athletes, and she was named state player of the year. Colleges all over the area began to flood our mailbox, inviting Whitley to visit their school. Wyatt's wrist healed quickly, but the injury lingered longer than expected. He took the summer off playing baseball. I think Wyatt needed a break from baseball and the expectations. He spent his time enjoying the lake and drinking way too many beers. My parents warned Whitley and me to avoid him or there would be consequences.

Rocky Point Fire

Wyatt made the newspaper late in the summer for all the wrong reasons. Wyatt, Troy, Whitley, and a few other girls burned down Rocky Point Pier when they all drunkenly passed out before putting out their fire. Troy and Wyatt were not formally charged since John Angelo struck a deal with the boys. Troy and Wyatt agreed to forty hours of community service at the fire station. Sylvia Russell also agreed to a sizable donation. The last month of the summer, Wyatt and Troy spent their Saturdays from seven in the morning to seven at night doing odd jobs for the fire department.

My sister's name was held out of the paper, but her punishment would be worse. My mom and my reluctant dad decided to send her to an all-girls school for her senior year. She would miss her senior year at Swansville High School. The soccer coach was devastated. His chance for another state championship vanished with Whitley. My parents began to distance themselves from each other too. They stopped going everywhere together, and my mom was absent from our family night dinners. My senior year was awkward without Whitley. I became a focus for the first time in my life. My dad and I actually began to have conversations with each other that did not involve Whitley. Our breakfast conversations were no longer dominated with Whitley's soccer recap. I learned an all-new respect for my workaholic dad. His every move was for our family. I had not noticed all he did, and I took for granted the little things he had sacrificed over my life. His vibrant smile was gone. He knew in less than a year both Whitley and I would be gone.

Wyatt later confided in me that he went to Rocky Point Pier frequently because he continued to attempt to contact EELNEB

259

with the Ouija board. He told me, "I have not made contact with EELNEB since our first attempt six years earlier." He went on to explain he never understood why EELNEB said *pain*. It had haunted him since our camping trip. The night of the fire, he played it with Troy, my sister, and the other girls. He told me all this while he was shaking, and his voice cracked. I asked him, "What did EELNEB say?" He said, "When everyone played it, nothing happened other than Troy being goofy, but just after midnight, Whitley and I tried one last time." He went on to tell me what EELNEB told them. "It spelled out *fire*, then *agony*, then Whitley asked who, and EELNEB responded, 'You 2.'" He then said, "EELNEB said *agony* over and over." His eyes told me he was more concerned with the second word.

He reminded me I had told him when we were twelve years old that I did not think it was real. I never told him I was scared too. He told me after EELNEB said agony for the fourth time, he threw the Ouija board in the fire, which was nearly out. He and Whitley went to sit on the dock to finish off the remaining beers. They fell asleep under the stars by the moonlight shadow of the "No Jumping" sign. He rarely spoke of my sister in such a calm way.

Whitley also told me the details of the fire. She shakenly said, "I woke up and kicked Wyatt to wake him up. The flames were getting closer. I could feel the heat on my face. Wyatt told me to jump in the lake. We both hit the water at the same time, then we frantically swam to the shore. Troy and the others were surrounded by fire and the collapsing oak tree. Wyatt ran through the flames to wake everyone up. He grabbed one of the other girls, then ran her out of the flames. He shouted at me to stay, and I obeyed as he went back for Troy. He carried Troy back to safety." When I asked Wyatt about it later, he jokingly described his bravery as fueled by Busch Light. Whitley told me she watched as she heard the faint sound of a fire truck. John Angelo and the fire department arrived just as Wyatt was running through the flames with a drunk Troy in his arms. Wyatt dashed back into the flames, ignoring John Angelo's warning, to retrieve his dad's bat. Wyatt said, "I can't leave it behind." Everyone was safe as the smoldering pier began to vanish into the brown water along with Troy's boat.

The headline of *The Swansville Orator* read, "Slugger Burns Down Abandoned Pier." The newspaper portrayed Wyatt and Troy as spoiled brats. Several local fishermen were quoted voicing their displeasure for Troy and how he did not respect the lake. Garret Sink told the paper, "Troy thinks he owns this end of the lake and it is his personal playground." The article insinuated Wyatt felt like he could get away with anything because of his local stardom. The article even referenced his game-winning Little League World Series home run.

Wyatt's heroics did not make the paper. John Angelo, my sister, Troy, and I were the only ones that knew the truth. Wyatt asked me to promise him I'd never expose the truth. I agreed; one more secret would not be hard to keep. Wyatt called *The Swansville Orator* and demanded they never put his picture on the front page again, and they agreed.

The summer before our senior year seemed to go by too quickly, and it abruptly ended with a funeral. The last weekend of the summer, David Luck found Cecil Bane dead in his shack. The war veteran had a heart attack, and only his hound witnessed his passing. My dad demanded Whitley and me attend the funeral. My dad explained Cecil deserved a proper burial. I watched my dad give the funeral home director an envelope that was surely full of cash. I assumed my dad had secretly paid for Cecil's funeral.

The graveside funeral was small, with only a few people from town in attendance. Everyone in town knew Cecil, but only a few ever spoke to the large man. Cecil was a town fixture, and it would be odd driving through Swansville without seeing him pushing his shopping cart full of cans. My dad offered to say something, but he struggled. He fought back tears as long as he could before he officially choked up. It was odd to see my dad so emotional over someone I believed he barely knew. Wyatt walked up to my dad and put his hand on his shoulder, then he eloquently finished reading my dad's speech. My dad buried his face in his hands and openly sobbed. I felt awkward and embarrassed. Wyatt finished reading my dad's speech, then he opened a jar of muddy brown water and poured it on Cecil's casket. Wyatt finished by saying, "A little brown water to make you feel at home." Cecil was laid to rest beside his family. My dad purchased Cecil's house and donated it to the town to one day be a museum for Swansville.

Horizon

Our senior year, Wyatt had an up-and-down season. He would have games where he would dominate and no one could stop him. Wyatt still looked like a phenom at times, and other times he seemed indifferent; then he began to strike out. Wyatt hated getting out prior to our senior year, and now he just calmly went back to the dugout. He seemed complacent, and our coach assumed he had somehow tamed Wyatt. He never blamed his wrist, but I knew something was off or missing. We only won two playoff games, and the summer started sooner than ever. The town lost baseball fever as quickly as they had caught it years earlier.

Wyatt was still named to the all-state team despite hitting half the home runs. The stands for every game were filled with both college scouts and scouts from the big leagues. Occasionally, I thought they might see something in me too. I started at second base, and I batted leadoff. I led the team in stolen bases, but I was far from being a prospect even for a lowly division 3 college. My career would end whether I liked it or not. Wyatt and I hung out less and less as our senior year passed. Once upon a time, he was at my house every day and he seemed like he was part of the family. My mother's hateful gazes intensified after the fire, and he stopped coming around as often.

Whitley was banished to Virginia for her senior year. She did not take my parents' warnings seriously, and so they sent her to a private school in Virginia. The Rocky Point fire was the last straw, and my mother was finally able to talk my dad into sending her away. She led an all-girls school to the state title and dominated soccer in another state. Whitley went out on top, but I did not attend her triumphant final high school soccer match. *The Swansville Orator* covered her success, and she was the talk of the town despite being 230 miles away. She was an All-American, and *Sports Illustrated* even did a short sports biography on her. The soccer prodigy had grown up. *The Swansville Orator* chronicled her success from when she was a child soccer prodigy at eight years old. The front-page headline read, "Still Magical." My dad's office was decorated with all her accomplishments and a team photo of the Little League World Series team.

Whitley thrived in Virginia, and she made a new set of friends. She rarely came home during the school year. Whitley only attended a few of my baseball games, but she would talk to the locals more than watch the game. Each day I checked the mailbox, eagerly anticipating my college acceptance letter. I was disappointed each day, and the mailbox was flooded with Division 1 scholarship offers for Whitley among T-shirts and hats to schools throughout the Southeast. I believed, wherever Whitley chose to go to college, she would stay and never return to Swansville. She had outgrown the Brown Water.

Whitley returned for the summer, but she made trips to see her new friends in Virginia every couple of weeks. She had changed drastically in the year she was gone. Whitley did not seem consumed with soccer anymore, and she started living a more carefree lifestyle. Whitley even began to smoke, much to my dad's displeasure. He blamed the habit on my mother, who had secretly smoked all our lives. She had grown even more rebellious, and she openly disobeyed my parents, especially my mother. Whitley began to call our mother Emily instead of Mom, and the two fought all summer. The halo Whitley was born with was gone, and our mom saw the eighteen-year-old beauty for the bully she had always been. Whitley even dyed her blond hair to a dark black in defiance. It gave her a sinister look, and my mother constantly said, "Whitley looks like a witch." Whitley shrugged off the insult. She stayed away from our house as much as possible all summer.

Wyatt, Ogre, and Ruby were reunited on the baseball diamond for one last season. The three Little League superstars played on the local legion baseball team. They had not shared a dugout since we left Williamsport. Wyatt and Ruby openly argued in games just like they had done six years earlier. The two never ran out of insults. If Drake had been on the team, it would have been a perfect reunion, but he was gone.

Ruby was more arrogant and obnoxious at eighteen years old than he was when he was twelve years old. He transformed back into the narcissistic giant when he entered the halls of a new school without Wyatt or Whitley to keep him in check. Ruby was still a dominant pitcher, and he had signed to play baseball at Mars Hill University. I believe Ogre was glad Ruby and Wyatt fought all summer, because it allowed him to slip back into the shadows. Ruby still went by the nickname Wyatt had given him when we were twelve years old. He only wore the ruby-red cleats when he was scheduled to pitch. Ruby would get upset with Wyatt when Wyatt obnoxiously called him Travis.

Wyatt found his swagger during the summer, and he seemed to hit a home run every game. The three former teammates won the state legion baseball title. Wyatt was the North Carolina Legion Player of the Year. Both Ogre and Ruby pitched in the championship game, and Wyatt hit a three-run home run in the third inning as they cruised to the 9–2 win. The newspaper's article featured a picture of the three baseball stars from when they were twelve years old looking up to a current picture of them. The headline read, "Big Things to Come." The picture was uncanny, and it would be the last picture of the three together for a long time.

We all had grown up, but I still remembered them as twelve-year-olds. When Ruby and Wyatt argued, I remembered back to when the rivals were just innocent kids. Their insults now seemed to cut deeper, but neither of them would show the wounds. I watched them dominate from the stands due to my torn ACL. I was a footnote in Wyatt's and Ogre's story. My baseball career ended, and I never got another hero moment. I would have to settle for the day I became Lightning.

Goodbye

Baseball was over, and now summer could not end fast enough. I was ready to leave Swansville. I limped around all summer, and I could not wait to leave the Brown Water. I had grown tired of the town, and I believed once I left, I'd never return. I wanted a place where my sister and my best friend would not be on the front page of the newspaper. I wanted to blend in, and I was annoyingly tired of answering questions about Wyatt's home runs and Whitley's soccer accolades. I was only special because of my connection to the two of them. I wanted everyone to see Carson Smith's talents and to ask how I was without bringing up Wyatt or Whitley. I had grown selfish.

Leaving Swansville had been my goal for the last year. I was excited to leave Cubbie Cove. I closed my speech as I stared out over my classmates, "I will miss you all and this place." My valedictorian speech was full of lies. I had begun to pack for college before the last day of school. Wyatt, Whitley, and I all felt the same way; more adventures lay ahead.

Whitley and I rarely spoke or hung out all summer. She stayed away. My mother was happiest when Whitley was not around; thus, she allowed her to roam and go wherever she pleased. My parents gave up trying to control her. One of our last conversations was about when she caught our mom day-drinking while our dad was at work. Whitley never got over the fact that, as she put it, "Emily was living a lie." Our parents also began to no longer be seen as one person like they had our entire lives. While Whitley was away at school, our dad never missed any of her games and our mom stayed home. My mom began to change. I ignored it until it was too late. Less than a year later, our mom moved in to a small lake house and our dad stayed behind to run the business. They were rarely seen together again.

I loaded up my car and I left for college, but not before I stopped in one last time to see Frankie and to grab a Cheerwine for the drive. Frankie struggled to maneuver the old bait shop, and now he just sat in an old blue lawn chair behind the register. Frankie still looked the same as he did six years earlier; he had evaded time. Frankie, per usual, was listening to the Braves game, and he boastfully said, "This is their year!" I had heard the old man say that for a decade. He would be wrong again. We walked out to the dock, and he complained of the extra trash drifting down due to the renovation of Rocky Point Pier. He cursed under his breath, "Those two dumb-ass boys have ruined Cubbie Cove, and now trash will cover the shoreline." Then he said, "Next summer Cubbie Cove will not be the same." Time would prove the old man right.

Frankie pointed in the distance at the last ripples of a boat's wake, then said, "You just missed your friend."

I asked Frankie, "What did he have to say today?"

Frankie responded, "The same ole thing."

Troy always complained of the new, bigger boats ruining our lake. Frankie always voiced his displeasure with Troy, but deep down the two were just alike and they both viewed themselves the keepers of Cubbie Cove. Troy was just a small figure on the horizon as he headed out to the big water. Troy never took to the big-water mind-set, and he generally stayed on the safe waters of Cubbie Cove. He had made the Brown Water his home despite being forced to assim-ilate to Stoney Creek. He stayed loyal to the Swansville side of the lake. The lake was his sanctuary, and the hum of boats called him each day. He would stay lost at sea. I doubted if he would ever leave his beloved lake. I wondered if he was headed to the Hole in the Wall or if he was searching the lake for a new hiding place.

I said goodbye to Scarborough Memorial Park from the store's dock. I knew if I went any closer, the memories would flood back and I'd stay too long and drown under the memories. I would want to walk out to right field and see the sun disappear behind the pine trees. I did not have time to enjoy one last moment on the old field. I was ready to go to a place where no one knew we had won the Little League World Series.

Ogre and Wyatt pulled up in the Black Stallion before I reached my car. The Black Stallion was bursting at the seams with everything Ogre was taking to college. He did not want to leave anything behind. He tried to pack the entire town in his Bronco. Wyatt had moved most of his stuff a few weeks prior, and he only had a duffel bag with his remaining clothes, and his father's bat awkwardly stuck out. Ogre said, "I came to say goodbye to my uncle." It was a lie. He could not hide his real motivation for stopping by to see Frankie. He wanted say goodbye to the field one last time too. We chatted for a while about what we expected college to be like. Shadows were starting to creep in, and the field began to be covered in darkness.

Ogre was dropping off Wyatt at the airport before he reluctantly headed to college. He did not want to leave his home. Outside of Swansville, Ogre was just another giant, but in Swansville, he was normal and just another kid. Everyone he knew was here, and he did not like strangers. Jack wanted his son to get an education and to experience the real world. Ogre told me, "I do not know why he wants me to get a degree. I just want to be like him." Ogre was content with his baseball career ending at eighteen years old. His father had run out of space to display Ogre's home run balls. Ogre was ready to give up hitting any more. He begged his father to let him stay.

We all three stared in the direction of right field, and we began to run out of things to say.

Wyatt said very little, and it was the quietest I had ever seen him. I think Wyatt knew the baseball field we stared at was what allowed him to assimilate into our town. He was once an outsider, but now he was the face of Swansville. Leaving the Brown Water had to be scary for Wyatt. He had to start over somewhere else, and the feat must've seemed more impossible at eighteen years old than when he confidently walked into Mr. Troutman's class six years earlier. He knew and likely desired the spotlight to follow him to his next destination. I felt like the day he arrived, my life began, because I don't remember much before he was here. My memories of my life before Wyatt seem like dreams I can't describe the next morning.

Whitley sped into the parking lot of Scarborough Memorial Park, then she did a U-turn as she headed back to Virginia. She must've known we were there. I had not seen my sister in three days, and we did not get to have a proper goodbye. In the last year, I felt Whitley and I were no longer friends. We were more like distant relatives than twins. Her car windows were down, and I could see she had dyed her hair back to blond. The faint sound of the Fleetwood Mac song "Go Your Own Way" drifted from her car. Whitley sped by and honked her horn, and we all three gave solemn waves.

I jumped in my car as Ogre and Wyatt walked in Winslow's. The three of us never officially said goodbye. My eyes filled with tears as I drove off. I wondered when I would see them again. Summer and our childhood felt like it had ended. We all went opposite directions. I went west, Ogre east, Wyatt south, and Whitley north.

No Ducks on the Pond

Jim Duckworth forgot more about baseball than anyone you knew, or at the very least that was what he told everyone. I believed him. Duckworth died five days before the beginning of the 2006 MLB season and just in time to complicate Green and Clean Day. His funeral was held the same day. His stomach could not handle cancer any more than he could stomach another Cardinals world championship. He was like most folks in the South, and he adopted the Atlanta Braves after their success in the 1990s. He despised the Cardinals as much as the Yankees. Deep down I always believed he was a Cubs fan. He knew way too much about their history and the big city. Duckworth had once eloquently told me of the curse of the billy goat when I was eight years old.

I wish I had visited him in the hospital, but I had a version of Duckworth in my head and I wanted it to stay that way. My version of Duckworth was laughing while hitting infield, shouting "Field with your feet!" and "Alligator hands!" not the frail, sickly man he had become. Drake never left his father's side, and they listened to the Braves last spring training game. Duckworth's blind allegiance to the Braves had faded, and he had become a realist when discussing his favorite team. He told Drake, "It would be a long summer in Atlanta, and the team would not see October." His crystal ball proved to be correct, because the Braves' run of division titles ended. I felt I had abandoned my friend and my beloved coach. Duckworth died holding Drake's hand while clenching a picture of Donnie in the other. Principal Duckworth and Ashton quietly sobbed outside the hospital door with Wyatt's mother. Patti Hartley was on duty the night he died. She had cared for the dying coach for the past three weeks.

Duckworth religiously followed the phenom's career. He did not try to coach Wyatt because he knew Wyatt was a natural. Wyatt laughed and sarcastically repeated Duckworth's baseball cues. Duckworth tried to teach Wyatt to be humble and respectful. Wyatt respected Duckworth, but not many others. The gregarious coach let Wyatt be Wyatt and only tried to reel him in when it was necessary. The combination worked. The two and Drake finished on top as Duckworth landed Wyatt in the next draft, and he finally went undefeated. They won the championship, and I saw Drake Duckworth smile that day for the last time on a baseball field. Duckworth coached his last game and was a sideline coach most of the season after having shoulder surgery. He was no longer even able to throw a baseball or do his favorite thing and hit infield.

After Drake had won that championship, his focus shifted and he started down a new path. Drake decided to pursue his father and brother's dream. Drake had reached a baseball pinnacle, and now he wanted a new challenge. Drake became a standout basketball player in high school and went on to win a Division II National Championship at Bowie State University in Maryland. Drake told me once he was sick of everyone asking, Was he as good as his brother, Donnie? So at fourteen he set out to be. He started concentrating on basketball. Jump shots became the new self-prescribed medicine he forced on himself. Drake shot free throws at Scarborough Park every night. He did not want people to think less of his father or the ghost of his brother.

I remember his first varsity game as a sophomore, when he pulled off his warm-up suit: the crowd was silenced, and many had tears roll down their cheeks when they saw him wearing his brother's retired number, 24. Drake's quiet confidence on the baseball field had turned into a smile on the basketball court. He seemed to enjoy the game, and his dimples returned. The crowd did not stay silent long as Drake set a school record for consecutive three pointers. The crowd chanted, "Duckworth, Duckworth!" and the familiar sound broke Jim Duckworth and he hastily walked out of the gym to hide his tears. The Duckworth chants became echoes again, and they only lasted that one magical season.

After our sophomore, year Principal Duckworth took a job three counties over, and just like that, Drake was gone. Duckworth gave Drake the option to remain at Swansville High School, but he was ready to move on. Duckworth was able to see his son become a star, but at another school. Drake did not have to play basketball at a gym with a memorial of his brother hanging on the gym wall. Two years later, Drake led his new school to the state title, and he was named MVP. His number was retired, while his brother's jersey still hung in the Swansville High School gym.

When Principal Duckworth took Drake away from Swansville, he became our missing piece and, more importantly, our excuse. We learned to say, "If we only had Drake." He was the only former teammate we said that about while we navigated high school. Neither Jaxon nor I was able to fill his shoes on the baseball field. We missed his calmness the most, and we became more defiant without Duckworth around.

I still remember my quiet friend leaving school for the last time. He knew that his stepmother had taken a new job and he would be leaving Swansville, but no one else did. It was odd for Drake not to walk out of school with our group of friends, but on the last day of school our sophomore year, he stoically walked just ahead of us. He never dropped his head, and his eyes seemed focused on the horizon, as if he was headed toward a mirage. He did not even look back or wave. He was leaving behind not just us but the sadness that tormented him. He wanted to go somewhere the ghost of his brother would not haunt him.

When Duckworth passed away, the news spread faster than the rumors at Winslow's. The most unlikely person started the phone tree. Coach Alex was the first to call me. I could hear the tears rolling down his face as he told me his longtime Little League adversary had passed away. Alex simply said, "He's gone." He knew what Duckworth meant to us all, especially the Ducklings. Deep down, Alex wished he could've been loved like Duckworth. Alex coached using fear, and now years after he retired, he saw the beauty in Duckworth's coaching style. I thanked Coach Alex for letting me know as quickly as possible to try to silence my own tears.

Despite expecting the tragic news any day for the past couple of months, I broke down. I decided to go to Scarborough Memorial Park, and I stayed into the night, sobbing on the tailgate of my truck. The field was empty except for the shadows in the right field. I walked out onto the field and mimed a throw from second to first, then I trotted the bases, reliving a home run moment that never happened. Without Duckworth, the field did not seem to have the same magic, and I was instantly embarrassed. I ran off the field before anyone could see me foolishly running the bases. I half-expected to see someone in the bleachers as I touched home plate; instead, I saw lights on at Winslow's. The rumor was, the once-lively bait shop had been purchased. Frankie died three years earlier, and his store had closed. Time was starting to catch up with the old men of my youth.

Drake called me the next day and asked me to be a pallbearer and to speak at the funeral. He told me, "My dad asked about you all the time." He told me Duckworth specifically said, "Get Worm to say something at the service. He's the smart one." Drake told me his dad's new, outlandish stories now involved me. Drake said his father's favorite story was the day a worm transformed into the lightning, and his daughters had heard the story many times. Drake and I continued to chat, and the small talk seemed to have a purpose. It was awkward. It was the most I had heard him say since we were nine years old. He finally asked, "Would you get the service details to everyone?" I agreed, and I started calling my old teammates, some of whom I had not seen or heard from since high school. So at twenty-six years old, we all went to our first funeral together, except for Wyatt.

Wyatt was training nearby, and everyone assumed he would be at the funeral. Wyatt and Duckworth had a special relationship that few understood. I believe Duckworth saw Donnie in Wyatt. The folks in town still treated Wyatt like the superstar he should've been. The night before the funeral, he called me then asked to meet him at Rocky Point Pier. The place still gave me chills, especially at night. It was no longer a forgotten fishing access, so I parked my truck in the parking lot of what was now called Rocky Point Beach. It was one of those annoyingly rainy nights. It was just enough rain for my wipers to smear the green pollen and distort my view. He was dropped off a hundred feet away under the original streetlight that still glowed yellow. The car sped off once he got out. He looked like a guilty man that was out of alibis, with nowhere else left to go. His shadow made him look like an invincible giant as he paced the shoreline. He was no giant, of course. I watched him walk around for a few minutes before flashing my lights.

He jumped in, and he smelled like beer, which was not a surprise, since he had an open twelve-pack of Coronas. He asked me, "Do you want a beer?" but before I could answer, he said, "Damn, she was supposed to leave me the bottle opener." I handed him mine, and he cracked two.

I said, "We need to get out of here."

He laughed, then said, "No shit."

Wyatt believed he should have been forbidden and the place had some type of curse. We spent a portion of our youth being chased out of here, and I did not want to do it tonight with two open beers in my truck. I asked him, "Who dropped you off?"

He did not answer the question, using one of his many misdirection tactics he had used on me since the sixth grade. He burped and only said, "Duckworth," then looked out of the window. We rode in silence while he drank beer after beer. I drove us out to one of the new communities under construction to have some privacy and not get arrested. A new BMW sped past us once we arrived at the community of Cascade Creek, and I felt like we were being watched.

I asked Wyatt, "Would you read my speech at the funeral for me?"

He declined without hesitating, then told me, "I am leaving." He would not make it to the funeral. He said, "I am trying to recapture some baseball magic, and I think I have." The injuries were beginning to pile up, and he knew he needed to maximize what was left of his baseball career.

Duckworth was not as important to Wyatt as he was to me and a few others. I expected the flags to be at half-mast, but Duckworth was only that important to the Ducklings. Most of the world and Wyatt Hartley would not blink back a tear, but the rest of us would. Wyatt told me he was leaving for Japan in the morning and that he had signed to play for the Hanshin Tigers. I dropped him off at his uncle's house. I wished him luck and shook his hand. He winked at me, then drunkenly said, "Thanks. Who needs luck?" I felt like he was running from something, and I did not know if or when I'd see him again. He had to continue his baseball odyssey, and I had to go to a funeral.

The morning of the funeral, it rained and it made me think of a time Duckworth said, "At least the rain stopped our losing streak for one day." The funeral was jam-packed. Ogre and Jack Wilson greeted everyone at the door. Ogre and RJ would serve as pallbearers. The expected attendance made it necessary to have his funeral in the Swansville High School gym. The entire town seemed to come to his funeral, and many folks would stand in the back. Donnie's memorial seemed to look over the funeral. The gym had to have exceeded the number of people allowed per the fire code, but this was Jim Duckworth, and John Angelo was not going to turn anyone away.

Before the funeral, I paced along the back of the gym just out of the rain's reach and practiced my speech. The rain and my tears dotted its pages. There was no way I could read it without breaking down. Minutes before the funeral, Ruby saw me pacing, then asked, "What are you doing?" I told him the dilemma, and he offered to read it. He looked it over and said, "No sweat." I thanked him, and I told the preacher of the altered plan.

Drake looked calm as always, and his wife was pregnant. She was due any day. Drake felt like my big brother for most of my life despite that I was six months older than him. I was closer to Duckworth growing up than my own dad. I looked around and saw many men that probably felt the same way I did about the old coach. I had not seen Drake in a long time, but he had begun to be distant long before he left. His eyes still looked at the horizon. He and I barely spoke. We only gave each other an awkward hug, then I said, "Sorry. Heaven must need a coach." If I had to say more, it would have poured more from my eyes than my mouth. I missed my friend and my teammate.

Those of us that played baseball with Drake came face-to-face with our older counterparts that Duckworth had coached in basketball a decade prior. It was like looking into our own future. Their heads were starting to show gray, and wrinkles were in their faces. They remembered a much younger Duckworth, one that made ours look tame. His energy and drive were manufactured for us, while it was still natural for them. They knew they were luckier than us. Smelly Kelly oddly represented the older guys at the funeral, but he was now a quasicelebrity since taking over the sports page for *The Swansville Orator*. He now shook hands with pride and definition. We were thrilled with the broken and aging Duckworth, because that was all we knew. Their tears flowed while we fought ours. We were still young enough to not want to show our real emotions. Tears were our enemy for the day.

The service was short but full of laughs. I felt insignificant because Duckworth had an impact on so many in such a short time. I was called to the podium to give my speech, and I nervously walked up while motioning for Ruby to join me. Although I was a couple of inches taller than the now-round Ruby, he still was a menacing giant in my eyes. He casually strolled to the podium, and each step's click-clock echoed off the gym walls. I introduced him. "I would like to thank Travis Harrison for reading a speech I prepared." Then I shrank back into his shadow. It was odd calling him Travis and not Ruby.

Ruby grabbed the speech and began.

My speech detailed all the times Duckworth had made me laugh when I felt like crying. It began, "Duckworth was the kind of man you named a street after." I told the story of the day the worm transformed into lightning and how he made me feel like a hero. My speech described how Duckworth would shout "Lightning!" at me years later, and it always made me smile despite being embarrassed. I mentioned all his crazy baseball sayings and how I believed everything he said. My words seemed foreign coming out of Ruby's mouth. He spoke clearly and eloquently, but it was difficult to believe him. He did not love Duckworth, and he showed very little emotion until the last few lines. His voice cracked, and his dark eyes filled with tears when he read, "The world does not need one less Jim Duckworth. It needs more. More great men, more father figures, more hero makers, more mentors, and more coaches." My speech ended with the familiar Duckworth saying, "I love you, and God loves you, and I am proud of each one of you." I stood in Ruby's shadow, trying to hold back and hide the tears. I was not strong enough, and the tears trickled down my cheeks. I thought about the kids that did not know him and the ones that never would. I decided then and there to become like Duckworth or, as he would have said, the lesser version he would have traded away.

My tears flowed down my cheeks, and my former teammates hid their tears until it was time to file out of the gym once the service ended. The Kenny Rogers song "The Greatest" played, and everyone's tears began to let go.

The Greatest

> *Little boy, in a baseball hat*
> *Picks up his ball, stares at his bat*
> *Says I am the greatest the game is on the line*
> *And he gives his all one last time*
> *And the ball goes up like the moon so bright*
> *Swings his bat with all his might*
> *And the world's so still as still can be*
> *And the baseball falls, and that's strike three*
> *Now it's supper time and his mama calls*
> *Little boy starts home with his bat and ball*
> *Says I am the greatest that is a fact*
> *But even I didn't know I could pitch like that*
> *He says I am the greatest that is understood*
> *But even I didn't know I could pitch that good.*

Everyone's tears were easily camouflaged as we giggled at the same time. The song reminded us all of how Duckworth never let us feel like we had played poorly or made an error. Now all that was left was for me to try to fill his large shoes.

It was still raining when we stepped out of the gym, and now the sun was brightly shining. I expected a rainbow was somewhere just out of my view. Those of us that did not prepare for the rain sprinted in our dark suits to our cars. Duckworth requested the funeral procession to drive by Scarborough Memorial Park before heading out of town to an old church cemetery. A new soccer field was under construction; thus, the funeral procession had trouble navigating the parking lot filled with construction equipment. It was comical watching a hearse and two limousines trying to maneuver.

The procession was delayed, and I spent time in a little traffic jam, staring at the field. Nearly ten years earlier, I said goodbye to it and thought I would never return. I looked at the field now and knew it was where I was meant to be. Eventually, the procession was finally able to hit the road toward the small church where Duckworth would be laid to rest beside Donnie. Tears continued to roll down my face until I saw the makeshift memorial of a dirty giant Donald Duck holding a rose inside a Corona bottle. A spray-painted note was above it on the back of the 1980 state championship sign, reading, "One less duck on the pond." I wondered if my former teammates laughed through tears as I did while driving to lay the colorful coach to rest.

A Different View

Wyatt only lived forty-one miles away, but it seemed like one thousand. If you took the old bridge, it would take about an hour and fifteen minutes, but now the trip took less than an hour because of a new bridge. The new bridge was built five years earlier. It connected everything, but I still decided to take the old roads. I was reminded of the town of Hopewell. Businesses on what was once the new four-lane highway looked like a ghost town. Many of the businesses relocated to downtown, and the Swansville Gas and Tackle was being remodeled for the fourth time in six years. The next owner had high hopes despite the store's recent demise after the new bridge was complete.

The old roads were quiet, and the drive was pleasant. The only cars and people I saw on these roads lived nearby. These roads were only traveled by the locals. The hour-long ride gave me time to reflect and prepare what I would say to Wyatt. He stopped coming to town long ago. I had not seen him since the night before Duckworth's funeral ten years earlier. He spent a small fortune becoming a young recluse. He finally retired at the old age of thirty-six. He used his local fame and what money he had saved to buy the most secluded property on the lake.

The property was never for sale since it was the mouth of the river, and it was always off-limits. The terms of purchase he agreed to allowed emergency vehicles to access the river's mouth by using his driveway. He built his own private gated entrance. It took five minutes or more to traverse his gravel driveway, which stretched about a mile, and this was after turning off the main road that looked like it led to a place to dump bodies. If you wanted to hide in plain sight,

Wyatt had found it. The road was hidden between tall pine trees. It was the only place on the lake that had a sign showing the height of the water due to the volatile river water filling Pisgah Lake. The water was a dark purple instead of the dirty brown I was accustomed to, and it was the first section where trash entered the lake. He had no lakeside dock, but his house sat atop a mini mountain. He could see the majority of the lake, especially Cubbie Cove. His view looked directly across the lake in the direction of Swansville, and it was a straight line as the crow flies to where the muddy dock of where Winslow's once had stood.

I nervously made the trip. I drove up his driveway. I felt like I was being watched by the buzzard colony that sat atop a power line in the distance. The grass was high on both sides of the road, with the occasional wild honeysuckle bush. Wyatt's private road made it seem as if I was headed to an area that took special authorization to enter. The rode split at a large magnolia tree, and I had to decide which road to take. One of the roads looked far less traveled. I decided to take the road that looked like it had seen some recent action. I reached his private gate, which was overtaken by yellow bell bushes, and I thought for a minute about what to say and I had second thoughts. I pushed the button to be buzzed in, and I waited. I waited with the windows down for what seemed like an hour, and the air was thicker and a dull gray on this side of the lake. Two minutes later, when the gate clanged open, it made me jump and I nervously shook. It was as if I were on unsteady ground. The closer I got to his house, the slower I drove, and I felt tears filling my eyes and it became hard to swallow. My estranged childhood best friend was just around the next corner, and I had no idea what I would say.

The eerie feeling went away when I turned the corner, and I saw flowers everywhere. The flowers had a pattern, but it was diffi-cult to decipher. Pink carnations and gardenias lined his front porch. I chuckled when I saw rhododendrons along the side of his house below what was likely the master bedroom window. Daylilies lined the path to his front steps. A giant blue hydrangea welcomed me. His front porch looked like something from a magazine. The porch was lined with four white rocking chairs, and each chair had a small table beside it with the a different, brightly colored hibiscus plant. The contrast of colors and the white rockers seemed like something only an artist could capture. Other than the flowers, the house seemed bland.

His house was big, but not what I expected. It was not unique, and it was designed without a woman's touch. The only thing that stood out was the decorative glass on his front door, which was in the shape of a baseball. I parked my car, and I felt like I could see my breath as if it were the middle of winter and not June. When I got to the door, it was ajar. His house was open but was uninviting, with only few pieces of furniture. It was evident he had lived a bachelor's nomad lifestyle for over a decade.

A familiar voice rained down from upstairs, and my nervousness was gone. Patti Hartley shouted, "Who the hell is here?" Wyatt motioned for me to come in, and I closed the door and at the same time we spoke over each other, stating my arrival. I stumbled and said, "It's me, Carson Smith, Mrs. Hartley." Meanwhile, Wyatt simply yelled, "Carson!" I heard her faintly giggle, but she never came down the stairs.

He stopped at his kitchen counter, then looked at me in silence, just as tailor would if he was about to measure me for a new suit. Other than Wyatt announcing my entry, it was the longest I had ever heard him not talk. I spoke first, although he knew why I was there. I asked how his mother was. Before he answered, he gave me the same grin that I saw for the first time when he shook the earth. He knew what I was thinking, and he was one step ahead of me, just like he'd been with every pitcher he faced. He said, "She's great." Then he took over the conversation as I knew he would. He sternly asked me, "Why are you here?" He answered his own question with, "I know why. It's been twenty-five years, and someone sent you." He was right, but I played coy.

Sports Illustrated wanted a cover story, and they had heard I knew him best. He had been all over the world, and somehow, I was still identified as his best friend. He looked me in the eyes and said, "I'm done telling the story. Y'all were all there. You tell it." He had told the story for his entire career, and now he was done repeating it.

I asked him, "Why do you never come to town?"

Then he bellowed a villainous laugh. The echo from the top of his mini-mountain home made me feel like his accomplice in a crime. I spoke as if in a race just to beat the next words out of his mouth. I said, "Never mind that." He looked me in the eyes again, then sternly said, "Tell me who sent you." I ignored his request.

Wyatt smiled, then said, "My whole life, everyone wanted to know how I could do the things I could do on the baseball field." I nodded in agreement. I had watched reporters and his peers marvel at his abilities. I knew Wyatt did not take them for granted, but I also knew he could not explain it. He had something special. He finished by saying, "I could tell you wanted to know how I could do it too, but you never asked me, and it made me respect you even more."

I replied, "Wyatt, I can tell you want to ask me something right now and not about why I am here." He nodded while trying to hide his excitement and fear. It was obvious he wanted to ask about her. I simply said, "She's fine."

I told him my sister was doing well and she was living in Charlotte with her son, Ryan. These were facts I was sure he already knew. I told him I rarely saw her, and she seemed gone for good. She had packed up her BMW and moved to the city. She had outgrown the Brown Water for a second time. Whitley had become Charlotte's top realtor, and she was raising her nine-year-old alone.

He then asked again in a harsher tone, "Who sent you?"

Patti yelled down from her upstairs perch, "Let it go!"

He yelled back, "I wish they would!" but that was not what she meant.

The world had asked him over and over to retell an event that happened when he was twelve years old, and it meant nothing to him. She meant everything to him, and he felt like he should be able to ask about her.

He casually walked to his back deck, past what was surely his father's and uncle's urns. I followed him despite what looked like the threat of rain. The clouds were rolling upriver. We sat down on his patio furniture, on his massive deck. I felt like I could see all the way to Elizabeth's Lakeside Restaurant. It was like looking at the past, the present, and the future at the same time. His view was beautiful, and the yellow and dark-red canna lilies lining his gazebo only magnified the beauty of his view.

I asked him, "Why do you look back at Cubbie Cove?"

His head dropped, and he replied, "For two reasons: I try to see her, and the other is so I can come up with a way to forget her." I understood why it was so hard to look back at Winslow's and try to see her, because the world had looked back at him his entire life. Neither of those chapters of his life ever closed.

The bottom fell out, and the rain forced us inside.

Wyatt looked at me and said, "My life would've been different if I had not hit that home run. I wish it never happened." At that moment, I looked at my old friend, who looked ten years younger than me, and I understood his life in that one sentence. The most magical moment of my youth was just another home run to him.

I selfishly told him, "All our lives would've been different." I was instantly ashamed after saying it.

We walked down to his basement, which was his nearly empty trophy room. It did not have one trophy or accomplishment of himself except one. He had his father's bat behind the bar, and the bat's handle had his initials as well as my sister's. He hit his first Major League home run with it, then he promptly retired it. An out-of-place painting of purple tulips was beside the bat. We walked out to his covered back patio and stood. We talked while we waited for the rain to stop. The faint smell of my wife's favorite flower filled my nose. His house was almost perfect, and I pictured myself living here.

Wyatt and my sister were the same side of a magnet. They were drawn to each other, but they needed to repel each other. Opposites attract for a reason, but they were not opposites. They made each other miserable and happy at the same time. When they were not together, they both likely obsessed over each other. I was their link, and I had been since we were twelve years old.

My parents blamed me for their bond. I was the one that introduced them. When he came over to see me, he ended up arguing with her. It was a playful joke while we were in middle school that he only came over just to see her. My classmates began to question if he and I were friends at all. It seemed Wyatt and Whitley were oil and water, until one day, I realized they were something more dangerous. The two were actually gasoline and fire. They were destructive, and the path that followed was ashes.

I knew of their secret bond long before it was ever public, and I knew neither of them wanted anyone to know. I remember Whitley giving him a good-luck hug and whispering something in his ear as he went onstage at *The David Letterman Show*. I don't think that was the actual moment he knew he was in love with her, but it was the moment I knew. Wyatt seemed nervous, and her hug and secret message somehow calmed him. I later asked Whitley, "What did you say to him?" and she replied, "Just something silly."

It became evident in high school that it was a bad idea to have a union of the best-looking and most talented two people. Their accolades made their heads swell, and they were always trying to be the main attraction. The stage only had room for one star at a time. Neither Whitley nor Wyatt liked to share the spotlight. They became equally difficult with each other as well as us all. It seemed they argued only to reconcile a day later. It was exhausting to follow their stock-market relationship.

My sister and Wyatt were Division 1 athletes, and their careers sent them in opposite directions. She signed with University of Virginia, and he went to University of Florida. As soon as he arrived at Florida, he was requested to tell about the Little League World Series championship. He obliged, and he became an instant celebrity on campus when the school newspaper's headline read, "A Baseball Legend Arrives." The article referenced his *David Letterman* appearance and how Letterman called him Home Run Hartley. The nickname and the story followed him everywhere. He always tried to deflect the attention to Ogre's and Drake's heroics that summer, but they always focused on him. He would go on to tell the story at every stop on his baseball odyssey. He always pointed out how Ruby, Ogre, and Drake made the summer magical. Reporters wanted a hero, and they barely referenced the team, much to Wyatt's disappointment.

Wyatt's freshman year was streaky. He had stretches of batting over 400 and stretches batting under 200. He was named to the second-team all SEC and was freshman of the year. Agents began to swarm Wyatt. He was drafted, but he decided to stay in school.

Whitley decided to transfer to the University of Central Florida after her freshman year to be closer to him. She had to sit out the season due to the NCAA transfer rules. Wyatt began to shine, and no pitcher was safe. He dominated his sophomore year, and he became an All-American. Whitley ruptured her Achilles before the year was over, and she would miss another season. Wyatt was drafted by Texas Rangers in the second round. He signed and was set for life, but he left her behind.

He followed the typical bonus-baby path from A ball to AAA with the Arizona Fall League sprinkled in. At each minor league stop, he was featured for his heroics from when he was twelve years old. Minor league scoreboards would play the video of his home run between innings when he was due to bat. He must've relived that moment ten thousand times. He struggled his first year in the minors. Whitley's soccer career ended prematurely due to her injury. She left college to join Wyatt in the minors. My dad was devastated that she had given up her soccer career. My mom was upset that she would have a daughter labeled a college dropout. Wyatt's career accelerated as no one in AA could get the ex-phenom out. He was a September call-up, and he homered in his first at bat. He became the star of Swansville that Whitley was destined to be before he walked in Mr. Troutman's math class.

Whitley spent three years with him in the minors, and she watched him dominate at every level. Just after his second call-up to the Rangers, she left him. She unceremoniously came back to Swansville. He told me she left him without saying a word and only left a note saying, "The best don't need luck." He pulled the faded note from his wallet and showed me. He told me, "I believed it," then put the note back in his wallet. Some people are made for the main stage, and she was one. She was the main character in her own story, not a secondary character in his. He fell apart after she left, and he bounced between AAA and the majors.

A year later, Wyatt played an AAA playoff game in Charlotte, and I made the trip to watch my friend. It was the first time I watched him play since the state legion championship game. It felt normal to be in the stands to watch him. He saw me among the crowd, and he immediately headed my direction. He waved me down, and the crowd looked at me to see why a professional baseball player was making a fuss over a fan. I stuck out my hand for a handshake, and he pulled me in for a hug. I awkwardly grabbed him by the wrist as he pulled me close. We chatted before the game. He asked how everyone was doing and winked at me, then said, "You old dog, I heard the news." I bashfully shook my head. He told me he missed me. It felt authentic as he hugged me tight.

I never got to watch him play. Just before he crossed the right field chalk line, he turned and walked backward while shouting, "Lightning, see you on the Brown Water!" A rogue ball rolled under his right foot as he turned to join his teammates. He tripped. He caught himself before eating a face full of grass. He grimaced in pain, and the old break in his wrist shattered for the second time. Some wounds just don't heal. His catching days were over. His career was sidetracked, and he spent six months back home rehabbing and learning to play left field and first base. He became a ghost, and I rarely saw him. Our friendship began at a lunch table, but our bond was because of baseball. For the first time in our lives, neither he nor I had a baseball to hold us together.

Whitley tortured Wyatt while he was home. He begged for her attention at first, but she ignored him. In the three years she had been back home, she had taken over my family's real estate business. She spilled more Dr. Pepper on the lake, and the ants returned. Whitley's smiling face was plastered on billboards at every intersection. He had trouble going anywhere without seeing her face. Whitley's green eyes seemed to follow him everywhere. She paraded every eligible guy in front of him.

Wyatt did everything possible to hide. He stayed at the house he had bought his mother. He rarely left the house other than to work out. He never waved back when I drove past him jogging down the road. He acted as if he did not see me. Wyatt and I had a brief encounter when I saw him using the middle school field to take batting practice. His uncle lobbed balls in his direction while he bounced them off the gym wall while he effortlessly swung his father's bat. I watched in awe, as the game was still easy to him. I asked, "Will you be ready soon?" He replied, "I sure hope so." It was like I was talking to a stranger, and I left him to his task of hitting baseballs.

When he left this time, I doubted I would ever see him again. He became a baseball nomad. He spent another year bouncing between AAA and MLB before deciding to go to Japan after Duckworth's death. He played in Japan for two successful seasons while the heroic story was translated. He came back, and he still had the magic he took with him to Japan. He told me when they chanted "Home Run Hartley" in Japanese, it made him want to come home to her. After he won the Japanese league MVP, he came back to the United States and signed with the White Sox, where he became an all-star. His success was short-lived, and the following year injuries found him again. He was never the same, but he caught on as a pinch hitter and he bounced around the big leagues for few more years. He eventually won a World Series with the Marlins. At thirty-six years old, he decided he'd rather come home than go to spring training. He finished his MLB career with 199 MLB home runs, and I was here to ask him to tell the story one more time about the one he hit when he was twelve.

We talked over Coronas, and the rain finally stopped. We went back out to his deck. We removed the faded watermelon-print pillows from his patio furniture before sitting back down. His lawn took a deep breath, and steam seeped out of his perfectly manicured green lawn. The sunflowers at the edge of his lawn looked like an old man trying to stretch, as they were still slightly slumped over due to the weight of the rain. The sun began to set, and the sky turned pink over Swansville. I had never seen it look so beautiful, nor had I seen it from this vantage point.

I asked him, "Why did you come back?"

He looked in the direction of Swansville and took a deep breath before responding. He said, "Everywhere else, I am the kid that hit that home run. In Swansville, I am the dumb-ass that burned down Rocky Point Pier, mockingly called a giant Ruby and broke my wrist falling out of a window. She drew just as many second looks. Here I can be myself, flaws and all. This town saw my wounds before they were scars. So when you ask me to tell the world again about a home run I hit when I was twelve, I tell you, I barely remember it. She floods my memories. The moments I remember the most were not my home runs. It was when she told me she loved me. I remember the first time and the last time."

I swallowed then simply said, "Just one more time. We will all be there."

He looked back at me and said, "Except for Duckworth."

We both nodded and looked toward Winslow's. A moment later, he said, "Under one condition."

A spring must've popped under him, because he jumped up and ran downstairs. I waited and stared in the direction of Swansville. When he returned with his bat, his eyes were glazed over. I did not feel like he saw me when he said, "Give this to her." I pleaded with him not to give up his bat, but he insisted. His voice cracked when he said, "I could only make it do what it did when she was in my life." I told him I would try, but she would likely refuse it, and then he said, "Give it to her kid, then, or you keep it. Maybe it can bring someone else luck." I reluctantly agreed, and I took his bat.

When he hit that home run, it was as if baseball had a clock and he stopped it. It stopped for him that day too. The heroic home run put the spotlight he craved on him the rest of his life. He spent his life reliving what he did when he was twelve years old. She was the only one that knew how he really felt, and she bathed in her own light. The light was shining his direction again, and the first thing he thought of was her.

I left, then told him, "Thanks. I will be in touch."

Reunion

The *Sports Illustrated* article reunited us all for the first time in twenty-five years. We met at Scarborough Memorial Park on a sunny afternoon. I had barely seen some of my old teammates and rivals over the last twenty-five years. Their eyes all looked the same despite the wrinkles in their faces and the first appearances of gray hairs. Time had caught up with us all, and the boyish faces I remembered looked like fathers instead of sons. About half of the guys had moved away, and a few of us still stayed in touch. Those of us that stayed in Swansville became the storytellers of that summer of 1994. Our small town had ballooned to over twenty-nine thousand people. The ants recently returned for a third time. My sister led them this time. The folks that moved to the Brown Water after that summer took pride in telling everyone about the summer of 1994 like they were there. Ogre and I spotted the frauds all the time.

I never thought I would live in Swansville as an adult. I left for college, but I returned home to finish at nearby UNCC. My dream of being a lawyer was sidetracked when I came home for spring break during my junior year. Wyatt shook the earth when I was in the sixth grade, but Ella Huggins made my heart stop. I instantly thought back to the summer of 1994, when I dreamed of her and I stole glances of the older beauty.

Ella was working at Queenie's Salon when I needed to chop off my shaggy hair to attend a dinner party with my mother in my father's absence. She recognized me and hugged me as if we were old friends. We chatted while she made me presentable, and she asked, "How long will you be in town?" I told her, "One week." I nervously asked her when I was paying if she would like to properly catch up.

She agreed. I did not want to return to school after one date. I sent her a gardenia plant after I got back to Vanderbilt. When I came back to see her two weeks later, she wore one of the white flowers in her hair on our second date. Before I knew it, I was transferring from Vanderbilt and majoring in history to be a teacher.

Ella's blue eyes drew me back to the Brown Water. Ella had a set of twin two-year-old boys when I transferred back home to be with her. My parents disapproved of my decision to leave Vanderbilt for a girl. My mother adamantly disapproved of Ella. She told me, "That family is trouble." I took a job two years later at Swansville Middle School. I was back in the Brown Water for good. I coached Ella's boys in T-ball, and I did my best impersonation of Duckworth saying, "Field with your feet!" and "Alligator hands!" Dalin and Davin only played baseball for two years. My sister corrupted them by giving them soccer balls for their fifth birthday. They only wanted to kick around the soccer ball, and my heart broke.

I continued to coach other parents' children as I waited for my own children to play. Jacklyn Danielle, or JD as we call her, looked like my wife, but she was built like my sister. JD was a fast learner, and she took to the baseball field, and at eight years old, she was the best player her age. She was difficult to coach because she picked up things quickly. All the drills I learned growing up were useless on her. She was a natural, and all the other parents laughed when she instructed, "Just throw the ball." I knew she would topple giants and tame the wildest of beasts one day.

When I arrived, Drake Duckworth was on the field with his three daughters. All three girls were dancing aimlessly without any choreography around their father. Drake just watched them and shyly smiled. It was no surprise that Drake had become a lawyer in Maryland, nor did it surprise anyone when he gave it all up. Drake decided at thirty-four he no longer wanted to deal with the pressure of being a criminal lawyer, so he decided to move to a small town to become the town planner. After his father passed away, Drake felt like he was missing his daughters' childhood, and he wanted to enjoy it with them. His wife did not make the trip since she was pregnant with a boy that would be thirteen years younger than his eldest sister.

Coach Alex and Ruby uncharacteristically arrived early. Coach Alex was in a wheelchair with a breathing machine. He was still arguing with Ruby. The two had not changed except it seemed Ruby was winning the arguments now. It was beneath Ruby to come to Swansville. Ruby owned a new car dealership near the new, trendy lake on the other side of Charlotte. Ruby looked like his father from twenty-five years ago, except he was taller and rounder. Ruby had two girls and a stepson. Ruby forced his stepson to attend.

Alex said very little. Alex coached a few years after Ruby aged out. I believe he learned, after his son was no longer on his team, how to have fun. He no longer had a giant to give him the advantage, and he learned to lose. The old coach stood up and walked out of his wheelchair, then unhooked his breathing machine. The smell of the late-summer baseball field made him cough. Ruby shouted, "What are you doing?" at his father. Ruby sat his dad down and hooked him back up to his breathing machine. Ruby loudly said, "I dominated everyone on this field, didn't I, Carson?" He was not wrong, so I nodded to his stepson.

Ruby was a star pitcher for Mars Hill University. Ruby's fastball suddenly became hittable after he was drafted by the Pittsburgh Pirates. Ruby bounced around the minor leagues for a few years before deciding to give up baseball. He blamed his father's health. The story he told everyone was, he was about to be called up when his dad collapsed. He flew home and never left. The truth was, he never made it past single A.

Anthony and Preston simply walked over from the fire department. They had flip-flopped their father's positions, and now Preston was the fire chief. Anthony shot up after high school and was now bigger than his father. Preston walked with a slight limp due to a knee injury caused by a fire rescue. Preston jumped from the second floor of an old farmhouse to save a six-year-old boy. He was deemed a hero. He received pats on the back everywhere he went.

Anthony became a celebrity when the two firemen in training went to New York to assist with the search after the September 11 terrorist attack on the World Trade Center. Anthony dived between the rubble and pulled out one of the last survivors. The story of the

New York City orphan returning home to become a hero put himself and his best friend on the cover of *The New York Times*. The clippings from the *Swansville Record* and *The New York Times* were posted in the post office. Neither man ever spoke of their heroic moment, but both would tell you about the Little League World Series if you allowed them.

Coach Ross and RJ both showed up well dressed, with Missy shouting, "Oooweee, look at y'all boys now!" as soon as she had stepped out of the car. RJ's football career only lasted through high school before he realized he needed to put on a pair of blue bike shorts and hit the sidelines with his dad. He became his dad's top assistant, and the two built a powerhouse in Hendersonville, North Carolina. The father-and-son coaches won two state titles. Coach Ross was in the North Carolina Sports Hall of Fame.

RJ returned to the Charlotte area and coached at a private school that averaged about three wins a year. RJ was still bouncing around. He sounded just like his dad as he had transformed into Coach Ross after his dad retired. Coach Ross made the trip up from Myrtle Beach. RJ was married with four boys, and he could not wait until they played for him. Every time Swansville had an opening for a head football coach, RJ was the first person they called. He always turned down his alma mater. I assumed he did not want to hurt his father's legacy if he could not build a winner.

Coach Ross was the first to spot Jaxon, and he immediately shouted in his deep coach voice, "Get over here, mophead!" as soon as Jaxon stepped out of his Mercedes. Jaxon lived the farthest away and moved to Florida after the military. He was a pilot for Southwest Airlines. He was Captain Leonard. Coach Ross had taken the troubled boy under his wing. Jaxon rewarded him by following his advice and enrolling in the military. Jaxon moved in with RJ after his grandmother died. He was tired of bouncing between his mom and father. Jaxon became Coach Ross's all-district quarterback in high school. His retired number 5 jersey hung in the field house. Jaxon enrolled at VMI. He was the first starting quarterback to lead them to back-to-back bowl wins. Jaxon Leonard was a name everyone in the surrounding counties knew.

Jaxon's dad was still alive and living in Swansville. Jaxon returned every year to see his dad and to bring up his two daughters. He had barely aged since high school. Jaxon looked like he did not belong in our small town. He looked like he should live on the big water. He dressed like a man headed for a wedding, not for a baseball reunion. He walked tall and looked you in the eye when he spoke to you. He was not conceited, and his confidence had transformed him into a leader.

Troy Russell docked his boat at Elizabeth's Lakeside and walked over. He wore a tank top and a faded swimsuit. He never left Swansville, and he lived in his mom's pool house. He worked at the old marina. He was loyal, and he never went to work for the new, nicer marina just off the new bridge. Troy knew I invited everyone to the photo shoot and the reunion, but he still loudly asked the folks from *Sports Illustrated* who was in charge of this circus. Troy still looked like a young man, and he still acted like one. Ella and I constantly had to remind him not to say inappropriate things in front of our children.

Troy was Ruby's connection to those of us that stayed at Swansville High School. We all enjoyed Troy's company more as we got older. He threw parties and took everyone out on his boat every weekend. He rarely invited Ruby because Ruby would almost always somehow ruin the fun. I wish Troy were not content with his life, but he had no ambition. The lake had a spell over him, and he never wanted to leave it. He rode Ruby's coattails in high school, and he did not need to give 100 percent. He was now a fixture at Elizabeth's Lakeside. His face was still young, but his cheeks were red all the time.

Dale and Curt pulled up at the same time, and both let out what seemed like a clown car full of kids out of their minivans. Their kids scattered to their favorite playground. Dale and Curt married sisters and lived in their wives' town, about forty-five minutes away. Dale decided to adopt. He had a very diverse family. Curt said, "My greatest achievement in life is making David the Pop-Pop to four wild kids." Our paths crossed all the time as my stepsons played soccer against his sons. We always reminisced while watching our kids play. He occasionally called me Worm or Lightning.

The two friends worked for the county parks and recreation. If you had a problem with an umpire or a field, you called Dale or Curt. They were the driving force of the new athletic complex built in the county. I felt like I had allies patrolling the fields of Swansville. Any time I saw Curt in town, he would make sure our conversation led to the Little League World Series or about the Hole in the Wall. His chest poked out for either story.

Jack and Ogre drove over from Jack's house. Ogre's high school baseball days were just like his Little League days: he dominated. Ogre went away to a small college, only to return home after his dad had a car fall on him, nearly crushing him. Jack survived, but he would struggle to run his business, so Ogre came home. It was an easy decision for Ogre to return. Jack never officially retired, and Frankie's chalkboard sat in his front yard since Winslow's closed after Frankie died.

Ogre married and had two boys. His boys inherited their father's size, but not his shyness. No one was surprised Ogre's boys were the best baseball players in the county, but they were surprised when Logan and Lance told you they were. The two had finished their Little League years, as they were now a freshman and a sophomore in high school. The two boys fell one run short of representing North Carolina in the regionals. Their red hair gave away their mother's identity. Kandi and Ogre were town fixtures. The large man and tiny redhead were an odd match. She still spoke for them both, as he still said very little.

Mitch O'Neal ran a funeral home in Greenville, North Carolina. Mitch stayed in Greenville after attending East Carolina. I missed seeing him and how eloquently he was able to tell the story of what he called the world's worst bunt. Mitch only played baseball one more year as he regressed after he was drafted by Coach Alex. Ruby bullied him and stole his confidence. Mitch's mom caught the eye of a salesman of one of the new lake communities. She married and quit cleaning houses. She now lived on the big water.

I had only seen Mitch a few times since he moved away, but we spoke regularly. He played in a small band in Greenville called Cured Potion. His hair was jet-black and past his shoulders the last time I saw him. He sent me a Christmas card every year and always included a sealed letter for Wyatt. He instructed me to mail the letter to wherever Wyatt was living. I never opened the letters, and I always wondered what it said. Mitch called, telling us he was running late. He said it would be over an hour before he arrived.

While we waited, we walked over to Elizabeth's Lakeside diner to grab a drink. Drake stayed behind. I thanked everyone for coming back, and I told them I missed them. I was ignored, as everyone had already started their own side conversations. Wyatt and Jaxon sat beside each other, looking at wine menu written in chalk just above where Frankie always sat. The old bait shop seemed to be filled with echoes of our youth, and if we held our heads just right, we might be able to hear ourselves updating Frankie with our scores.

Ruby quietly walked up to Wyatt and extended his hand. The two childhood rivals awkwardly shook hands. Ruby told Wyatt, "Thank you. You changed our lives."

Wyatt looked up at the giant. "Travis, thank you. Iron sharpened iron."

Ruby was caught off guard by the compliment, and he loudly laughed while he quickly wiped his eyes. Ruby told Wyatt, "I prefer to be called Ruby. My nickname connects us." They gently tapped their bottles in celebration.

Mitch finally arrived and apologized for being late. The bachelor jokingly blamed his pregnant wife. I rounded everyone up to leave. Wyatt paid the bill. We all waited for cars to pass before crossing the once-dead-end street. Wyatt brought up the rear, defiantly carrying his bottle out of the restaurant.

We took a team picture under the 1994 Little League World Series Championship sign, and the flash made us blink, so we took another one. Wyatt tried to hide in the back with Drake, but he was the main attraction and the cameraman put him in front. Wyatt wanted the team to be the focus and not his heroic moments. Our sign stood beside the faded state championship sign. Seven years earlier, the green in our sign was starting to show its age, then the town determined it was time to replace it. No one in town wanted to let that magical summer fade away.

The article did not focus on Wyatt's Roy Hobbs-esque home run or his dominant pitching debut, as every other article had done for the last twenty-five years. Wyatt's contribution in the article was more about his successful career and how he had come back to Swansville. The reporter asked, "How does it feel after all these years?" He was at a loss for words at first, then he chuckled to hide his lack of confidence. He said, "I have not had that question before." He paused and scratched the gray stubble of a beard. His voice wavered. "It seems like it was yesterday. I wish I could recapture the feeling. My heart stopped, and I felt vulnerable. My confidence disappeared, all the while I felt like I was floating above everyone. I still do not know how to act at times, and now it seems like it was my destiny." When asked in the article why he came back to Swansville, he simply said, "For the same reason." The reporter assumed it was because of his memories of the summer no one would let him forget.

The article did detail how Ogre and I were carrying on the Swansville Little League tradition and the league had grown to twelve teams. The county built an athletic complex on the other side of Cubbie Cove that had four baseball fields, two soccer fields, and a brand-new member's-only pool. Scarborough Memorial Park became the secondary park for the league. Two years prior to the article, the town had baseball fever again as Ogre and his sons nearly won the state. Ogre and I coached the team. We were one player short from making another long run. Ogre's boys had made names for themselves. Ogre let me take the credit when the reporters came for interviews. We both knew we had success because of his boys, and I did little to affect the games.

The article's main focus was how, without our team, baseball would have been on life support. Mark McGwire and Sammy Sosa would not have had a sport to save five years later. Baseball would've been dead. Once we made it to the championship, every baseball fan in America tuned to cheer for one team for the first time in its history. The article said we gave America hope that baseball could be fun again. Wyatt's and Ruby's antics were documented as fun-loving kids, not the rivals that despised each other.

After the photo, everyone scattered back to where from which they came and back to being an adult, but for a few hours, we had the pleasure to experience the spotlight that had followed Wyatt for twenty-five years. We were special when we were twelve, but now we had to go back to being teachers, coaches, firemen, mechanics, car salesmen, and fathers, among other things. Ogre and I walked back over to Elizabeth's Lakeside to relive our glory days. Jack slowly walked over and sat in the dugout. Troy waved goodbye as he sped out of Cubbie Cove. Wyatt walked down the once-dead-end street, swinging a stick, without a care in the world, heading to an unfamiliar destination. Drake stayed behind again, and for a moment, in the magic of the setting sun, I believed he felt twelve years old again, because I saw him mime a throw over to first base and then pump his fist in triumph. His daughters giggled, then ran up and hugged him, then all four danced. Their dancing shadows now seemed to have a purpose.

The *Sports Illustrated* photographer later mailed me his first attempt at our team picture when we all blinked. Wyatt's eyes were wide-open, and the reflection of the flash off the Little League World Series Champions sign was bright enough to create a shadow on our faces. It is hard to look at the flawed picture and not be taken back to the that amazing summer. The shadow over our faces helps hide our wrinkles and scars of the last twenty-five years. When I squint and look at the picture with the right set of eyes, I do not see old men; I see an artist, a giant, an ogre, and a conqueror. The picture is my prized possession.

The time between the games is what I remember the most. Twenty-five years later, it is like looking back through a fog, and every pitch and hit gets harder to see and recall. When I brush the fog out of the way, it feels like it was a dream, but the moments off the field are clearer with each passing day. I want to go back to the summer of 1994 and plead for time to slow down. It is maddening, and it is like grasping at smoke. That last summer was full of laughs and tears. I wish I could bottle that feeling and drink it up whenever I need a youthful elixir. I've longed for those long hot summer days. Now that summer follows me everywhere: I taste it every time I drink a Cheerwine, I smell it when the fragrance of honeysuckles drift my way, I drive by it when I pass our road sign, I hear it when the big-water locals tell our story, I feel it when I swim in the brown water of Cubbie Cove, I say it when I repeat Duckworth's stolen baseball lines, and I see it in the my daughter's green eyes the most. It's everywhere, and it never seems to end, thankfully.

Maybe baseball does have a clock after all.

About the Author

Chan Howell grew up in the small town of Denton, North Carolina. He married his beautiful wife, Mary, in 2006. They have three sons: Duke, Rus, and Trader. He is a graduate of East Carolina University, where he studied English literature and exercise sports science. His busy life includes a full-time job, owning a local business, coaching baseball, football and basketball, along with writing.

Chan is many things to many people: son, brother, husband, coach, friend, or foe (depending on who you ask). He writes to reflect and pay tribute to the many mentors and coaches of his life. Chan's passion for sports, especially baseball, was born in the backyard while he played baseball with his older brother, Chris. His love for storytelling began at an early age, when he would excitedly recap his older brother's baseball exploits to anyone that would listen.

Chan is a gregarious character that is known throughout his hometown, and the local youth gravitate to his fun-loving character. His writing is inspired by the children he coaches, their parents, along with many past and present associates. *The Last Summer* is Chan's debut novel and his love story to baseball.